BEHIND THE
WHITE HOUSE DOORS . . .

"Gentlemen," the President began. "I want to apologize for getting you out of bed at this hour, but Tom called me an hour ago with some very disturbing information concerning the future of NASA. With that, I leave it with you, Tom."

Pruett exhaled. "Thank you, Mr. President. Gentlemen, all of you are aware by now of the problems NASA's *Lightning* is facing in space. First, one of the main engines failed during the lift-off stage. Less than an hour later the OMS engines, the Orbital Maneuvering System engines, failed. The cause of the malfunctions cannot be truly determined until *Lightning* gets back down and NASA scientists get a chance to take the engines apart and inspect them. Gentlemen, I stand here before you with the statement that *Lightning*'s problems were not due to malfunction, but to sabotage."

SIEGE OF LIGHTNING

*A novel of technological conspiracy
in the tradition of Clive Cussler
and Robert Ludlum*

SIEGE OF LIGHTNING

R.J. PINEIRO

BERKLEY BOOKS, NEW YORK

SIEGE OF LIGHTNING

A Berkley Book / published by arrangement with
the author

PRINTING HISTORY
Berkley edition / April 1993

All rights reserved.
Copyright © 1993 by R. J. Pineiro.
This book may not be reproduced in
whole or in part, by mimeograph or any other
means, without permission. For information
address: The Berkley Publishing Group,
200 Madison Avenue, New York, New York 10016.

ISBN: 0-425-13787-2

A BERKLEY BOOK ® TM 757,375
Berkley Books are published by The Berkley Publishing Group,
200 Madison Avenue, New York, New York 10016.
The name "BERKLEY" and the "B" logo
are trademarks belonging to Berkley Publishing Corporation.

PRINTED IN THE UNITED STATES OF AMERICA

10 9 8 7 6 5 4 3 2 1

SIEGE of Lightning is dedicated to two very special people in my life:

To my beautiful wife, Lory, a friend for all seasons.

To my son, Cameron. Thanks for letting me rediscover the world through your eyes.

I would like to thank Kay Grinter from the National Aeronautics and Space Administration Public Affairs Office at Kennedy Space Center for her significant help in providing massive amounts of technical information on the orbiter, mission events, crew systems, and general operations at KSC. Any technical errors in this novel are mine and only mine.

For his help and valuable feedback in the early stages of the manuscript, I would like to thank Gary Muschla.

For being there to listen to my frustrations, complaints, and ideas, I thank my wife, Lory, whose patience never ran out during those long nights and weekends when this novel was written—and rewritten.

For their constant encouragement, I thank my parents, Rogelio and Dora. You were right. I could do it.

Special thanks go to the Wiltz family: Mike, Linda, and Michael, Jr., who were always there for me.

Thanks also go to Bill Moser, who gave me my first spy novel almost thirteen years ago, opening the eyes of a teenager to the world of fiction.

We Roman-Catholics seem to have a specific saint for just about everything. The saint for the impossible is St. Jude. Since getting a novel published comes very close to that, I chose to pray to him a while back. I guess it paid off. Thank you, St. Jude.

Finally, I would like to thank the two people that made this novel possible. My agent at William Morris, Matt Bialer, and my editor at Berkley, Andy Zack. Without their full support, help, and guidance this story would have never left my word processor.

Thanks.

R. J. Pineiro
Austin, Texas, 1992

SIEGE OF LIGHTNING

PROLOGUE ★

BAIKONUR COSMODROME, EASTERN KAZAKHSTAN

Bathed in the soft ruddy glow of an autumn sunset, the Russian cargo spacecraft *Progress VI* trembled as the engines of its four strap-on boosters and central core ignited with the thundering roar of thousands of gallons of highly pressurized kerosene reacting with liquid oxygen, unleashing a combined thrust of 400,000 pounds against the flame-deflector pit.

Engulfed in a pillar of blaze and smoke, the rocket hesitated for a few seconds as the monumental upward drive fought the gravitational force pulling down on its 300,000-pound mass, until slowly the unmanned ferry gained the momentum necessary to achieve lift-off. The four "tulip" stabilizer arms, cradling the three-stage rocket over the concrete stand, fell back to their retracted position through the action of counterweights as the deafening RD-107 engines thrust the craft clear of the launchpad.

On-board computers issued hundreds of commands per second to the attitude-control boosters to keep the ferry from drifting off course as the launch vehicle broke through the sound barrier in forty-five seconds.

Leaving a long billowing trail of smoke, the boosters fired for another eighty seconds before separating from the central core, which continued to fire as the second stage for an additional two hundred seconds.

Forty seconds into second-stage firing, the abort rockets on the shroud tower ignited and the protective third-stage shroud separated into two halves along its longitudinal axis, exposing the spacecraft inside.

At an altitude of ninety miles, the second stage separated, and the RD-461 third-stage booster kicked into life with a final thrust of sixty thousand pounds for 240 seconds, injecting *Progress VI* into an east-to-west elliptical orbit 150 miles in perigee and 310 in apogee. The flight plan called for the spacecraft to remain in that orbit for seven hours and fifteen minutes, after which *Progress VI*'s main engine would start the first of three orbital burns to approach Space Station *Mir*.

The Olympus 6-F8 oceanography studies satellite continued its low-Earth orbit of 150 miles with an inclination of eighty-two degrees while performing a surface-imaging survey of the waters off the Venezuelan coast. Its central processing unit temporarily switched tasks in response to a priority-one signal sent from a tracking station in French Guiana.

The signal ordered the processor to run a one-time algorithm, which would erase itself from memory after execution, programmed to jettison a cylindrical-shaped white object that had remained concealed since the satellite's launch several months back.

The five-hundred-pound cylinder did not house any of the infrared and microwave imaging gear that filled most of the parent satellite. Aside from six tubular solid-propellant rockets around its one-foot diameter, a homing sensor, and a transponder radio, the five-foot-long object contained three hundred pounds of HEP, High Explosive Plastic, connected to a fuse with a brief time delay. The radar-absorbing fluorocarbon resins coating the entire cylinder made it nearly invisible to its creators as well as to the Russian tracking stations controlling *Progress VI*.

The rockets fired, propelling the cylinder into a highly elliptical two-hundred-by-three-thousand-mile orbit, but the cylinder never reached its apogee. It never even came close. As the accelerating object reached its maximum velocity, its homing unit detected *Progress VI* in its own orbit one thousand miles away.

The high-speed chase did not last long. Traveling at nearly thirty thousand miles per hour, the cylinder closed the gap in minutes and struck the rear section of the Russian craft with a relative velocity of five thousand miles per hour. On hitting the target, the cylinder fractured and its explosive filling spread like a pancake around the Russian craft, detonating a split second later. Stress waves propagated along the length of the craft, sending hundreds of metal fragments traveling around the interior of *Progress VI* at lightning speed, and puncturing the liquid oxygen and kerosene fuel cells housed in the rear.

On-board impact sensors registered the attack but were unable to transmit the data to Earth. The blast that followed dwarfed the initial explosion. Thousands of gallons of propellant and liquid oxygen ignited creating an inferno that lasted only a few seconds, but long enough to destroy *Progress VI.*

KOUROU, FRENCH GUIANA

The operator sitting behind the green CRT display read the Orbital Termination message flashing on the top left-hand corner of the screen. The message marked the end of the drone satellite's transponder radio signal, indicating that the drone had been successful in reaching its target and detonating.

The operator shifted his gaze to the circular radar screen to his left and verified that the Russian craft had disappeared from the display. Satisfied, he continued processing the surface images collected by the Olympus satellite.

ONE ★

New Beginnings

There can be no thought of finishing, for 'aiming at the stars,' both literally and figuratively, is a problem to occupy generations, so that no matter how much progress one makes, there is always the thrill of just beginning.
—Dr. Robert Goddard

LAUNCH COMPLEX 39, PAD A. KENNEDY SPACE CENTER, FLORIDA

Gleaming and pristine, *Lightning* stood quietly perched above her concrete stand, pointing at the heavens. Expectant, waiting, she seemed to be a mighty bird of prey poised to rise into the air on pillars of flame produced by her powerful twin Solid Rocket Boosters. Her external fuel tank was an unsightly but necessary blemish on her otherwise perfect white skin, composed of over 21,000 thermal protection tiles individually placed in their unique spots on the orbiter—a multimillion-dollar jigsaw-puzzle task.

The furnacelike late-morning Florida sun had already elevated outside temperatures well into the nineties. Mission Commander Michael Kessler glanced at the launch complex as he taxied a Gulfstream II jet onto Runway 33, the fifteen-thousand-foot-long runway of the Kennedy Space Center's shuttle landing facility. The jet had been extensively modified by NASA for practicing "dead stick" landings.

Kessler gently applied full throttle. The dual Rolls-Royce Spey 511-8 turbofans came to life unleashing nearly twenty thousand pounds of thrust, propelling the fifteen-year-old craft down the sizzling concrete surface. Kessler kept the nose aligned with the center line as airspeed increased. One hundred knots . . . One-ten . . . One-thirty.

Kessler pulled up when he read 150 knots. He spoke into his voice-activated headset.

"Kennedy, Gulfstream niner-four-six, over."

"Niner-four-six, go ahead."

"Climbing to forty thousand. Dead-stick approach plan, over."

"Niner-four-six, you're clear to forty. Winds from the east at ten knots. Altimeter two-niner-point-zero-six and rising."

"Roger."

Kessler put the craft on a thirty-five-degree angle of climb while making wide circles over the runway.

"Hate doing spiral climbs and simulated dead-stick landings," Mission Pilot Captain Clayton "Tex" Jones complained from the copilot seat. "They bore me to death."

Kessler smiled. Jones, an old friend from the days when Kessler was stationed aboard the U.S.S. *Constitution* in the Persian Gulf, was Air Force, but Kessler didn't mind that. He considered Jones the last of the down-to-earth American officers. "I doubt you'll say that during the real thing, Tex. Based on what I've been told, Earth re-entry is hardly child's play."

"Haven't been afraid of anything all my life, Mike. I'm not about to start now."

Ten minutes later Kessler eyed the altimeter as it shot above 38,000 feet.

"Almost there."

With the sun to his right, Kessler cut power to idle and put the craft on a twenty-degree angle of descent heading for the ocean.

"This is peaceful. Can't believe you think it's boring."

Jones simply shook his head.

Kessler made a 180-degree turn ten minutes later and saw Runway 33 ten miles away. He checked the control panel. Altimeter, ten thousand feet; speed, 220 knots. Just a dash above the perfect glide approach of 215 knots. Kessler adjusted with slight backward pressure on the control stick. The hydraulically powered elevators in the T-tail responded by forcing the tail down and the nose up. Kessler watched the airspeed decrease. From the time the dead-stick approach began at forty thousand feet, changing speed could only be achieved by changing the rate of descent, not by adjusting throttle.

"Looks like you got it down to a science," Jones commented.

"I sure hope so. Once we're in *Lightning,* if I screw up the approach I won't be able to correct with throttles."

"Well, so far so good. Runway's seven miles straight ahead. Eight thousand feet at two-one-five knots. Looking good."

"Kennedy, Gulfstream niner-four-six, over," Kessler said.

"Niner-four-six, we have you on radar and on visual, go ahead."

"Requesting permission to land, over."

"You're cleared for a straight approach to Runway 33, niner-four-six. Winds are from the east at ten knots. Altimeter's at two-niner-point-zero-seven."

"Ah, roger, Kennedy."

"Three miles, five thousand feet, holding at two-one-five knots. Not bad for a Navy boy," Jones said.

Kessler grinned. "You haven't seen anything yet."

Kessler's left hand firmly gripped the control stick. His fine adjustments in heading and speed kept the Gulfstream on the specified glide path. With the turbofans on idle, and with the large vertical fins NASA had added under the narrow fuselage, the craft was supposed to "feel" like an orbiter.

"One mile, two thousand feet," Jones said.

Kessler nodded and pulled back lightly on the stick. Airspeed decreased to 190 knots.

"Fifteen hundred feet, half mile."

Kessler slapped the gear handle. The landing gear dropped. Kessler lowered the nose a dash to compensate for the added drag. The speed remained glued to 190 knots.

The trainer approached the end of the runway. The light crosswind pushed the craft toward the grass to the left of the runway. Kessler nudged the stick to the right. At the same time, he pressed the left rudder pedal to compensate for the crosswind. That had the effect of tilting the wings by a few degrees, giving the impression that the craft was turning into the wind. Kessler let it turn a few degrees before the left rudder forced the craft in a straight path, bringing the Gulfstream's nose on line with the approaching center of the runway and holding it there.

"You're a little low, niner-four-six. Pull up."

Beads of perspiration rolled down Kessler's face as he pulled the control stick toward him. He eyed the attitude indicator. Twenty-three degrees . . . twenty-one . . . twenty . . .

Kessler checked the altimeter. Two hundred feet. The runway came up to meet him as the craft gracefully glided over the patch of grass at the end of the tarmac. With his concentration now at a climax, Kessler kept his eyes fixed on the center line and continued to make fine adjustments.

"Twenty feet . . . ten feet . . . five . . . three . . . touch-down!"

Kessler felt a slight vibration as the rear wheels came in contact with the runway. He held the stick back and let the nose drop by itself as airspeed decreased below one hundred knots.

"Niner-four-six, you're clear to taxi to the ramp."

"Roger."

"Think you had enough of this?" asked Jones.

Kessler exhaled. "Guess so."

"Good. I'm starving."

Kessler rolled his eyes. "I guess you have a piece of red meat in mind, huh?"

"Not just *any* red meat, partner. Sixteen-ounce rib eyes medium rare. Nothing else comes anywhere near."

That drew a laugh from Kessler. "Whatever you say, pal. It's your body you're polluting with all that cholesterol and nicotine." Jones was also a light smoker.

"And what a happy body it is."

Kessler shook his head. "Fine. I guess rib eyes it is. We'll go eat right after the briefing. Otherwise I don't think I'll hear the end of it."

Jones nodded and headed aft. Kessler smiled. Jones was a true Texan.

Five minutes later they were in the Astrovan and headed for the briefing room. With a press conference scheduled for the day before the launch, NASA administrators wanted to ensure that both astronauts were prepared to respond to questions from reporters.

On the way, the astronauts sat in silence. Through the tinted windows Kessler stared at the octagonally shaped launchpad, which covered roughly a quarter of a square mile.

The actual launchpad section had two major components. The fixed service structure, located on the west side of the hardstand where the space shuttle assembly rested, consisted of an impressive 247-foot-tall tower with connecting arms to the orbiter crew hatch. The rotating service structure pivoted one-third of a circle, from a retracted position well away from the shuttle to the point where its payload change-out room doors met and matched with *Lightning*'s payload bay doors. Besides being used for installation and service of the payload, the rotating structure also supported the weather-protection system that shielded *Lightning* from rain and hail while on the pad.

Kessler inhaled deeply and shifted his gaze toward the beach. *The sea.* Kessler sighed as he stared at the vivid blue hue that outlined the coast. His thoughts drifted to his years with the Navy, Kessler's family and home for most of his life. Memories of fellow pilots flashed through his mind: the friendships, the laughter . . . the supersonic nightmares. Kessler knew they would always be with him filling a special chamber of his soul. He knew he belonged to a special breed: naval aviators. Not Air Force pilots. Navy pilots. Men for whom the end of a mission came only after jockeying a thirty-ton jet going two hundred knots onto the heaving flight deck of a carrier. *No room for mistakes. No room for exhausted pilots,* he thought.

From the day he got his private pilot's license at seventeen, Kessler had decided to make a career out of flying. Going against his father's wishes that he become an electrical engineer, Kessler earned an aeronautical engineering degree from Florida Institute of Technology in three years while continuing to log hours as a flight instructor. Upon graduation he applied and was admitted to the Naval Air Training Center at Patuxent River, Maryland, where he quickly distinguished himself from the rest of his classmates with his aggressive style of flying.

Kessler never flew slow if he could fly fast. Nobody would ever catch him going for a shallow turn or climb. He always pushed; always took his craft to the outer limits of the manufacturer's specifications. He had a simple logic: Either I push my craft and win the dogfight or the enemy will. If I bank at forty-five degrees and the enemy banks at sixty, I'll lose. If I fly one-point-five Mach and the enemy flies Mach two, I'll lose. Kessler knew only two kinds of pilots: "the quick" and "the dead." Throughout his career he fought hard to make sure he was always "the quick." His engineering degree gave him a knowledge of aerodynamics that enabled him to comprehend the manufacturer's specifications better than any of his classmates. He knew about the so-called safety margins in aircraft designs, like how much additional stress an air surface could really take beyond a specified number of Gs without sustaining structural damage. That allowed Kessler to "safely" push his craft for maximum performance, gaining an edge over his classmates.

After graduation, Lieutenant Commander Kessler got the commission of his dreams: flying F-14 Tomcats from the carrier U.S.S. *Constitution,* where it didn't take him long to earn the respect of his fellow pilots during Operation Desert Storm. He shot down two Iraqi MiG-23s using guns and a single Sidewinder a few months after his arrival, during a time when everyone still considered him a "newcomer." That episode plus several others during his years with the Navy earned Kessler an appointment as Commander Air Group and gave him a national visibility that led NASA to recruit him later on.

NASA. Kessler glanced over his left shoulder at the Solid Rocket Booster refurbishment and subassembly facility as the Astrovan continued down Kennedy Parkway North on its way to the KSC's Industrial Area. The facility could turn SRBs around in under six months from the time of recovery 140 miles off the eastern coast of Florida to the time of integration with an External Tank and an orbiter.

Kessler looked at Jones, who had his eyes closed and his head leaning against the side window glass. The Air Force captain continued to maintain an ice-cold attitude about the entire ordeal—something that Kessler could not understand. Especially with the launch less than forty-eight hours away.

The driver turned left on NASA Causeway East, and made another left on C Avenue. The Astrovan came to a stop on the side of building M6-339, the KSC's Headquarters.

"Wake up, Tex. We're here."

Jones abruptly opened his eyes and took a deep breath. Kessler reached for the side door and slid it back.

They walked into the briefing room a few minutes later.

PARIS, FRANCE

The light late afternoon breeze blew gently, giving motion to the branches of a nearby tree layered with a colorful assortment of flowers that seemed to bring life to the mellow tunes of the young saxophone player performing beneath it. A hat lying by his feet displayed the generosity of the day's crowd. To his right, a street vendor held up short sticks of French bread to pedestrians, who appeared more interested in watching a child learn to ride a bicycle on a patch of grass to the left of the sax player.

"François! François! Faites attention, François!" Cameron Stone heard the child's mother scream at her accelerating youngster, who was apparently making a last-ditch effort to get the basics down before the day ended. The nervous woman finally caught up with him on the other side of the small park, and shouted something Cameron could not understand. Cameron smiled as he inhaled the cool, invigorating air. It felt good to be in Paris again.

He had left the American Embassy and stepped into one of the most relaxed cities in the world. Definitely a change of scenery from the depressing streets of Mexico City, where he'd spent most of the past five years.

He checked his watch and proceeded to the Metro station by the Place de la Concorde, the east end of the long avenue next to the gardens behind the Louvre. Cameron quickened his pace; he only had thirty minutes to make it to the Left Bank before seven o'clock that evening. He crossed the rue Royale and reached the steps leading down to the Metro hall.

After purchasing a ticket from one of the automatic ticket machines, Cameron followed the signs down an oval-shaped concourse layered with white brick.

He made his way across the crowded platform, and managed to squeeze his slim but muscular body into an already packed second-class car, leaving barely an inch between his face and the closing doors. He grabbed the overhead railing with his left hand and kept his right hand under his coat, firmly holding his holstered Beretta, more to prevent a pickpocket from snatching it than out of fear of needing it. Cameron didn't feel like having to explain to his new CIA case officer that he had had his weapon stolen, especially during his first day under the man's jurisdiction.

As the crowd pressed against him Cameron could feel the three small manila envelopes inside a waterproof pouch sewn in to his coat liner. One contained three fake passports and matching driver's licenses, the other two his emergency money. Cameron never went anywhere without them . . . and his Beretta.

The rocky ride lasted two minutes. Then Cameron switched to a southbound train, which turned out to be just as crowded.

Cameron's current assignment, given to him by his case officer that morning, was to meet with the widow of a French rocket scientist killed in an auto accident the day before. The widow had contacted the Agency and requested the meeting. Ordinarily, such a seemingly unimportant request would have been dismissed by the CIA or, at most, passed on to the French authorities. But the widow had used a CIA emergency code—albeit an outdated one—when contacting the embassy, and that fact alone had had a few CIA officials concerned enough to activate a field operative.

Cameron got out at the Saint Michel exit, went up to the street, and turned left at rue de Cujas.

An unusual street, he reflected as he stared at the two- and three-story stone buildings, some probably dating back to the seventeenth century. The widow had asked for the meeting at an out-of-the-way location.

Cameron walked up the narrow street on the left side. The sun was setting, and the street was already dark. He eyed the vertical sign of the Grand Hotel Saint Michel opposite him. The hotel could not have been any wider than thirty feet, but someone had thought it large enough to have "Grand" preceding the name. *An odd place to meet,* he thought, considering that her late husband, the famed French rocket scientist Claude Guilloux, had been among the most respected and wealthiest men in Paris. Claude Guilloux had also been one of the leading scientists of the European space agency Athena, the pride of the European Economic Community.

Athena. Now, there's a big corporation, Cameron thought. Athena had been around for years, he recalled from the file his case officer had given him that morning, but the agency hadn't become the corporate giant of today until after the *Challenger* explosion several years back. Within days of the NASA disaster, communications companies and weather agencies from large and small countries alike had flooded the European space agency with satellite-deployment requests because of NASA's inability to perform. Backed by the EEC, Athena had grown from less than five hundred employees to over fifteen thousand, and from a few launches every year to a tight weekly schedule engineered to cope with the world's increasing demand for its services. Athena, now a very powerful and wealthy agency, had a brand-new state-of-the-art launching facility operating in the coastal city of Kourou, French Guiana, and had recently announced plans for a European space shuttle and permanent space station. With Guilloux's death, Marie Guilloux, also a noted scientist, a main contributor to the development of the guidance system in the reliable Athena V rocket, would inherit most of her late husband's fortune.

Cameron exhaled. The secrecy and strange meeting place didn't make sense. Nevertheless, he crossed the street and pushed open the single glass door of the hotel.

Right away, the strong cigar smell sickened him. It came from the other end of the long and narrow entrance hall. He noticed a sitting room to his right, through a pair of double glass doors. He walked in and spotted a couple of sofas and chairs scattered around the small square room. Cameron stepped back to the narrow entrance hall, and walked along the hardwood floors to the other end, where he saw a small elevator to his left and what had to be the hotel's front counter off to the right.

He approached the counter and saw an old woman lying on a small bed behind it. A cigar burned on a metallic ashtray next to the bed.

"Pardon, madame."

The old lady opened her eyes, grunted, and slowly got up. She snatched the cigar and let it hang off the edge of her mouth. Cameron detected a foul body odor; at first hidden by the cigar smoke, it became much more noticeable as she got closer.

"Oui?" she responded in a voice as coarse and unfriendly as her appearance. Her sunken eyes studied Cameron through the smoke.

"Bon soir, madame. Quelle est la chambre de Madame Guilloux?"

"Un moment." The woman put on a pair of glasses and flipped through the hotel's registry.

"Madame Guilloux n'est pas ici." The woman turned away.

"Ah . . . pardon, madame . . ."

The woman ignored him and walked back to her bed.

"Madame?"

"Madame Guilloux n'est pas ici! Fiche-moi la paix!"

Cameron still remembered enough French to realize that the old woman had just told him to shut up. He clenched his teeth in response to the rude remark, and was about to cut loose with the worst of his French when he noticed someone to his left.

"You're five minutes late," said a deep but extremely feminine voice in flawless English.

Cameron turned his head and saw the tall, trim figure of Marie Guilloux across the hall. She wore a pair of tight-fitting blue jeans and a San Francisco Hard Rock Cafe sweatshirt, and was holding the elevator door open.

"Are you just going to stand there, Mister . . . ?"

Cameron walked in her direction. "Name's Cameron Stone and I'm still a few minutes early, Mrs. Guilloux."

"Marie, please. I never liked being called that even when my husband was alive. Come, let's go upstairs before someone spots us."

Cameron stepped into the tiny elevator, barely big enough for the both of them. Marie closed the door. With his body almost pressed against hers, Cameron heard the old elevator make a few worrisome noises before it finally started moving upward. He just stood there, uncomfortably still, his face only inches away from hers. He kept his eyes trained on a spot on the wall, but felt Marie's eyes on him. She studied him.

"You speak without an accent," he finally said, trying to break the ice and pretend he was not bothered by her nearness.

"That's because English is my native tongue. I was born and raised in Florida, Cameron. My maiden name is Roberts."

The elevator stopped on the third floor. She opened the door and got out. "This way."

He followed her to the end of the corridor. She pulled out a key, unlocked the door, and pushed it open. "Not bad for twenty-five dollars a day," she said as she opened the windows overlooking rue de Cujas.

"You are going to have to forgive me, but this is not at all what I expected this meeting to be like."

She sat on one of two beds and gave him a puzzled look. "Oh, why is that?"

"Well, for starters this place, and your attitude. It all appears totally out of character for the grieving widow I read about in the papers this morning."

"You're the one that's going to have to forgive *me*. It should be obvious to you that the reason I'm meeting you here is because I didn't want anybody to know I was talking to the CIA. Perhaps the Agency sent the wrong person for the job."

Cameron frowned. "Look, lady, the reason I said that was because I was told this assignment was only a simple deposition. If it's something more than that, I'd like to know right now."

"Why? So you can leave?" She got up and walked toward the windows.

"No. So I can determine if this place is safe enough, and also find out exactly how you got here. Just because you're dressed like a tourist and you're staying in this dump doesn't mean no one followed you."

She turned around and faced him. "All right, all right. I apologize. For a moment I thought—"

"I'm a trained operative, not a psychic. Now tell me, what was so important that it forced you to use the emergency code you gave us. And how did you get it? As far as we can tell you're not associated with the Agency."

"From my late husband."

Cameron frowned again. "Well, here I am. Now, what is it that you wanted to tell us?"

Marie turned around, put both hands on the windowsill, pulled her chin up, and let the breeze swirl her long black hair. A very attractive woman, Cameron noted.

"It's about the night before he died," she said, her back still to him.

"*Hmm* . . . what about it?" Cameron sat on the bed and loosened his tie.

"He'd just spent a week trying to work out some launch problems in Kourou, and was on his way back here when he called from the plane. He sounded worried, concerned."

"Well, a man in his position. So much responsibility. It would seemed natural to be—"

"No, it wasn't like that. Claude and I worked many hours together, both here in Paris and in Kourou. As a matter of fact, developing the guidance system for the Athena V is how we met in the first place, and over the next few years we learned to work effectively under the enormous pressures associated with keeping to a tight launch schedule.

Sure, he had his bad days with Athena, and so did I, but the other night was different. He wasn't upset or angry, or worried about anything expected; instead he seemed unusually nervous. For a few moments I even recognized an ounce or two of fear in his voice."

"Look, this is very hard for me to say, but I don't see why the CIA needs to be involved."

"Please let me finish." She turned around and faced him. "After he managed to calm down, he told me that the rumor about the Russian craft was true. Then he gave me the CIA code in case something—"

"Wait. Back up. What rumor? What about the Russians?"

Marie ran a hand through her hair, briefly closed her eyes, and sat on the windowsill. "A few months back a Russian spacecraft exploded soon after reaching orbit. The rumor some of us at Athena heard was that it had accidentally collided with one of our own satellites. One of our technicians at Kourou Mission Control had spotted an Orbital Termination message on one of the screens. No one had thought much of it at the time. After all, during the testing stage of the Athena V we'd placed several satellites in orbit which Athena now uses to monitor weather patterns prior to launches. Now and then one of those satellites falls down to such a low orbit that it becomes useless. We usually terminate it by firing its rockets and letting it burn during re-entry. After we got news of the Russian craft exploding at roughly the same place and time as one of our satellite terminations, rumors began floating around the agency that we had accidentally blown up the Russian craft. But the board of trustees quickly squashed those rumors without much investigation, officially closing the matter. Claude seemed particularly distressed by this. He wanted to find out if indeed Athena was at fault, but the termination records appeared to have been erased from the memory banks of the tracking computer."

"All right, what are you trying to tell me?"

"I don't think his death was accidental, the way the papers said."

"You're saying someone killed him?"

"I think so. Claude told me that he and a few other scientists managed to retrieve part of the data that had been erased from memory. He said that the bits and pieces of data they recovered indicated that the Russian craft didn't blow up accidentally at all. It was intentional. And he claimed to have proof that incriminated Athena's upper management."

"What did the French police have to say about Claude's death?"

"The police were useless. They said the death was accidental. I told them I didn't agree with their conclusion and gave them my reasons. I told them that they were closing the case too quickly and that they should do more work investigating."

"And? What did they say?"

"An inspector by the name of Philippe Roquette called me a half hour after I finished talking with the initial investigator. I told him what I'd told the investigator, and he assured me that the situation had been professionally and thoroughly handled. He said that he'd approved the official statement, that Monsieur Guilloux had indeed died in a car accident. Then he said he had other business to deal with and hung up."

"That's it?"

"Yes. Do you see now why I contacted the American Embassy?"

"Well, perhaps you should have . . ." Cameron stopped and walked toward the door.

"What's the—"

"*Shh.*" He held up his left hand and grabbed the Beretta with his right. Slowly he dropped to a crouch and pressed his back against the wall next to the door. The footsteps had stopped again. He had heard them outside several seconds ago. Whoever it was had gone up and down the hall twice.

Maybe a maid, he thought, but quickly discarded it as a possibility. *Kind of late in the day for maid service. A lost tourist? Perhaps, but why stop in front of this door twice?*

Cameron felt his heartbeat increase as adrenaline rushed through his veins. He signaled Marie to get down and hide behind the dresser next to the windows. She complied. Then he slowly extended his hand and unlocked the door. The latching mechanism snapped.

Staccato gunfire burst through the wooden door. Cameron jumped back and rolled next to Marie.

"Don't move!" he screamed while training the 9-mm automatic pistol on the large hole in the center of the still-closed door.

Just as suddenly as it had started, the firing stopped. A second of silence, quickly followed by screams coming from nearby rooms. Cameron didn't flinch. He focused on the door and kept the forward and rear sights of the Beretta perfectly lined up with the center of the hole. Nothing.

He looked at Marie. She was shuddering, her green eyes wide open, her lips quivering.

"Calm down and don't move. As long as—"

A pear-shaped object flew through the hole in the door and skittered across the floor.

Grenade!

Instinctively, Cameron embraced Marie and rolled toward the other side of the room.

It went off. Cameron heard the loud blast. He closed his eyes and waited for the shrapnel, but it never came. He opened his eyes and found himself blinded by thick smoke. Marie coughed. Cameron's eyes stung. The Beretta! His hands fumbled over the worn carpet. Nothing. He heard footsteps approaching.

"Quick, follow me!"

"I can't see! Oh, God, my eyes, they . . ."

Ignoring her cries, Cameron grabbed her right wrist and pulled her behind him. He got up and raced for the window.

He reached it, crawled on the windowsill, and inhaled deeply. Through tears he spotted a thick copper pipe running vertically next to the window. Cameron grabbed it firmly with his left hand.

"Put both arms around my shoulders! Quick!"

"I can't see, my eyes . . ."

The footsteps had stopped.

"Dammit! Do it!"

He felt her embrace from behind.

"On the count of three hold on tight and wrap your legs around my waist. Got it?"

"Yes, I—"

"One—two—three!"

Cameron brought his right hand around and grabbed the pipe as he jumped off the sill with Marie pressed to his back.

He heard the door being kicked open.

The strain on his arms became nearly unbearable. He began to slide down to the street as fast as he could, knowing that it would not take their attacker more than a few seconds to realize how they had escaped.

"Mon Dieu! Mon Dieu!"

Cameron looked toward the street and spotted the old lady from the hotel counter screaming at the top of her lungs by the front door.

"Shit!"

Several pedestrians came from both sides of the block and gathered around the hotel. Cameron looked up toward the window and spotted a gray-haired man with a gray beard looking straight at them.

"Hang on," Cameron said. He instantly felt Marie's grip tighten.

Cameron loosened his hold on the pipe and rapidly slid the last ten feet before crashing against the wet sidewalk. Marie let go on impact, and they both rolled over on the wet pavement. His right shoulder stung as he slammed against the bumper of a parked car, but he forced himself to look back up toward the window. The bearded man had disappeared.

In a blur, he noticed three youngsters gathering around Marie, who appeared unconscious a few feet away. Cameron got up. There was no time to spare. Any second now the gunman would come running out of the hotel.

"Allez-vous en!" Cameron shouted to the startled trio, and shoved them aside as he bent down and pressed the middle and index finger of his left hand against Marie's left wrist. Cameron felt a pulse. He quickly lifted her slim body, hung it over his left shoulder, and raced up the street. The kids stood aside as Cameron brutally kicked his legs, struggling to put some distance between him and the assailant. The wind swirled his short thin hair. Marie's weight quickly became more noticeable. His shoulder burned. So did his legs. He ignored it all and kept running.

"Wait! Wait!"

Cameron glanced back and spotted the bearded man standing by the entrance to the hotel waving them back. Cameron ignored him and turned the corner. He continued down that street and turned left into a dark alley.

TWO ★

Countdown

KENNEDY SPACE CENTER, FLORIDA

After two exhaustive hours going over the proper responses to possible media questions, Kessler left the briefing room and headed for his quarters. With his body and mind totally drained, he could not care less about the press at that moment. The vision of a warm bed filled his mind, and he used what little energy he had left to propel his body down the long and narrow dim-lit hall. He spotted his room at the other end.

Nearly asleep on his feet, Kessler made his way along the dark, glossy-tiled surface. Retrieving his key, he inserted it in the lock, turned it, and pushed the door open.

Inside the air felt warm and stagnant, but that didn't matter to Kessler. He shifted his gaze to the only object important to him, the bed next to the windows on the other side of the spacious room. He approached the bed, untied his shoes, kicked them off, and lay down. Then he frowned, got up, reached for the AC window unit above the bed, and turned it on. The rush of cool air caressed his face, quickly drying the perspiration that dripped from his creased forehead. Now he could sleep.

He lay on his back and closed his eyes. It didn't take much time before he began to drift away. He inhaled deeply and relaxed. His heartbeat decreased and his breathing steadied.

"Hey, Mike! You in there?"

Kessler started at the sudden intrusion. He shook his head and smiled. "It's not locked. Come in!"

The door inched forward. Behind it stood his Texan pilot at over six feet tall and nearly two hundred pounds, wearing his sunglasses. Ray•Bans. Air Force pilots always wore Ray•Bans.

"Ready to eat?"

"Give me a minute to rest," Kessler responded.

"What did you think about the briefing?" Jones closed the door behind him, grabbed a chair from beside the metal desk, spun it around, set it next to the bed, and straddled it like a horse. Kessler smiled wearily. "I couldn't give a damn about that press conference right now. I'm drained. If NASA wants us to fly on schedule they better slow down the pace. Say, did you go see the doctor this morning?"

"Yep."

"And? What did he have to say about your knee?" He noticed the smile disappear from Jones's face.

"No problems."

"Glad to hear that. For a while I thought NASA was going to assign another pilot for the mission."

Jones had been shot down during an F-111B sortie over Iraq years before. An Air Force E-3A Sentry AWACS had detected a pair of Iraqi MiG-23s headed for the two-seater F-111B strategic bombers as they returned to Saudi Arabia. Due to a lack of Air Force fighters nearby, Kessler and his wingman were called in for cover, but when his wingman experienced hydraulic failure, only Kessler could comply with the request. Kessler turned to intercept, but his RIO (Radar Intercept Officer) had trouble with his radar and could not get a good vector to the F-111s from the AWACS crew. After a frustrating two minutes, Kessler managed to intercept and destroy the two MiGs, but not before one of the MiGs had opened fire on Jones's plane. A shell pierced the fuselage of Jones's strategic bomber and exploded inside the cockpit, instantly killing Jones's navigator. The blast set Jones's legs ablaze as shrapnel tore into him. Only Jones's disciplined reaction—grabbing a fire extinguisher and dousing his blazing flight suit—saved his life. He then managed to eject.

Although Jones blamed the incident on the fortunes of war, Kessler couldn't help but feel responsible for the navigator's death and the subsequent pain that Jones had had to endure from his injuries.

"You mind?" Jones pulled out a pack of Marlboro Golds and a lighter.

"Nope. Go ahead. They're your lungs, not mine."

"Well, this is the way I see it. If those damned Iraqis couldn't kill me after filling my plane with lead, then I doubt this little cigarette has a chance in hell of doing much to me."

Kessler smiled broadly. "I guess some things just never change."

"Well, for your information, some things *do* change. This is the first smoke I've had since yesterday morning. For a guy that used to smoke a pack a day a year ago, I'd say that I've come a long way."

Kessler threw his arms up in the air. "All right, all right. I apologize."

"Good," Jones said. "Then let's eat."

PARIS, FRANCE

With his mind racing, looking for a reasonable explanation, Cameron paced back and forth in the small room on the second floor of St. Vincent de Paul Hospital.

The incident at the rue de Cujas certainly gave Marie's story some credibility. Enough for Cameron to share his information with his case officer back at the American Embassy. His case officer had not been pleased. This wasn't supposed to have been anything serious. The French police, on the other hand, had been most polite under the circumstances. They had given him back his lost Beretta, after determining that it had not been fired the night before. The police had listened to his entire story while taking massive amounts of notes. Cameron did find out one interesting fact about the case: The police had found a dead man in Marie's hotel room, who'd turned out to be Inspector Philippe Roquette. He had been shot in the back. Roquette was the same inspector that Marie had talked to about her husband's death. That had Cameron baffled. *Why was he there? To warn her about the gray-haired assassin? Or was Roquette the assassin himself?*

He stared at Marie, sleeping peacefully across the room in a bed next to the window. The doctor had said she had a minor concussion and would be out for several hours.

"Mmmm."

Cameron saw her stir in her sleep. He walked across the tiled floor and sat at the edge of her bed. She moaned softly, slowly moving her head from side to side, clearly upset even though unconscious.

Cameron walked to the small sink on the opposite side of the room, wetted the small towel hanging next to it, and walked back to Marie's bedside. He folded the towel in two and gently pressed it against her forehead.

"Hmmm . . . mmmph . . ." She relaxed. Cameron smiled. Marie was indeed a very beautiful woman. Naturally beautiful.

He pressed the towel gently against her cheeks and neck. "You'll be all right, Marie. Relax. Everything is going to be fine." Cameron stared at her face and suddenly felt ashamed of himself. Her husband had died less than forty-eight hours ago and here he stood feeling strongly attracted to her. He shook his head and exhaled. It felt strange. He had not been with a woman for years, not emotionally, that is. His first and only love affair had occurred nearly two decades earlier, in Vietnam. Although GIs had been officially prohibited from becoming involved with the locals, Cameron had fallen quickly for a petite nineteen-year-old named Lan-Anh Binh, the daughter of a prosperous Saigon businessman. The secret affair had lasted for six months, ending abruptly when her father's store fell victim to a terrorist incendiary bomb while Lan-Anh worked the cash register. Her body had been burned beyond recognition. Cameron, devastated, had turned in a request to be transferred to Special Forces where in those days the survival ratio was very poor. He'd spent three tours with Special Forces, participating in covert operations behind enemy lines. Those three years had toughened him up, both physically and mentally. They'd been his wild years. Booze, women, and war had filled his life. Solid friendships had been begun and lost quickly in those days. The more reason for the booze and the women. He had managed to survive Vietnam, had spent more time with the Army as a basic training instructor, and eventually had been recruited by the CIA. With the CIA in Mexico he had gone out with a few embassy secretaries and some locals, but nothing serious had ever developed. His work never left him enough time to have a proper relationship. He knew that for a forty-two-year-old his sex life had not been all that bad, but his love life had been way below average.

A knock on the door made him reach for his Beretta. He pulled it out of the Velcro-secured holster.

"Stone? You in there?"

Hiding the weapon behind his back, Cameron approached the door and opened it. Outside stood two large muscular men in their late twenties, dressed in two-piece suits and overcoats. One held a can of soda in his left hand and a paperback in his right. The second man kept one hand inside a coat pocket while holding up two identification cards with the other.

Amateur hour, thought Cameron as he briefly eyed each of the rookies and checked their IDs. *Never compromise your hands.*

"I'm heading back to the embassy to get some sleep," Cameron said, holstering the Beretta. "Call me if she comes around, and *please* do me a favor and stay frosty. Trash the reading material, keep your hands free at all times, and split up. One outside in the hall and the other near her bed, but away from the windows. Switch places every half hour." Without waiting for a response, Cameron grabbed his coat and walked past the startled duo.

Cameron arrived at the American Embassy thirty minutes later. He used the elevators instead of the stairs, like most everyone else in the building. Tired and nauseated from lack of sleep, he didn't feel like exerting the additional effort, especially after fighting a petulant morning crowd in the Metro. He pushed the button and the elevator doors closed.

Cameron briefly closed his eyes and yawned. His mind automatically began to go through the list of possible explanations for last night's incident, but he shook the thoughts away. *Rest first, then analyze.*

The doors opened. Cameron stepped away from the elevator, turned left, and walked toward his room at the other end of the narrow hall. As he pulled out his key, he noticed a white piece of paper folded in half and taped to his door. Cameron pulled it off and read it. A note from his case officer. A meeting with the French police had been set up for later that day at the hospital. *A meeting? What's going on? Are these the same cops who didn't have a clue about the shooting last night? Could they have really come up with something useful since then?* He exhaled and accepted the fact he would have to wait for a few more hours before finding out. He unlocked the door.

Although he had a fairly small room, he didn't have to share it with another operative as had been the case in Mexico City. Cameron reached for the small Sony stereo system next to the single bed and tuned into Armed Forces Radio, one of the few English-speaking radio stations in

Europe. He barely heard the music as his eyes drifted toward the only photograph in the room, a black-framed eight-by-ten standing over the stereo. It showed him and three members of his old platoon in Vietnam. Three that never made it back alive. Cameron's eyes filled when he focused on the blond skinny kid with one arm around Cameron's neck. A young private by the name of Jim Skergan, a good kid from the steel towns of Pennsylvania. Cameron had known him for only a few months.

Cameron instantly regretted the thought. The memory came rushing back, just as it had hundreds of times before. Skergan's eyes pleaded with Cameron. *Go, Cameron. You can . . . make it on your own. I'll hide . . . and wait . . . for you to . . . come back.*

Cameron managed to shake the thought away, and his eyes focused on his war decorations, also framed, next to the photograph. His hypocritical ribbons and medals, as he thought of them. Decorations given to him after he had left Skergan to die at the hands of the savage Vietcong. Cameron didn't deserve them, Skergan did. The private had been the one that had offered to die to save Cameron. He had been the one that had convinced Cameron to save himself.

War decorations. Nothing but meaningless scraps of cloth and metal that reminded him of his past, yet he had kept them for all these years. He loathed their sight, but he had hung on to them to remind himself of past sins. Cameron saw them as a path to atonement, a path to redemption through self-inflicted mental punishment.

Cameron glanced at the photograph once more. As he eased himself on the bed and closed his eyes, Skergan's face filled his mind again. *Go, Cameron. You can make it on your own . . .*

THREE ★

SSMEs

LAUNCH COMPLEX 39, PAD A. KENNEDY SPACE CENTER, FLORIDA

A tall female senior engineer walked past the guard station that led to the Mobile Launch Platform. She flashed her badge and waved at the guards, who smiled and waved back.

"Morning, Vera."

She knew them both. Vera Baumberger had been a Rocketdyne engineer from the beginning of the space shuttle program back in the summer of 1972, when Rockwell International won the 2.6-billion-dollar contract to design and build the space-shuttle orbiter, mandated to fly one hundred times each, and capable of sixty flights per year. The contract, Vera recalled, included system-integration responsibility, where Rockwell would guarantee that all components—including Martin Marietta's External Tank, Morton-Thiokol's Solid Rocket Boosters, and Rocketdyne's Space Shuttle Main Engines—worked together.

She limited herself to saying "Hello" as she made her way under the colossal platform resting on six twenty-two-foot-tall pedestals over the concrete pad. Kennedy's three MLPs, initially built for use in the Apollo/Saturn V program, were 160 feet long, 135 feet wide, and stood twenty-five feet high. The single square opening in the center of the platform that allowed hot exhausts from the Saturn V to escape into the flame trench during lift-off had long been replaced by three openings—two for Solid Rocket Booster exhaust and one for SSME exhaust. Vera walked toward the orbiter engine-service platform, which had been positioned beneath the MLP and raised by a winch mechanism through the SSME exhaust hole to a position directly beneath the three engines.

Vera approached the base of the service platform and started going up the steps. This section of the pad was fairly crowded, and with good reason, she decided. With the launch less than forty-eight hours away, people moved in all directions performing final checks. Each inspection team had responsibility for a specific section of the orbiter. In Vera's case, she was the team leader responsible for all three Space Shuttle Main Engines.

Vera had been with the SSME design and test team from the start of the project back in 1972. From that point on the engineering crew had faced an uphill battle to iron out numerous flaws in the original design of the powerful engine, particularly in the turbopumps. The SSME was essentially an engine which put out highly pressurized steam obtained by burning liquid hydrogen and liquid oxygen. The high pressure was generated by the rapidly burning fuel going through the nozzle and erupting at the throat of the engine at very high velocity. This concept required special pumps to accelerate the liquid oxygen and liquid hydrogen through the nozzle. Rocketdyne's solution to the problem became the high-pressure turbopump, which, although it worked beautifully on paper, turned out to be plagued with design flaws. The pump had two main problems: a whirl mode—instability caused by vibration of the turbo blades when rotating at very high speeds—and a lack of adequate cooling for the bearings. These two problems tended to mask each other and were extremely difficult to identify. To make matters worse, the only way to check the results of a design improvement was by test-firing an engine.

Vera frowned when she recalled the dozens and dozens of SSME firing tests she'd participated in at the National Space Technology Laboratories in Bay St. Louis, Mississippi. The pump experiments caused SSME explosion after explosion, damaging so many engines that NASA had to double the number originally ordered. By 1980 the whirl problem had been resolved and Rocketdyne had developed an efficient way of delivering a sufficient amount of coolant to the bearings to avoid the disastrous turbopump overheating.

Vera shifted her gaze up and watched three members of her team standing on the elevator platform that extended upward to the engine bells. From that platform, several access scaffolds went up to the base of the engines.

"Hi, Vera," said one of her technicians when he saw her.

"How's the systems check going?"

"Fine. No problems yet."

"Good. Let me take a look." She easily climbed up the twenty-foot-tall vertical ladder to the elevator platform, walked to the access scaffold under the number-three SSME, went up the scaffold, and reached her team on the platform.

"All right. Let me take a look at the manifold valves. You and you, get a lifter and bring my equipment up here."

"Right away," responded two members of her team as they went down the scaffold, leaving her with one young technician still in training. Almost ignoring him, she moved around him on the platform and leaned over and peeked inside the space in between the nozzle's base and the open heat shield. Her hands moved automatically, doing what they did best. She manually performed one final check as her trainee looked on.

"We've already checked the entire system three times today," he noted.

"You can never check these engines enough times. Now hand me a flashlight, please."

Her subordinate handed her a black flashlight. Vera grabbed it with her right hand and trained the flashlight on the manifold valves that controlled the flow of liquid hydrogen through pipes that ran all around the nozzle. They appeared normal. Next she inspected the high-pressure turbopumps. The larger one for liquid hydrogen, the smaller for liquid oxygen. They looked normal. She lowered the beam of light until it reached a black box. It had a tube coming out of the front. The tube went into the hydrogen turbopump at one end and came out the other, returning to the back of the box. The tube carried precious coolant to the pump's bearings. The black box was the coolant pump.

Vera raised an eyebrow when she noticed a small white cylinder strapped to the side of the coolant pump, almost out of sight. The cylinder—whatever it was—definitely did not belong there. She set the flashlight over a wide pipe to her right and used both arms to pull herself through the one-meter opening.

The main engine compartment was crowded with pipes and wires. Recovering her flashlight, she trained it on the small cylinder, and blinked twice in silent astonishment when she realized what it was. The cylinder had a small digital readout indicating 00:04:00. She had found a timer with a small actuator motor. The arm of the motor was connected to the manifold valve on the side of the coolant pump that controlled the flow of coolant to the liquid hydrogen turbopump's bearings. If her guess was correct the timer would shut off the valve four minutes after lift-off, at a time when *Lightning* would be at a very critical phase of its ascent. Without coolant the bearings would overheat in a fraction of a second, overheating the turbopump and inducing a fire which would result in a tremendous explosion. She had seen those explosions many times before.

"This is sabotage," she murmured.

"Excuse me?" said the trainee ten feet below her.

"Ah . . . nothing. Just talking to myself. Hand me a pair of wire cutters, would you?" Vera decided this was highly classified information. Someone had definitely attempted to sabotage the orbiter and she would make sure the information reached the appropriate authorities, namely the center's director.

The technician handed her the wire cutters. Vera disconnected the small cylinder from the valve, put it in her pocket, and shook her head. Whoever did this knew exactly what to do. Since the timer would not kick it until after liftoff, the General Purpose Computers would not diagnose a problem. *Damn!*

"Wait here for the others and tell them this engine is fine," she said as she walked to the edge of the platform.

"All right."

She was about to reach for the rail to crawl down from the scaffold when she felt a shove from behind. Before she could react, her body flipped over the short safety rail.

"Ahhh!" Vera twisted her body in midair and slapped both hands against the array of pipes hoping to grab one, but failed. She hit the welded steel edge of the elevator platform with her back, bounced, and fell for another thirty feet, finally crashing headfirst against the concrete stand.

LANGLEY, VIRGINIA

In one of twelve cubicles inside a computer room on the third floor of the Central Intelligence Agency headquarters, George Pruett removed his thick glasses and rubbed his eyes and the bridge of his nose. Grimacing, he looked at the heavy lenses, the result of ten years of staring at computer screens.

Working for the Office of Computer Services within the Directorate of Science and Technology, George had been given the colossal task of writing and debugging a series of algorithms designed to detect patterns in a variety of government agencies related to job-switching, promotions, resignations, and several other parameters, including deaths. He knew the reason the Agency had given him such a task was the same reason the CIA had lured George from his previous job with the NSA a year ago by doubling his salary: George was a computer genius. There was no algorithm he couldn't write, no computer he couldn't break into, and certainly no programming language he couldn't master in a fraction of the time that it would take one of the other CIA senior computer science analysts, like the ones working behind the Sun Sparks workstations in the other cubicles of the large room.

George also sat behind a Sun, which not only had access to the CIA mainframe computer in the adjacent room, but also had its own stand-alone hard disk—the place where his programs resided.

He put his glasses back on and gazed at the array of small half-inch-by-half-inch icons, seven across by nine down on the screen. Each icon had a three-letter acronym that described a government agency. Some acronyms were straightforward, like IRS. Others he'd learned as his program evolved. The INS, for example, stood for the Immigration and Naturalization Service. In the instances—which were quite a few—where three letters were not enough to describe an agency fully, the acronym described only part of the name. George knew the meaning of all of them.

The icons were color-coded according to the "relevance" of the pattern as defined by the algorithm, which he had programmed to detect and accumulate events for the previous month only. A white-bordered icon meant there were no significant changes in that particular government agency. Yellow was borderline, a possible pattern probably worth investigating. A red border meant the algorithm had definitely detected a pattern of some sort that might or might not be significant to the user, and had flagged it.

George looked at an icon in the center of the array. It had a yellow border—the third such icon he'd seen in the past two hours. He read the letters NAS. George wondered what was happening at NASA.

His right hand reached over the mouse connected to his workstation. He slowly dragged it over the mousepad and brought the screen pointer inside the icon. He clicked the left button on the mouse twice. The screen suddenly changed. All of the icons disappeared as the screen displayed "NASA" across the top. On the left-hand side of the screen he read the list of possible pattern-generating parameters. He noticed the DEATHS parameter blinking.

George grunted his curiosity and grabbed a cup of coffee next to the Sun. He took two small sips and frowned at the coffee's bitter taste. He set the cup down and placed his hand on the mouse once more. He moved the pointer to the DEATHS parameter line and clicked the left button on the mouse once. Again the screen changed.

George studied the new display, which included two names, brief biographical descriptions of the individuals named, and a cause of death for each. The first one was Claude Guilloux, a well-known French rocket scientist who had been killed a few days earlier in an auto accident. *Interesting,* thought George, wondering why his algorithm had grabbed someone who was not associated with NASA. Then he smiled when he remembered that his program would enter not only anything associated with a particular agency itself, but also any relevant occurrences in that agency's field.

George had begun to read the second entry when he was interrupted by the analysts in the other cubicles getting ready to leave for lunch.

"You sure you don't want to come, George?" asked a fairly new female analyst as everyone headed for the glass door on the left side of the rectangular room.

George got up and glanced at her over the short cubicle wall. "Ah, no, thanks," he replied. "I've got a few errands to run."

"You kidding?" asked a man in his late thirties as he zipped up his jacket. "That'll be the day when George joins us for lunch. I gave up on him about six months ago."

George raised an eyebrow and grinned. He had better things to do with his free time than spend it chewing the fat with CIA analysts talking about their problems at work and at home. He heard enough of that just by sitting in that room with them, and besides, George already had had more than his share of problems in life. His father, a former senior CIA operative, had mysteriously died almost ten years before in East Berlin, shortly after George's seventeenth birthday. When his mother sustained permanent injuries in a tragic hit-and-run accident four years later, George had been forced to become the head of the household practically overnight, taking care of her and his two younger sisters. While working two jobs to help support his family, George had finished college and gotten his degree before he turned twenty-three.

No, George decided, he definitely didn't feel like listening to his coworkers' problems during his free time. With his mother in a wheelchair, George and his two sisters took turns going home during lunch to look after her. During the days when one of his sisters went home for lunch, like today, he spent his time enjoying the only other activity that filled his life besides computers: reading spy novels. George read them by the dozens. He simply couldn't ever get enough, even as a teenager, when he'd visualized his own father playing the roles of the main characters. A love for clandestine work had been part of the reason he'd chosen the intelligence field after college. He had wanted to be a field operative, follow his father's footsteps, become a Cold War master spy, but reality had fallen far short of expectations when George had failed the rigorous physical examination required for all operatives. He just wasn't the physical type, and that revelation had nearly crushed him. But he had hung in there. He'd still wanted to be a part of it, to live up to his father's memory. And so, with a computer engineering degree and a minor in political science, he had joined the National Security Agency right out of school.

As the lunch group left, George sat back down and read the second entry in the computer list. Vera Baumberger, a Rocketdyne engineer working at Kennedy Space Center on the new orbiter *Lightning,* had accidentally fallen off a platform at the launchpad and died from a fractured skull.

George leaned back in his swivel chair. He read both entries once more looking for something else that could indicate a possible connection, but nothing seemed obvious. The incidents appeared to be totally unrelated. *Hardly a pattern,* George thought, but that was the reason why the program only highlighted the icon in yellow—a *possible* pattern.

He clicked back to the main screen. So far he had nothing relevant for Clandestine Services, the department George reported to, which also happened to be headed by his own uncle, Thomas H. Pruett.

George didn't mind indirectly working for his father's older brother. In his mind, George knew the Agency had hired him for his top-notch computer skills, but as in any other large corporation, he was concerned about rumors of favoritism spreading around the Agency. As it turned out, in the year since his arrival at Langley, George had only seen his uncle a few times, mostly outside work, when Thomas Pruett visited George's mother. As head of Clandestine Services, his uncle was a busy man.

Also known as the Directorate of Operations, Clandestine Services was primarily composed of the so-called "area" divisions. These divisions corresponded roughly to the State Department's geographic bureaus. His uncle had explained to him on his first day that it made a lot of sense, since most CIA operators in foreign countries worked under State cover. The largest division was Far East, followed by Europe and Western Hemisphere. George worked indirectly for Western Hemisphere and Europe since his algorithm concentrated mostly on aspects of those two areas. His data—assuming he came up with anything of significance—would first go to the office of Chief Europe Ronald Higgins, who also happened to be acting as Chief Western Hemisphere, and if the information was deemed significant, it would then be presented to the elder Pruett.

George had stopped by his uncle's office the day before to drop off a small birthday present from his mother, but his uncle's secretary had told him that Pruett had been out of the country for almost two weeks and would not be back for another day, something that didn't surprise George one bit.

George locked his system and headed for the parking garage.

PARIS, FRANCE

Cameron eyed the young CIA agent guarding Marie's door, and nodded approvingly at the rookie's hands-free-and-ready posture. He went into the room and smiled when he saw Marie sitting up, eating a bowl of soup. The second agent sat next to her bed drinking coffee and reading the paperback. Cameron shook his head. The agent quickly got up and left the room.

Cameron stopped halfway to her bed. She wore a white hospital gown.

"How are you feeling?"

She looked up and studied him briefly. "Fine. Much better. Do you believe my story now?"

Cameron exhaled. "Yes. We believe your story."

She smiled. "Good. Thanks. Your two colleagues told me what you did. I guess I owe you one."

"No problem. I was just doing my job."

The door opened. Cameron's case officer, Richard Potter, walked in the room. A couple of inches shorter than Cameron and forty pounds heavier—most of it around his waist—Potter gave the impression of someone who spent too much time behind a desk. The CIA official closed the door and approached the bed.

As Cameron went through the introductions, the door opened again. A middle-aged, well-built man wearing a suit under a brown overcoat stood in the doorway. The man briefly introduced himself as the Prefect of the Paris police. Cameron could barely see his lips move underneath a thick but well-kept mustache.

The Prefect removed his coat, set it on a chair next to Marie's bed, and faced his audience of three.

"I'm afraid our initial assessment that the single-car collision was purely accidental was incorrect," he began to say. "We think Monsieur Guilloux was murdered—"

"Damn! I knew it! I told you, Cameron," Marie said. She turned to the Prefect. "I also tried to convince Inspector Roquette, but he wouldn't believe me. I think my husband was killed because of what he had discovered at Athena."

"That's possible. You do know that Inspector Roquette was killed last night at the hotel?"

"Yes," responded Marie. "I found that out from the CIA agents outside. How was he involved in all of this?"

The Prefect briefly ran a finger over his mustache. "We have reason to believe that Inspector Roquette was responsible for your husband's death."

"Well, that makes some sense," noted Cameron. "That would certainly explain why he brushed Marie off when she asked him about the investigation."

"That's right . . . bastard!" exclaimed Marie. "Wait a second. Who killed Roquette then?"

"We're working on that right now," said the Prefect. "We have a couple of good descriptions from witnesses. They all saw a man with gray hair and beard running out of the hotel."

"That's right," agreed Cameron. "I saw him too. You think he killed Roquette?"

"At this point we're working under that assumption."

Cameron tilted his head. "Do you think he was killed to break the link with the people that actually wanted Guilloux dead? According to Marie, they could be Athena's upper management."

"We're trying to establish that right now. That's all I'm at liberty to say at this moment, but please rest assured that the police are handling the case under my direct supervision. There is no need for your agency to be involved any further."

"Just answer this," Cameron pressed further. "If Marie's suspicion is true, and her husband was killed because he had information that incriminated Athena in the destruction of the Russian craft, then wouldn't that make it an international incident?"

"If that's true, yes," the Prefect responded. "But until that is established, I can't talk about the case any more. This is a French police matter. We appreciate the help you have given us, but I'm afraid the matter no longer concerns you."

"The hell it doesn't!" Marie snapped. "The last time I was told by the police that matters were being handled was the day before Roquette tried to kill me! And the only reason I'm still alive is because the CIA came to my rescue. Now after all of that you're telling me you want the CIA out of it?"

"I'm afraid the Prefect is correct," Potter said, cutting in. "This matter is not for the CIA. Not yet anyway."

Although not very pleased, Cameron accepted Potter's decision. The police would handle it for now.

The Prefect grabbed his coat, mentioned to the group that two of his men would be there within the hour to replace the CIA agents, and left the room.

Potter glanced at Cameron. "Ready?"

"In a minute, sir. I'll meet you down by the car."

"Two minutes. Remember, the French are in charge now. It's their show."

"Yes, sir."

Potter left the room. Cameron waited until the door was closed. He sat by the edge of the bed. Marie frowned and stared out the window. Her room overlooked the Observatorie de Paris.

"You okay?"

"I guess."

"Well, I've been ordered to stay out of it, but that doesn't mean I can't keep in touch. You should be out of here by tomorrow." He reached into his coat pocket. "Here's my direct number at the embassy. If there's anything you need, *anything,* please give me a call. All right?"

She turned and looked at him. He felt overwhelmed by her dazzling eyes. Even without any makeup, Marie was a beautiful woman. Slowly, her frown changed to a slight smile. "All right. Thanks. Thanks a lot for everything."

"My pleasure." He put his hand over hers. "Bye now." He got up.

"Au revoir."

Cameron smiled. *"Au revoir,* Marie." He turned around and walked outside.

FOUR ★

Clippers

We have seen many vessels pass through the water, but never saw one which disturbed it less. Not a ripple curled below her cut-water, nor did the water break at a single place along her sides.

—*A reporter aboard the clipper*
Lightning *on her maiden voyage*

LAUNCH COMPLEX 39, PAD A. KENNEDY SPACE CENTER, FLORIDA

Michael Kessler had always loved the sea as much as he enjoyed flying. He dreamed of the times when discoverers like Columbus, Cortez, and Balboa went against all odds and set forth to find new worlds, challenging the powerful and dangerous ocean in wooden ships that would make today's sailors tremble with fear. *Those were the days,* he reflected. *The days of the real sailors. Men with nerves of steel.* Most of the famous explorers were considered lunatics by their peers, or were labeled as dreamers and not given any respect. Only after much ridicule did men like Columbus and Magellan, men ahead of their time, finally receive ships, which often looked so old and battered they appeared hardly able to reach the harbor's mouth, much less endure the cruel Atlantic Ocean or the even more dangerous Pacific. Crews were made up mostly of prisoners, men sentenced to death who would be pardoned by the crown only if they cooperated and survived. Ships' crews were large in those days, mainly because one in four would die during a given voyage. Those were the odds given to the inmates prior to sailing: a seventy-five-percent chance of coming back alive with their crimes forgiven. Most took the opportunity, though the sea was far from forgiving.

Scurvy was the primary cause of death. Caused by a lack of Vitamin C, it resulted in the slow rotting of their bodies, starting with their gums and calves. The disease, if not immediately treated, evolved into gangrene and eventually death. The men tried just about everything—from opening their gums and skin with knives to bleed the blackened blood, to savage amputations. *Mere delays of inevitable death,* thought Kessler. *How ironic. While the ocean's clear waters flowed under the hull and fresh air caressed the main deck, the crew would be literally rotting away.*

With time, cures for such diseases were developed, sailing ships grew in size and speed, and by the middle of the nineteenth century safe and fast transatlantic voyages were possible thanks to a new breed of vessels, initially called the "tall ships." Sails hung higher and higher on massive masts in order to maximize the driving power of the wind. Below the waterline, their reinforced hulls could endure the savage punishment of the sea as water and wood clashed at speeds in excess of twenty knots.

It was the golden age of sailing, the age of the clippers, and the American-built *Lightning,* one of the largest and fastest clippers ever made, a long, graceful yachtlike vessel, beautifully painted and rigged, ruled the seas. *Lightning*'s first captain was "Bully" Forbes, notorious for refusing to reduce sail area when the winds were strong, setting records during his voyages between America, England, and Australia while surveying routes to deploy submarine cables for telegraph communications. The fear in those days was that strong winds would increase the likelihood of smashing rigging, but Forbes knew how much to push *Lightning* without exceeding the builder's specifications. *Lightning*'s shrouds, four inches in diameter, provided the strength to support a 160-foot-high mainmast. In addition, *Lightning* became one of very few ships that regularly used a moonsail—a sail above the uppermost sails. *Lightning* had the muscle, and Forbes simply took advantage of it, setting record after record in one of the last of the great American clippers.

Lightning. Kessler read the words painted in black on the starboard wing. It was nighttime, but the entire area was brightly lit, and he stared at the thermal-protection system covering the basically aluminum orbiter. The system, composed mainly of two types of reusable insulation tiles and thermal blankets, protected *Lightning* against the brutal aerodynamic heating during re-entry. The two types of tiles, consisting of pure silica fibers made of sand and stiffened with clay, differed only in thickness and surface coating to provide protection for different temperature regimes. The thicker tiles—ranging from one to five inches in thickness—were coated with a mixture of tetrasilicide and borosilicate glass, which gave them their glossy black sheen. These tiles protected the orbiter's entire underside, part of the nose, and all leading edges against temperatures reaching up to 2300 degrees centigrade. The thinner tiles and thermal blankets—ranging from one-half to three inches thick—had a coating of aluminum oxide and white silica compounds. Rated for up to twelve hundred degrees, these white tiles and thermal blankets protected the upper fuselage and all leeward surfaces.

Thermal tiles—a logistic nightmare. Each tile had to be individually cut and fit to a specific location on the orbiter. After bonding, the tile was pull-tested to determine how tightly it adhered to the skin. Pull-testing was critical to ensure that *Lightning*'s thermal-protection system would be able to withstand the extreme rigors of lift-off and re-entry heating.

Kessler continued to stare at the orbiter. In less than

twenty-four hours, hundreds of thousands of gallons of liquid hydrogen and liquid oxygen would be pumped into the External Tank, from the propellant storage facility located on the northwest corner of the launch complex, at the rate of ten thousand gallons per minute, making *Lightning* ready for business.

Ready for business. Kessler lowered his gaze, suddenly overcome by a feeling of inadequacy, of not being ready for the responsibility. *But what about all of the months of training I endured at Johnson Space Center's Shuttle Mission Simulator? All of the "dead stick" landings at Kennedy? The hundreds of hours practicing EVAs in the WET-F pool? Doesn't that count for something? And that's not counting the flying I did for the Navy. Doesn't that qualify me as mission commander?*

Kessler watched in silence as the colossal Rotating Service Structure slowly rolled back, exposing *Lightning*'s closed payload bay doors. Launch minus thirty hours. Kessler felt his heartbeat increasing. *Relax, Michael. If you can handle one of those Tomcats landing on a moving carrier, you shouldn't have any problems bringing that craft back home.*

Kessler closed his eyes and visualized him and Jones on the day of the launch at the Operations & Checkout building eating the classic steak and eggs breakfast prior to the weather briefing. Then it would be time to suit up and leave the O&C building at T minus two hours, thirty minutes and head for the launch pad. Upon arriving at the white room at the end of the orbiter-access arm, white-room personnel would assist them in entering the orbiter, where they would conduct air-to-ground communications checks with Launch Control at Kennedy and Mission Control in Houston. Then *Lightning*'s hatch would be closed.

God, he pleaded, *please don't let me screw this one up.*

Kessler turned and headed for his quarters. He had two more hours of rest before the press conference later on that morning.

• • •

A mile away Captain Clayton "Tex" Jones walked up to the Vehicle Assembly Building, looking for Kessler. The VAB, originally built to assemble the Saturn V moon rocket under the name Vertical Assembly Building, was at the time the largest building in the world, covering eight acres with an enclosed volume of 129 million cubic feet. The structure could withstand winds of up to 125 knots, a necessity to protect the space vehicles properly against the temperamental Florida weather.

The titanic bridge cranes lifted the orbiter *Atlantis* off the floor. They would hoist 150,000 pounds of orbiter onto the 154-foot-long, unpainted, rust-orange External Tank. Its dirty-looking primer contrasted with the pristine white of the Solid Rocket Boosters and the gleaming orbiter, but NASA had made the decision long ago—after the second shuttle flight—to stop painting the disposable tanks, thus saving the taxpayers the cost of a fifteen-thousand-dollar paint job, and lightening the tank's weight by almost six hundred pounds.

The entire shuttle assembly took place over one of the Mobile Launcher Platforms.

Jones stared at the colossal assembly. The high-precision hoisting unit had successfully brought *Atlantis*—in a vertical profile—within inches of the External Tank. NASA technicians now worked laboriously at connecting the hardpoints on *Atlantis*'s underside to the steel assembly built onto the side of the External Tank.

The Herculean effort to prepare a shuttle for launch never failed to fascinate him. He'd watched for hours while *Lightning* was readied. He couldn't wait to ride her into space.

ANDREWS AIR FORCE BASE, MARYLAND

Inside the small aft lavatory of the Boeing 707, Thomas H. Pruett felt another convulsion and couldn't hold it any longer. On his knees, Pruett placed his face over the toilet and let it all out. In the past he'd only felt nauseated during the few occasions when a crisis forced him to travel by Air Force fighter to "hot spots," but as his digestive condition worsened, Pruett found himself unable to tolerate even jet-liner flights.

"Let's go, Tom. The limo's waiting."

Chief Europe Roland Higgins banged impatiently on the lavatory door. To Pruett, Higgins seemed all too eager to get back to the office after returning from a South American tour designed to let Higgins get acquainted with most of the Western Hemisphere field houses. Since the early retirement of the previous Chief Western Hemisphere, Pruett had been filling in while searching for a permanent replacement, but after several months without being able to find the right individual, Pruett had decided to give his younger, ambitious, and very confident Chief Europe a shot at managing both divisions.

"Give me a second."

Their last stop had been French Guiana. Not a very high place on Pruett's list, but Higgins had insisted on visiting all the field houses. Not because he'd expected any real surprises—after all, Pruett always kept extremely close contact with his people—but because Higgins had argued that a face-to-face meeting was the best way to keep a good working relationship with faraway field offices.

Pruett turned on the faucet over the diminutive sink and splashed cold water on his face. He inhaled deeply and stared at his own image in the mirror. *Not a pretty sight,* he decided with a frown. The circles under his bloodshot eyes and tousled hair were not in character with a man in his position. Two weeks of nonstop traveling had definitely taken a toll on his fifty-year-old body. *Not a young gun anymore,* he thought. Ten years ago he would have already been in that limousine headed for the CIA headquarters.

Pruett dried his face with a paper towel, pulled out a comb from his pocket, and brushed his brown, thinning hair back, making a receding hairline much more obvious and a square wall of forehead a bit more rectangular, but also giving him a somewhat distinguished look. At least that was what his secretary, Tammy, had told him. At his age he was beyond flattering remarks from young members of the opposite sex. He admitted he had kept some of the attractive characteristics of his youth, especially his large frame, which had given him the right to date just about any girl he wished as captain of his school's wrestling team, and his full lips, which blended into a square jaw—his father's jaw—gave him a kind of rugged geniality.

He rinsed his mouth several times, straightened up his tie, and rolled down the sleeves of his still-white shirt. He smiled. After a decade of stomach problems, Pruett had gotten good at getting sick without messing up his shirt or tie. Just a few minutes in a private rest room and he would emerge looking like new.

He unlocked the door, pushed it open, and spotted his subordinate closing his briefcase. Higgins was about six feet tall, a couple of inches shorter than Pruett. He looked impeccable, dressed in a double-breasted suit, which went well with his pale complexion and carefully clipped mustache.

"You should see a doctor," Higgins said as he walked up the aisle toward the forward section of the craft.

Pruett frowned, snagged his briefcase and coat, and followed him. "Doctors don't know shit."

Higgins shook his head as they walked down the stairs toward the limousine waiting to take them to Langley.

FIVE ★

Personal Sacrifices

LANGLEY, VIRGINIA

Pruett set his briefcase down on his large desk and walked toward his mini-bar. His secretary always made it a point to keep his small refrigerator stocked with one of Pruett's favorite items: milk. He drank it by the gallon to help his ailing ulcer. He opened the refrigerator and smiled when he saw two fresh cartons, one of whole milk, one of skim. He snatched the whole milk and eyed the expiration date, just in case. Satisfied, he opened the carton and took two large swigs.

Loosening his tie, he walked back to his desk, and eased himself into his leather swivel chair. The chair had belonged to his previous boss, the former Head of Clandestine Services, killed on the job several years back. Pruett, Chief Western Hemisphere at the time, had been asked by the CIA Director to fill the position until the Agency could find a replacement, but after several successful months, the Director had made Pruett's temporary assignment permanent.

He noticed a small gift-wrapped box on the right corner of his desk. Pruett eyed the calendar and smiled. He had missed his own birthday. He shrugged and picked up the box. Like a curious youngster, he shook it twice but could not make out its contents. He removed the red wrapping paper and opened the box.

Pruett smiled as his eyes filled. He lifted out a clear paperweight with a three-by-five color photograph inside it, a photo of his brother's family, Pruett's only family besides his two kids. All his older relatives were long gone, and his job had never really given him the chance to start another relationship after his wife had left him nearly two decades before. His two kids never got to see much of him anymore. As they'd been raised by their mother and stepfather, Pruett had been pretty much kept out of it. *That's just as well,* he reflected as his fingers fumbled with the square piece of Plexiglas. He'd always been on some assignment, and wouldn't have been able to spend the time with them anyway. *You're better off this way, Tom . . . or are you?* It was certainly the price he had paid to get to his current position. He took another sip of milk and wondered if his large personal sacrifice had really made a difference. Did his contributions to the Agency compensate for the fact that his own kids—his flesh and blood—were practically strangers living across the country on the West Coast? *Go easy on yourself, Tom!* he told himself. *That was a decision made long ago. It's too late to go back.*

Pruett managed to shake the thought as he looked at the photo, and made a mental note to check on his nephew's progress over at Data Collection the following day. He was a good kid, he decided, picking up where his father had left off at such a young age. Pruett felt a little guilty for having seen George only a few times since his arrival at the Agency, but his job . . . *hell, it's always the job.*

The burning pain in his stomach lessened as he continued to drink directly from the milk carton. The soothing effect was better than what he got from the antacid tablets he carried with him at all times. *It's also healthier,* he thought, staring at the Plexiglas paperweight.

PARIS, FRANCE

It took Cameron Stone one hour to walk the stretch of the beautifully landscaped gardens between the Place de la Concorde, across from the American Embassy, and the Louvre. He'd decided to spend his day off discovering Paris all over again, especially after the turmoil of the past couple of days. As the noontime sun warmed up the air, tourists gathered in front of the huge glass-and-steel pyramids in the center square of the Louvre. The controversial pyramids had been built several years back to modernize access to the museum's different wings.

Cameron got in line to follow the tourists down the escalator that would take him to the underground reception and ticket area, the place from which all museum tours started.

He suddenly felt a hand on his shoulder. Startled, he spun around.

"Marie!"

She was dressed casually, just a plain pair of Levi's and a long-sleeve white T-shirt. Her long hair was tied in a ponytail and she wore large gold earrings.

"Hello, Cameron."

Once more, Cameron felt strongly attracted to her, and a bit guilty because of it. "You . . . are you all right? How's that head wound?"

"What head wound?"

Cameron smiled, but the smile quickly vanished. "Did you follow me here?"

"Cameron, there's something you must know. It's about the rumor at Athena I told you about the other night."

"C'mon, you know I can't get—"

"Please listen to what they have to say. The information they have is very disturbing."

" 'They?' Who are you talking about?"

Marie shifted her gaze to the left. Cameron turned his

head and spotted the man with the gray beard. The man from the rue de Cujas.

Instinctively, he reached under his coat. Marie put her hand over his. "Relax. He's on our side."

Marie waved at the man. He approached them.

"Hello, Monsieur Stone. My name is Jean-François. I was Monsieur Claude Guilloux's bodyguard."

Cameron blinked twice. Bodyguard? "Is that what you were doing back at the hotel? Protecting Marie?"

"Trying to, *monsieur*. Simply trying to conform to one of Monsieur Guilloux's final requests. Come now, please."

"Where? I'm not going anywh—"

"This won't take long," Marie said. "You'll hear for yourself why Athena killed my husband."

Cameron hesitated. The operative in him told him to stick to the rules. *Contact Potter and get approval.* But his instincts told him otherwise. Marie had talked of possible corruption in Athena's ranks. If Athena had indeed destroyed the Russian spacecraft, then in Cameron's logical mind, the problem demanded CIA intervention. Although Cameron seldom deviated from the book—he'd known too many who had and had died—his experience told him this was an exception. Going through proper channels to obtain approval might take too long. Potter might not even sanction further intervention. Cameron made his decision, and followed Marie and Jean-François to a parked car next to the Louvre's west entrance.

Five minutes later, with Jean-François at the wheel, a worn-out Renault sped down the rue de Rivoli toward the Place de la Bastille, where Jean-François turned south and continued on Avenue Daumesnil.

Cameron sat in the back with Marie. He simply stared out the window wondering if he'd made the right choice by coming along. He knew that in doing so he had disobeyed a direct order from Potter.

The car came to a full stop in the middle of a long block on the right-hand side of a deserted street. Large warehouses on their side of the street bordered the Seine. Between the warehouses Cameron could see the river's peaceful waters. The warehouses across the street blocked the view of the city's skyline. Jean-François turned his head.

"Here we are. Please wait for my signal."

"Where are we?" asked Cameron.

"Please, *monsieur*."

Jean-François got out and walked across the cobblestone street to a warehouse on the left. The warehouse had a huge metal sliding door. It was closed, but Cameron spotted a smaller door next to it. Jean-François checked both sides of the street, pushed the smaller door open, and disappeared.

Cameron turned to Marie. "I don't like being inside this parked car. We're too exposed."

"Want to get out and wait next to the warehouses?"

"That sounds like a great—"

"There. He's giving us the signal. We can go in now."

Cameron glanced back toward the warehouse. Jean-François was waving his right hand at them.

Cameron quickly got out and helped Marie. "Let's go." He warily scanned both sides of the block. All clear. They crossed the street and followed Jean-François inside.

The stench of urine and mildew struck him like a moist breeze. Cameron saw no one as Jean-François led him and Marie across the warehouse. He spotted a door at the other end. Jean-François took out a key, unlocked the door, and pulling it open, motioned Cameron and Marie to go through. He followed, locking the door behind them.

Cameron stopped. The room was pitch black.

"Where are we?"

Before Jean-François could answer, bright lights came on, almost blinding Cameron. He found himself under the scrutiny of three well-dressed older men sitting behind a long wooden table.

"Who are you?" he asked, perplexed.

"Our names are not important, Monsieur Stone," replied

the one in the center. "All you need to know is that we were Monsieur Guilloux's colleagues."

Cameron didn't like this game. As he scanned the room for possible avenues of escape, he chastised himself for allowing himself to be trapped. The room had no windows and no visible doors except for the one they had come in through. It looked about sixty feet deep and at least two hundred feet long. The ceiling was as high as the rest of the warehouse. Several fluorescent lights hung from it.

Cameron stood in the middle, Marie to his right. "All right. What is this all about?"

"I'm afraid it concerns the future of your space agency," said a distinguished-looking gentleman seated at the table.

Cameron thought a moment. "You mean NASA?"

"Oui, monsieur. We were all dismissed from our positions at Athena Aerospace, where we worked with Monsieur Guilloux. We were lucky. None of us pressed the issue to the point he did. For that he was murdered. Still, we know what he discovered and cannot allow him to have died without purpose.

"The directors of Athena are planning to sabotage NASA, just as they sabotaged the Russians last month."

Cameron stared at the hardened face of the man across the table. "Sabotage? Murder? Do you realize what you're saying? The implications? The reaction from my government?"

"Oui."

"All right. Go back to the beginning. Tell me everything you know. I want to know *everything.*" Cameron stared into the man's sunken eyes. He saw fear.

The man started, slowly. Every once in a while he would stumble onto a word whose meaning he knew only in French. He would use the French equivalent, pause, and wait for a reaction from Cameron, who would simply nod and motion him to continue. It took only a few minutes. When the man finished, Cameron closed his eyes and simply inhaled and exhaled deeply several times, trying to come to terms with what he had just learned, forcing his logical mind to assimilate the incredible revelation. He turned to Marie. Her eyes were on him, waiting for his reaction. He glanced back across the table.

"So, let me get this straight. Athena tested this . . . killer satellite on a Russian spacecraft to check its accuracy before trying it on an American orbiter?"

"Oui."

"How long before Athena launches this satellite?"

"Three days."

"How long before *Lightning*'s launch?"

"Tomorrow—"

A blast. An ear-piercing blast, instantly followed by a powerful shock wave that sent Cameron flying across the room. A shower of glass from shattered lights fell everywhere. Cameron braced himself as he crashed hard against the far left wall. He bounced and landed on his back on the wet concrete floor, rolling as trained reflexes took command.

He saw several dark figures enter the room through the large hole blasted in the opposite wall. Their silhouettes were sharp against the bright sun gleaming through the opening. Cameron couldn't see much at first. He lost precious seconds trying to discern the long thin extensions at the ends of the figures' hands.

Automatic weapons!

He reached for his Beretta as his eyes scanned the room. Marie had to be somewhere. *But where? Where was she before the blast? Standing to my right. My right, my right. That means she has to be in front of me somewhere. Between me and the guns.*

He heard one, two, three muffled shots. Detected the spitting sounds of a suppressed automatic. He gazed around the room, found their origin. A figure lay still on the floor in the middle of the room.

Bastards!

He counted six intruders. The Beretta had fifteen rounds,

and he didn't have an extra magazine. It was his day off. No more than two rounds each. Cameron spotted the long table lying on its side ten feet away.

He heard three more spitting sounds followed by a low cry. Another two spits. Another cry.

Cameron rolled toward the table and stopped inches from its wooden surface. He rose to a deep crouch. Clutching the Beretta with both hands, he used the edge of the table for support.

"Fuck off, you assholes!" Cameron looked to his right. *Marie!*

His gun sights sought the dark form standing in front of Marie. Fired once. Twice. Both rounds aimed at the midsection. The target came up off his feet and fell to the left as both 9-mm Parabellum rounds transferred their energy. As he fired, Cameron quickly rolled away from his position. His weapon did not have a flash suppressor or silencer attachment. By firing he'd given his position away. The remaining five targets brought their weapons around and fired where he'd been merely seconds ago.

He had to get closer to Marie. Get to a new position and perhaps take out one or two more targets. His right shoulder crashed against the wall. Something gave; not the wall.

Damn.

He brought the Beretta around and trained it on a man still firing into the table, now twenty feet away. One shot. The target fell to his knees. Before he collapsed, Cameron already had another one lined up in his sights. He fired once more. Three down.

"Cameron . . . here . . ."

He heard her words, heard her pain. She was hurt. Cameron bolted up and raced the ten feet that separated them, sliding in beside her, next to the first target he'd killed. He looked to his left and spotted two targets leveling their weapons at him. Instinctively, Cameron grabbed the body of the dead target and pulled it up in front of him as he protected Marie with his own. He braced himself but death never came. Instead, he heard four loud blasts.

Confused, he focused on the right side of the room, where he'd seen the muzzle flashes. *Jean-François!* Relief fell victim to dread as three silenced shots foretold the end of Jean-François.

Cameron spotted the target. He trained the Beretta on him and fired twice. Both rounds hit. The man fell. Cameron scanned the room once more but saw no more targets. He turned to Marie.

"Are you hurt?"

"No, I think just bruised. Don't feel anything brok—" Her words were cut short by the sound of blaring sirens in the distance. Help. But not for him. This was no longer a local matter. He needed his case officer, needed to report. He remembered what he'd been told. Remembered a Roman candle called *Challenger*. Remembered a young schoolteacher and a country grief-stricken.

They left the warehouse through the hole blasted by the intruders and ran to the end of the block, slowed down, and walked casually for several blocks. The embassy was thirty minutes away. Help was there, *support* was there. He needed them. The future of America in space depended on them.

KENNEDY SPACE CENTER, FLORIDA

Kessler and Jones approached the mob of reporters. They had been briefed by NASA officials on what they could and could not say in public.

The NASA administrator standing by the mike looked in their direction.

"Ladies and gentlemen, I present to you Michael Kessler and Clayton Jones, the crew of *Lightning!*"

The audience of reporters and NASA personnel began to applaud. Kessler looked at Jones, who rolled his eyes.

"This is incredible, Mike," Jones whispered. "I mean,

look at them. They all think we can walk on water. I doubt we can do any wrong in their eyes."

Kessler smiled.

The administrator pulled out a single sheet of paper.

"Ladies and gentlemen of the press. Launch time for *Lightning*'s maiden flight has been set for tomorrow morning at 6:54 Eastern Standard Time. Navy Captain Michael Kessler will be mission commander. Mission pilot will be Captain Clayton Jones from the Air Force. With that I'll open for questions."

"Captain Kessler," a lady asked from the back of the room. "Martha Warren, UPI."

Kessler approached the mike. "Yes, Ms. Warren?"

"Isn't it a little strange for you to go up in space as mission commander?"

Kessler narrowed his eyes. "I'm not sure what you mean."

"Well, rookies like yourself usually get their feet wet by going up as mission pilots before commanding a shuttle."

Jones was about to step up to the mike when Kessler motioned him to calm down. Kessler stared at the reporter. He spoke slowly, his words measured. "I have to agree with you in the sense that it isn't common for an astronaut to go up in space for the first time as mission commander, but on the other hand, why not? Look at the facts. Look at the training we've received. The hundreds of hours spent inside the Shuttle Mission Simulator at Johnson Space Center going over the launch, ascent, orbit, docking, deorbit, landing, and quite a number of emergencies that could occur in space. The simulator is by far much more demanding than the real shuttle. It tested us with situations that were far worse than anything that has ever happened in flight to date. We've gone over every problem faced by previous missions. In addition, both Jones and I have logged over five hundred hours of dead-stick approaches on the Gulfstream trainer, which also happens to be more demanding than the shuttle in terms of control and stability. We're ready, we're going up, and we will succeed. Next question, please."

Before anyone could ask a question, the same woman spoke again. "That still doesn't explain why you're going up so soon when there's a long list of astronauts waiting for their chance to go. Some have been waiting for over a decade. Isn't it a little unfair for you to go up so fast? It would seem that you haven't paid your dues yet."

Kessler was about to respond when Jones stepped up to the mike. "I'd like to respond to that if you don't mind, Mike." Jones turned in the direction of the reporter. "Listen, Ms. Warren. I have no idea what you're driving at, but I'd like to say—for the record—that this guy here's the best damned pilot I've ever seen in my life. He's going up because he's the best, and *Lightning* deserves nothing *but* the best at the helm. I'm very proud to get the chance to go up with him in what's going to be the most successful of the shuttle missions to date. Now, why don't we stick to real issues about the mission and stay off the trick questions?"

The room fell silent for several seconds. Kessler closed his eyes and exhaled.

"Next question, please," Jones said.

"Robert Kinsley, ABC. How many days is the mission to last?"

Jones smiled and turned to Kessler. "I guess I'll let you answer that. After all, you're the mission commander."

Kessler smiled in return. "The current schedule is to remain in orbit for four days."

"What is the main purpose of the mission?" the same reporter asked.

"The first priority is to get *Lightning* checked out for commercial and military use. Captain Jones and I will go through a comprehensive series of tests to verify *Lightning*'s functionality in space. This is the main reason for the crew of two. There will be no mission specialists aboard on this trip . . . yes, the lady in the second row."

"Is there any spacewalking scheduled for this mission?"

"No."

"But *Lightning* is carrying the latest spacewalking gear, correct?"

"Every orbiter, regardless of the mission, always carries two sets of EVA gear even if there are no plans to go outside. In the event that we have to EVA for whatever reason, both Captain Jones and myself have spent hundreds of hours training to do so."

Kessler looked at Jones as a dozen hands went up. Jones raised his eyebrows and smiled.

LANGLEY, VIRGINIA

George Pruett put down his paperback and raised an eyebrow when the yellow-bordered NASA icon suddenly turned red. His right hand reached for the mouse and he clicked his way down the list to a new entry.

He read on for a few minutes and exhaled.

"Sweet Jesus!"

"You okay, George?" asked one analyst looking over the short cubicle wall into George's small office.

"Ah . . . yeah, yeah, I'm fine, thanks."

The analyst gave him a puzzled look before going back to his work.

What does it mean? George asked himself. *Three former Athena scientists gunned down during an assault on a warehouse? Two of them shot in the head point-blank? Who did the shooting? The other seven unidentified dead men found there maybe? All had automatic weapons. None carried any identification papers.*

The report was short but concise. It had originated with a daily summary of Surete activities provided by CIA analysts.

"Hmm . . ."

Now this *is interesting,* George thought as he selected the print command from a list of options on the right side of the screen. *First Claude Guilloux and now more scientists from the same space agency?* A few seconds later the Hewlett Packard laser jet printer kicked in with a light hum. A single sheet of paper was sucked in from the paper tray and came out at the other end. George snatched it and carefully read all three entries again. His analytical mind now told him that Guilloux had also been murdered. *What about the accident at NASA?*

George couldn't help himself. Perhaps he'd read just too many spy novels, or maybe he simply wanted his algorithm to come up with something of significance, but he grabbed his phone and called information for the number of the public affairs office at Kennedy Space Center. He got it and redialed.

Ten minutes later, he hung up and set the Sun into a continuous loop so that nobody could access it without the appropriate password. Satisfied, George got up and headed for the fax machine across the hall, where the public affairs official at KSC faxed him a copy of the formal report on the accident.

George walked back to his cubicle, sat on his swivel chair, and slowly read the two-page report. It seemed as if Vera Baumberger had lost her balance while climbing down from one of the shuttle's main engines—according to a young technician working with her at the platform, who also happened to be the first one to get to the spot where she'd fallen. George still didn't like it, but decided to leave it at that for now. The matter with the Athena scientists, however, definitely needed some attention.

He briefly checked the six-digit counter on the side of the laser printer and wrote down the number on the printout. He then made an entry on the printer's logbook. The number of entries in the logbook matched the number of single-sheet printouts. That way no one could get hard-copy information from his system without him knowing about it.

George typed a short memo using a small electric type-writer on the side of his desk, grabbed the computer printout, and headed for the Records department of Computer Services on the second floor. He walked through the double doors and handed the papers to the Records clerk.

"Please route copies to the European section and file the originals."

"Right away," she responded, getting up and walking to the copy machine.

"Thanks." George checked his watch and headed back to his Sun.

PARIS, FRANCE

After three Metro transfers and a short walk, Cameron unlocked the door of their hotel room and let Marie through. He checked both sides of the long hallway before stepping inside and locking the door. They had had no problems finding a hotel room. Tourist season was almost over.

Exhausted, they both collapsed onto the double bed. Cameron flashed briefly on the impropriety of being this close physically to his charge, and guiltily recognized that he didn't give a damn. His training told him that two people, often two agents, were inclined to become physically involved during high-stress assignments, but something told him that if it happened to him and Marie, stress would have less to do with it than her stunning beauty.

Priorities. Cameron knew they were clean, that they hadn't been followed from the warehouse. And he'd specifically chosen not to seek refuge in the embassy when he noticed a gray-paneled truck parked next to the side gate. He wondered for a moment if the embassy was aware of the surveillance, then began to think about a safe contact point to meet his case officer. Marie's voice broke his train of thought.

"So, what's next?"

"Huh?"

"What do we do next?"

"Oh, I contact Potter and get him to pull us in."

"How?"

He smiled. "Trust me."

"What about the French police?"

"I'm not sure how to handle that yet. Let's get to safety first and talk it over with our people. I'm sure there's a way to work that out."

She frowned. "How do you think Potter is going to react?"

"Oh, he'll be pissed off at first and will probably curse me out for a couple of minutes. After that I think he'll listen to what we have to say."

"When do you plan to . . ."

"I spotted a couple of public phones a block away. I just wanted to get you out of harm's way first."

She smiled again and touched his arm in gratitude.

A strong woman, Cameron thought. Going through what she had gone through and still managing to keep her cool and not fall apart. Guilloux had indeed been a lucky man.

Cameron got up. "I'll be back in a few minutes."

"Please be careful."

Cameron smiled and left the room.

LANGLEY, VIRGINIA

On the second floor, Higgins picked up the phone and stared out the window. "Higgins here."

"Hello, sir. Rich Potter here. Sorry to disturb you."

"Don't worry about it. What's wrong?"

"I might have a problem with one of my operatives. I'm not sure yet."

"Go on."

"The name's Stone—Cameron Stone. He contacted me a few minutes ago and requested immediate cauterization," Potter said, referring to the recovery of compromised agents.

"His reason?"

"He claims there's an organization set out to sabotage NASA. Says it's going to destroy the new shuttle, to be more specific. He also thinks the French police might be involved."

Higgins inhaled and closed his eyes. He struggled to remain in control. "Did he set a pickup location?"

"Yes, sir."

"Very well then, bring him in and keep him well guarded. Let me know what he has to say. Got that?"

"Yes, sir."

"Good. When and where?"

"Botanical Gardens, five P.M. today. That's an hour from now."

"I'll be here. Call me when it's done, and remember. No mention of this to anyone else."

"I know, sir. Good-bye."

"Good-bye, and good luck." He hung up and pressed a fist against his jaw. *Damn! How can it be? How did Stone get that information?*

Higgins grabbed the phone and dialed a foreign number he had committed to memory.

PARIS, FRANCE

Cameron stood next to the window and looked out. The sky was becoming dark and overcast, indicating an impending storm. He inspected the street below. All appeared normal. He checked his watch. An hour before the meeting.

"So, Cameron, you seem to know quite a bit about me. What's *your* story?"

Cameron looked at Marie, still lying on the bed. "I'm not sure you want to hear it. It's pretty boring."

"It's okay. Go ahead."

Cameron smiled. "It all started when I graduated from high school and left for the war."

"Vietnam?"

"Yep. Spent four years there."

"Why four? I thought that you were only required to do one year."

"True, but after my first tour I went home to find out that there were no jobs. The American people weren't that sympathetic to soldiers in those days. So I went back, and remained in the military after the war. I was with the Special Forces for a few years before the CIA snatched me, and here I am today."

Marie sat up and hugged her knees close like a child. "With all that activity going on I guess a private life was out of the question."

Cameron didn't respond. He lowered his gaze as the image of Lan-Anh's charred body filled his mind. "There was someone once. It was a long time ago. I was only a kid. Had just turned twenty. Her name was Lan-Anh. She was killed in Saigon."

Marie left the bed and came to him. Touching his arm gently she said, "I'm sorry."

"There's nothing to be sorry about. Like I said, it happened a long time ago."

"Cameron . . ."

He lifted his eyes and met hers.

"What was it really like over there?" she asked.

He looked away. "You don't want to know."

"I lost a brother over there, Cameron. Yes, I *want* to know."

Cameron sat against the window sill and stared at Marie. *Who are you, Marie Guilloux? What is happening to us?* Cameron tried to suppress feelings he had not felt for years. He had felt physical attraction from the day he saw her. But this went deeper than that. He felt comfortable in her presence. He trusted her. She was not just another pretty face but a woman of substance.

Very well, Marie. You asked for it. Cameron began to speak. His voice was ice cold, his words strong. He told her about the pain, the frustration, the sorrow. He explained to her how young soldiers had died useless deaths mainly because of lack of training. Gunfire would erupt and they would just freeze and fall on their faces seconds later, filled with lead. It was madness. Then his tone changed. He dropped his voice by a few decibels and began to speak in between deep breaths. His fists were tight. His body rigid. He was back. The jungle surrounded him. *Go, Cameron. Make a run . . . for it. You have a chance . . . by yourself. Get help . . . and come back . . . God, why did I leave him? But I did come back. I did!* But too late. The Vietcong had gutted Skergan like an animal and left him hanging from a tree.

His mind was too cloudy to continue. His words became incoherent. Cameron turned to stare out the window, embarrassed, guilty, unable to face her. Marie was the first person he'd ever told the story.

He felt her hands on his shoulders, her fingers gently pressing. They reached his neck and massaged it. Cameron closed his eyes for a few moments, feeling his body relax.

"It's all right, Cameron. It's all right."

Cameron turned around and stared into her eyes. He saw tears, felt mesmerized by her. She understood the way he felt. She understood his pain.

"Thank you," he said.

"No. Thank *you*."

ATHENA AEROSPACE HEADQUARTERS MUNICH, GERMANY

The long and narrow conference room, built to accommodate the large table covering most of the marble floor, had all of its windows facing the city's skyline. It fit his image of a world leader's center of government, noted Frederick Vanderhoff as he scanned the occupants of fifteen of the forty black leather chairs that followed the contour of the oval-shaped mahogany table. The men present that afternoon formed his inner circle, a handful of visionaries who, like Vanderhoff, were among the most powerful financial leaders of the European Economic Community. He considered them the backbone of the EEC's space agency,

Athena, and the only ones willing to risk what it would take to make Europe the leader in space by the end of the century.

But Vanderhoff was more than just an investor. He had started as a scientist with a nose for good business ventures during the seventies and eighties, when he'd made his fortune by using his engineering talents to help develop weapons like the Armbrust man-portable anti-tank system, along with a variety of Heckler & Koch light weapons. He'd then used his negotiating skills and factory contacts to arrange sales of weapons to a number of Middle Eastern, South American, and African countries.

Vanderhoff glanced at an empty seat to his left, the one that had belonged to rocket scientist Claude Guilloux. Although very bright technically, Guilloux had lacked the commitment and resolve needed to achieve Vanderhoff's vision for the European space community.

After the *Challenger* disaster, the EEC had invested hundreds of millions of dollars to modernize Athena's launching facility in Kourou, French Guiana, and to improve the quality of its rockets. With the large amount of capital available, Vanderhoff had hired the best scientific minds in Europe to design an improved launch vehicle with advanced guidance systems and capable of multi-satellite deployment on a single mission. The end result was the Athena V, a three-stage, 130-foot-tall rocket capable of carrying single payloads into geosynchronous orbit or multiple payloads into low Earth orbit. Seven years after its debut, fifty Athena Vs had been launched without a single malfunction, establishing the European space agency's credibility. With fees of sixty million dollars per low orbit launch and a hundred million per geosynchronous orbit launch, Vanderhoff and his ring of investors had collected a hundredfold on their original investment, and in the process had provided the European economy with an overnight boom in state-of-the-art industries manufacturing everything from satellites to components for Athena's rockets.

But a dark cloud loomed over Athena's profitable venture, threatening not only to take away the obscene profits Athena had grown to enjoy, but most importantly, to ruin Vanderhoff's plans for European domination in space. The new NASA. An improved NASA. A reborn space agency with a real vision: to regain the status it had held in the late sixties and early seventies, to establish itself once more as space leader. The *Challenger* setback had only resulted in a new, vigorous agency willing to go the extra mile to achieve the dreams of Presidents Eisenhower and Kennedy: to make space travel routine, an everyday occurrence. Vanderhoff knew that was the philosophy behind the American space shuttle program. It was the reason NASA had stepped away from brute-force methods of reaching space and opted for sophistication, for a reusable spacecraft capable of taking off like a rocket and landing like an airplane, routinely transporting its passengers and cargo to orbital stations built from materials also ferried into space by the advanced orbiter. That was the shuttle's mission and, in Vanderhoff's mind, the future.

But Vanderhoff believed the future in space belonged to Europe, not the United States, and not even the independent republics of the former Soviet Union, which remained united behind Russia's leadership when it came to space exploration. Athena already had plans for its own shuttle and space station, but needed time to develop the projects. Time that Vanderhoff knew would not be available if NASA remained successful in maintaining its aggressive new schedule of shuttle launches, a large number of which would be used to ferry modules of Space Station *Freedom* into orbit.

Vanderhoff eyed General Marcel Chardon sitting to his right. Chardon was the second-in-command of all French armed forces and the most powerful military player of Vanderhoff's coalition.

Like the two high-ranking German Bundeswehr officers sitting next to him, General Chardon had chosen to join Vanderhoff's conspiracy for tactical reasons. The sixty-two-year-old general was certain that Europe would be threatened by competing U.S. and Russian space stations, which would be used—Cold War or no Cold War—as test bases for Strategic Defense Initiative weaponry.

SDI. Vanderhoff exhaled. He strongly shared Chardon's belief that Europe had to take immediate steps now to position itself as the leader in space with the end goal of becoming *the* world superpower. Vanderhoff, like Chardon, cherished the dream of Europe being the strongest power on Earth, and space supremacy was a critical step toward achieving that dream.

Vanderhoff and his allies had the financial means to back all of the research needed to build Athena's revolutionary *Hermes* shuttle and the *Columbus* space station, but time was running out. NASA was coming back too strong. The prototype modules for *Freedom* were already completed, and with *Discovery, Atlantis, Columbia, Endeavour,* and now *Lightning,* the American space agency had plenty of muscle to ferry all the hardware necessary to permanently establish itself in space before the end of the century.

Athena needed time and Vanderhoff knew how to get it. He had already tested his stealth killer satellite on the Russians, and now it was the Americans' turn. He began the meeting.

"We have two major issues to discuss. The first is in regards to a CIA operative named Stone. Apparently this agent was responsible for the debacle at the warehouse. He seems to have taken Madame Guilloux under his wing." Vanderhoff saw Chardon's face hardening. "I have just received a call from our contact inside the CIA and he has given me information that assures us of Mr. Stone's termination. Once he is done away with we will find Guilloux's wife and terminate her as well, just as we killed her recalcitrant husband and the other scientists who opposed us. We can't afford a leak before *Lightning*'s launch."

Chardon shifted his two-hundred-pound body on the chair and exhaled.

"Something bothering you, General?"

"Stone should have been dead by now, *monsieur*. He never should have left the warehouse alive."

"Well, just make sure your people are in place at the Botanical Gardens, and that he doesn't escape this time. Any problems with the local police?"

"No," replied Chardon. "We own the Prefect of Police."

"Well, just make sure everyone involved knows that this time there can't be any mistakes. Understood?"

"Oui."

Vanderhoff paused to look around the table and saw several heads nodding in assent. He had driven the point home. He leaned back in his swivel chair and forced his expression to relax somewhat.

"Gentlemen, the second issue up for discussion is Athena's future in space in the post-NASA era. I have met with my scientists down in Kourou and their progress has been outstanding, largely due to the major injection of capital into our research and development division. Here are the fruits of our labor." Vanderhoff rose and walked to the side of the room, where he pulled off a white cloth covering mock-up models of their space shuttle and space station.

"This is a model of the shuttle *Hermes,* gentlemen, a space vehicle that takes state-of-the-art technology one step beyond the American space shuttle. Our shuttle will be capable not only of returning from space and landing like an airplane, but also taking off like one."

Right away, Vanderhoff noticed people murmuring among themselves. He waited for silence and continued.

"Before Guilloux's elimination, he had devised a revolutionary and clean method of reaching space. You see, gentlemen, three-fourths of the launch weight of the American shuttle is nothing but liquid oxygen—the heavy oxidizer vital to achieve combustion with the liquid hydrogen fuel. Most of that oxidizer is consumed during the first three minutes of flight, when the shuttle is still within the Earth's atmosphere. Guilloux came up with an interesting thought.

Why carry all that oxygen along when there is plenty of oxygen in the atmosphere? And so Guilloux proposed a rocket engine that would breathe oxygen during the atmospheric portion of the flight, switch to on-board liquid oxygen right before reaching space, and in the process, severely cut back on weight and complexity while increasing cargo area. Simple and elegant."

"But feasible?" asked Chardon.

"Our scientists are working on that. That's why we need to slow down NASA. We need the time to overcome two major obstacles. One is the development of an air-breathing jet engine capable of attaining speeds in excess of Mach ten to achieve space injection. The second is to develop an active fuselage cooling system. Unlike the tiles of the passive thermal-protection system of the American orbiter, our system will cool the entire fuselage by running liquid hydrogen under the craft's skin using a technology similar to the one currently used for cooling conventional rocket-engine nozzles. We feel the cooling issue will be straightforward, but the jet engines—they're going to take time and plenty of money to develop. Once done, however, we will have a true space plane."

"How much time?" asked Chardon.

Vanderhoff pointed at the engines in the rear of the three-foot-long plastic model of the streamlined *Hermes*. "A conventional jet engine extracts oxygen from the atmosphere, but it is not suitable for speeds above Mach three. We have developed an engine that uses the ramming effect of the plane's supersonic speed to compress the air in the combustion chamber prior to its mixing with fuel. This is what we call a ramjet engine, and we have determined that ramjet technology will get us up to Mach six. Beyond that, we have designed—on paper—a special type of ramjet engine in which supersonic air flows through the combustion chamber. This technology, gentlemen, is what will get us the speed necessary to break away from the Earth's gravitational force. The heart of *Hermes* is the supersonic combustion ramjet or scramjet, but to develop it we'll need time and money. We have the money. With *Lightning* out of the way we'll buy the time." Vanderhoff paused to let the information sink in.

"Is our launch on schedule?" asked Chardon.

"All is in place. An Athena V with an explosive drone attached to a communications satellite is scheduled to lift off at 11:35 P.M. local time the day after tomorrow, but remember, gentlemen, the satellite is just a contingency. We don't expect *Lightning* to reach orbit."

"Any problems at NASA?"

"No. All is in place there as well."

Chardon leaned back and nodded. The room fell silent.

"Very well, then," concluded Vanderhoff. "General, you'll handle Mr. Stone. I'm flying back to Kourou immediately to supervise the launch. Call me the moment you have news. Meeting adjourned."

SIX ★

Games of the Trade

PARIS, FRANCE

The storm arrived sooner than Cameron had expected. Flashes of lightning temporarily illuminated the dark afternoon sky. Ear-piercing thunder shook the soft grass beneath him. Secluded yet open, the park offered several escape options. Closing time was only a few minutes away, and most of the strollers had already left to get out of the rain.

Marie was not with him. He had talked her into waiting outside the park's walls, out of sight by the Seine. He would get her after cauterization was complete.

Cameron watched the light drizzle turn into a heavy rainfall as he stood a hundred feet from the Quai Saint Bernard, the four-lane street that separated the gardens from the enraged waters of the Seine. The powerful winds drove three- and four-foot waves savagely against the century-old retaining walls. Water exploded in a cloud of white foam that seemed to engulf the tourist boats docked nearby, but somehow the brightly colored crafts emerged time and again from beneath the maddened waves, refusing to surrender to their much stronger adversary.

Cameron pulled up the collar of his trench coat, leaned against an oak, and watched a single deer peacefully taking refuge from the storm inside one of several man-made caves

built as part of their caged habitat. Cameron smiled. He had
not been at a zoo for some time. Actually he didn't expect
to see animals here. According to the sign outside, JARDIN
DES PLANTES, he was in the Botanical Gardens, yet in
the short time he'd been moving around waiting for Potter
to arrive, Cameron had seen enough wild animals in cages
and enclosures to fill a small-sized zoo.

He checked his watch once more. It was past five o'clock
and still no sign of . . .

Cameron spun around. His ears had registered a new
sound, almost imperceptible against the thunder. A gunshot.

He reached for the Beretta 92F, pulled it firmly to free it
of the Velcro strap, and curled his fingers around the black
alloy-framed handle. He turned and headed into a cluster
of trees. Who was the shooter? Was it Potter? Was his
case officer corrupted? Anything seemed possible at this
point.

His thoughts quickly vanished as bark flew off the trees
under the impact of a high-velocity round. He squinted but
couldn't see anything through the heavy rain. The report
came a second later as he rolled away over the muddy soil
toward cover.

The cold rain quickly seeped under his coat and soaked
his cotton shirt. The wet fabric clung to his chest. His back
hit the trunk of a cedar tree hard. He burrowed into the
foliage, quickly surrounding himself with cover, temporarily safe. Smeared mud covered his face. His hair felt heavy
with it. Cameron turned his face to the sky and let the
rain wash it clean. Crouched, uncomfortably still, he raced
through his options. *A second,* he thought. A second for the
sound of the gunshot to reach his position. The shooter had
to be about a thousand feet away, Cameron estimated as he
unsuccessfully scanned the area. Already darkness and the
rain made it impossible to see anything out beyond thirty
feet away, except during lightning flashes. But he also
knew that the shooter could most likely spot him during

that time also. His night vision lost to a lightning flash, Cameron waited for a moment, until it cleared. He raced forward, away from the protection of the trees, across the clearing to where an animal cage, the ape pen, stood in the middle.

One, two, three bullets ricocheted loudly off the wet concrete walk a mere two feet from him. Close, too close, he decided, suddenly realizing his mistake. The shooter didn't need the infrequent bolts of lightning to illuminate his target; he had a night-vision scope. Cameron was safe as long as there *was* lightning, when the bright sky would literally blind anyone using night-vision gear. The scope would amplify the surrounding lightning by a hundredfold, blinding the user with very high-intensity flashes, and rendering the equipment useless.

Darkness returned. Two more shots. Two more splashes. *Bingo.* Cameron spotted the bright muzzle flashes through the rain, coming from the mound next to the distant aquatic garden.

He reached the rotunda in the center of the park and hid behind a three-foot-tall concrete wall; waited in the dark. Lightning gleamed and he jumped over the low wall, tripped on something, and landed headfirst in a puddle of water. Involuntarily, he inhaled, choking on muddy water. He snorted and coughed to clear his airway, and breathed deeply for several moments to catch his breath.

Night resumed. Two more shots. Another bolt of lightning. The two seconds of light revealed what had tripped him. Bile rose in his throat as he experienced a field operative's worst fear: the compromise of his case officer. It wasn't Potter shooting at him. *Who?*

Darkness came as suddenly as it had departed. Cameron rested against the concrete wall as water dripped down his forehead. He tried to come to terms with Potter's death, with the breaking of his link to the CIA. Only Potter could officially pull him in, but the next lightning flash showed a hole the size of Cameron's fist in Potter's chest. Not only high-velocity, but also jacketed hollow-point as well, he decided. One good shot and the game had ended.

Cameron wiped the cold water off his face with his quivering hands. Soaked to the skin, he began to shiver. But Cameron knew he couldn't let that slow him down. He tensed, ready to move, when a bullet struck the Beretta just forward of the trigger casing, missing Cameron's index finger by a fraction of an inch. His hand stung from the impact, which brought memories of Little League bats held too loosely. He instinctively let go of the weapon, watched it skitter across the wet concrete. The gunfire had come from his right.

A second shooter!

Cameron ran as fast as his legs allowed him. He disappeared into the small forest, stopping when he estimated he was at least a hundred feet away from the clearing. He cut left and headed toward the back of the park, reaching the edge of the woods a minute later. He found the rear gate already closed, the security guard gone. Cameron had not expected to be there so late. The deserted four-lane street and the Seine extended beyond the six-foot-tall, ornate wrought-iron fence.

Cameron inhaled deeply and broke into a final run. He felt light-headed but persisted, concentrated on reaching the fence. Nothing else mattered. The black fence. The winds and rain intensified, blowing him to the side. He forced his aching legs to continue running, positioning his body against the rain falling at nearly a forty-five-degree angle, pushing harder and harder against the wrathful storm until he managed to curl his fingers against the thick metal bars at the top of the fence.

He glanced backward. Through water and mud, he saw two figures exiting the woods. Cameron kicked his legs, pulled himself up and over the fence. He landed on his feet and rolled on the sidewalk.

He got up and raced across the street, reaching the other side in seconds. He looked back, saw the figures halfway up the fence. Cameron darted down the concrete steps that led to the Seine's shore, sought a place to hide.

As he reached the bottom of the stairs, Cameron bolted upstream, remaining a few feet away from the edge of the concrete retaining wall. The ferocious waves continued to pound below him.

Lightning flashed. The shots came once more, muted by the thunder but clear. The sound remained in his ears long after the ground exploded to his right. Cameron could not outrun them. It was just a matter of time before the men caught up with him and finished him off. Cameron felt weak. His pace slowed. He had to take a chance, the choice not pleasant but the alternative less so. Jump and maybe die, don't and be certain of it.

Cameron cut to the right and kicked both legs as hard as he humanly could against the weathered edge of the concrete wall, diving directly into a four-foot wave. He heard a shot while in midair but felt no impact.

The water came, sudden and cold, yet somehow soothing. He went under, below the boiling, wind-torn surface. The pain from his limbs began to subside, dulled by the cold water or perhaps because he was losing consciousness. *Air.*

The waves and current dragged him downstream fast. He surfaced and spotted the shooters over a hundred feet away, still scanning the area where he'd jumped. Cameron continued drifting away, farther and farther. Again he felt light-headed. He fought it. He needed to somehow get the word out about Athena's plans to destroy *Lightning*, but the physical abuse had been severe. His body demanded rest. He struggled to reach one of the boats but his aching legs refused to respond. He battled the waves for a few more minutes until he felt drained, totally drained, well past the brink of exhaustion. He tried to kick his legs to remain afloat, but failed. Cameron slowly went under. His last conscious feeling was a hard tug on his arm. He had found silence. He had found peace.

LANGLEY, VIRGINIA

Higgins let the secured telephone ring three times before answering. He knew who was calling, and also knew why he was calling. The coded message from the Paris station faxed to him just minutes ago indicated that only one man had died at the Botanical Gardens. There were supposed to have been two found dead, Case Officer Potter and Operative Stone. Yet the CIA flash report indicated that only Potter had been killed, by a direct hit to the heart. There was no mention of Stone.

He pounded both fists on the smooth wooden surface of his large desk. Stone should have never left that park alive. Now he was a loose cannon. Angry and probably confused. Not knowing who to trust.

"Yes?"

"Hello." Higgins heard Vanderhoff's cold voice on the other end. "This is—"

"I know who you are. How did this happen? I thought you had it under control."

"Missions are not always successful, Mr. Higgins. A man in your position should know that."

"Are you out of your fucking mind, Vanderhoff? Do you realize the implications? Now Stone probably thinks there's a leak in the CIA, and if he remembers anything about standard procedure, he'll have realized by now that the only person Potter could have made contact with was me, Chief Europe—unless he also thinks someone was tailing Potter. We have to find him."

"Chardon thinks he drowned."

"Did you find the body?"

"No, but . . ."

"Then we must assume he's still alive." Higgins closed his eyes and rubbed a finger against his left temple.

"I know."

"I have no other choice but to frame him for Potter's

death, to mark him for termination. I'll need Chardon's help in gathering the proof I need to convince my superior."

"All right. I'll make sure the French handle their side before midnight tonight."

"Good. The game has changed and we must adjust. Call me back if there are any problems. Otherwise I'll assume Chardon will handle his end. One more thing, any sign of the woman?"

"No, but we have people looking for her."

"All right. Good-bye." Higgins hung up the phone and rubbed his chin with the side of his index finger. He then made a fist and lightly pressed the knuckles against his lips. The situation was getting out of control. He had to act decisively. If Stone was still alive, he could expose them.

Higgins's hand reached for the next memo on the pile of papers in his in-box. He made it a personal goal to go through his in-box daily, and never let the paperwork accumulate. In his line of work he couldn't afford to fall behind.

Higgins read the short cover letter. It was from George Pruett, his boss's nephew working at Computer Services, routed to him from the European desk. Higgins groaned. Did he have to personally review every piece of paper the analysts couldn't easily plug into one of their little cubbyholes?

The one-paragraph memo told Higgins that George had written an algorithm that searched for isolated incidents and attempted to look for patterns. He flipped to the second page and froze. *What? How in the hell did he put these events together so fast?* He read the list once more in disbelief.

Great! Just fucking great! On one side he had Vanderhoff, a scientist-turned-investor trying to play the intelligence game. And on the other side a little genius who writes software that picks up all the relevant killings out of hundreds of killings every day around the world.

Higgins drove a fist into his palm, then rose from his chair and paced back and forth. He needed to calm down and be objective. Solve one problem at a time. First was the problem with Stone. He thought he had an answer to that one. A simple and straightforward answer. He just needed to convince his boss to give the order for termination. Only Pruett could label an operative "beyond salvage."

That much should go fairly smoothly, he decided. Once labeled, Stone would be as good as dead. The standing orders would be to exercise extreme prejudice. Shoot to kill. Period.

What had Higgins concerned was the second issue. His boss's nephew. How could he stop George Pruett's algorithm from stirring up more trouble? From adding more pieces to the puzzle?

Suddenly, an idea came. Higgins reached for the phone and dialed a local unlisted number.

SEVEN ★

The Laws of Physics

Everything in space obeys the laws of physics. If you know these laws, and obey them, space will treat you kindly.

—*Wernher von Braun*

LAUNCH COMPLEX 39, PAD A. KENNEDY SPACE CENTER, FLORIDA

"T minus four minutes and counting. Preparations for main engine ignition. The main fuel valve heaters have been turned on. T minus three minutes, fifty-seven seconds; final fuel purge on Lightning*'s main engines has been started."* The NASA public affairs commentator was broadcasting over numerous loudspeakers and through the orbiter's communications system.

Kessler closed his eyes and desperately fought against the excitement that slowly consumed him.

"Heart rate is up to one hundred twenty beats a minute. Relax, Michael." Kessler heard Neal Hunter's reassuring words through his helmet's built-in headset. Hunter was Mission Control's capsule communicator, or CapCom, for STS-72, the number of their mission.

"Trying . . . I'm trying." Kessler inhaled deeply and looked over to his right. Jones sat rock still, apparently frightened. That helped Kessler relax. He had never seen Jones scared before.

"Say, Tex," Kessler commented. "I thought you boys from Texas weren't scared of anything."

Jones turned his head and looked at Kessler. "Say, guys, what's my heartbeat?"

"Ninety-two beats a minute, Jones. You're doing just fine."

Kessler frowned. Jones was indeed ice cold.

"Just think of something pleasant," Jones said to Kessler.

"T minus three minutes, thirty-five seconds."

Kessler watched *Lightning*'s General Purpose Computers responding to commands from the Launch Processing System—the KSC's ground computer network at the launch site—by moving the elevons, speed brake, and rudder to ensure that they would be ready for use in flight. The control stick barely moved in all directions. LPS had taken control of the launch sequence at T minus twenty minutes, and it would remain in direct control of the GPCs until thirty-one seconds before launch.

"T minus three minutes, twenty seconds. Lightning is now on internal power; however, fuel cells will continue to receive fuel from the ground-support system for one additional minute."

He looked through the heat-resistant glass panels. Nothing but blue skies; another beautiful day in central Florida.

Kessler decided that the wait prior to the launch had to be the worst part of the flight.

"T minus two minutes mark. It's gonna be smooth sailing, baby."

Easy for you to say, Kessler thought. The NASA announcer was not the one sitting over several million pounds of volatile chemicals. Kessler decided to follow Jones's advice, and closed his eyes and thought about the sea, about the clippers, about the courageous Captain Forbes and *Lightning*. For a moment he felt ashamed. Ashamed of being scared. He had to force his mind not to be afraid of something for which he knew he was more than adequately trained. He was ready, he was prepared. But what if something goes wrong and . . . *dammit, Michael! Stop it! If something goes wrong you will have to deal with it. You are in charge here. You make the calls. Just like Columbus on the* Santa Maria *or Henry Hudson on* Discovery. *You are the captain of your vessel. Start acting like one!*

He inhaled deeply and opened his eyes. The sky was so blue. So peaceful. He admired it through the 1.3-inch-thick transparent center pane. Although the sun was in his field of view, it didn't bother him. The outer surface of the pane was coated with an infrared reflector that transmitted only the visible spectrum. Kessler closed his eyes once more and relaxed.

"Heartbeat's down to one hundred three, Michael."

Kessler's lips curved upward. He was in control. He was the mission commander.

"T minus one minute mark and counting. Sound-suppression water system is being armed . . . it has been armed. T minus forty-five seconds and counting."

Kessler could not help himself. He felt his heartbeat increasing once more. But this time he was not afraid; he was still in control of his own thoughts and movements. His senses sharpened to an all-time high.

"T minus thirty-five seconds."

The Launch Processing System switched off. Its last command enabled the automatic launch-sequence software of *Lightning*'s five General Purpose Computers.

"Switching to redundant sequence start. T minus twenty seconds. T minus ten . . . nine . . . eight . . . seven . . . six . . . we've gone for main engine start . . . we have main engine start!"

The rumble. The powerful, soul-numbing rumble of *Lightning*'s three main engines pounded through the orbiter as they savagely unleashed a combined 1.2 million pounds of thrust against the jet-blast deflectors of the launchpad. The turbine blades of the SSMEs' turbopumps accelerated to 37,000 RPM, pressurizing the volatile chemicals to three thousand pounds per square inch. Liquid hydrogen and liquid oxygen savagely clashed in the nozzle section and exploded in a ferocious outburst of highly pressurized steam. At the same moment, the sound-suppression water system poured water onto the bottom section of the launchpad at a peak rate of 900,000 gallons per minute, protecting the orbiter and its payload from the damaging violence of the acoustical energy reflected off the Mobile Launcher Platform.

The SSME boost was titanic, but not strong enough to launch the shuttle into its maiden flight. It needed additional power, additional force. It came a millisecond after the General Purpose Computers verified that all three engines had reached the required ninety-percent thrust level after three seconds of operation. Kessler felt the vibrations reach his soul the moment the two Solid Rocket Boosters kicked into life with a savage roar, shaking not only *Lightning,* but the ground itself for several miles around. Kessler clenched his teeth as the pounding shock waves of six and a half million pounds of thrust thundered across Cape Canaveral in a howling, ear-piercing crescendo. Suddenly the blue skies disappeared. *Lightning* had been engulfed by the wake of its own engines.

The GPCs verified that both Solid Rocket Boosters had ignited properly before initiating the eight twenty-eight-inch-long explosive bolts anchoring the shuttle to the platform. The GPCs started the on-board master timing unit and mission-event timers. *Lightning*'s main engines throttled up to one hundred percent.

"*Lift-off! We have achieved lift-off of America's* Lightning*!*"

Kessler noticed upward movement, felt a light pressure pushing him down against his seat. *Out of my hands,* he thought. No human could ever provide the precise thruster controls to achieve a smooth lift-off. The thousands of microscopic adjustments issued by *Lightning*'s powerful computers every second kept the orbiter on track.

"*The shuttle has cleared the tower!*"

In the cockpit, Kessler and Jones monitored equipment and instruments as *Lightning* rose higher and higher into the blue sky. A billowing trail of exhaust marked its path.

"Twenty seconds, all systems go," commented Kessler in a controlled monotone. He noticed something happening to him. The fear was gone. "Roll maneuver starting." The shuttle began to roll clockwise 180 degrees. "Twenty-five seconds. Roll maneuver completed."

NASA's ground-tracking stations received Kessler's S-band radio transmission before relaying it to Houston. During the liftoff and ascent phase, *Lightning*'s S-band system transmitted and received both communications and systems-status information through the Merrit Island, Ponce de Leon, and Bermuda ground-tracking stations.

"Zero-point-six Mach and rising," Jones remarked. "The ride is very smooth, Houston."

"Forty-five seconds. Approaching Mach one. Throttling engines down for Max Q," Kessler reported as the computers reduced thrust for a moment to relieve the tremendous strain on the structure as *Lightning* approached the speed of sound. The entire cabin glowed from the light of the engines far below.

Suddenly ice, accumulated over the upper section of the external fuel tank, began to break off as the orbiter cruised through Mach one. Pieces exploded against the flight deck's forward windows, but the sound of their impact was lost in the low, hard roar of *Lightning*'s engines eighty feet behind.

"Mark one minute, Houston," Jones reported. "Five nautical miles in altitude, twenty-three nautical miles downrange, velocity twenty-three hundred feet per second."

"Roger, Lightning. You've passed through Max Q. Looking good to throttle up the engines back to one hundred percent."

"Roger, throttling up," responded Kessler.

"One minute and forty-five seconds. Negative seats, Lightning. Repeat, you are negative seats."

"Roger, negative seats," acknowledged Kessler. *Lightning* had passed the altitude for safe usage of ejection seats.

"*Looking good,* Lightning. *Mark one minute, fifty-five seconds. Twenty-one miles high, five thousand feet per second. Initiate Solid Rocket Booster separation.*"

"Roger, Houston. Starting SRB sep."

Kessler watched the pyrotechnic display as both SRBs simultaneously separated from the sides of the external tank.

"*Confirm separation,* Lightning.*"

"Smooth as glass, Houston, smooth as glass."

"*Good,* Lightning. *Two minutes, fifteen seconds. Press for MECO.*"

"Roger, Houston. Press for MECO," acknowledged Kessler as *Lightning*'s on-board guidance system converged, steering *Lightning* for its precise window in space for Main Engine Cut-Off. *Lightning* was now thirty-five nautical miles high.

"Okay, Houston, the engines are coming down and looking good," reported Jones as he monitored the main engines' status on the control panel to his left.

Lightning rose higher and higher as its speed blasted past six thousand feet per second. The communications link between the orbiter and Houston switched from NASA's ground-tracking stations to one of three satellites from the Tracking and Data Relay Satellite System in geosynchronous orbit 22,000 miles above the Earth. *Lightning*'s data, acquired by the five-thousand-pound satellite, was transmitted to the TDRSS ground station at White Sands, New Mexico, where it was relayed to Johnson Space Center.

"Lightning, *Houston. You're looking good at three minutes.*"

"Roger, copy looking good at three."

The sky began to darken. The colorful blue of just a minute earlier had turned into one of a less vivid hue, as the orbiter scurried through the Earth's stratosphere at nearly ten times the speed of sound. Kessler had only been exposed to a maximum of three Gs during Max Q. Quite a contrast from his days as a naval aviator when pulling seven or eight Gs in a twisting, turning F-14D Tomcat was an everyday occurrence.

"Mark three minutes, fifty-five seconds, Lightning. *Mark negative return. Repeat, negative return. You're a go for space!"*

"Roger, Houston." Kessler eyed the instruments. Fifty-eight miles high at eight thousand feet per second. He looked over at Jones, who smiled and gave him a thumbs-up. He stared at Jones for one more second before he felt a strange vibration. Something he had never felt before. *Lightning* began to tremble.

"Houston, *Lightning* here. I think we've got a—"

His words were cut short by a powerful blast. It shook the entire vessel. Images of *Challenger*'s explosion flickered in front of his eyes as what once was a clear view of the cosmos was suddenly engulfed in a ball of flames. Kessler felt momentarily disoriented. He wasn't sure what had gone wrong.

"SSME failure! SSME failure!" screamed Jones.

"Shut it down, Lightning! *Shut down number-one SSME now, NOW!"*

Kessler reached with his right hand for one of three covered switches located in the middle of the wide center console. He lifted the cover and shut off number-one Space Shuttle Main Engine as they left the wrathful flames behind and free space was in plain view once more. "Number-one SSME off."

"Lightning, you are to press to ATO! Repeat, press to ATO!"

"Press to ATO? Please confirm order, Houston," Kessler requested. Although *Lightning* was flying on two engines and could still reach orbit by performing an Abort to Orbit maneuver, Kessler could not justify in his mind to continue.

No one had a visual on number-one SSME. There was no telling what the blast could have destroyed without a visual. *Why continue? Why not abort to Rota? Shit, the storm,* he thought. NASA had access to the landing strip at Rota Naval Air Station in Spain in case of shuttle emergencies, but a powerful storm had all but closed the base. *Lightning* couldn't land there.

"Lightning, *you must press to ATO immediately or risk missing your window!*"

Kessler exhaled. There was no other way. Return to launch site had not been an option since four minutes after the launch. With the storm over Spain, *Lightning* was committed for space flight. "Roger, press to ATO," he finally responded.

Kessler throttled up the two remaining main engines to 109 percent. He turned to Jones.

"Enable the OMS engines, Tex."

"You got it." Jones armed the two Orbital Maneuvering System engines, which were not intended to be used until after External Tank separation, right before orbital insertion. Instead, *Lightning* would use a large portion of the OMS engines' fuel to provide enough energy to reach orbit.

"Fire on my mark. Now—now!"

At each OMS pod, highly pressurized helium reached a titanium-layered tank filled with 4500 pounds of hydrazine, and another tank packed with an oxidizer. The helium gas—performing the same role as an SSME turbopump—forced both propellant and oxidizer through an array of pipcs and valves leading to the combustion chamber. The chemicals ignited on contact in a hypergolic reaction, generating a combined thrust of twelve thousand pounds.

Kessler felt the light kick and quickly eyed the helium tank's pressure of each engine: 4700 PSI. He nodded approvingly.

"Houston, *Lightning* here," Kessler said. "Two-minute OMS burn. Number one and two OMS engines nominal.

Sixty miles altitude, five hundred miles down range, velocity twenty thousand feet per second. What in the hell happened?"

"Can't tell for sure, Lightning. Computers are running diagnostics on number-one SSME."

"Probably a leak of some sort," said Kessler.

"How can you tell, Lightning?"

"Just a hunch, Houston. What else could have caused such an explosion?"

"We'll continue the diagnostics run, Lightning."

"Roger, Houston. Press to MECO in one minute, thirty seconds. Systems remain nominal."

"Roger, we copy, Lightning."

Everything appeared normal once more, but Kessler knew that could be deceiving. The explosion could have loosened some of the heat-resistant tiles that protected the orbiter from the extreme temperatures during re-entry. He was not that concerned about losing tiles on the upper fuselage, but it would be critical if tiles underneath were missing, where temperatures would reach over two thousand degrees during Earth re-entry.

"Houston, MECO in fifteen seconds."

"Roger, Lightning."

"MECO in five . . . four . . . three . . . two . . . one . . . MECO! Seventy miles at twenty-seven thousand feet per second," Kessler called out as both operational main engines shut down. Kessler also shut off the OMS engines after having used a large portion of the available fuel in the integral tanks. OMS helium pressure decreased to 2500 PSI on both tanks. He then proceeded to prepare *Lightning* for External Tank separation.

"Five seconds for ET sep. Four . . . three . . . two . . . one . . . we have ET sep." Kessler performed an evasive maneuver by moving below and beyond, and translating to the north of the External Tank. He watched it moving away from the side window. He relaxed. They would reach orbit. A low orbit, but nevertheless an orbit. With their current speed he estimated *Lightning* would achieve an egg-shaped orbit of 140 by 110 miles, the balance point between the Earth's gravitational pull force and *Lightning*'s centrifugal force.

"Lightning, *Houston here. We just double-checked all computer outputs before launch. All systems showed nominal.*"

"So what do we do now?"

"*You're in low Earth orbit. Second OMS burn. Ignition in fifty-three minutes, ten seconds.*"

"Roger, Houston."

Kessler unstrapped himself and removed his flight helmet, but held onto it. They were in zero G. Jones did the same. Both were about to go aft simultaneously.

"You first, Mike."

Kessler used a single arm motion to lift his body off the flight seat, and gently pushed himself toward the aft flight deck station. He threw the payload bay doors' switch on Panel R13L, and noticed the talk-back indicator light underneath the switch changing from CL to OP, showing that *Lightning*'s General Purpose Computers had received his directive. The starboard door slowly opened first, gradually giving Kessler a partial view of the orbiter's vertical fin. The port door followed sixty seconds later, and he noticed a few white tiles missing over the OMS pods.

"Damn," Jones said. "I hope the tiles underneath are intact."

"No shit." Kessler nodded as he briefly enjoyed the spectacular view of northern Africa overhead before flipping the two radiator-control-release switches on the same control panel to deploy the thirty-foot-long environmental-control-and-life-support-system radiators, incorporated over the forward inside sections of both doors. Talk-back lights showed proper deployment and nominal circulation of Freon-21 coolant looping from both sides of the radiator panels for heat rejection by *Lightning*'s systems, including the heat that had built up on the orbiter's skin during the ascent phase. Without the radiators, the life-support system could not maintain a suitable temperature inside the crew compartment.

"Let's go below and get rid of these flight suits."

"In a minute. I want to see something." Kessler turned on the payload bay's floodlights and visually inspected the sixty-foot-long compartment.

"Looks in pretty good shape," commented Jones.

"Yep. Looks that way. I guess we won't know for sure until we get a chance to go out there and take a closer look."

"But first things first. Let's get into more comfortable clothing. These flight suits are too bulky. See you down there," Jones said as he pulled himself through one of the two interdeck access hatches on the flight deck's floor. Below was the mid-deck crew compartment, where most everyday living activities took place, from eating to sleeping. "Boy! This weightlessness beats the heck out of the simulated stuff on those parabolic KC-135 flights."

Kessler shook his head. The Air Force captain was in space for the first time in his life and seemed determined to enjoy it as much as possible, even if the mission wasn't going as planned.

Kessler watched Jones disappear through the hatch. He shrugged and dove after him.

EIGHT ★

Sanctimonious

> *Beware of false prophets, which come to you in sheep's clothing, but inwardly they are ravening wolves.*
> —*Matthew 7:15*

LANGLEY, VIRGINIA

Tom Pruett pinched the bridge of his nose and briefly closed his eyes as he walked toward the windows behind his desk. He stared at the overcast sky. An unseasonably low thirty degrees had brought an early frost to the Virginia countryside. Winter was setting in before summer had ended and even before autumn had gotten a chance to get started. It was like that worldwide. This would be one very cold, hard winter. But Pruett's depression came not from that realization. He had just heard the most amazing story about a mole in the Paris office. Someone Pruett knew from his days as a case officer. He turned around and stared into Higgins's intelligent but cold eyes, wondering how his subordinate had managed to detach himself emotionally from all this.

"Are you absolutely certain of this, Roland?"

"Beyond doubt. Stone killed his case officer, Richard Potter, during a meeting Stone had called. He'd claimed he had some vital information regarding something of national importance that could not be discussed over the phone, and that he couldn't come into the station because it was under surveillance." Higgins's tone indicated disbelief. "Potter agreed to the meeting, and following standard procedure, he let me know of it before he left," Higgins continued. "The bullet found in his chest has been confirmed to have come from a rifle which had Stone's fingerprints. Also, we have depositions from two police officers on duty at the park during the incident. They both picked out Stone's photograph from a stack of nearly one hundred mugshots. It all fits."

"Yes, I can see that. It all fits too perfectly." He walked to the bar, opened the refrigerator, and grabbed a small carton of milk. "Tell me, what would you say was his motive?"

"We're working on that. Perhaps money? We're not sure."

"You better find out, and fast. I know Stone. I doubt money was his motive." Pruett noticed his words had a strong effect on his subordinate. Higgins blinked twice, exhaled deeply, and looked away.

"I can understand where you're coming from," Higgins said. "But the evidence! It's all there. And the incident earlier that day. We have reason to believe that he was involved in the murder of three French policemen during a shoot-out in a Paris warehouse. The bullets extracted from the bodies match Stone's Beretta found in the park. Stone is a dangerous man. He must be stopped."

"When will we get an official French police report with all the evidence?"

"Within the next couple of hours. We'll need an additional hour to translate all the relevant portions."

"Very well, you bring me the evidence. We'll review it together and then I'll make the call."

"Sure, Tom." With that Higgins turned and left the office.

Pruett was concerned. He had never labeled anyone beyond salvage in the years he'd been Head of Clandestine Services. And he didn't want to now, especially someone he knew personally, but if the evidence was indeed as irrefutable as Higgins had indicated, Pruett knew he would have no choice but to issue the field alert. He still felt uneasy, even after Higgins's convincing words. *What are you up to, Cameron? Killing a bunch of cops and then your own case officer? Why? What's your motive? Who are you working for?* In another time he would have guessed the Russians, but not in this day and age. Then who? And why? It simply didn't make sense.

One floor above, George Pruett noticed an icon turning yellow. It was the personnel icon. He clicked it and eight new icons appeared on the screen, one per area division. All were white except for the European Division. He clicked it and read about the death of Case Officer Richard Potter from the Paris office. The report had indicated that he had died from a gunshot to the chest.

Paris? The same place where the Athena scientists were killed. He leaned back on his chair without taking his eyes off the screen. *What's going on? Europe is supposed to be quiet these days.* He shifted his weight uneasily, not sure what to make of the new finding. *Is there a connection?*

George switched from his algorithm to the CIA's databanks and requested more information on Potter's death. The system came back a few seconds later with the statement that more information would be available within the hour.

George checked his watch and returned to his algorithm.

PARIS, FRANCE

For Cameron the nightmare had returned. Lightning engulfed him once again as the rain and the wind savagely pounded against his exhausted body. Triple-canopied jungle funneled streams of water onto him; insects fed on exposed flesh. They'd been running from the VC—just the two of them, the only survivors of a bloody ambush that had taken the lives of twenty others—for three days. Cameron and Skergan had survived by hiding under their comrades' bodies, remaining still for hours, waiting for the VC to move out. They had escaped during the night, under the cover of darkness. For two days they had not seen the enemy; then late on the third day Skergan stepped on a VC mine. His leg was taken off at the knee. Cameron tied it off with a tourniquet and managed to bandage the leg as best he could, and they continued struggling south. But the explosion had given their position away. The VC got closer and closer. Skergan kept slowing them down. With the bottom half of his leg missing, their progress was slow. Despite the tourniquet and makeshift bandage, he continued to lose blood at a staggering rate. It was just a matter of time. They stopped and stared into each other's eyes.

Go, Cameron . . . you'll have a chance . . . on your own, Skergan told him, but Cameron couldn't bring himself to leave Skergan to a certain death. The soldier persisted. *You must . . . Cameron. You have . . . a chance by yourself. I'll . . . hide and wait.* It made sense. If he could leave him hidden and then run for help, perhaps the two of them could make it. So he did. Cameron left him hiding under a large log, and moved south for a half hour before guilt overwhelmed him. He had left a comrade in arms behind. He had committed the ultimate sin of a warrior.

Cameron turned around and headed back—too late. By the time he got there the VC had already killed Skergan. Cameron found him hanging naked from a tree. He had been emasculated. Later that same day Cameron ran into an American recon platoon and was airlifted to safety. The same day. *Oh, Jesus! I could have saved him. We could have made it alive together.* The guilt finally consumed him whole when he visited his friend's family after the war. A young wife and two boys. Memories of Lan-Anh's death flashed in his mind as he stared at the anguish in their faces. The sadness in their eyes was beyond anything he could bear. Cameron left the house minutes after he'd arrived. He had destroyed them. He was responsible. He had sinned, caused pain. He would carry that burden forever.

With rivulets of sweat rolling down his forehead and neck, Cameron woke up with the worst headache of his life. His eyes scanned the room he was in. It appeared modest but clean. A single light bulb dimly illuminated the wooden walls and ceilings.

He turned his head. A plain table bearing a large white bowl stood beside his small bed. Beside the bowl was a pitcher. Aside from a single chair next to the table, the room was empty. He managed to sit up and looked out the small window over the bed. The waters of the Seine flowed peacefully under a bright, clear sky.

How long have I been here? Hours? Days maybe?

Inexorably, his mind drifted back and relived the encounter at the Botanical Gardens. The shooters had been undoubtedly sent by Athena to prevent him from revealing the plan to destroy the new NASA orbiter. *But how did they know?*

His case officer was dead, and he was isolated. If his case officer had used proper CIA procedures, then Chief Europe had to be in on it since he was the only other soul that knew about the meeting . . . unless the call had been intercepted. Cameron knew he could not afford to gamble. Chief Europe was not an option. Who then? Who could he approach with his information? Anyone at the Paris station? How? He hardly knew them. Whom could he trust? And Marie, where was she? She was supposed to have been waiting by the Seine. Did she get captured?

The door screeched open.

"Cameron! Thank God, you're awake!"

Marie ran to him and gave him a hug. He didn't know how to respond. He hesitated. Part of him wanted to return the hug, but the professional in him pulled him back. As much as his feelings for Marie were growing, he had to remain emotionally detached. He needed his trained, logical mind to help him survive. Feelings and emotions would only cloud his judgment. He had to remain focused.

"Yes, yes. I'm fine." He gently pushed her away and saw tears in her eyes.

"Oh, my, oh, God. For a while I thought that you . . ."

"It was close. Too close. How did I make it here? I remember the waves. The water was cold . . . then everything faded away."

She sat next to him. "I thought I heard some shots, but wasn't sure if it was just the storm. Then I saw you running down the steps. There were two men following you. I saw you dive in the river. You drifted in my direction. I waited until you got close enough and jumped after you. I pulled you to the shore and managed to get some help from a tourist boat captain. He helped me bring you here."

"Where is here?"

"A small hotel a few blocks away from the Botanical Gardens."

Cameron looked at his battered body and then back at Marie.

She smiled. "Don't worry. This place rents rooms by the day or the hour. No one cares what you do up here or what you look like. We're safe for now."

"You saved my life," Cameron said without taking his eyes off her. "Thank you."

"I'm so glad you're all right." She hugged him again.

This time Cameron returned the hug. "So am I."

"What—what happened? I thought it was supposed to be a simple meeting."

"I found Potter dead. Someone set us up."

Marie's face became serious. "Dead? What do we do now?"

"Where's my coat?"

Marie gave him a puzzled look, got up, and walked to the other side of the room. "Here it is. I almost threw it away. It's nearly torn apart."

Cameron snatched it and rubbed his right hand over the side of the coat. The waterproof pouch was still there. He looked into her eyes and smiled.

LANGLEY, VIRGINIA

Higgins read the faxed report from his contact in the French police and smiled. The report detailed in no uncertain terms the French government's conclusion that Stone had orchestrated the murders of Potter and the three French police officers. Stone *would* be labeled "beyond salvage." If he was still alive, he was as good as dead. No one would dare touch him without killing him first. No one would listen to the shallow words of a marked man, who would most likely say anything to save his skin.

He got up and headed for Pruett's office. He had removed the last barrier for the Head of Clandestine Services. With or without a motive, his boss would have to give the order. And Higgins would have more than earned what was due him.

George Pruett noticed the same CIA personnel icon turning yellow again. Just as suddenly, NASA's icon turned red once more. He clicked his way down the CIA personnel icon and found a new entry in his list. There were no additional deaths in the operative world, but somehow Potter's assassin had been identified. Cameron Stone had been labeled "beyond salvage."

Shit, George thought. *That guy's as good as dead.*

He went back up to the main menu and selected NASA's icon. Again, he clicked his way down until he reached the list. It had a new entry. His eyes opened wide in surprise when he read the name Cameron Stone. He was suspected of killing, not the three Athena scientists, but three policemen at the scene. The bullets from the three slain bodies matched Stone's handgun found near Potter's body.

Wait a second! What's going on? That's not the way it happened. George tilted his head. Something didn't seem right.

He went up the NASA list and started reading the third entry. His recollection was that there had been three Athena scientists dead and seven unidentified men. If that was the case, then where did the three policemen that Stone killed come from? Did he kill them afterward?

Those thoughts faded away when his eyes read a different report from the one he had originally read. The "new" third entry indicated that three policemen and four unidentified men had been found at the warehouse along with the Athena scientists.

What the hell?

George blinked twice in surprise and read the entry once more. *Shit! Someone changed it and my algorithm picked up the change and replaced the old one.* Something was wrong. He could feel it.

His heart rate increased as a rush of adrenaline flooded his system. This just looked too much like a novel, yet it was actually happening.

With the palms of his hands already sweaty, he placed the cursor on the print command and clicked the left button on the mouse. A few seconds later the laser printer started humming away. He pulled out the sheet from the paper tray and read it once more.

"Pretty fucking incredible."

"Talking to yourself again, George?" said the voice from the other side of the cubicle wall.

George ignored it. He simply locked the system and headed for the Records department.

He thought about taking the elevators but decided against it. He had been sitting at that chair for most of the morning and needed the exercise. George turned right and hurried toward the stairs at the end of the long hall. *Who could have done that? If the new report was accurate and they were indeed policemen, then what do the French have to say? What do we have to say? And who changed it? The French?* He didn't think so. The information had to go through a strict CIA screening before it was allowed inside

the Agency's data banks. That meant that someone in the
Agency had entered it. Could it have been a simple clerical
error? Two operators entering data at separate locations?
One writing over the other's information?

He shook his head, finally understanding the reason for
his uncle's digestive problems. Too many questions and
never enough answers.

He pushed the heavy door open and headed downstairs,
reaching the second floor in seconds. He opened the door,
exiting from the stairwell. Records was on the right.

"Hi, George."

George stopped in mid-stride, turned, and stared at Roland
Higgins. "Wh—oh, hello, sir," he responded. *Where did he
come from?*

"So tell me, your algorithm coming up with anything
new? I saw the report you sent to the European desk."

George hesitated for a moment or two. All of his information had to be filed before leaving the Office of Computer
Services. "Well . . . in a way, sir, but . . ."

"Hmm . . . tell me. I'm interested."

"I'd like to, sir. But you know, the rules say I should go
to Records before . . ."

Higgins laughed out loud. "I know the rules, George. I
make most of them. You won't get in trouble. I'll go talk
to Records afterward. Now, tell me. What's new?"

George reddened. He felt silly, trying to quote a CIA
regulation to someone as high up as Higgins. "This, sir." He
pulled out the folded piece of paper from the back pocket
of his pants. "The algorithm just picked it up."

Higgins took the sheet of paper from his hands and read
it for about a minute.

"Good information. It is indeed too bad that you have to
be exposed to this, but that's the reality of things. These
kind of problems don't always just happen in the movies.
They occur in the real world."

"I know, sir. It's a terrible thing. Does that really mean
that . . ."

"Yes. The standing orders are for termination with extreme prejudice. It sounds cold, but trust me, the evidence against him is overwhelming. We have to stop him."

"I understand, sir. There's one observation I'd like to point out to you."

"Yes? What's that?"

"Well, it regards the third entry, sir. It's changed from the last time I printed it." He noted that Higgins remained quiet for a few minutes and stared at the sheet of paper.

George felt uncomfortable. Chief Europe finally raised his gaze. "When did you find out about this?"

"About ten minutes ago, sir. I was on my way to Records to file it and—"

"Don't. I mean, I'll handle it. I'll talk to Records. You don't need to get involved anymore. Is that understood?"

George noticed the warmness in Higgins's eyes was gone, replaced by a fierce intensity.

"Yes—yes, sir. No problem. No one knows about this."

"George, you have done the Agency a great favor. I can't tell you anything else beyond that. Rest assured that this information along with your observation will go to the appropriate persons. Good job."

"Thank you, sir."

Higgins turned around and disappeared around the corner. George headed back to his office with a truckload of questions and concerns. Why had Higgins reacted like that when George told him about filing the report with Records? Was he up to something? George wasn't sure about that, but he felt certain that someone somewhere had changed his story and got caught doing it, and Higgins's reaction only added to George's suspicion. *Calm down, George! Think objectively. Objectivity. That's the answer.* He'd read or heard that somewhere, perhaps in one of his novels; perhaps he remembered his father telling him that once. *Step aside and look at the problem as a bystander, George. You dug up conflicting information and you presented it to one of your superiors, who didn't react too positively when you told*

him about filing the conflicting information with Records.
On top of that Higgins had pretty much ordered George to
keep a lid on it.

   *All right, George, what can you do if you don't trust the
person that has the information? Easy. Pass that same info
to someone you* do *trust. Who?*

   George headed for his uncle's office.

The moment Roland Higgins reached his office, he walked
directly to the metal trash can next to his desk. He took the
glass lighter from his desk and set George Pruett's sheet
of paper on fire. He let it drop inside the trash can, where
he'd burned the two stapled sheets from George's previous
finding the day before.

   He reached for the phone. *It has to happen today,* he
reflected, staring at the burning paper. Today he would
settle his problems.

NINE ★

Cover-up

JOHNSON SPACE CENTER, HOUSTON, TEXAS

Neal Hunter walked outside Mission Control to have a short meeting with the press. He had been thoroughly briefed by the NASA administrator at the Cape on what to say and definitely what *not* to say. *Lightning* was the benchmark of the new NASA, the latest orbiter packed with the latest technology. The last thing the space agency needed at that point in time was bad publicity.

He pushed open the double doors and faced a mob of reporters and their camera crews. Selected members of the press had been present inside the guest room behind Mission Control, separated by a soundproof glass panel. They had been able to see the lift-off and hear the voice of the NASA public affair's commentator at the Cape, but luckily for NASA, communications between the orbiter and Mission Control had not been live after the first few critical minutes. The members of the press may have noticed the commotion inside Mission Control, but had not been able to hear a thing besides the NASA commentator's recap of the successful launch.

Hunter pulled out a white sheet of paper. "Good morning, ladies and gentlemen. *Lightning* has successfully achieved a low orbit. Two OMS burns are pending to get it to its target orbit. Mission Commander Michael Kessler and Mission

Pilot Clayton Jones report that all systems are nominal. They will commence their test schedule in five hours after achieving a stable orbit and after a three-hour rest period. That is all for now. We will issue press releases in one hour and hold a formal press conference in two hours. Thank you, ladies and gentlemen." Hunter turned around and headed back to the control room.

"Then what was all the commotion inside the control room a half hour ago, Mr. Hunter? Is *Lightning* in any danger?"

Hunter stopped and slowly turned around. He narrowed his eyes and scanned the crowd in front of him for a few seconds before answering. "*Lightning* is fine! Everyone is always very tense during lift-offs, and for reasons that should be obvious to all of you, we were all particularly tense about this flight because of what it stands for. As I said earlier, a full press conference will take place in two hours, after *Lightning* reaches final orbit. Now if you'll excuse me, I have work to do. Thank you."

The mob of reporters blasted a fusillade of questions that Hunter politely dodged as he walked back into Mission Control.

LIGHTNING

Kessler strapped himself into his flight seat and watched Jones do the same. He felt much more comfortable now that they had removed their bulky rust-brown-colored emergency ejection suits—a requirement during lift-offs and landings—and had put on their blue intra-vehicular assembly clothing—flight overalls with lots of pockets and Velcro for attaching small items.

Kessler reached for the ballpoint pen tucked in a pocket on the side of his left arm. The pen was not ordinary. Because of the lack of gravity, the pen had been pressurized to force the ink to the ball. He grabbed the notepad floating over the control panel. A string kept it secured to the panel to prevent it from wandering around inside the flight deck. He made an entry of the current time and brief flight status.

"Houston, you there?"

"Roger, Lightning. We copy you loud and clear," Kessler heard Hunter respond through the speakers.

"Second OMS burn in two minutes, mark."

"Roger."

"Any more news on the problem on number-one SSME?"

"Ah, negative, Lightning, but it shouldn't matter. The moment you shut the SSME off, the fuel lines to the engine got cut off. The only concern over here is for the possible damage to the orbiter."

"Same over here, Houston, but we won't know until we go outside. By the way, we made a visual check from the aft windows. The payload bay appears normal."

"Good. We were just about to ask you that. How are you guys doing otherwise?"

"No problems. Just a little tired, I guess. One minute mark."

"Well, as soon as you reach your new orbit you'll have a reduced rest period before EVA. Sorry, guys, we're cutting your first break to three hours instead of eight. We all need to put our minds at ease about your situation, but without a visual we won't know for sure."

"No offense, Houston, but Jones and I prefer to start EVA as soon as we reach the new orbit. Thirty seconds to ignition."

"Continue with countdown, Lightning. We'll discuss this issue after the burn."

"Roger. Twenty seconds. OMS firing sequence started. Fifteen seconds."

Kessler could not explain it, but he felt relaxed. He had things under control. "Five seconds, four . . . three . . . two . . . one . . . ignition!"

Kessler felt the light kick of the two six-thousand-pound-thrust Orbital Maneuvering System engines. *Lightning* accelerated under its own power to change its current egg-shaped orbit to a circular orbit of 160 miles.

"Thirty seconds. Systems nominal. Integral propellant tank down to forty-percent level," Kessler said. Under normal conditions, they would have more fuel in the OMS hydrazine tank. "One minute. Fuel and oxidizer pressure nominal. Helium pressure at . . . Houston, we have another problem." The General Purpose Computers automatically stopped the OMS engines when helium pressure dropped below 460 PSI on the left OMS. He looked at Jones.

"Shit. OMS warning lights are red for both engines," said Jones.

Kessler checked control panel F7 and confirmed Jones's observation. The OMS engine Fault Detection and Identification system told him that in addition to losing helium pressure on one OMS engine, both OMS engines had failed the chamber pressure and velocity tests. He eyed the helium pressure on the right OMS engine. It showed a nominal two thousand PSI. He reached for panel C3 and disarmed both engines.

"Lightning, *Houston. OMS burn stopped thirty seconds early. New orbit one-four-five miles.*"

"Houston," Kessler began. "Helium pressure continues to drop on the left OMS . . . four hundred PSI . . . three hundred. What's going on? I've already turned off both engines."

"*Stand by,* Lightning. *We're checking.*"

Kessler simply sighed, not believing all of what was actually happening to him. He took off his voice-activated headset. Jones did the same.

"What do you think, Tex?"

"I'm not sure, but I'm beginning to get a little worried about this bird. If this had happened during re-entry we'd be in a shitload of trouble."

Kessler frowned. Jones was right on the money with that. If the OMS engines failed during re-entry burn, there was no telling where *Lightning* would actually reach Earth.

Most likely too far away from the nearest qualified landing strip, and that's assuming they somehow managed to make it through re-entry without burning up while entering the atmosphere at the wrong angle and speed.

"But heck," Jones continued. "I guess we won't have to worry about that since the fucking engines won't even start anymore."

Kessler slowly shook his head and exhaled. "Damn!" He put the headset back on. Jones did the same. "What's going on, Houston?"

"*Lightning, diagnostics is coming up with a major leak in the feed line from the left helium tank to the left OMS engine. We also just noticed that the propellant level on the left OMS tank is dropping.*"

"I hope to God it's leaking to space and not internally," Kessler remarked as he read a propellant pressure of 120 PSI instead of the normal 250 of seconds before. Panel F7 now had a few more warning lights on.

"Shit!" Jones yanked off his headset, unstrapped, and propelled himself toward the aft windows. He turned on the lights inside the cargo bay.

"*What was that, Lightning?*"

"Jones's checking to make sure there are no leaks inside the cargo bay. I share his concern about remaining in one piece, Houston." Kessler shook his head at the thought of volatile hydrazine propellant floating inside the orbiter. Unlike helium, hydrazine would ignite the moment it came in contact with any gas containing oxygen.

"*We feel it's leaking into space, Lightning.*"

"Hey, Mike," Jones screamed from the back. "Tell them I can't see any leaks back there. All appears normal."

"Houston, Jones can't see a leak internally. It must be leaking outside. Left OMS hydrazine pressure below fifty PSI and dropping. Helium pressure's down in the mud too. Any ideas?"

"*Confirm nominal reading on right OMS tanks.*"

Kessler eyed the levels. "Right OMS shows helium at

two thousand PSI. Hydrazine also nominal at two-six-five PSI."

"We're running diagnostics, Lightning, but based on the warning lights, it looks like a major OMS malfunction. Both engines show as failures."

Kessler knew very well what that meant. The OMS engines were the primary means *Lightning* used to decelerate for atmospheric re-entry. "Any chance of using the four aft RCS primary jets for deorbit burn?" he asked, referring to the Reaction Control System jets usually used only for attitude maneuvers.

"We'll run some simulations, Lightning. In the meantime get some rest. Start EVAs in four hours."

"Lightning requests permission to commence EVA right away. We are pilots, sir. We must know the condition of our vessel immediately."

"Stand by, Lightning."

Kessler waited.

A minute later, Hunter's voice crackled through his headphones. *"Negative, Lightning. Get your rest first. We're having enough bad luck as it is. You don't want to add fuel to the fire by working exhausted. Now go get a meal and some sleep. I'll wake you guys up exactly four hours from now. That's an order."*

"Roger, Houston. We copy." Kessler removed his headset and unstrapped his harness. He followed Jones down to the crew compartment.

LANGLEY, VIRGINIA

Tom Pruett walked down the short aisle between the two rows of cubicles in George's work area. He saw no one there. He checked his watch. *Lunchtime.*

He raised his eyebrows and stared at the piece of paper in his hands—the short but intriguing message George had left him earlier today, when Pruett was in a meeting. George claimed to have found conflicting information regarding a shooting in Paris involving Cameron Stone. That alone had been reason enough for Pruett to drop everything and head down to his nephew's office.

He spotted George's nameplate on the last cubicle to the left, next to a note saying that he would be back at two o'clock. Pruett walked inside the small cubicle and noticed that the system was off, contrary to what the sign taped to the side of the twenty-inch monitor said. His nephew had prohibited anyone from turning off the system, but there it was. Not only off, but Pruett noticed something else. The hard disk was missing. Although he was no expert in computers, Pruett had been around them enough to know that the CPU usually incorporated a hard disk.

A closer inspection of the system showed that someone had actually torn the disk out of the workstation. He clenched his jaw as he felt his stomach begin to burn. *What in the hell is going on here?*

He walked up and down the aisle, checking each cubicle. All of the other workstations appeared to be fine. He gave the room one final glance, stepped into the corridor, and walked straight for the security post on that side of the hall.

George, where are you?

At the opposite end of the hall, Higgins peeked around the corner and watched his superior approach the security post. He slowly exhaled through his nostrils. Another close call.

He checked his watch. He had an appointment to keep.

BETHESDA, MARYLAND

Harold Murphy, Master Sergeant, U.S. Army, Retired, pushed his brand new lawn mower out of the garage. This was to be the final mowing of the season and Murphy could not be any happier. He detested mowing the lawn, particularly because he lived across from the Pruetts, whose son, George, used a landscaping service to keep his mother's

home looking like one out of *House & Garden.* That forced
Murphy to at least keep his yard in halfway decent shape
so that he didn't look like the bum of the neighborhood.

In reality Murphy liked the young Pruett, a good kid
who had managed to stay off drugs and had gotten through
school while working two jobs after his father had passed
away and his mother had become unable to work. From
what George's mother had told him a few days before,
George Pruett was doing a magnificent job at the CIA.
Good for him, thought Murphy.

A year earlier, George had bought an old Porsche 356
convertible. Murphy, who owned a ten-year-old Porsche
911, had helped George get his new car in proper shape.
That was one of the things Murphy missed about never having been married, not having kids of his own. That's why
he always looked for ways to help kids in the neighborhood
with their bicycles, motorcycles, or cars. An expert mechan-
ic while in the Army, he now kept a garage loaded with
tools and a hydraulic lift. A day never went by without a kid
stopping by to fix a flat, grease a bicycle chain, or change
the engine oil. Over the years his garage had become the
central point for repairs of all sorts of kids' vehicles in the
neighborhood. He'd earned the title of "Mr. Fixit." Murphy
was proud of that.

He eyed George's 356 convertible parked in front of the
house and checked his watch. *Lunchtime.* Murphy smiled.
That was another reason he liked George. The kid had
always taken good care of his mother after that unfortunate
car accident that put her in a wheelchair for life.

The front door opened and George walked outside and
waved at Murphy, who quickly returned the greeting and
continued to push the lawn mower along beside the house.
As he did so, he noticed a car accelerating down the street.
He stopped his lawn mower, and was about to yell at
the driver to slow down when he noticed the windows
quickly being rolled down and made out what appeared
to be a rifle.

Murphy, a fifty-five-year-old veteran, surprised himself with his blazing-fast reactions. His years with the Army had forced him to stay in shape.

"Run for cover, George! Quick!" Murphy screamed at the top of his lungs, as the sedan, a gray Mercedes, came to a screeching halt behind George's car. Without waiting for a response, Murphy raced for his garage, where he kept a gun cabinet. He pulled on the handle, but it didn't turn. *Locked.* He always kept it locked. Kids played in his garage. It was the safe thing to do.

Gunfire!

He heard shots and glanced over his shoulder. George was running up the side of his house. Murphy drove his fist through the thin glass door of the cabinet. He pulled out a Colt .45 automatic, his favorite handgun. He snatched two magazines, snapped one in place, and ran back to his driveway.

There were four men. Two had remained with the car and faced the Pruetts' house. The other two he could only assume had gone after George. Murphy did not take any chances. The Army had taught him that when outnumbered by the enemy, it was wise to fire first and then ask questions. He reached a line of knee-high bushes that ran along the side of his driveway and hid behind them.

He crawled toward the street until he reached the curb. The two men by the car were less than forty feet away. One leaned against the hood, the other against the trunk. Murphy leveled his weapon at the man by the hood, cocked it with his thumb, and lined him up between the rear and forward sights of the stainless-steel weapon.

"Leave me alone! Get your hands off me, you bastards!"

Murphy shifted his gaze to his left. Two men were dragging George Pruett down the lawn and toward the parked car. Murphy exhaled in relief. *He's still alive.*

Murphy made his decision and lined up on the man to the right of George. He fired once. The man flew backward, propelled by the impact of a hollow-point round traveling at nearly two thousand feet per second. Before the second man escorting George had a chance to react, Murphy fired once, twice, aiming at the man's chest. Another hit. The man arched back and landed next to the first gunner. George froze, obviously not knowing what to do.

"Get back in the house, George! Call the cops! Hurry!" Murphy screamed, but before George could take a single step, Murphy heard two shots, quickly followed by George falling on the lawn.

"Aghh . . . my legs . . ." Murphy heard George cry as the young man rolled over on the grass.

You bastards . . . you damn bastards!

Murphy watched both remaining men level their weapons at him, and he went into a roll, trying to reach the safety of his garage. Gunfire broke all around him. Bullets ricocheted off the concrete driveway.

He felt a burning pain from his leg and knew exactly what had caused it, but he kept on rolling, rolling as hard as he could. His elbows and back stung from the roll. Another hit, this time on his left shoulder. The impact lifted him off the ground and nearly flipped him in midair. He crashed against a metal tool chest.

Stunned but conscious, Murphy looked in his right hand, surprised that he still clutched the Colt. He had fired three rounds. *Twelve left.* He would not go down with a nearly full magazine. He briefly eyed the shoulder wound. Blood gushed out from it. He knew from past war experience that he had maybe a minute or two before he would pass out from blood loss.

The gunfire stopped. The gunmen were out of sight behind the line of bushes, but he knew the general location of the Mercedes. George was wounded but still alive. *If I can only keep them away from George . . .*

Murphy aimed at a spot in the bushes where he estimated the Mercedes would be and started firing. His index finger brutally pounded against the trigger, one shot after the other. He developed a rhythm he had not felt in years. He anticipated the Colt's recoil and kept it trained for shot after shot until it was empty.

Silence.

Murphy set the gun down, and tried to withdraw the second magazine from his pocket but couldn't. His arms wouldn't respond. He had overestimated his strength and quickly became dizzy, light-headed. His vision blurred, but he could still see as a translucent figure approached George.

"You? You fucking traitor!" George screamed.

With unbending determination, Murphy inhaled deeply and forced his hand to move, to reach into his pocket. His fingers trembled around the magazine, and he persisted until he got a strong enough grip to pull it out. He set it next to the Colt. He didn't have much time left. The gunman was now next to George with the weapon leveled at the young man's head.

Calling upon the last of his strength, Murphy lifted the Colt, released the empty magazine, and placed the weapon in between his legs. Then he forced his quivering hand to grab the full magazine and pushed it into the butt. He heard it lock in place and tried to cock it, but could not get his thumb to pull the hammer back. Murphy desperately fumbled with the hammer and somehow managed to pull it back—too late. He watched in helpless horror as the man fired twice into George's head. *Mother of God, no, no!* All the years with the Armed Forces, all the weapons in his garage, and he had failed. George was dead.

With the sound of the Mercedes accelerating down the street, Murphy silently cursed his stupidity as he squeezed the trigger and fired one last time. The weapon fell from his hand. Then everything went dark.

In the back of the Mercedes, and with his pants stained with George's blood, Roland Higgins tensed as the side window shattered under the impact of a bullet, showering him with glass. His face, neck, and arms stung from multiple lacerations. He felt a numbing pain coming from his left shoulder. For a second he thought he had been hit in the shoulder by the bullet. He covered his bleeding face with one hand and probed the area over his shoulder wound with the other. It had not been a bullet but a large piece of glass.

"Dammit!"

"Are you all right, sir?" asked the driver.

"Son of a bitch! My face, my shoulder . . . damn!"

"Should I go to a hospital, sir?"

"Ah . . . no, no. Take me to the—safe house and get some—bandages—oh, damn!"

Higgins breathed heavily and tried to force his body to relax. He had to remain in control in spite of the terrible pain.

LANGLEY, VIRGINIA

Pruett walked into his office and noticed his secretary's pale face. "What's the matter, Tammy? You look as if you've just seen a ghost."

"Oh, dear. Oh, my!"

"What? What is the matter?"

"I'm sorry, Mr. Pruett. I'm so sorry."

Pruett inhaled deeply. The burning pain in his stomach came back. "What, Tammy? Can you tell me what in the world you're talking about?"

"It's about your nephew, sir, your nephew George."

"What about him?"

"He's been killed, sir."

"Wh—what? George? When—when did it happen?"

"Just a few minutes ago, sir. Your sister-in-law just called. There was a shoot-out in front of her house in Bethesda."

"Call my sister-in-law and tell her I'm on my way there!"

"Yes, sir."

Pruett ran inside his office to get his car keys and ran back outside. He reached his car in minutes and drove off.

PARIS, FRANCE

Cameron Stone stood by the front entrance of the hotel dressed in a pair of Levi's 501s, a white long-sleeved shirt, and a black leather jacket. That, plus the black horn-rimmed glasses he'd picked up at an optical store several blocks away, made him feel a little less paranoid.

"I want to go with you, Cameron."

"You'll be safer here, Marie. Trust me. There are a lot of people looking for us. Besides, you don't have a passport."

She shifted her gaze toward the Seine. Her eyes filled. "I feel safer with you. I'm scared."

He smiled reassuringly. "Don't be. Everything will work out. No one will find you in this hotel. I'll contact you as soon as I get some help. Remember, don't trust anybody, not even the CIA. It's better to play it safe for now until I figure out who can be trusted."

She took his hands in hers. "This is very awkward for me to say, Cameron, but I'm also scared for you. I care about you. I don't want to see you getting hurt again."

Cameron locked eyes with her. They remained like that for several seconds. He rubbed a finger over her cheek and gently brushed off her tears. "I'll be back. I promise. I'm not one to voice my feelings, but I can tell you that I care about you too. That's exactly why I can't let you come. It's too dangerous. I'll be back. You can count on it." He kissed her forehead gently.

Without another word, Cameron turned and headed down the stairs that led to the street. He looked up and down the Quai Saint Bernard. Street vendors filled the sidewalk, selling everything from miniature Eiffel Towers to cheap reproductions of Da Vinci's *Mona Lisa*.

He spotted a taxi and waved it down. The cab stopped a

few feet from him. Cameron briefly scanned the street and got in the back seat.

"*Bonjour, monsieur.*"

"*Bonjour. Conduisez-moi a l'aéroport Charles De Gaulle.*"

"*Oui, monsieur.*"

The taxi leaped forward. Cameron was pressed against the back seat and closed his eyes momentarily. He had allowed himself to become emotionally involved—a mistake. Feelings and logic did not mix well. He had to put Marie out of his mind for now. She was safe.

He reached into his leather jacket and retrieved two manila envelopes. He opened the first one and extracted a half-inch-thick stack of one-hundred-dollar bills. Half of his emergency money. Marie had the other half in the second envelope.

He placed half the bills in his wallet and stashed the rest back in his jacket's inside pocket. He opened the last envelope. There were three sets of passports and matching driver's licenses. All American, all his, but under different names. Two sets had been given to him by the CIA as part of his cover. The third was a contingency passport and license he had had made in Mexico by a top counterfeiting artist for a handsome amount of money. At the time he had thought it would be worth it one day. Cameron smiled. He'd been right.

The taxi dropped him off by the Air France entrance. He proceeded through the revolving doors and stared at the long ticket counter across the wide hall. Cameron counted eight check-in stations, each handling a line of passengers. Each station had two clerks. He smiled when he found what he was looking for: a single customs agent nearly running from station to station stamping passports. Cameron reached into his jacket and pulled out his contingency passport. Although he knew the fake passport was a work of art, it didn't have a stamp showing when and where he had entered the country. He had traveled into

France using his standard diplomatic passport, which he'd left at the embassy.

Keeping his head low, he approached the shortest of the eight lines. A middle-aged couple with two young daughters stood in front of him. They were Americans. The mother played with the girls while the father pushed a load of suitcases forward.

Both clerks serving his line became available at once. The family headed for one. Cameron for the other.

"Bon soir, monsieur," a man well into his fifties said from behind the counter.

"English?"

"Of course, *monsieur*."

"Blair, Steve Blair."

"How may I help you, Monsieur Blair."

"I need to get back to the States as soon as possible. When is the next available flight?"

"To what destination, *monsieur*?"

"Washington, D.C."

The clerk punched several commands on the keyboard, waited a few moments, and punched a few more. He looked at Cameron.

"Were you planning on leaving today, Monsieur Blair?"

"Yep. The sooner the better."

"Well, I'm afraid that might not be possible. All of our flights out of the country are booked for the next five days. It's the end of the tourist season, *monsieur*. Everyone wants to go home." The clerk pointed to the crowd lined up in front of the ticket counter. "Most of these people made reservations months in advance."

"Are you absolutely certain of that? It's very important that I leave today. There must be some flight available."

"Perhaps with another airline, *monsieur,* but not with Air France."

Cameron reached for his wallet, pulled out three one-hundred-dollar bills, folded them twice, placed them on the counter, and put his hand over them. *"Hmmm . . .* that's strange. I could have sworn there was at least one first-class seat available on the next flight. I even remembered it being a non-stop flight." He slid the hand over the counter toward the clerk, who looked in every direction and quickly placed his hand over the table.

Cameron kept his hand on the money. The clerk gave him a puzzled look. "Well, is there such a seat available?"

The clerk inhaled, his eyes trained on Cameron's hand. "Why don't I check one more time, *monsieur*."

"Yeah, why don't you?"

The clerk typed more commands and paused several times for the next couple of minutes. He shifted his gaze away from the keyboard and looked at Cameron again.

"It appears that you're in luck, Monsieur Blair. There just happened to be a last-minute cancellation on Flight 1143 leaving in twenty minutes from now. You can still make it if you hurry. It's not direct, though. You will have to change planes at JFK International. Is this acceptable?" His eyes briefly looked at Cameron's hand once more.

Cameron smiled. "Of course that will be all right. I appreciate your patience." He lifted his hand off the table. The clerk quickly slid his over, pulled the money toward him, and continued working on the keyboard. Cameron eyed the family to his right as the father placed two large suitcases on the scale between the counters. He noticed the small tray on the counter with their passports, and also saw the customs agent hastily walking toward them.

Cameron pulled out his passport and quickly flashed the first page to the clerk, who briefly checked the photo, nodded, and pointed to the tray. Cameron tossed it in a few seconds before the customs agent, a short, heavy man with greasy black hair, arrived and grabbed the tray. Cameron could hear the fat man breathing heavily as he quickly checked photos and expiration dates before stamping all five documents in quick succession, throwing them back on the tray, and racing as fast as his short legs could carry him for the next station.

Cameron slowly exhaled as he snagged his passport off the tray.

The clerk addressed him. "You're confirmed for Flight 1143, leaving Paris at 6:40 P.M. and arriving in New York at 9:00 P.M. local time. There the flight changes to 477 leaving New York at 10:30 P.M. and arriving in Washington at 11:46 P.M. The fare for a one-way, first-class ticket will be three thousand one hundred eight dollars, including local taxes."

Cameron pulled out a stash of bills, counted the appropriate amount, and handed it to the clerk.

"*Merci, monsieur.* Your gate number is 22A in the international section. You have exactly twenty minutes before boarding. Do you have any luggage?" He passed the ticket to Cameron.

"Ah, no. Thanks for your help." He grabbed the ticket, walked away from the counter, and headed for his gate. As he approached the line for the security checkpoint, Cameron spotted two intense-looking young men staring at him by the TWA counter. The men began to walk toward Cameron. He recognized them as the two rookie operatives who were with Marie at the hospital. Both reached into their dark-gray trench coats.

Instinctively, Cameron began to walk the other way. The CIA men picked up their pace. Cameron did the same to keep them from closing the fifty-foot gap. He walked as fast as he could without calling attention to himself; just another traveler trying to catch a plane at the last minute. Cameron glanced backward. Their hands remained inside their coats.

Forty feet. The men were getting closer. Cameron needed a diversion. Something that would give him enough time to lose them and reach his gate. He checked his watch. He had to hurry. He saw a pair of doors leading to the covered parking garage.

Cameron cut right and disappeared through the doors, instantly breaking into a run for several seconds before crawling underneath a blue sedan.

Just as he'd expected, the double doors swung open and Cameron heard their footsteps getting closer.

"Where in the hell did he go?" one voice said.

"Dammit. He's gotta be here somewhere," the other responded.

Cameron pushed himself over the oil-stained concrete floor toward the front of the sedan to get a better view of his attackers. He peeked from underneath the front bumper and saw one of them clutching an automatic with a silencer attached to the muzzle. That alone told Cameron plenty about their intentions. Field operatives seldom carried bulky silenced weapons unless they were working on a termination order.

But there was no time for those thoughts now. *Where is the second man?* he asked himself as he continued to stare at the first man near the double doors. Cameron looked at his watch. Time was running out. He had to act quickly or risk missing his flight.

The first CIA operative began to walk down the twenty-foot-wide aisle between two rows of cars running the length of the garage. Cameron noticed the operative checking in between the cars and also . . . underneath!

Then he heard a second set of footsteps behind him, and Cameron understood their tactic. One operative was checking the front of the cars while the second checked the rear. They were going to sandwich him!

He knew he had only one choice. *Stay here, Cameron, and you'll be shot.* At least running he had a "sporting chance" of getting away. *Oh, if I could only have my Beretta!*

He glanced toward the CIA man checking under a car fifty feet away. *Fifty feet.* He estimated that the silencers reduced the accuracy of their weapons by over sixty percent.

Cameron made his decision and, in a blur, rolled from under the sedan and rocketed across the aisle toward the adjacent row of cars. To his surprise, gunfire did not start right away, but it did come. The shattering windshield of a compact car next to him definitely confirmed his fears. The CIA men had fired without warning, without asking him to give himself up. Cameron knew then that he had been labeled for termination.

Cameron heard a shriek . . . *a woman!* Then a yell from a man. Security forces would come. A round ricocheted off the concrete floor and crashed through the plastic grill of another compact car.

The screams seemed amplified inside the concrete structure. Cameron came to the next aisle, crossed it, and reached the next row of cars. He dropped to a crouch and cut left, moving up the aisle behind the cars. Cameron heard other voices and screams in the distance as he counted fifteen cars. He abruptly stopped and hid in the space between two vehicles, moved near the front tires, and searched for the operatives.

He spotted one running down the aisle away from him. The second moved in his direction but with the weapon trained on the row of cars across the aisle from Cameron. The man had not seen him yet.

Cameron dropped to the ground and listened intensely for the footsteps. He waited. The man continued at the same pace. Cameron shrank back. The footsteps got louder. The figure loomed in his field of view.

Cameron plunged forward with both arms in front. The rookie operative spotted him and began to turn the weapon in Cameron's direction. *Too late.* Cameron intercepted the man's arm with his right hand, and gripped and twisted the man's wrist, keeping the weapon pointed away from him. In the same motion, he rammed his left hand against the operative's face, two fingers extended like a snake's tongue. The operative instantly released the weapon and brought both hands to his face with an agonized scream. Cameron drove his right knee into the man's groin and watched him fall over and curl into a fetal position on the concrete floor.

Cameron snagged the suppressed automatic—a Colt .45—
and spotted the second agent bringing his weapon around.
Cameron leveled the Colt on the operative and fired twice.
The CIA agent fell with a scream, dropping his weapon
while reaching down to his wounded thighs.

Sirens blared in the distance.

Cameron reached down and grabbed the first agent by
the lapels.

"Why? Why are you trying to kill me?"

Cameron saw blood coming out of the man's eyes. "Fuck
you, Stone. Go . . . ahead. Kill me . . . you bastard. Kill me
just . . . like you killed Potter."

Potter? What in the hell is going on?

"Tell me who gave the order! Tell me!"

"You're as good as . . . dead, Stone."

"Tell me, you fucker! Who gave the order?"

"You don't . . . get it, don't you? You're . . . beyond salvage, asshole."

Cameron released his grip. The agent fell on his back.
Beyond salvage?

The sirens got closer. Cameron dropped the Colt and ran
for the double doors. The airport lobby seemed undisturbed.
Cameron mixed with the crowd and headed for his gate. He
briefly checked his watch. The entire incident had taken
under two minutes. He still had time to make his flight.

TEN ★

Revelations

*And you shall know the truth, and the truth shall make
you free.*

—*John 8:32*

LANGLEY, VIRGINIA

After spending a revealing thirty minutes in the Records
department of the Office of Computer Services, Pruett
stormed into Higgins's office but found his subordinate
wasn't there. He checked his watch. *Five-thirty in the afternoon. Higgins always stayed past six. Where could he possibly be?* He walked back outside and spotted Higgins's secretary coming out of the ladies' room. He approached her.

"Where is he?"

The secretary, a middle-age woman known to the entire
department as a closet smoker, tried to remain far away
from Pruett. One sniff and Pruett realized she had been
smoking in the bathroom again. Under a different set of
circumstances he would have reprimanded her, but there
were more pressing things on his mind.

"He went out, sir."

"Beep him for me, would you?"

"Right away, sir."

"Thanks. There's something very important I need to
discuss with him." Pruett walked back into Higgins's office,

his own old office from years back before he'd gotten the promotion. Higgins had definitely remodeled it quite a bit. Most of Pruett's old furniture was gone and replaced with more modern stuff. In the CIA department heads were given a certain budget to furnish their offices. The higher up one went, the larger the budget got. In his case, Pruett had declined the opportunity to purchase new furniture after his last promotion. His old boss, who'd been assassinated, had been a good friend of his. Pruett had kept the office almost intact for sentimental reasons, and also out of respect. To this day he still used the same leather swivel chair and oak desk as his predecessor.

Pruett smelled something burning and immediately thought Higgins's secretary had been smoking in there. After a few seconds he decided the smell was not that of cigarette smoke, but left over from something that had been burned inside the office. Pruett recognized the odor because he had sometimes burned highly classified material and confidential information until he'd gotten his own personal paper shredder. Before that he had been too lazy to walk halfway down the hall to the closest paper shredder to dispose of security trash. Some of his peers used the security trash cans located just about everywhere in the building. He never did. He didn't trust them. Instead, he'd opted for burning letters and small documents in a metallic trash can he'd left to Higgins when he'd gotten the paper shredder.

Pruett briefly scanned the room and spotted the trash can next to Higgins's desk. He walked toward it and spotted a few burnt sheets of paper inside. He had been right. Higgins had picked up one of Pruett's old bad habits.

Pruett knelt down next to the trash can, tilted it, and took a closer look. Whatever it was had burned thoroughly. He spotted two sheets of paper, totally blackened and curled up but not yet collapsed. He noticed a staple on one corner holding them together. A third sheet had already crumbled. Pruett couldn't help himself. It made sense. While investigating George's murder and the sabotage of the Sun workstation, he'd had a short discussion with the filing clerk of the Records department of the Office of Computer Services, where Pruett had found the computer printout and cover letter that George had filed a day earlier. A small note attached to the cover letter indicated that one copy was made from it and passed to the European desk. From there it must have found its way to Higgins. The computer printout contained three events in a possible NASA pattern—the deaths of Claude Guilloux, the Rocketdyne worker, and the Athena scientists. Now Pruett wanted to find out why Higgins hadn't discussed that with him prior to the issuing of Stone's termination order.

Pruett felt the heartburn returning. He had just finished chewing two antacid tablets, and realized it was going to take more than that to placate his upset stomach. He reached into his pocket, grabbed the pack, and popped another tablet in his mouth.

Too many questions, too many things he didn't understand. He exhaled. Why did Higgins tell Pruett that three of the dead men in the warehouse were French police officers when George's printout clearly indicated that they were "unidentified men"? *Is this the conflicting information regarding Cameron that George mentioned in his note?* Something wasn't right.

He stood up and stared at the curled, blackened sheets of paper. *Could that be the copy of the printout and cover letter that George sent to . . . ?* He narrowed his eyes, shifted them toward Higgins's pile of mail on his desk. *What if Higgins never got a chance to read George's memo?* Pruett reached for the two-inch-thick stack of papers on the corner of the desk and quickly browsed through it. The memo wasn't there, which meant that unless the filing clerk had made a mistake, Higgins *had* to have read it. Pruett's eyes drifted back to the trash can.

"Damn. I can't believe you're gonna do this, Tom," he murmured as he took a white sheet of paper from Higgins's personal stationery. He knelt next to the trash can once more and tilted it to a forty-five-degree angle. He slid the white sheet of paper under the burnt ones and at the same time slowly set the trash can on its side. The burnt sheets softly rested over the white one. Pruett slowly pulled the white sheet out, curling up the edges to keep the burnt sheets from falling off. He got up and shook his head, disappointed in himself for not trusting Higgins. But under the circumstances . . .

He straightened the trash can with his foot and slowly walked outside.

"Have you reached him yet?" he asked the secretary.

"No, sir. I've already beeped him twice. I'll keep trying."

"Thanks . . . say, is that stack of mail on his desk from yesterday or today?"

"All from this morning, sir. Mr. Higgins always goes through his daily mail before leaving the office in the evening."

"Thanks again."

Strange. Very strange. Why didn't he mention George's findings to me yesterday? And why isn't he answering the beeps? Higgins was supposed to be on call twenty-four hours a day—the reason he carried a satellite pager.

Pruett headed toward his office, walking very slowly, attempting to minimize the risk of disturbing the fragile pieces of paper. Someone with the right tools might be able to retrieve some of the information as long as the sheets remained in one piece, but if they collapsed and disintegrated, all bets would be off.

He made it to his office.

"Hello, sir," Tammy said. "My, my, what is that you're—"

"Get me the FBI," Pruett interrupted, "the Microscopic Analysis Unit. Hurry!"

He pushed open the door of his office and carefully walked to his desk, where he gently set down the white sheet of paper. The burnt sheets were still in one piece.

Pruett stared at them. Innate curiosity had surpassed his sense of trust. He had to find out what was on those pieces of paper, and the FBI had just the tools to do it.

SOMEWHERE OVER THE NORTH ATLANTIC

Cameron set the headphones down and leaned his head back. The movie was as boring as the flight. He had tried unsuccessfully to fall asleep twice in the last hour, but the excitement of the past few days remained with him, the adrenaline still in his system. So far he had been lucky. He had managed to remain alive in spite of someone's plan to have him killed. Once again his mind explored the possibilities. One suspect was Chief Europe Higgins, for the simple reason that Higgins should have been the only one Potter would have contacted prior to the cauterization job. Under such an assumption, Higgins would know that Cameron was familiar with CIA cauterization procedures; therefore, when the assassination attempt at the Botanical Gardens only accomplished half the job, Higgins would have to assume that Cameron assumed that Higgins was the only other person who knew about the meeting, which meant that Higgins was to blame. *But what if someone intercepted Potter's call to Higgins? Or maybe my call to Potter?* Cameron thought, recalling the gray truck parked next to the embassy's side gate. In that case, Higgins would not be at fault. *Maybe Potter was dirty and he got killed because he knew too much about Athena's plans. Maybe someone in Athena thought of him as a liability.* Cameron briefly closed his eyes. *Possibilities.*

Something else that bothered Cameron was the issuance of the termination order—that kind of power only existed at the directorate level. In his case, only someone like Tom Pruett or someone above him held the power to issue such an order. Cameron shook his head, refusing to believe his old case officer could be up to something like that, unless . . . unless all Pruett knew came from information carefully fed by the mole. Someone could have altered the facts and given them to Pruett in such a way as to leave no doubt that Cameron had to be terminated.

It made sense, he decided. It certainly made sense, and since at that point not too many things did make sense, Cameron had to follow that theory. He smiled. His analytical mind knew just one way to do that.

GEORGE WASHINGTON UNIVERSITY HOSPITAL, WASHINGTON, D.C.

Pruett left Murphy's room on the second floor and headed for the elevators. The retired Army sergeant remained unconscious. The doctors feared that Murphy had brain damage from lack of blood and oxygen. They had performed several CT scans on him without much luck. And while all of the test results showed normal brain activity during sleep, which indicated no major damage, they could not answer the question of whether or not Murphy would ever wake up.

Too many questions. Even after going through the entire set of incidents several times and analyzing them objectively Pruett still could not come up with an explanation for why Higgins had withheld George's information, which conflicted with one of Higgins's reasons for accusing Stone. In addition, Higgins still had not responded to repeated electronic paging. The longer it took for him to get hold of Higgins, the more suspicious Pruett became.

He headed back to Langley.

WASHINGTON, D.C.

Just before twelve-thirty in the morning, Cameron slowed down as he entered the quiet suburban neighborhood. He didn't want to attract any attention to himself, particularly if there was some kind of neighborhood watch program set up. The flight from Paris had arrived on schedule at

New York's JFK. After minimum difficulty he'd gotten through Customs with nothing to declare, and had left the International terminal a mere thirty minutes after landing, giving him plenty of time to catch his connecting flight to Dulles Airport. Without any hassle, he had landed in Washington less than an hour ago. With the fake driver's license, Cameron had rented a car at the local Hertz.

Although he had not been in Washington for a few years, Cameron remembered clearly the multiple occasions when he had flown up from Mexico for meetings with his old case officer, then Chief Western Hemisphere. Several of the meetings had taken place at Pruett's home.

LANGLEY, VIRGINIA

Exhausted, frustrated, and still in pain, Higgins approached the door to his office at twelve-thirty in the morning. Although his face showed just a few cuts, the brown turtle neck sweater he wore covered a dozen lacerations on his neck and upper chest. The cut on his shoulder was by far the most painful of all, but bearable after being properly bandaged. In a way, Higgins guessed he should feel lucky. After all, he had managed to terminate George, and although he'd lost two of his men in the process, the police would never be able to learn anything from their bodies. Like himself, Higgins's men had carried nothing that could link them to the CIA.

Needless to say, Higgins had not carried his CIA-issued beeper either, so before going into his office, he stopped by his secretary's desk to check the messages he knew would be there.

He found several messages. Most could wait until the following day. His fingers stopped moving when he reached a small note from his secretary. It said that Tom Pruett had stopped by earlier, and that she had beeped Higgins several times at Pruett's request. He saw another message in

Pruett's handwriting requesting Higgins to call him immediately, regardless of the hour.

Higgins ran a hand through his hair. In all the years Higgins had worked for Pruett, the Head of Clandestine Services had come to his office only a handful of times. At the CIA, the mountain never went to Mohammed.

Does he suspect?

"Shit!" He rushed inside his office and carefully scanned the room. All appeared in order. The picture on the wall over his safe was just as he had left it, and no one else knew his combination. Not even Pruett. Higgins had been careful enough to get his combination lock changed after he moved in without his superior knowing about it. But even that didn't matter. Higgins had always been extremely careful not to have any written record of his own dealings. He committed it all to memory. Pruett could have benefited from nothing in that office, even if he'd looked. But after Pruett had found the sabotaged computers and learned about George's termination, his visit could only mean one of two things. Either he was suspicious, or he wanted Higgins's help in the ongoing investigations. After all, Higgins was officially Chief Western Hemisphere. It was his turf.

Suddenly his door opened.

Higgins turned around, his hand reaching into his coat. He kept it there.

"Jesus Christ! Don't do that again. You scared me."

"I'm sorry, sir. But it's time to pick up the trash," said the cleaning lady.

The trash? The trash! Shit!

Higgins raced for the metallic garbage can next to his desk. The burnt papers were there . . . or were they? He had burned three sheets of paper. He lifted the can up and emptied it on the carpet.

All that came out was barely enough burnt paper to make up one sheet. He glanced at the cleaning lady, who wore a puzzled look.

"Is everythin' all right, sir?"

"Yes . . . yes, it's all right. As you can see, I'll also need my carpet vacuumed."

The cleaning lady shook her head. "Whatever you say, sir. I'll go and get my vacuum—"

"Not now. Later! I have to work now."

"Then it won't be until tomorrow, sir."

"Fine, fine. Tomorrow is fine. Bye."

The cleaning lady frowned, turned around, and closed the door after herself.

Higgins tightened his fists. He now felt certain of the reason Pruett had come to his office. His superior was suspicious of him. Why? *Did he get a chance to talk to George before I terminated him? Or did he decide to go and check with Records and find the first computer printout?* It didn't matter. The fact still remained that somehow Pruett had become suspicious of him. Enough to come into his office and remove those burnt pieces of paper, which were probably being analyzed at that very moment. If the analysis was successful, Higgins knew Pruett would nail him to the wall.

He walked outside and headed for his car. He had to find a public phone booth right away. He had to reach Vanderhoff immediately.

Tom Pruett walked to the windows behind his desk and gazed out at the parking lot. He blinked in surprise when he spotted his subordinate. *Roland?* It was him all right, heading for his car.

Strange, he decided. Especially after Pruett had left a note with Higgins's secretary that he needed to see him immediately.

Pruett narrowed his eyes. Perhaps . . . He walked to the hall and continued down the long corridor, reached the end, and turned right. Higgins's office was halfway down the hall. A cleaning lady was vacuuming the carpet about thirty feet from the entrance to the office.

"Excuse me."

"Yes, sir?"

"I'm Tom Pruett, Head of Clandestine Services. Was Mr. Higgins here a few moments ago?"

"Yes, sir. He was in his office. Crazy man, he yelled at me and then began dumping trash on the floor."

Pruett inhaled deeply and felt a knot in his stomach, quickly followed by a burning sensation. "Is that it?"

"Yes, sir. He left a little after that."

"Have you cleaned his office?"

"No, sir. Not yet. I need to—"

"Leave it alone for now. Don't touch anything in there!"

"Yes, sir."

Pruett walked away. Higgins was indeed covering up something, but what?

He headed back to his office, hoping that Tammy had found the time to stock his refrigerator with a fresh carton of milk.

ELEVEN ★

Old Faces

WASHINGTON, D.C.

Feeling both furious and tired, Pruett turned the corner and slowed down as he approached his house, the third on the right side of the tree-lined street. It was one in the morning, and he was getting no answers. The FBI lab report on the burnt paper had come back negative. The first page didn't even make it to the lab. It collapsed soon after leaving the CIA. The information on the second page could not be retrieved. The technician claimed to have tried every known restoration technique without luck. The thin, cheap paper had burned all the way through. In addition, the print on the page had come from a laser printer, which left no hard impressions on the paper, just a surface coating of ink. After that evaporated with heat, nothing remained. If the paper had come out of a dot matrix printer or a typewriter, or had been handwritten, the verdict would have been different, since those three printing methods used impact or pressure to force the ink into the paper. Pruett exhaled as he pulled into his driveway, turned off the engine, and got out.

He struggled up the steps of his one-story house and unlocked the door. Pruett closed the door behind him, walked across the tiled foyer, past the living room, and into the kitchen. He reached for the light switch, but the overhead came on before he got a chance to flip it.

"Hello, Tom. It's been a long time. Perhaps too long."

Pruett looked in the kitchen but saw no one. He then remembered that the lights could be turned on from the formal dining room on the other side of the long kitchen. The voice . . . he knew the voice. He hadn't heard it for a long time, not since he was Chief Western Hemisphere. It belonged to one of the brightest young agents under his jurisdiction, a young Vietnam vet who had loved his country enough to dedicate his life to serving it. The agency had recruited him out of Ft. Benning, Georgia, much to the relief of the raw young recruits he drilled to exhaustion on a daily basis.

After a brief probation period, the Career Trainee had been sent to "The Farm," the establishment near Williamsburg, disguised as a Pentagon research-and-testing facility, where Pruett had first met him. Very young and ambitious, Pruett remembered. The young CT had undergone light-weapons training, explosives and demolition training, and a full course in parachute jumps. *Should have excused him,* Pruett remembered thinking. *He could have* taught *those courses.* From there, Pruett had taken his young recruit to a CIA training facility in North Carolina for advanced courses in explosives and both light and heavy weaponry. Pruett had nurtured his CT until he'd become a full operative a year later, completing a four- to five-year training course in less than two. After a brief period in France to acquaint the new operative with Cold War espionage techniques, Pruett had assigned him to Mexico City to spy on the Soviets and the Cubans. His missions had been tough, his results top-notch. One of the hardest things Pruett had experienced after his promotion was the loss of contact with the men and women in the field. Head of Clandestine Services could not be directly involved in operations. He had a full staff of risk-takers like Higgins to do that for him. Yet now he was in contact again. The voice could be no one else's. Pruett's thoughts were confirmed when he spotted the tall, slim figure in the doorway to the formal dining room.

"Cameron?"

"Hello, Tom. Or should I say Mr. Pruett?" He stepped from the shadows and into the bright kitchen.

Pruett noticed that Cameron had not aged much. He still had an unlined face. The hair looked darker than Pruett remembered, but it was him all right. Pruett held up both arms, palms facing outward. "Look, Cameron. I know what you've gone through, but—"

"Do you?" Cameron kept walking slowly in his direction. "I don't think so. I think you have no *fucking* idea what it's like to be completely cut off. To be labeled beyond salvage. *Beyond salvage!* How could you, Tom? After all that we went through together! How could you? Didn't all those years mean something?"

Cameron got within two feet of him. His burning eyes and contorted face displayed his intentions. Pruett knew he had to act quickly or risk being killed by an operative he himself had helped train. But he was too late.

"*Beyond salvage,* you bastard!"

Pruett felt the blow, the powerful palm-strike to his mid-chest area. It sent him crashing against the wall. He slid down and landed on the floor.

"How could you, Tom? Why?"

"*Ahgg* . . . my chest, stop, Cameron! No!"

Cameron grabbed Pruett by the lapels, lifted him up, and pressed him against the wall. He let go and Pruett fell to the floor again. Cameron walked to the countertop next to the kitchen sink. A set of steak knives filled a wooden block. Cameron curled the fingers of his right hand around the black handle of one of them and pulled it out of the wooden stand. He turned to Pruett. Emotionless, ice cold.

"I will give you something you failed to provide me with. I will allow you one minute to try and explain to me why you did what you did." He checked his watch. "One minute. The clock is ticking."

Pruett continued to massage his bruised sternum as his mind raced through his options. How could he explain what he'd done? Part of him wanted simply to apologize. After all, he no longer was sure the evidence against Cameron was valid. He questioned Higgins's data, but he knew he could not just come out and say that. That would most certainly make Cameron very suspicious. *One moment beyond salvage, the next I welcome him with open arms? No way.* Pruett knew Cameron would not buy that for a minute. He decided to play it differently.

"I did what I did for a reason," he began. "It wasn't personal. As a matter of fact, whether you believe me or not, it was one of the hardest decisions I've ever made. You see, those years *did* mean something."

Pruett noted that Cameron's intelligent brown eyes displayed neither fear nor affection, but he thought he saw a trace of curiosity in them. Pruett continued.

"Evidence was presented to me. I acted accordingly. The reports that I read indicated that you'd killed your case officer and three poli—"

"I was framed! All of that was fabricated to destroy me because of what I know."

"Prove it." Pruett noticed a hint of hope in Cameron's eyes. "Prove it or kill me. If you can prove that to me, then I'll change the order, but I will not buckle to a corrupt operative. I'd rather die first. It's your choice."

Cameron inhaled and exhaled deeply several times. He then threw the knife into the sink and drove a fist into his palm. He looked at Pruett.

"Dammit! I have no physical proof! Just my word and these wounds." He rolled up the sleeves of his shirt. Pruett noticed the multiple bruises.

"You could have gotten those anywhere."

"True, but I got them during my meeting with Potter. I spent most of the time rolling and crawling on the ground. Someone put a bullet through his chest and tried to do me as well, but I managed to escape."

Pruett frowned and stared at him. "Why would anyone want to do that?"

"Because of what I know. Because of what those Athena scientists told me before a group of assassins stormed the warehouse and killed them."

Pruett inhaled deeply as he remembered the conflict between George's computer printout and Higgins's report of the incident.

Cameron exhaled. "All right, Tom. Let me start at the beginning."

Pruett got up, leaned back against the wall, and continued to massage his chest. "Go on, Cameron. I'm listening."

Cameron cleared his throat and began relating everything he knew, from the initial meeting with Marie Guilloux to what the Athena scientists had told him at the warehouse, to the incidents at the Botanical Gardens and at the airport. His voice was low and calm, his words measured. By the time he finished, Pruett's eyes were closed in remorse. His mind screamed in its anger at Higgins; his heart ached with grief for young George. The fire in his belly consumed him.

PARIS, FRANCE

Carrying a small bag of groceries she'd purchased at an open market several blocks back, Marie Guilloux approached her hotel wearing blue jeans and a T-shirt underneath a leather jacket. Although she seemed physically calm, her mind was in chaos. It was eight in the morning. Fourteen hours and still no news from Cameron. *Where are you, Cameron? Did you make it out of Paris? Did you reach help? Damn!*

Her thoughts were interrupted when she spotted three men wearing overcoats following her. *Where did they come from?* She quickened her pace and the men did likewise. Marie dropped the grocery bag and raced for her hotel. Two other men, also wearing overcoats, now stood by the entrance to the building. They started walking in her direction. She stopped and glanced back. The three men ran toward her. One of them held an ID up in the air.

"Mrs. Guilloux?"

As the men got closer Marie recognized the ID. *CIA! They've captured Cameron and now they're coming for me!*

Instinctively, she broke into a run across the street. The CIA men raced after her.

"Please! Stop! You don't understand!" she heard one of them scream, but all her mind saw were images of the assassins chasing Cameron by the river.

The morning's cool air filled her lungs as she ran over the soft lawn of a narrow stretch of grass on the other side of the street. Her legs ached, but she kept on, taking in deep breaths as the patch of grass turned into a small park. The trees to either side of her melted into a wall of green as she tried to increase the gap, but she was getting weak, light-headed. She didn't have the conditioning to keep her current pace for much longer. She had to slow down . . .

Suddenly, a strong hand gripped her from behind and pulled her down and behind a line of bushes next to the trees. Marie viciously kicked her legs as her left hand unsuccessfully tried to reach behind her and grab her attacker: a clump of hair, an ear, perhaps scratch his face, throat . . . anything. But her attacker kept one hand tightly fixed around her mouth and another one holding a lock on her right arm.

In full rage, Marie felt the strong arms turning her around.

Animals! You're all a bunch of animals!

She pulled her right arm loose and tried to scratch him across his throat, but her clumsy move was effectively blocked by a fast forearm. Still light-headed from the short but exhausting run, and ignoring whatever it was the CIA man was saying, Marie continued trying to kick and punch the operative, who easily blocked all of her blows.

"Mrs. Guilloux, listen to me!" she finally heard him say as the man held her shoulders. "It's all right! Cameron is fine! We've come to take you to him. He's safe in Washington, and soon you'll join him."

Marie's vision was blurry. She thought her mind was playing tricks on her, making her believe what she so desperately wished would be true. She fought against believing her ears, but then she heard it again.

"Please, listen to me! Cameron is safe, and so are you now! Calm down and let us take care of you. Please, Mrs. Guilloux."

Marie couldn't fight it anymore. The CIA man had won.

As her tense body relaxed, the man's face slowly came into focus—the face of a stranger, but the eyes showed compassion and warmth, and Marie needed that to take her away from this insanity.

"Everything is going to be all right, Mrs. Guilloux."

She rested her head on his shoulder and silently wept.

THE WHITE HOUSE

Although it was his third time inside the Oval Office, Pruett felt a knot in his stomach as he faced a sleepy President and a very irritable Defense Secretary, the Secretary of State, and the Chairman of the Joint Chiefs of Staff. The Director of the CIA, currently on leave hunting in the mountains, could not be reached in time for the meeting. Cameron sat on a sofa next to the Defense Secretary. Pruett knew his title alone didn't give him enough pull to get these government officials together in a room on such short notice. It was the respect Pruett had earned for his performance during previous crises that had gotten the President out of bed. Pruett knew the President had a high regard for his opinion.

The President sat against the edge of his oak desk across from the sofas. He was dressed casually, a pair of light gray slacks and a white polo shirt. Pruett stood on the side in front of a small corkboard supported by a tripod.

"Gentlemen," the President began. "I want to apologize for getting you out of bed at this hour, but Tom called me an hour ago with some very disturbing information concerning the future of NASA. With that, I leave it with you, Tom."

Pruett exhaled. It never got any easier. Twice in his life he had stood before the leaders of the nation, and twice his ulcer had numbed his entire chest and nearly clouded his senses. He felt the heartburn intensifying and clenched his teeth, but quickly managed to force a relaxed face as all the eyes in the room shifted in his direction.

"Thank you, Mr. President. Gentlemen, all of you are aware by now of the problems NASA's *Lightning* is facing in space. First, one of the main engines failed during the lift-off stage, and then—"

"We can read, Tom," Carlton Stice, the Defense Secretary, suddenly said. He waved the confidential memo that Pruett had hand-delivered to the President. It detailed the current condition of the orbiter.

"Please bear with me, sir."

"Go on, Tom," said the President.

In spite of his digestive problem, Pruett smiled inwardly. Coming from this President, that meant don't fucking interrupt him again until he's finished!

"Thank you, sir. Less than an hour later the OMS engines, the Orbital Maneuvering System engines, failed during a maneuver that was meant to put *Lightning* in a higher, safer orbit. Fortunately, the engines didn't fail until after *Lightning* had achieved enough speed to reach an orbit somewhere between its previous orbit and the desired orbit. The cause of the malfunctions cannot be truly determined until *Lightning* gets back down and NASA scientists get a chance to take the engines apart and inspect them. Gentlemen, I stand here before you with the statement that *Lightning*'s problems were not due to a malfunction, but to sabotage." There was an immediate reaction from those listening. The Secretary of Defense talked briefly to the Chairman of the Joint Chiefs while the Secretary of State closed his eyes and rubbed his large forehead.

Stice then addressed Pruett. "Tom, how do you know this?"

"From one of my operatives, Mr. Secretary. Cameron Stone."

Pruett looked at Cameron and then at each of the others in the room. They all stared at him, the President included. Pruett cleared his throat and started speaking, telling the story right from the beginning: Claude Guilloux's mysterious auto accident, Marie Guilloux's revelation about the destruction of the Soviet spacecraft, the shooting at the hotel, the information conveyed to Cameron by the Athena scientists, the shooting at the warehouse, and the subsequent incidents involving the CIA directly. Pruett told it all as best he could. He finished with a brief description of Athena's launching facility in French Guiana.

The room was quiet.

"How, Tom? How can you buy into such an idea without concrete proof?" asked Stice.

Pruett didn't flinch, but stared the Defense Secretary in the eye. Although the heartburn was nearly numbing his senses, he managed to put it behind him, cleared his throat, and addressed the group. "Gentlemen, I have provided you with evidence that tends to corroborate Mr. Stone's testimony. I'll admit that I can't give you incontrovertible proof, but the reality of things in the intelligence field is that oftentimes we don't get such proof. We generally start with a series of facts. From there we must build theories and test them against the facts until we find the one theory that matches best. We then adopt it and hope the future facts continue to fit it. In this case, I have to admit that I was hesitant at first, but after our people at NASA informed me of the problems *Lightning* was facing . . . well, gentlemen, it became apparent that something was seriously wrong. At this point we can do one of two things. We could close our eyes and ignore it, and hope that NASA will be able to handle it, or we can accept the situation for what it is and do something about it. That is your choice, gentlemen.

I'm merely presenting the information to you."

More silence. Pruett noted Stice staring at the floor. He had slammed the door on the Defense Secretary.

"Is this place in French Guiana near a beach?" asked the Chairman of the Joint Chiefs.

"What do you have in mind?" asked the President before Pruett got a chance to point to the map of French Guiana pinned to the corkboard.

"I would just like to explore all our options, Mr. President."

The President nodded and looked at Pruett, who stepped to the side of the board and pointed to the coastal city.

"Yes it is, sir. It's near Devil's Island, approximately forty miles from Cayenne, the capital."

"Can we confirm deployment of the rocket?"

Pruett smiled and pulled out two satellite photographs. "These were taken exactly an hour ago during a KH-11 pass. This is the launch complex." He pointed to a structure in the right side of the photo. "And this in the center is the rocket itself. My analyst has confirmed it as an Athena V rocket, capable of putting payloads into geosynchronous orbit. Very powerful rocket, sir. And extremely reliable too. It's scheduled to be launched at exactly 11:35 P.M. local time, 10:35 P.M. our time." Pruett checked his watch. "Exactly sixteen hours and fifteen minutes from now."

"God almighty," the Chairman of the Joint Chiefs said. "We have to move right away, Mr. President. If Tom's information here is as good as it has been in the past, we must act immediately."

"What if it's not?" asked Stice. "All Tom's got is conjecture. There is no physical evidence, only Stone's testimony. No offense intended, Stone."

Cameron frowned. "None taken. But I would like to point out, sir, that Marie Guilloux, who happens to be on her way here from Paris, will back my story. She's a scientist herself, and she was also there when the other Athena scientists were killed."

"We know that." Stice exhaled and turned to the President. "From what we know, sir, Athena is about to deploy a very sophisticated satellite for the Australian government. We are looking at two hundred million for the satellite and another thirty million for the rocket. We can't just go in and blow it away, can we?"

Pruett inhaled deeply; his ulcer was growing out of control. He desperately wanted to reach in his pocket for the pack of antacid tablets, but decided against it. "Conjecture? I think not," he responded in a tone as casual and controlled as he could make it. "It all depends on how you look at the data, Mr. Secretary. I don't believe in coincidence, and there have been just too many related incidents to ignore them and write them off as coincidence. Also, let's all remember the fact that *Lightning* is in trouble just as the evidence indicated it would be. In my opinion, *Lightning*'s problems are all the physical proof we need. Gentlemen, the data here is telling us that something is definitely wrong. Cameron Stone's—and Marie Guilloux's—testimony simply brings it all together."

The President, Pruett, and Cameron remained quiet as the others explored the alternatives and gave their various opinions on how the situation should be handled.

Finally, the President got up and walked toward the bullet-proof windows that looked out on the White House Rose Garden. The yellowish light from the halogen floodlights outside filtered through the Armorlite glass. The President simply stared outside, chin up, hands behind his back. The room was now quiet. Each person there knew that the President had listened to all that he'd cared to, and was now in the process of formulating his own response to the crisis.

The President turned around and faced Pruett. "Has anyone notified NASA of this?"

"No, sir."

"What about the FBI? Do they know anything about this?"

"A couple of technicians from the analysis lab were involved in the investigation to find the mole, sir."

"All right, I'll make sure the appropriate people know about this, if that's the route we take. In the meantime keep a lid on the whole thing."

"Yes, sir."

"Tom, like always, you have explained the situation clearly and concisely. Damn good briefing."

"Thank you, Mr. President."

"And also thank you, Mr. Stone."

"You're welcome, Mr. President."

"Now, if you don't mind, I would like to discuss our options with my staff. Go back to Langley. I'll get the word to you on our decision."

"Yes, sir."

Pruett left the map and photos on the board and simply grabbed his briefcase and signaled Cameron to follow him.

They closed the door behind them. Pruett dropped the briefcase and reached into his pocket.

"Tom?"

"Yeah," he responded as he chewed on the tablets.

"I think my involvement in this is over. I did what I was supposed to have done. Now it's up to you guys to—"

"Stick around for a little while. Who knows, things might get interesting."

"That's exactly what I'm afraid of."

"Stick around anyway. Besides, if things do get interesting, we'll also need Marie's help."

"Why her? I think she's already been through enough."

"She used to work at the Kourou site, right?"

"Yes, but—wait a second, Tom. I don't want to expose her to—"

"Relax. All we might want is some intelligence on the launch complex before we move in, if we move in at all."

Cameron sighed and checked his watch. Marie's plane was due to arrive between noon and one P.M.

DULLES INTERNATIONAL AIRPORT, WASHINGTON, D.C.

Cameron paced back and forth by the gate as the passengers from the TWA DC-10 left the craft. Although he felt very excited about seeing Marie, the professional in him kept him from showing it externally. Pruett was right. As much as Cameron wanted to end his involvement in the case, the problem was still far from over. A conspiracy threatened to destroy America's future in space. Cameron knew he had to hang on for just a little while longer.

Then he stopped his pacing and turned toward the gate. The eyes, the face. He saw her smile the moment Marie recognized him and rushed past startled travelers and into his arms. Cameron closed his eyes and inhaled deeply, feeling Marie's body pressed next to his. No words were spoken.

"I was so afraid," she finally whispered in his ear. "I didn't know if you—"

"*Shh.* I'm fine, Marie, and so are you."

"You don't know what it was like to—"

"Don't worry. I won't leave you again. I promise."

Marie hugged him tight. Cameron didn't resist. His logical side could wait while his soul bathed in the love he had not felt for nearly two decades.

TWELVE ★

EVA

My God, the stars are everywhere, even below me.
—Michael Collins,
Apollo 11 astronaut

LIGHTNING

Inside the airlock between the mid-deck and the payload bay, Kessler helped Jones into his Extravehicular Mobility Unit, a self-contained life-support system and anthropomorphic pressure garment that provided not only thermal protection to the astronaut during extravehicular activities, but also protection against micro-meteoroids. Usually astronauts put these suits on without assistance in free space, but Kessler figured Jones could use the help during his first time suiting up in a weightlessness condition. Three main parts made up the suit—the liner, the pressure vessel, and the life-support system.

Jones didn't need Kessler's help to get into the suit liner, similar in appearance to long underwear. The liner was made of stretchable nylon fabric laced with over three hundred feet of plastic tubing to circulate cooling water around Jones's body.

Jones took a final breath of one-hundred-percent-pure oxygen from a plastic mask. The one-hour pre-breathing procedure prior to EVA was necessary because the normal atmosphere inside the orbiter consisted of seventy-nine percent nitrogen and twenty-one percent oxygen at a pressure of 17.4 pounds per square inch, the same as sea level. Jones's pressure suit, for ease of movement, operated at a reduced pressure of only four PSI with one hundred percent oxygen. Pre-breathing removed all of the nitrogen from Jones's bloodstream, preventing bubbles of nitrogen from forming and expanding in his blood when his suit's pressure dropped to four PSI. The nitrogen bubbles could cause nausea, cramps, and severe pains in the joints.

Kessler held on to the legs of the lower torso section of the pressure vessel. Jones dropped into it feet first, guiding his legs into the legs of the multilayered garment that protected the lower half of his body. The outer shell of the garment was made of tough Ortho fabric—a blend of Teflon, woven Nomex, and Kevlar Rip Stop—that served as an abrasion and tear-resistant cover as well as the primary micro-meteoroid shield. The other layers were alternating Aluminized Mylar Film and Dacron Scrim that insulated the wearer from the extreme temperatures of outer space.

Jones held on to the metallic locking ring of the lower torso section of the EMU suit while Kessler grabbed the upper torso section from the rack behind him.

"Ready?"

"You bet."

Kessler lowered it over Jones almost like a T-shirt. Jones put his arms through the holes until it floated over his shoulders.

"Damn! This is great. One hell of a lot easier than down where the buffalo roam."

Kessler smiled. Donning this 250-pound suit on Earth was a formidable task, yet in the weightlessness of space it became simple. Kessler locked the pants and upper torso with the metallic ring connector.

"How does it feel?"

"Great. Just great." Jones moved around the air lock and checked the flexibility.

Kessler put on Jones's gloves and connected them to the arms of the upper torso section. Jones moved his fingers.

"Will do."

"All right, turn around. Got to hook you up to the PLSS." Kessler removed the Primary Life Support System, the backpack unit used to provide oxygen, pressurization, and ventilation to the pressure vessel, from a rack on the air lock wall.

Kessler strapped the PLSS on Jones's back and then connected a few tubes to the suit. He moved to Jones's front.

"Time for your Snoopy cap. Stand still." Kessler put a skullcap on Jones's head. It held a microphone and earpiece that Jones would use for communication. "And this is in case you get a little thirsty." He inserted a small in-suit drinking bag filled with water. It had a drinking tube with a suction-actuated valve.

"Thanks, but to tell you the truth, I kinda prefer Jack Daniels."

"You mean to tell me that you're nervous?"

"Not really, but right now I think I'd give up my left nut for a cigarette."

"Sorry, pal. Being here does come with some sacrifices."

"You're telling me! All right, let's crank this puppy up."

Kessler attached the PLSS's display panel and control unit to the front of Jones's suit and activated the system. Cool water began to circulate around his body through the plastic tubes of the suit liner. At the same time the system began to spew oxygen for breathing and attempted to pressurize the suit.

He reached for Jones's helmet, a rigid, one-piece hemisphere made of ultraviolet polycarbonate plastic. He locked the helmet in place, and also the gloves. Now hermetic, the suit quickly pressurized to four PSI, equivalent to roughly

34,000 feet in altitude. One of the major challenges during the design of the shuttle space suit was to make it flexible enough to allow EVA activities without extreme physical exertion. NASA had answered that challenge by stitching tucks in the shoulder, elbow, wrist, knee, and ankle areas. This allowed Jones's joints to flex without excessive muscle fatigue.

Kessler elevated the pressure inside Jones's EMU to eight PSI and shut off the oxygen supply. He waited sixty seconds before reading the digital display on Jones's chest-mounted control module, and verified that the suit's pressure had not dropped by more than 0.2 PSI, the maximum allowable rate of leakage of a shuttle EMU. Satisfied, Kessler turned the oxygen supply back on and brought the suit's pressure back up to air-lock pressure. He checked his watch.

"Thirty minutes to go."

"Yep," Jones responded as he began the final pre-breathing session before the pressure in his suit would be permanently lowered to four PSI.

Kessler grabbed the plastic oxygen mask that Jones had used and also began to breathe pure oxygen, conforming to NASA's regulations requiring a backup astronaut to be ready for EVA in case of an emergency. Because Kessler had been too busy running dozens of diagnostic algorithms to determine the extent of the shuttle's damage, he had failed to follow the pre-breathing rule, and now he tried to at least partially comply with it.

A half hour later Kessler removed his oxygen mask and slowly lowered the pressure of Jones's EMU to four PSI before securing the visor assembly over Jones's helmet. The visor provided protection against heat, light, and impact. Finally, Kessler strapped a TV camera just above the visor, positioning it along the same line as Jones's own line of vision.

"You're ready."

"I know, but you're not. You better get your unprotected little ass back inside the crew module. I'm ready to get out there."

"Listen. Be careful with that MMU," Kessler said, referring to the Manned Maneuvering Unit, the fifteen-million-dollar jet-propelled backpack system designed to provide completely untethered transport for an astronaut during EVA. "It's supposed to be much more sensitive than the one we practiced with at the WET-F pool. In there at least we had water resistance. Up here there's nothing to counter our movements except for the jets."

"You worry too much. Now how about you letting me go around the ship and find out what kind of shape we're really in."

Kessler pounded lightly on Jones's shoulder. "Careful, this is the real thing, man. Later."

"Later."

Kessler went through the D-shaped opening and into the mid-deck compartment, closed the aluminum-alloy hatch, and locked it in place. He pushed himself up through one of the openings connecting the flight deck to the mid-deck compartment, floated into the flight deck, and stood in front of the aft control panel.

He brought his left hand down to the bottom left section of panel 13L and flipped the switch to deploy the Ku-band antenna system. The servomotors of the seven-foot-long antenna, gimbal-mounted on the starboard sill longeron in the payload bay, responded to Kessler's command by deploying the antenna until it formed a sixty-seven-degree angle with the orbiter's longitudinal axis, while turning the three-foot-wide parabolic dish at the end of the graphite-epoxy structure toward the closest TDRSS satellite in geosynchronous orbit.

Kessler nodded as he saw the Ku antenna's talk-back indicator light confirming deployment. *Lightning* now had Ku-band communications capability with Houston through the TDRSS-White Sands Ground Terminal link. The Ku-band system could handle much higher quantities of audio, video, and telemetry data than the S-band system.

Kessler reached the UHF-mode control knob on Overhead Panel 06. He turned the knob to the EVA setting and flipped one of three UHF switches above the knob to select a frequency of 259.7 Mhz, linking Jones, *Lightning,* and Houston for audio communications.

"How are you doing, Tex?"

"All systems appear nominal. Getting ready for EVA."

"Hold on. Let's check your video signal."

"Camera's on," responded Jones.

Kessler moved over to an array of switches and talk-back lights controlling *Lightning*'s five payload bay cameras and the two cameras mounted on the Remote Manipulator Arm. He turned on the keel/EVA switch, disabling all video inputs except for the one coming from Jones's camera. Kessler glanced at the two black-and-white TV monitors on the adjacent panel. The ten-by-seven-inch monitors were arranged one over the other. Kessler activated the top one.

"I'm receiving a good clear image from Jones's camera, Houston. Do you see it?"

"Roger, Lightning. *The image is crystal clear."*

"Copy, Houston. Go easy, Tex. Remember to stay clipped to something until you reach an MMU."

"Relax, Mike."

"Lightning, *Houston here. Listen to Kessler, Jones. Go extremely easy, particularly because it's your first space walk."*

"Ah, roger. Well, here I go . . . Oh, man! This is terrific. What a feeling!"

"Now, close the hatch behind you and be careful," Kessler said. "Go directly to the MMU and strap yourself in." Kessler watched Jones through the aft view windows. Jones gracefully floated toward one of two Manned Maneuvering Units, briefly inspecting it before backing himself against it.

"Strapping in . . . there! All right, let's turn this puppy on."

Kessler watched Jones reach with his left hand for the on/off switch located on the MMU's right-hand side, over Jones's shoulder. He saw the locator lights come on. The MMU appeared to be in working condition.

"All systems nominal," Jones noted. *"Will check the engine section first and then the underside."*

"Roger," responded Hunter from Mission Control in Houston. *"Copy for initial check of the SSMEs followed by a visual of the OMS pods and the underside."*

Kessler shifted his gaze to the black-and-white screen monitor.

"Ready for EVA."

"Go for it, Tex."

Jones slowly propelled himself to the aft section of the orbiter. Kessler noticed he was going unusually slow. *Good. Tex's being cautious.*

He reached the tail section and went around it, panning the camera on *Lightning*'s main engines.

"Damn! You guys seeing this?"

Kessler held his breath for a moment as he realized just how close they had come to total destruction. Number-one SSME was destroyed, along with most of the exhaust section, including the protective tiles around it. The orbiter looked like it had come with only two SSMEs and the two smaller OMS engines above.

"Houston, are you there?" asked Jones.

"Ah, roger. We're still here."

"Any comments?"

"Not yet. Could you pan in closer?"

Kessler saw Jones disappear behind *Lightning*. He shifted his gaze back to the screen. The camera panned in on the area where number-one SSME had been. Now there was only a mangled mess of pipes and loose cables.

"That's as close as I can get."

"Hold position."

"Hot damn, Houston! Looks like one of the turbopumps was blown to hell."

"Yes, we can see that. Can you tell if it was the liquid hydrogen or the liquid oxygen turbopump?"

"I can't remember which is the smaller of the two, but the one blown here's the larger one. The other pump's in one piece."

"That's the liquid hydrogen pump."

"Well, the pumps are pretty darn delicate pieces of equipment. I guess a failure was bound to happen sooner or later."

Kessler frowned. Jones was correct.

"Houston, *Lightning* here. You guys have any ideas?" Kessler asked.

"*Lightning, we've just pulled out the maintenance records of the SSME, and it shows that all three engines successfully fire-tested for a full one thousand seconds each prior to installation on the orbiter. The report from the twenty-second Flight Readiness Firing last week shows nothing out of the ordinary. Based on the way the engine blew, our only guess at this point is that perhaps the turbopump somehow overheated, or maybe the blades simply came apart under the stress. Again, those are guesses. We won't know for sure what caused it until we perform a thorough inspection.*"

Kessler exhaled.

"*Jones, please pan onto the left OMS engine next.*"

Kessler saw the image moving over to the left Orbital Maneuvering System engine. It looked nominal.

"*Can't see anything wrong here.*"

"*Pan closer.*"

Jones placed himself between the OMS exhaust and the vertical fin. "*Sorry, boys, but there's no apparent damage here.*"

Kessler got to within inches of the screen. It looked normal. The thermal tiles surrounding the OMS engine appeared intact.

"*Well, Houston?*" asked Jones.

"*We'll have to continue running diagnostics. Give us a look underneath.*"

"All right . . . oh, shit!"

Kessler watched the image on the screen rotating. Something had gone wrong. "Tex, what's your situation? Tex?"

"Oh, man! Can't control this thing!"

Kessler did not have a visual on Jones since he was behind *Lightning*. He could only see the image on the screen, which showed *Lightning* rotating along its center line and moving farther away. That meant Jones was rotating and moving farther away, apparently out of control. Kessler finally saw him, above the tail and spinning along all three axes.

"Close your eyes. Relax!"

"Don't fucking tell me to relax, man! This thing's got a mind of its own. My hands aren't even on the damned controls and the jets are firing like crazy. What in the hell's going on?"

"Jones, Houston here. Shut the MMU down. Shut it down!"

Kessler saw what he feared he would see. Jones, still spinning, was coming straight back toward *Lightning*. *Jesus! He's gonna crash against the orbiter!*

"Tex! Shut it off! God, please, shut it off!"

"Dammit! I'm trying, I'm trying!"

Kessler watched Jones's left hand savagely striking the section of the MMU above his right shoulder in a desperate attempt to throw the switch off before he disappeared from Kessler's field of view. Kessler immediately shifted his gaze toward the screen. The image of the left OMS nozzle grew larger and larger.

"Oh, God. Nooo!" Jones screamed.

The screen went blank.

"Tex? . . . Tex? . . . Tex! Oh, Sweet Jesus!"

"Lightning, what's going on? Our screen just went blank. Do you have a visual on Jones?"

"He just crashed against the left OMS engine nozzle. The MMU's still active. He's spinning and moving away from the orbiter!" Kessler watched Jones continue to rotate in all directions as he began to move away from *Lightning* again.

"Fucking MMU!" Kessler removed his headset, dove for the mid-crew compartment, pressurized the air lock, and floated inside it. He moved quickly, closing the interior hatch, stripping in seconds, and donning the suit liner. He reached for the lower torso section of the pressure suit and pulled it up to his waist. He then dove into the upper section and joined it to the lower section with the connecting ring.

"*Lightning? What is going on? What is the status of Jones? Is he moving?*"

Kessler, his senses clouded by the sudden rush of adrenaline flooding through his system, barely heard Hunter's voice coming through the speakers. Every second counted. Every damned second. He'd let Jones down years before in Iraq. Kessler was determined not to do it again. As mission commander, Kessler was responsible for the craft and its crew. Jones was his crew.

Kessler backed himself into the PLSS backpack unit and strapped it on, also securing the control and display unit on his chest. *Gloves, gloves . . .* He scanned the shelf to his left.

There!

He snapped the gloves into the ring locks and put on the skull cap and communications gear. He activated the backpack unit and before he read the displays, he reached for the helmet and lowered it in place. He locked it and eyed the display on his chest. The backpack system was nominal. Kessler lowered the visor assembly over his helmet.

"*Lightning, Houston here. Please acknowledge.* Lightning? Lightning? *Dammit, Michael. Answer me!*"

"I'm here, Chief," he responded through his voice-activated headset. "I'm going after him."

"*Not yet. You haven't fully pre-breathed yet.*"

"I know, Chief, but I don't have a choice. He's getting away!"

"Then be very careful. Try to relax as much as possible. Don't breathe any faster than you have to or you might throw up inside your suit."

"Roger." He depressurized the air lock, pushed the exterior hatch open, and floated into the payload bay.

Kessler quickly forced his mind to overcome the spatial disorientation so typical for first-time spacewalkers. For a brief moment it seemed that the hundreds of hours he had spent training in the 1.3-million-gallon Neutral Buoyancy Simulator tank at the Marshall Space Flight Center in Huntsville, Alabama, and at the Johnson Space Center's WET-F pool had been insufficient. *Well, almost insufficient,* he admitted, as his senses finally adjusted to the orbiter's upside-down flight profile. A large portion of the South American continent appeared to hang overhead as Kessler looked up through the gold-coated visor of his space suit and past the opened doors of the payload bay.

Kessler shifted his gaze to the left, above the orbiter's vertical fin tip. He narrowed his eyes and inhaled deeply as his heartbeat increased.

"Don't get nervous, Michael. Take your time breathing that oxygen. Let your body adjust slowly. Hold it in as much as possible and exhale slowly," said Hunter.

"Trying, Chief. Starting EVA," Kessler said over the radio as he took a shallow breath and held it in. He briefly inspected the second MMU on the right side of the payload bay, checking for nominal propellant and battery levels before backing himself into it. He strapped himself in and threw the power switch located over his right shoulder. The MMU's flashing locator lights came on. Before placing his hands on the thruster controls, Kessler went through the brief checklist he had committed to memory. Satisfied that all was in operating condition, he skillfully fired the MMU's thruster jets for one second. The twin tanks in the back of the MMU provided compressed nitrogen gas to the thrusters, which puffed out the gas in one direction and pushed him gently in the other. Kessler reached the rear section of the payload bay and affixed a "Stinger" to the arms of the MMU. The Stinger was a device designed to latch on to broken satellites. With that, Kessler headed out of the payload bay and into free space. He activated the TV camera for the benefit of Houston.

Kessler used the hand control to move away from the payload bay. He looked around him but didn't see Jones. Puzzled, he propelled himself roughly two hundred feet above and to the right of the orbiter. Still no sign of him. He piloted the MMU to within a hundred or so feet below *Lightning*. There! A white figure. Still rotating out of control. Kessler applied a three-second burst on the thrusters. Compressed nitrogen propelled him beneath *Lightning* into a sea of darkness. The missing tiles on *Lightning*'s underside distracted him momentarily, but his logical mind quickly put things into perspective. First get to Jones, then worry about the missing tiles.

He released the MMU's controls and continued moving in the same direction. Jones's limp figure grew progressively larger and larger. Kessler knew he was moving much farther away from *Lightning* than he should, but all of that was secondary. Who knew what kind of injury Jones had suffered in his collision with the orbiter? Jones appeared to be unconscious, since he didn't move his arms or legs.

Kessler approached within ten feet of Jones and slowed down, trying to achieve a similar translational velocity. He did so as he came to within five feet of him. Kessler noticed that Jones's MMU seemed dead, the compressed nitrogen supply probably exhausted. *No obvious damage to the EMU suit. Still pressurized. Visor intact, so no damage to the helmet underneath.* Kessler breathed easier. Hope filled him.

Kessler fired the reverse thrusters for one second and reduced his speed. Additional lateral thrusts allowed him to align the Stinger with the back of Jones's MMU.

Slowly, almost painstakingly, Kessler approached his rotating friend.

"Two feet and closing . . . one foot . . . contact, oh shit!" Kessler managed to place the Stinger's latching mechanism in contact with Jones's MMU, but he lacked enough force to snap the latch. His approach had been too slow. The Stinger and Jones's MMU momentarily transferred their respective translational and rotational energies and then separated. Kessler's forward motion caused Jones to wobble. In turn, Jones's rotating motion caused Kessler to rotate clockwise. In an instant, the Earth, space, orbiter, and Jones flashed through his field of view, changing positions as he tumbled away unpredictably on all three axes.

Kessler felt dizzy and disoriented. He tried to concentrate and remember the hours he'd spent in the multiaxis simulator. His hands fumbled for the MMU's controls, but spatial disorientation quickly set in, making it harder for Kessler's confused brain to decide in which direction to reach for the hand controls of the propulsion unit. His breathing increased. He tried to control his rising nausea.

"Close your eyes! Close them and hold your breath. Remember your training," Kessler heard Hunter say over the radio, but he began to panic. The orbiter seemed to float farther and farther away.

"Dammit, Michael! I gave you a direct order. Close your eyes and relax. You have plenty of compressed nitrogen to make it back from miles away. Breathe slowly, hold it for several seconds, and let it out slow. Concentrate!"

Hunter's voice was reassuring. Although designed to be used within three hundred feet of the orbiter, the MMU could get him back from farther away than that. As mixed images of Earth and space flickered in front of his eyes, Kessler managed to draw strength from his strict NASA training and forced his eyes to do something his natural instincts refused to let them do: He closed them. In a flash it all went away, as if someone had abruptly dropped a heavy gate in front of him, isolating him from the sudden madness that had engulfed him. *Peace.* His eyes stopped registering motion; his brain regained control; his body relaxed. Kessler's breathing steadied.

"Eyes closed."

"Good, Michael," said Hunter. *"Now listen carefully. I've got you in plain view from one of* Lightning*'s payload bay cameras. You're rotating clockwise about once every ten seconds. Counter with a two-second lateral thrust."*

Kessler almost opened his eyes to reach for the controls but caught himself. Instead, he felt his way down the MMU's arms, placed his hands on the controls, and fired the right-side jets. *One-thousand-one . . . one-thousand-two.* He released the trigger.

"Good, Michael. Now, you're also rotating backward at a slower rate . . . hmm, about once per minute. A one-second forward thrust should do."

"Roger," Kessler responded as his confidence began to build up again. He complied with Hunter's order and fired the jet.

"All right, now what?"

"Open your eyes."

Kessler did so. "Jesus!" was all he could bring his lips to say when he realized how much he had drifted away in such little time. *Lightning* appeared to be a small white object no larger than a couple of inches in length. Jones floated roughly fifty feet away, rotating faster than before.

Kessler decided to take a different approach. He released the Stinger from the MMU's arms and then approached Jones. He stopped when he estimated he was five feet away from his rotating friend. Kessler removed the ten-foot-long webbed line hanging from the side of his MMU. It had tether clips on both ends. He clipped one end to the side of his own MMU and carefully tried to snag the other end to anything on Jones's space suit or MMU. He got within three feet. Jones's rotation turned him clockwise about once every five seconds. Kessler reached for the center of Jones's suit, the point of zero rotation, and managed to clip the end to one of the straps securing Jones to the MMU.

He slowly turned around and started to haul Jones back toward *Lightning*. The webbed line neutralized Jones's rotational movement.

Kessler eyed *Lightning*. He estimated they were at least a thousand feet away, over three times the maximum recommended distance for MMU EVA work, but Kessler knew that was just a precautionary specification. In actuality, as long as compressed nitrogen remained in his tanks, the MMU could take him as far away as he pleased.

He opted for a four-second thrust. The first second would put tension on the line and give him a hard tug, the other three seconds would be to compensate for Jones's mass and to propel them both toward the orbiter.

With both hands on the controls, Kessler thrust himself forward. As expected, the tug came and jerked him back, but he kept his hands on the hand controls, commanding the MMU to give him more forward motion. Slowly, it happened. Kessler began to drag Jones back to the orbiter.

A few minutes later they got to within one hundred feet. Kessler knew slowing down would be trickier than accelerating. The moment he slowed down, Jones would close the ten-foot gap and either crash against him or fly by him and pull him along. Without slowing down, Kessler glanced at the aft section of *Lightning*'s empty payload bay. He estimated his velocity at no more than two or three feet per second.

Kessler made his decision and directed the thrusters to propel him and his "cargo" toward the payload bay. He waited. Fifty feet separated them from the bay. Forty feet. Kessler readied himself to perform a maneuver he'd never done before. Thirty feet . . . twenty-five . . . now!

He slowed down a little. The webbed line lost its tension as Jones continued moving at the same speed and in the same direction. Kessler jetted himself upward, barely missing Jones, who flew past him a few feet below. He waited for the tug. It came. Hard. Jones pulled him toward the payload bay. Ten feet. Kessler fired the thrusters and managed to slow Jones and himself down to less than a half foot per second. Jones softly impacted the inside wall of *Lightning*'s aft payload bay. Kessler managed to stop a few feet from him.

Almost home. Kessler unstrapped Jones's MMU and secured it to the side of the cargo bay.

With Jones's bulky MMU out of the way, Kessler placed Jones in between the arms of his own and gently jetted toward the front, toward the still-open hatch that led to the air lock. They reached it in less than twenty seconds.

Kessler quickly unstrapped himself, temporarily secured the MMU, and dragged Jones into the air lock.

He closed the hatch and repressurized the compartment. Kessler unlocked his gloves and removed his visor and helmet, letting them float inside the compartment as he unstrapped the backpack and display unit. He unlocked the joining ring, kicked off the lower torso pressure suit, and twisted his way out of the upper torso section. Now he wore only the liquid cooling and vent garment.

He removed Jones's gloves and helmet, and powered down the backpack unit. Jones's eyes were closed. Kessler put a finger to Jones's nose. He was breathing. Kessler noticed a cut on Jones's forehead. *He must have hit the inside of his helmet on impact and knocked himself out.*

He finished undressing Jones and spotted bruises on his ribs. *Damn! Broken ribs.* Kessler frowned, but was not that surprised. Jones had crashed against the orbiter at great speed. He was lucky just to be alive. Kessler put on the comfortable blue, one-piece cotton flight suit and then carefully dressed Jones. He pushed the inside hatch open and gently dragged Jones to the mid-deck compartment, closing the hatch behind them.

"Houston, *Lightning* here. Do you copy?"

"What's your situation, Michael? How's Jones?"

"Jones is injured. He's got a head wound and I think some broken ribs. His breathing's steady and his pulse strong. I'm going to strap him in and keep him still."

"Copy, Lightning. Careful with the broken ribs. Jones could puncture a lung."

"Roger that. Also, I noticed several black tiles missing on the underside. They must have shaken loose during the explosion. That's bad news."

"Exactly how many tiles are we talking about here?"

"Uh, I guess about a dozen."

"We'll have to check if your tile repair kit can handle that much exposed area."

Kessler shrugged. Somehow that answer didn't surprise him. NASA had been putting less and less emphasis on tile repair kits since the early days of the shuttle, when tiles were falling off left and right during tests due to poor adhesives. Since then, better compounds had been developed that greatly improved the reliability of the thermal shield to the point that not one single shuttle mission had had the need to repair or replace tiles in space. For that reason, Kessler doubted that the epoxy foam that came with *Lightning*'s tile repair kit would be enough to fill a dozen holes, most of which were six inches square by five inches deep.

"Say, Michael, when was the last time you slept more than a few hours?"

"The day before the launch."

"Get some rest. We'll wake you up in a few hours."

"Roger, Houston."

Kessler reached for the orbiter medical system. The three-part medical kit, designed to handle simple illness or injuries, had some medications to stabilize severely injured crew members. He cleaned Jones's head wound and bandaged it. That was the easy part. The ribs were different. He played cautiously and decided to leave them alone for now. As long as Jones didn't move much, the broken ribs shouldn't affect his lungs.

Kessler brought Jones to one of three horizontal rigid sleep stations and unzipped the sleeping bag attached to the padded board. The station was over six feet long and thirty inches wide. Kessler easily guided Jones into it and zipped it up. In weightlessness the sleeping bag would hold Jones against the padded board with enough pressure to create the illusion of sleeping on a comfortable bed. Kessler wanted to do more for his friend, but was afraid that in doing so he could cause more harm than good.

"Sweet dreams, Tex."

Kessler crawled onto another horizontal station and tried to fall asleep but couldn't. Too many questions preyed on his mind. Too many things had gone wrong. First the number-one SSME had blown up, then the OMS engines had malfunctioned, and now a faulty MMU. He exhaled. Inspection of the SSME and OMS engines would have to wait until they returned to Earth, but the MMU . . .

Kessler bolted out of bed, floated inside the air lock, and donned a space suit. He closed the internal hatch, depressurized the chamber, and opened the external hatch. He had left Jones's MMU tied to the side wall on the other side of the payload bay. Kessler gently pushed himself in that direction without regard for a safety clip until he reached the MMU. He clipped one end of a woven line hanging from his suit to the side wall.

The nitrogen jets of the MMU had somehow remained open, sending Jones tumbling out of control. Kessler was only partially familiar with the MMU design, but he had an engineering degree and felt somewhat confident enough to unclip the rear panel door where the nitrogen tanks for the jet thrusters were located. He pulled back a square door and exposed a section of the tanks along with an array of wires coming from the hand controls. The wires were connected to mini-valves that controlled the flow of nitrogen through a number of tubes coming out of the tanks.

That made sense, Kessler decided. Each tube went to a specific jet. The opening and closing of a valve was in reality what controlled the flow of compressed nitrogen to a jet. The wires went through a translation circuit that converted the hand-control commands into valve commands, which in turn regulated the flow of nitrogen to a particular jet. The conversion was needed because the joystick-type hand controls provided digital pulses which then needed to be amplified and converted into an electric current capable of driving the small valves. The design was simple but reliable. Then again, Kessler thought, the reliability of the system was not any better than the reliability of the individual components.

The MMU had twenty-four separate jets. Twelve primary jets and twelve for backup. That meant twenty-four tubes coming out of the nitrogen tanks, controlled by twenty-four valves. The way Jones had gone out of control told Kessler that there had to be more than one jet misfiring; otherwise Jones would have had plenty of working jets to counter a malfunctioning jet. Also, Jones's nitrogen supply, designed to last for several hours in "normal" operation, had lasted but a minute. Those two facts told Kessler that something had overridden the hand controls and commanded the valves to open and close at random, quickly depleting the load of compressed nitrogen in the MMU tanks. There was no other explanation. Either that or several valves had malfunctioned at the same time. Kessler could accept one or two valves going bad at once, but more than that? He couldn't buy it. Something had overridden the hand controls.

Kessler shifted his gaze to a point to the right of the array of wires, where all of the wires converged before going in a number of directions to their appropriate valves.

What the hell?

Kessler blinked twice and refocused his vision on what appeared to be a small timer attached to the circuitry that translated the digital pulses from the hand controls into the electric current that drove the valves.

A timer? Why? Then he understood, and the revelation sent chills through his body. The small timer, its tiny display showing 0:00:00, had two wires coming out of the front. The wires were connected so that they would short-circuit the translator circuitry of both the primary and the backup jets. That meant that the moment the timer went off, the translator circuitry got roasted and the valves received random electric surges.

Jesus Christ!

Kessler inhaled deeply, held it, and then slowly exhaled. He spoke into his voice-activated headset.

"Houston? *Lightning.*"

"Michael? You're supposed to be sleeping."

"Houston, I'm afraid I've got pretty bad news for all of us, particularly for us two up here."

"What's that, Lightning?"

"Someone sabotaged Jones's MMU." Kessler closed the MMU back panel and secured it. He unclipped his safety line and gently pushed himself toward the front of the payload bay.

"What? Say again, Lightning."

"Sabotage, Houston. I have found a tampering device in the translator circuit of Jones's MMU. I'm in the process of checking mine." He reached his MMU and quickly opened the back panel. His eyes now knew what to look for. Nothing. His MMU had not been tampered with, at least as far as the translator circuit was concerned. "Mine appears clean, Houston. I think it would be best if we head back down to Earth as soon as possible."

"That's our thinking down here as well, Lightning, especially in light of what you just found out. We should have an answer on the missing tile situation within the next few hours. In the meantime get some rest. You'll need it."

"Roger, Houston."

"We'll wake you up in five hours. Sweet dreams."

"Yeah, right." Kessler floated into the air lock.

KOUROU, FRENCH GUIANA

Vanderhoff threw the copy of *The New York Times* against the wall. His initial plan had failed. *Lightning* had somehow reached orbit, but although the press did not mention any problems, he knew the orbiter was wounded. It had to be. The main engine sabotage was fool proof. It had to work. NASA was doing a superb job in covering it up. Vanderhoff was also certain that the contingent sabotage of the OMS engines had left the orbiter almost stranded.

He got up from the leather couch and walked toward the windows behind his desk. He rubbed his eyes and checked his watch. It was two-thirty in the afternoon.

He stared at the Athena V rocket nearly ready for launch. That would be the final nail in NASA's coffin.

He nodded as he visualized the headlines in the *Times*. *Lightning,* the failure of the decade, right behind the Hubble telescope. *The entire world will finally realize,* he reflected, *that NASA just doesn't have what it takes to prevent accidents from happening. No one will suspect sabotage as long as* Lightning *is destroyed.* Vanderhoff felt certain that if NASA's scientists ever got their hands on *Lightning,* they would discover the sabotage, but that, he decided as his lips curved upward, would not happen. *Lightning* would never make it back to Earth.

He turned around and stared at the Athena rocket once more. *Nine hours,* he reflected. *Nine hours and it will be all over.*

He frowned. There was still the issue of Higgins. The CIA official was in trouble. His phone call the night before had been distressful. The Head of Clandestine Services was after him, and Vanderhoff knew that if captured, Higgins could directly incriminate the network. The chain reaction that would follow such exposure would be devastating. A decade's worth of planning and investing to position Europe as the world superpower by the end of the century would go astray the moment European leaders discovered such a conspiracy right under their noses. No, Higgins had become a liability—the reason Vanderhoff had made an additional phone call after he'd hung up with Higgins. It had to be done. *Nothing personal,* he thought. The EEC's plans for the future of Europe in space came first.

WASHINGTON, D.C.

Higgins walked toward the rendezvous point, where Vanderhoff's people would be waiting to pull him out. A death would be staged. No one would look for a dead person. The idea had been Higgins's and Vanderhoff had loved it. Clean, professional, safe. A body would be planted in Higgins's place. A mutilated, charred body with no chance of physical identification. Higgins's personal items would be with the body. Care would be taken in making sure no one could trace the body for dental records. Beyond that, Higgins had no special body markings that would lead anyone to believe the planted body wasn't his.

What had amazed Higgins the most had been the fact that Vanderhoff would be able to pull it off on such short notice. Higgins had indeed underestimated the German's resources. But it didn't matter. In less than twenty-four hours he would be enjoying life in one of Vanderhoff's South American estates surrounded by as many luxuries as he desired. That was the reward for putting his neck on the line for the EEC and Athena. The EEC leaders would take care of him.

He approached a worn-down, abandoned red-brick building located in one of the worst neighborhoods in Washington, the warehouse where Vanderhoff's local contact had instructed him to go.

Wearing a gray jogging outfit and tennis shoes, Higgins walked through a large opening in the front, where a sliding gate once stood. He carried a briefcase with him containing the few personal items he couldn't leave behind. He'd left all his bank accounts alone. With Vanderhoff, money would be unnecessary. Besides, that way no one would notice anything out of the ordinary. A simple disappearance and then a body found in one of the city's worst areas. Higgins's body. He had no family, no wife, no kids. A clean break, simple, elegant. He'd left nothing behind that he would miss, yet plenty would be waiting for him with Vanderhoff.

He squinted and stared at the single light bulb on the far right side of the dark and humid cavernous room. It illuminated a small table. He frowned and walked toward it. He carried no weapons—another request from Vanderhoff. Higgins understood his logic. Do nothing that would arouse suspicion.

Higgins spotted some barrels on the left side of the otherwise empty warehouse, which was probably used by the homeless for refuge during the winter months. He noticed a briefcase on the table.

Strange, he thought. He reached the edge of the table and looked in every direction. Nothing.

He shifted his gaze back to the black leather briefcase and the note taped to the front of it. It said to check for instructions inside while a surveillance team made sure nobody was following him.

"Hmm . . ." He decided that Vanderhoff could be extremely careful when he wanted to be. He pressed the side levers on the front of the briefcase. Both latches snapped open at once. Higgins opened the briefcase.

His senses registered the loud explosion, accompanied by a split-second vision of fire. Then he could not see or hear anything, but he felt agonizing pain. He tried to move his arms and turn around but couldn't. His legs buckled, and he tried to put his arms out to stop the fall but they were no longer there. The heat intensified. Blissfully, he began to lose consciousness. An excruciating, burning pain engulfed him as the savage flames consumed his maimed body.

SOMEWHERE OVER THE CARIBBEAN

Dizzy and tense, Pruett surrendered himself once again to the humiliating agony of nausea over the small aluminum toilet in the lavatory of the VIP transport plane.

"Oh, God," he mumbled as his stomach forced nothing but bile up his throat. He didn't try to resist, and let it all out. His eyes watered as the overwhelming odor nauseated him even more.

Cameron knocked on the door. "You okay, Tom?"

"Ah . . . yes . . . I'm fine . . . it happens all the . . . oh, shit!"

Cameron heard Pruett's guttural noises and decided to leave him to his privacy. He walked back to his seat, next to Marie.

"Is he all right?" she asked.

"Looks like his stomach can't handle airplane flights anymore. His ulcers are eating him alive."

"Oh, God. How terrible. He should go see a doctor."

Cameron smiled. "Not the Tom Pruett I used to know. He'd rather die than go see a doctor."

Cameron heard the rest-room door opening. "Are you all right?" he asked Pruett.

"Damn, fucking planes . . . pardon the language, Marie," Pruett murmured as he eased himself into a seat a few rows ahead of them. The rest of the plane was empty. They were the only passengers.

Cameron shook his head and stared at Marie's bloodshot eyes. "You better get some sleep while you can."

She nodded, lifted the armrest in between them, leaned her head against his shoulder, and closed her eyes. A minute later, Cameron felt her breathing steadying. *Marie.* The only person that knew about his past, and to this moment Cameron still didn't know what had compelled him to tell her. *Maybe trying to ease my pain by bringing it out in the open? By sharing it with someone who would understand? Someone who seemed to care?*

He simply stared at the clear sky as they flew over the Gulf of Mexico. *Mexico,* he thought. In spite of what most people said about their large neighbor to the south, Cameron had enjoyed his years there, certainly more than the years in Vietnam, in hell, everyone trapped in his own world, not knowing who to trust and struggling not to make any friendships.

It seemed that in Vietnam death hid behind every corner, behind every bush. American forces became good at handling the dead. All properly body-bagged and tagged for their silent return. So many of his friends returned home that way.

Cameron checked his watch. One more hour before they arrived at Howard Air Force Base in Panama, where a Special Forces team would be waiting for Pruett's briefing.

Cameron sighed and continued gazing out at the blue sky as his thoughts drifted back to Marie, the beautiful stranger who had so abruptly come into his life and literally turned it upside down. He hadn't felt so comfortable in someone else's presence since Lan-Anh. There was definitely a chemistry between them. She understood the way he felt. That Claude Guilloux had been a lucky man indeed.

The thought faded away the moment Cameron closed his eyes. His past haunted him again. Marie's face was replaced by the face of Skergan. The pleading eyes cut through his soul. *Go, Cameron . . .*

THIRTEEN ★

Mambo

Discipline is the soul of an army. It makes small numbers formidable; procures success to the weak and esteem to all.

—George Washington

CANAL ZONE, PANAMA

The day was warm and humid, the sky clear. Firmly clutching a modified Colt Commando submachine gun, First Sergeant Francisco Ortiz moved through the dense forest slowly and warily. Every calculated step was preceded by a careful scan of the heavy foliage around him as he checked for anything that did not belong in the woods. An irregular noise, boot prints, branches broken at an unnatural angle.

Nothing.

Satisfied, he moved once more in a deep crouch, softly feeling the terrain with the tip of his boot before setting it down. The strain on his slim yet muscular legs was enormous but still bearable. Ortiz belonged to the 7th U.S. Special Forces Operational Detachment Delta, one of the elite squadrons made out of volunteers from the Green Berets, the 82nd Airborne, and the Rangers, trained specifically for tropical jungle warfare. The squadron of over a hundred men was divided into easily deployable platoons.

171

Ortiz's platoon followed his footsteps fifty feet behind. Fourteen others depended on how well he did his job. Ortiz was the eyes and ears of his platoon, code-named Mambo.

Ortiz sensed something foreign, but wasn't sure what it was. He stopped, raised his left hand in a fist, and silently dropped to the ground.

Which of his senses had detected something? Had he seen, heard, or smelled something? Ortiz wasn't sure, but he felt certain that there was something out there that didn't belong. He waited a few more seconds before slowly, almost imperceptibly, rising back up to a deep crouch.

There it was again. This time he decided it was a sound, almost masked by the swaying branches of a nearby rosewood tree. Ortiz smiled. Whoever was out there was good, but not good enough to get by his trained ears. Ortiz had worked hard at developing each of his senses to levels of equal sensitivity. Most jungle warriors had one sense they depended on more than the others. The problem with that, Ortiz knew, was that it imposed limitations on their abilities to adapt to different battle conditions. At night, even though he wore night goggles, Ortiz could also rely on sounds and smells. An enemy standing still at night in the forest would be very difficult to spot, even with the Sopelem TN2-1 goggles Ortiz would be wearing. But the enemy could make a slight noise, or his body give out an odor that could be detected by Ortiz's nostrils. Ortiz tried his best to avoid becoming too attached to the mechanical enhancements constantly used by other point men because, in the end, he knew one day he could find himself in a situation where it was just him, his hunting knife, and the forest against the enemy. No fancy electronic gear to protect him. Ortiz knew he would be prepared if the day ever came. In his mind there was no other way. A true jungle warrior could use the forest alone to stalk, attack, and retreat totally undetected, leaving the enemy wondering how it had all happened.

Ortiz moved toward the source of the noise, on the other side of a line of bushes beyond the narrow field of tall grass to his right. Ortiz floated through it, moving only when he felt the light breeze swirling down the hill. He stopped as the breeze died down, and moved forward with the next gust.

He reached the bushes a minute later, and slowly moved a branch with the Colt's muzzle. He spotted four guards standing about twenty feet away from him, all facing in the opposite direction.

These guys should be awarded the Pendejo *of the Year award for stupidity,* he thought. *If you're going to stand in the middle of a clearing, at least form a circle so that you can cover all directions.*

Ortiz smiled. He quietly extended the telescopic butt of the Colt and pressed it against his right shoulder as he lined up the closest guard on the cross hairs.

Then he fired twice. The Colt responded with a barely audible blip as the laser beam zeroed in on the remote sensors attached to the yellow vest of the guard. The vest's sensors picked up the beam and closed an electric circuit, powering up an array of red and yellow LEDs. The guard instantly lighted up like a Christmas tree. Without waiting for a reaction, Ortiz switched targets and fired again. Another hit. He swiftly changed targets twice more. Four quick kills. The episode had taken less than ten seconds.

"Dammit! Someone got us!"

"You're all dead, *amigos.* Better roll over 'n' learn how to play dead."

"Is that you, Tito?" asked one of the soldiers, calling Ortiz by his nickname.

"That's right, *amigo.* I've just killed you all." He approached them.

"Shit."

"Start walkin'. You're Mambo's prisoners."

Three other members of Mambo came out from the tree line and escorted their prisoners. One of them was Mambo's platoon leader, Lieutenant Mark Siegel.

"Good job, Tito. You really surprised those four."

"Gracias, jefe. They weren't too happy about it either. Looks like I caught 'em off guard." Siegel was a fair leader. A little new, but fair. Ortiz knew Siegel was trying to learn as much as possible from him and the other more experienced soldiers in Mambo. At the same time, Siegel tried to earn their respect. A tough position to be in, reflected Ortiz, who had already decided in his mind that the lieutenant was good, but lacked some of the innate qualities necessary for jungle warfare survival.

"Well, they got off easy, Tito. If these would have been the real thing . . ."

"Sí, jefe. I know."

Siegel turned around and talked on the radio.

"Coordinator, Mambo here, over."

"Mambo, this is Coordinator, situation report, over."

"Just captured the last of the yellow team. War game completed. Mark forty-five minutes. No casualties in our team."

"That's a new record. Congratulations, Mambo. Proceed to rendezvous point for airlift."

"Roger."

Ortiz reached the large concrete ramp at the edge of the exercise zone, where they were to meet the chopper back to Howard Air Force base for a well-deserved rest. He frowned. The chopper hadn't arrived yet. He sat down and simply stared at the sky. The sun was high overhead. Ortiz closed his eyes.

His mind filled with memories of his endless, bloody years in the *barrio.* Memories of gang wars, of his explosive youth. He had been careless back then. His life had belonged to his gang. He did what they did, behaved like they behaved. So many of his friends had died useless deaths during those days. So many had fallen victim to pointless wars fought to prove one gang's *machismo* over another's. To prove that the Rebeldes were better than the

Lobos. Or perhaps that the Pumas were superior to the Sangrientos. Or to claim a piece of land, which no one really owned in the formal sense of the word. It was a way to show everyone else that a gang controlled that section of the neighborhood and was willing to fight for it. Nothing else mattered. Sometimes a gang would grow in numbers and attempt to expand, which usually meant cutting into someone else's territory. Then wars would break out. Wars in the conventional sense of the word, with automatic weapons, grenades, and homemade bombs. Long gone were the baseball bats, chains, and knives. Gang wars were so feared by the police that at times the police department would stall on purpose before attempting to break them up, to avoid too much involvement in the actual confrontation. The police were mainly there to make a report of the incident, count the dead, and settle the last few fights with an overkill of manpower. That minimized the exposure of police officers to most of the danger, and allowed the gangs to do what they wanted to do in the first place: kill each other. It made sense, Ortiz decided. In the eyes of the police, gang members were criminals anyway, so gang wars did the police department the favor of exterminating criminals. Plain and simple.

Ortiz had spent almost four years with a gang after he'd tired of his father's constant beatings. He didn't want to take it anymore. Older and able to take care of himself, Ortiz lived on the street, learning the ways of the world. He also learned about human nature, friendships, blood oaths, treason . . . death. Ortiz experienced them all, until the day reality struck home. Ortiz came to terms with the fact that he was a survivor, and there just weren't any survivors within the gangs. No true winners. Most were destined to die or go to prison. Ortiz had seen many of his friends go both routes.

That was when he had left the streets. He'd left his beloved *barrio* and searched for another place to use his only skills. One day he'd walked into an Army recruiting office, and his life had taken a turn for the better. He had survived the *barrio*.

"Hey, Tito!"

Ortiz looked up to his right at Tommy Zimmer, another member of Mambo, also wearing a set of jungle-warfare-colored fatigues and black boots. Zimmer wore the fatigues a bit differently, though. He couldn't take the excessive heat and humidity of the tropical hell their superiors called Panama, and had cut off the sleeves. Ortiz liked Zimmer, a young black kid from the Bronx, a smart kid. Ortiz had met him at Fort Bragg, North Carolina. They'd become instant friends. Although they'd grown up on opposite sides of the country, they shared a common bond. They were ghetto survivors.

"Yeah, *hermano*. What's up?"

"We're moving out, man! Would you believe that shit? Our platoon's movin' out. We just got the order."

Ortiz leaned forward. "Movin' out? What are you talkin' about? We just finished bustin' our asses in this exercise. Where are we goin'?"

"Some place in South America. Don't know where. All I know is that some CIA honchos are gonna brief us. C'mon. The lieutenant wants to talk to all of us before that."

Ortiz stood up, wondering what in the world was going on. This side of the hemisphere was supposed to be quiet.

"Mierda! I don't like the smell of it, Tommy."

"Why not, man? Better that than just stickin' 'round here doin' nothin'."

"CIA means secret mission. And secret mission means that if we fuck up inside enemy territory chances are no one will acknowledge us."

"What are you sayin'?" Zimmer asked, lowering his eyebrows in a mix of curiosity and concern.

"That if we fuck up we're as good as dead and no one will come to our rescue. That's what it means."

"How do you know it's gonna be secret?"

"Well, CIA usually means that," Ortiz responded. "But I don't wanna scare you. Let's go and see what the lieutenant's gotta say."

Ortiz heard the low whup-whup sound of the transport chopper. They picked up their gear and joined the rest of the men standing by the LZ.

FOURTEEN ★

Game Plan

JOHNSON SPACE CENTER, HOUSTON, TEXAS

Hunter stepped up to the array of microphones. As far as the rest of the world was concerned, the mission was going as planned. He cleared his throat and began to read the short statement on the status of *Lightning*.

"Good afternoon, ladies and gentlemen of the press. First of all, I would like to say on behalf of NASA that we appreciate your patience while waiting here these last two hours. We apologize. The *Lightning* crew will be awakening from their rest period in another three hours, at which time we'll be able to provide you with live coverage of the interior of the orbiter. I would like to state at this point that *Lightning* will be joined shortly by *Atlantis* for an emergency drill. NASA's current plan—assuming Congress approves our budget—is to have all modules of *Freedom* ferried into space and fully operational before the end of the decade. This means far more frequent shuttle flights than ever before, which also means we must be better prepared and trained to handle emergencies in outer space if one should occur. Ladies and gentlemen of the press, the *Lightning-Atlantis* joint mission is to prove that we can indeed send an orbiter up in space at a moment's notice for whatever reason. We at NASA decided that a simulated emergency would be best. That's the end of my statement. I will take questions now."

Almost instantly three reporters raised their hands.

"Yes, the lady in the back?"

"Mr. Hunter, Ellen Nunez, AP. Why the secrecy? Why wait until now to tell us this?"

Hunter slowly shook his head and smiled thinly. "We are conducting a training mission in *emergency* procedures, Ms. Nunez. It would hardly be effective if there were advance warnings. Therefore it was essential that it remain secret until the very last minute."

"So, this is a drill then?" she asked.

"That's correct, and in the process, the astronauts in *Lightning* will check out the orbiter for commercial use."

"Is *Atlantis* carrying any commercial or military payload?"

"*Atlantis* is still carrying its scheduled payload."

Hunter inhaled deeply and forced his face to remain relaxed as he scanned the room and noticed several hands up in the air. He had lied to the world, and could only hope it would not come back to haunt him someday.

HOWARD AIR FORCE BASE, PANAMA

The hum of the air-conditioning unit disturbed Ortiz as he sat next to Zimmer in the brightly lit briefing room. Siegel kept checking his watch every minute or so as he continued to pace back and forth in the front of the room. The entire platoon had been waiting for the CIA officials to arrive for the past hour, but still saw no sign of them. Outside the brick building, each man's gear sat neatly packed in a row next to the entrance. They were ready, Ortiz felt. Day or night, he truly believed Mambo could handle anything.

"They're pretty late, *hermano*," he whispered to Zimmer, who had his eyes closed. The Bronx native opened his eyes, turned his head, and shrugged.

"Figures," he responded. "The grunts are always th' ones that gotta wait."

Ortiz rubbed his hand over his short-cropped black hair and felt a scar he'd gotten during a fight many years ago. Hair had never grown back on that particular spot of his skull. He thought of it as a constant reminder of his past.

Siegel's short barracks briefing an hour ago had been vague. All he knew was that they would be heading south of there, that it would involve jungle warfare, and that the operation would last up to twenty-four hours. Nothing else. No idea on what they were going after, no information on the size of the opposition's force, or on their weapons. Was it a rescue mission? Had a guerrilla group kidnapped someone the CIA deemed important enough to go in and rescue? Or was it an assassination mission of some sort?

Ortiz shook his head. Too many questions. He checked his watch. The CIA guys were really late.

Suddenly the door in the back of the room flew open. Several heads turned. Ortiz spotted the base's commanding officer, General Jack Olson, followed by two men and a woman. All three wore civilian clothes; Ortiz had never seen them before.

"Ten-*hut*!" Siegel called out.

The entire platoon jumped to attention.

"At ease, men," Olson said as he walked ahead of the three civilians, who Ortiz suspected were the CIA officials. One of the two men was much older than the other. The older one was a large-framed man with thin, brownish hair. The second was a bit shorter and thinner but muscular. The woman seemed to be in her late thirties, but very attractive. "All right, people, sit down and listen up." Olson began. "The following information is highly classified. Lieutenant Siegel's platoon has been selected for a very critical mission of great national interest. I want you all to provide your platoon leader with your fullest support and listen carefully to what Mr. Thomas Pruett has to say. He is Head of Clandestine Services, CIA. The gentleman to his left is Mr. Cameron Stone. He is the CIA field agent that uncovered the criminal activity that will be the subject of this briefing. Next to him is Ms. Marie Guilloux. She has visited the target area and might help answer some of your questions. I want to remind all of you that you belong to Special Forces Detachment Delta, and thus all of the information you are about to hear is confidential. With that, I'll turn it over to you, sir." Olson stepped to the side. Pruett and Stone took a few large black-and-white photographs from a briefcase and began pinning them to the corkboard while Marie looked on.

"Good afternoon, gentlemen," Pruett began. "I'll be brief since we don't have much time. I'll go over the basics of the operation here, and then I'll cover all the details and be more than happy to answer questions when we're in the air."

He walked over to the board and pointed at the first photograph. "In exactly six hours and twenty minutes, a rocket containing what is supposed to be a commercial satellite will be launched from this facility located in the city of Kourou, French Guiana." He circled the small city with his index finger. "Our intelligence data tells us that the actual purpose of that rocket is not to deploy a satellite in space, but to deploy a drone, a satellite lookalike, that is intended to collide with the space shuttle *Lightning.*"

Ortiz was stunned. He could hardly believe something like this was actually happening. Before anyone could say anything, Pruett continued.

"A C-145 StarLifter is scheduled to depart this base in ten minutes, gentlemen. The craft will take you to French Guiana, where you will parachute down in the jungle, destroy the rocket before it is launched, and quickly retreat to a rendezvous point, where a helicopter from the U.S.S. *Blue Ridge,* currently sailing near the Venezuelan coast, will be waiting for you. We'll cover mission specifics on the way over. We're short on time."

Olson walked back to the front of the room. "Men, this is a covert operation, and as such, we cannot force you to go along. The mission poses certain dangers, since you might run into some degree of opposition. How much? We have not been able to determine that exactly as of just yet—perhaps Ms. Guilloux might be able to give you some details on the way—but there will be some resistance at the launch site for sure. I'm telling it to you like it is, men. Most of you have heard of me. I'm not going to stand here and blow sunshine up your asses, but I will say that you're one of the Armed Forces' elite fighting units. This is what you have been trained for, but given the circumstances, if any of you wants out, you can simply walk to your barracks instead of to the plane. There will be no dishonor in it.

"Lieutenant Siegel tells me that all your paperwork has already been filed. Your selected beneficiaries will receive the proceeds from a CIA life insurance policy equal to your military policy, in case some of you don't make it back. For those of you who do choose to go, you will be temporarily removed from the Armed Forces' records until you get back. As far as the outside world is concerned you do not exist. As far as the U.S. Government is concerned you do not exist. Any questions?" He paused. "All right. Carry on, Lieutenant."

"All right, people!" Siegel said. "You heard the general! Everyone outside. Those of you who are coming along line up behind your gear. The rest back to the barracks. Fall out!"

Ortiz and the others got up and headed outside. As he reached for his Ray-Ban Wayfarers he noticed that every single member of Mambo stood at attention behind his packed gear. Ortiz's chest swelled and he raised his chin. He was Mambo, the best of the 7th U.S. Special Forces Operational Detachment Delta.

He snapped to attention next to Zimmer as Siegel and Olson came outside followed by the civilians. Olson looked at Siegel and then eyed the troops.

"Make us proud, men. Good luck."

"Thank you, sir," responded Siegel as he did an about-face and scanned the platoon. "Let's move it. Fall out! Everyone grab your gear and get in that truck. Move it, people!"

Ortiz followed the line of soldiers walking across the tarmac to a waiting truck. Things were happening too fast. He felt carried away by the emotion of the moment, by the possibility of combat. He'd always heard that when the call came, there was always hardly any time to react, hardly any time to think. Trained instincts, honed to a fine edge by Mambo, took over. He now understood the reason behind the exhaustive drills, the constant hell he and his fellow soldiers were exposed to daily in the inhospitable jungles of Panama. It had prepared him for this moment, for what his country now needed him to do. Ortiz smiled. He felt ready, capable, qualified to do the job, but the smile quickly vanished from his face. Although his instincts told him he was prepared, his logical side told him to beware of overconfidence, not to underestimate the enemy. Ortiz had learned two important lessons in the *barrio*. First, never underestimate the enemy. Always expect the unexpected. Second, *do* the unexpected, surprise the enemy, avoid predictability. Anyone who consistently followed this credo increased his or her chances of survival tenfold.

Ortiz jumped last into the back of the truck, pulling the tailgate up behind him. The truck started and headed down to the ramp. The trip took less than a minute. Ortiz didn't even have time to get comfortable.

"Fall out!" Siegel screamed as he came around the back.

Ortiz and Zimmer pushed the tailgate down and jumped off, hauling their gear. Ortiz looked over his right shoulder and stared at the blurry shape of the light-gray Lockheed C-141 StarLifter parked a few hundred feet away. The scorching plume of the four large turbofans, combined with the hot air rising off the blistering tarmac, made the StarLifter a wavy mirage in the sun, but Ortiz could still make out the open paratrooper door at the aft end of the cabin. A military police jeep carrying the CIA contingent rushed past them and stopped next to the craft.

"All right, let's go!" Siegel screamed.

Ortiz picked up his gear and followed Zimmer toward the waiting craft.

Cameron got out of the jeep and watched the line of soldiers approaching the craft.

"So, what do you think of Mambo, Cameron?" asked Pruett from the passenger side.

Cameron glanced at his superior, then at Marie sitting in the rear seat, and back at Pruett. "They look too young and unseasoned. None of them have experienced real battle before. Not even their commanding officer."

"General Olson seems to think they're the best."

Cameron sighed. "We'll see." He continued to stare at the soldiers now climbing inside the craft. The sight brought back memories. *Funny,* he thought. *Some things never change. Regardless of how much military technology advances, the real work is still done by the grunts.*

Nothing could replace the foot soldier for this type of mission. No fancy helicopters, armored vehicles, or fighter craft. The soldier in the field was the one who got the job done, Cameron firmly believed. He had learned that lesson in Vietnam. Sure, Air Force planes came in low and dropped load after load of napalm to clear the way for the advancing troops, but a hill was not assumed captured until the infantry took it.

As the last of the soldiers disappeared behind the opened paratrooper door, Cameron felt the old adrenaline rushing through his body—the uncertainty, the excitement, and the fear of battle—a unique feeling experienced only by those who participated in war. But beneath it lay grief, sadness. Boys would die today.

"Ready, Cameron?"

Cameron shifted his gaze back to Pruett and Marie.

"Yep. Let's go."

The three followed the soldiers into the plane.

LIGHTNING

The ear-piercing sound thundered through the entire vessel. Kessler jumped up and hit his forehead against the ceiling of the horizontal sleeping station. He felt momentarily disoriented. His head stung and his ears still rang, but not from the explosion. Alarms now blared in the flight deck as interior lights flickered off and on.

Now what?

Kessler bolted from the mid-deck up to the flight deck, where after a brief scan he realized the seriousness of their situation. The control panel warning lights indicated that two fuel cells had failed. *Lightning* had a total of three fuel cells. During peak and average power loads, all three cells came on line; during minimum power loads only two fuel cells were used. A profound sinking feeling rushed through Kessler. *Lightning*'s fuel cells generated electricity through the electrochemical reaction of liquid hydrogen and liquid oxygen. Each fuel cell had its own set of oxygen and hydrogen tanks, and an independent combustion chamber. Coolant flowing through the fuel-cell stack controlled the temperature inside the chamber. As the coolant left the stack, *Lightning*'s General Purpose Computers measured its temperature. No alarms or warning lights came on as long as the coolant temperature remained between 170 and 240 degrees Fahrenheit. The warning lights told Kessler that the cells somehow had overheated. The explosion that followed had not only destroyed the fuel cells, but had also resulted in the loss of all the oxygen from the tanks that supplied the damaged fuel cells, the same oxygen used by *Lightning*'s life-support system.

Puzzled that the GPCs hadn't automatically shut down the overheated cells to prevent an explosion, Kessler quickly switched from the two damaged cells to the third fuel cell, which they'd been holding in standby mode. The lights inside *Lightning* stabilized. Kessler knew that one fuel cell operating alone could not adequately power the on-board environmental-control and life-support system. The system was composed of three main subsystems: the atmosphere-revitalization subsystem that controlled the crew module's atmospheric and thermal environment; the food, water, and wastewater subsystem; and the active thermal-control subsystem, which maintained *Lightning*'s sensitive electronic components within manufacturer-specified temperature limits.

"Houston, *Lightning* here. We have another problem."

"Lightning, *say again,*" Kessler heard Hunter say.

"Ah, we have another problem, Houston. A critical one, I might add. We just lost two fuel cells."

Silence. Kessler sighed. Houston had put him on hold to prevent him from hearing their reactions. The radio came back on. Hunter's voice was calm.

"Lightning, *Houston. We have just received confirmation from the CIA that the orbiter has been sabotaged.*"

"Nice of them to tell us after we're up here."

"*It looks as if they've just figured it out.*"

"Any ideas on what else has been sabotaged?"

"*Ah, negative,* Lightning. *All we know is that someone is trying to destroy the orbiter.*"

Kessler shook his head. "Hell, that's just fucking great! And in the meantime we just sit up here and wait for something else to blow?"

"*We are running a computer simulation to determine the best course of action. In the meantime the CIA and FBI are going at it full blast. All we can do down here is try to get you guys back home safe. Status of third cell?*"

"I just brought it on line but it won't be enough to handle the entire life-support system. The cell is working at one-hundred-ten-percent capacity. I'm gonna have to unplug something soon to relieve the load. It's a priority call."

"Roger, Lightning, we copy. We have two Rockwell engineers with us in the room. Their suggestion is to disconnect the food, water, and wastewater subsystem, and see the effect of that on the loading."

"Just a moment." Kessler switched off the automatic life-support system which kept all three subsystems on line, and switched to manual. That way he could select the subsystem he preferred to maintain operational. "It's done, Houston. Cell operating at ninety-eight-percent capacity. I've also noticed a decrease in the oxygen content in the crew module. I'm afraid that even with the food and water subsystem off there isn't enough power to maintain a proper oxygen level, and even if there was enough power, remember that we just lost two oxygen tanks. Pretty soon there's not going to be much oxygen left for the system to circulate."

"*Lightning, our simulation confirms your suspicion. If our data is correct, it shows that you have less than twenty hours before the oxygen content drops to a hazardous level.*"

Kessler inhaled deeply and stared at the Earth slowly rotating overhead. Their situation was critical. In twenty hours they would have to suit up and rely on the oxygen inside their space suits. The life-support system backpacks came with a seven-hour supply of oxygen. Kessler estimated they each had used less than an hour's worth during the EVA. Damn! In less than twenty-six hours they were going to be out of air. They were stuck, marooned, their hopes for an early Earth re-entry dashed. Even though he could route the remaining helium and propellant from the right OMS tanks to the RCS primary jets to slow down the orbiter enough to achieve re-entry, *Lightning* would incinerate the moment it reached the upper layers of the atmosphere, since the payload bay doors were open and there were at least a dozen thermal tiles missing.

"Roger, Houston. Twenty hours, plus the six-hour supply in the PLSS backpacks."

"Don't forget the three rescue balls, Michael. There's a two-hour supply in each."

Kessler nodded slightly. Hunter was referring to the personal rescue enclosures, or rescue balls. Since there were only two space suits on board an orbiter flight, in the event of an emergency the rest of the crew—which in Kessler's case was none—would use the rescue balls. The problem with that, he reflected, was that the balls were zipped shut from the outside by another crew member. With Jones still unconscious, it meant that Kessler had to rely only on suits and Jones on the rescue balls. Even if Jones was awake, he decided, one of them still had to use the suits.

"I'm aware of that, Houston. In any case, it looks like thirty hours max. Any way we can close the payload bay doors with one fuel cell?"

"Stand by, Lightning.*"*

Kessler kept his eye on the oxygen level. Still within the normal range, but not for long. The only good news in this whole situation, he reflected, was that it was just Jones and him, and not six or seven occupants like so many other shuttle missions. Under those conditions, they would have been lucky to get more than ten hours' worth of oxygen.

"Ah, negative, Lightning. *A minimum of two fuel cells is required."*

"Great. Any news on whether or not I can fill the gaps left by a dozen tiles with the tile repair kit?"

"Bad news on that front also, Lightning. *The kit doesn't have enough epoxy foam to fill all the holes."*

"Well, Houston? Can't close the payload bay doors and can't repair the tiles. What's next?"

"Hang in there, Lightning. *We'll figure a way out of this one. In the meantime, try to keep still and relax to conserve oxygen. It's preferable that you even sleep. You will consume less oxygen that way. Also, shut off all lights and redundant systems to give the life-support system more juice. Perhaps you can last a few more hours than calculated. We will contact you in five hours."*

"Copy, Houston. Over 'n' out."

Kessler switched off most of the crew compartment's lights and all payload bay floodlights. *Lightning* was engulfed by the cold darkness of space. Kessler remained on his flight seat just staring at the Earth. Only his steady breathing disturbed the total silence in the flight deck, and that would cease soon unless NASA got very creative, but how? *How can they possibly help us out? Even if they somehow figure out a way to close the cargo doors, the missing thermal tiles will do us in during re-entry.*

The problem went beyond the fact that *Lightning*'s underside had several spots where its internal, all-aluminum skin was exposed. Those unprotected spots by themselves would account for some internal damage, but probably not enough to destroy the orbiter. Kessler's primary concern with the missing tiles was that the exposed aluminum would reach extremely high temperatures during the critical twenty-minute re-entry. The melting heat would propagate across the aluminum skin and cause adjacent tiles to become loose and eventually fall off. The process would degenerate into a massive tile loss and inevitable orbiter burnout.

Kessler rubbed his eyes and sighed. *There has to be a way out of this one.*

THE WHITE HOUSE

In the Oval Office, the President sat on his leather swivel chair and watched Carlton Stice across his desk working the phone to get all concerned parties on the line. The latest news from *Lightning* was distressing. The two astronauts literally were going to die from asphyxiation.

The President got up and drove a fist into his palm, startling Stice. Then he grunted and turned to the windows facing the south grounds. There must be something NASA could do. Something, but what?

"I think I have them on the line, sir," Stice said.

The President signaled him to press the speaker box. He did.

"Tom, can you hear me?" the President asked as he sat back down on his chair.

"Hello, Mr. President," Pruett said, his voice coming through.

"Good. Hold on, Tom."

"Yes, sir."

"Hunter, are you there?"

"Yes, Mr. President."

"Tom, can you still hear me?"

"Yes, sir."

"Well, gentlemen, we're talking on a secure line. I want to know everything that's going on. And when I say everything, God Almighty, I mean *everything*. Is that clear?"

"Yes, sir!" was the unanimous response.

"All right. Tom, what's your situation?"

"We left Howard two hours ago, sir. We expect to reach French Guiana in one more hour. The platoon has been fully briefed and armed."

"What's your confidence level as a special ops expert?"

"Well, based on what I've learned from General Olson, sir, this team—they call themselves Mambo—is about the best there is. In my opinion they have more than a fifty-percent chance of success."

"Fifty percent? Why so low? Didn't you just say they're the best?"

"Well, Mr. President, considering the short notice and their lack of familiarity with the base they are attacking, I believe that—"

"Don't we have satellite reconnaissance for that? And also, isn't the Guilloux woman providing additional intelligence?"

"Ah . . . yes, sir, and every man has had a chance to fully review the data on the compound as we know it."

"Then?"

"In the past—on missions that I've been involved in, that is—we were always able to build a mock-up of the target and run a week or two of simulated assaults prior to the real thing. That's the difference, sir. Without that familiarity factor the odds are almost against them."

"I guess I'll have to live with those odds since we're out of time. Hunter?"

"Yes, sir?"

"What's the orbiter situation?"

"*Lightning* has less than thirty hours of oxygen left, sir."

"What's the plan of action?"

"We're going full blast on *Atlantis,* sir, but it's going to be close."

"Explain."

"*Atlantis* was hoisted to the External Tank and Rocket Booster Assembly just two days ago, sir. It was not scheduled to launch for ten more days. Now we're trying to get up there in less than twenty-four hours. We'll do the best we can, but I hesitate to launch prematurely and risk more problems. By that I mean two stranded orbiters instead of one."

"How is the press being handled on this?"

"We're keeping them out of it under the pretext that *Atlantis* will join *Lightning* for an emergency rescue drill as part of NASA's overall strategy to get *Freedom* operational before the end of the century, sir."

"You think they're really buying that?"

"I think so, sir. The press conference went relatively well."

The President rubbed the tips of his fingers against his temples, inhaled deeply, and exhaled. He opened his eyes.

"Listen up, Hunter. We're out of time. The lives of two astronauts are in danger here. I want all of you to do whatever it takes to launch *Atlantis* as soon as humanly possible, without, and I repeat, *without* compromising the safety of *Atlantis* and its crew."

"Believe me when I tell you, Mr. President, we are doing all we possibly can to launch as soon as possible."

"I know, Hunter, I know. That will be all for now, gentlemen. Both of you have direct access to my office at any hour of the day. I may be tied up with other matters, but the Defense Secretary will be handling this issue in my absence. Remember that secrecy is of the utmost concern. Understood?"

"Yes, sir!"

"Thank you, gentlemen." The President hung up the phone and faced Stice. "What do you think?"

"Well, sir, you probably already know that I'm not very keen on the military operation. It's much too risky. Too many things can go wrong. What happens if some of our men get caught by the enemy? What should I do? Deny intervention?"

"Give me a call."

"What if you're unavailable and I have to make a split-second decision, sir?"

"You're gonna have to rely on your best judgment. Just keep in mind that although this is a covert operation, there are American lives involved."

"Yes, Mr. President."

"Good. Now get the Kremlin on the line."

"Excuse me, sir?"

"The Kremlin. I must speak to the President of Russia immediately."

Stice jumped out of the chair and reached for the phone.

FIFTEEN ★

Coalition

We believe that when men reach beyond this planet, they should leave their differences behind them.
—*John F. Kennedy*

MIR SPACE COMPLEX, 205 MILES OVER NORTHERN AFRICA

Commander Nikolai Aleksandrovich Strakelov switched off the radio after a ten-minute conversation with Baikonur Control, the primary cosmodrome for support of *Mir,* and the main center for rocket and satellite research and development. To his right was Flight Engineer Valentina Tereshkova. She looked at him and frowned. Things had not really been going well since their arrival at the space complex two months ago. First had been the problem with their heat shields flaring out of the space module during disengagement from the booster section while approaching *Mir;* then *Progress VI* had mysteriously blown up after reaching orbit, and now the standing order from Moscow meant another week-long postponement of a carefully planned schedule of experiments for their eight-month stay at *Mir.* Strakelov exhaled. They didn't have a choice. Their American comrades were in trouble and needed help.

He motioned Tereshkova to follow him into the *Kvant-2* module. The *Mir* complex was made up of modules that had been launched into space one at a time over a period of two years to achieve their current T-shape configuration. In the center was the original *Mir* module, which had a multiple docking unit on one end and a single docking unit at the other. Two modules were connected to *Mir*'s multiple docking end at 180-degree angles from one another. They were known as *Kvant-1* and *Kristall*. *Kvant-2* was docked at the single end of *Mir*. The Soyuz TM-15 spacecraft was docked at the other end of *Kvant-2*. The main living quarters were in *Mir*. The other modules contained a variety of laboratories and space observation gear. There was a temporary module also connected to *Mir*'s multiple docking unit: a cargo spacecraft, *Progress VII*, that had arrived two weeks ago, carrying water, food, air supplies, reading material, film, fuel, and new experiments for *Mir*'s crew. Strakelov and Tereshkova had nearly completed the long and tedious process of unloading *Progress VII*'s cargo, and were ready to use up the last of *Progress VII*'s fuel to push the *Mir* complex into a higher, safer orbit before jettisoning away the empty module to burn upon Earth re-entry. Now Moscow had given them new instructions: *Progress VII*'s remaining fuel would be used for another purpose.

Strakelov went through the docking tunnel and floated into *Kvant-2*. He turned and faced Tereshkova.

"What do you think?" he asked.

"I don't think Moscow realizes how dangerous it is for *Mir* to go to such a low orbit, Nikolai Aleksandrovich. It will take a great deal of propellant to bring the complex back up to a safe orbit."

"I know Moscow doesn't realize the implications. Our job is to comply with the order and then generate the request for another cargo ship loaded with fuel. But that will come later. For now we must comply."

"I understand."

Strakelov smiled. He had a lot of respect for the tall Frontal Aviation pilot. She had joined the cosmonaut training program only five years previously in spite of knowing that the odds were against her. The Cosmonaut Training Center was highly selective in the students it chose. The fact that she had not only been accepted, but had also managed to graduate, told Strakelov plenty. Only the very best were accepted for cosmonaut training, and unlike in the West, it took more than just top-notch flying to earn the right to become a cosmonaut. Or so he had been told by his superiors. Strakelov found it hard to believe in his heart that a great country like the United States would allow men without many years of education and training to pilot sophisticated reusable space vehicles. Strakelov loved the *Rodina*. He had loved it even during the days of communism, when he'd had specific concerns about some of the people that were in charge of key governmental positions. One of them had been the head of the Soviet space agency, someone whom Strakelov had not had a lot of respect for after the unfortunate accident that had nearly ended his cosmonaut career ten years earlier.

After graduating with honors from the Polbin Higher Military Aviation School in Orenburg, Strakelov was posted to the Baltic Sea, where he served as a Navy pilot until 1979. That year a representative of the Cosmonaut Training Center visited Strakelov's unit to actively recruit young pilots for cosmonaut training. Strakelov was among the few selected, and was immediately sent on to a test pilot's training course, where he mastered several different types of aircraft and was awarded the qualification of test pilot second class. He had everything going for him until the day of the unfortunate freak accident, during an exercise in an isolation chamber. He flipped a timer switch in the chamber that had somehow come in direct contact with an electrical line carrying 220 volts. Strakelov burned both hands badly and lost consciousness, also injuring his head in the ensuing fall. And the doctors monitoring the exercise were slow to come to his aid, assuming he had simply collapsed as a result of the exhausting exercise.

The head of the space agency tried to have Strakelov dismissed from cosmonaut training because of his injuries, but Strakelov persevered, and through numerous medical checkups, fought his way back to the cosmonaut ranks. A year later he went on his first Soyuz mission.

Strakelov and Tereshkova floated back into *Mir* and sat on the flight seats facing the complex's central control station.

"Baikonur's intercept solution has been fed to the computer system, Nikolai Aleksandrovich," said Tereshkova as she read the information displayed on the screen to her right.

"Time to fire?"

"Ten minutes, thirty seconds," she reported as fast as she typed the commands on the computer keyboard. Tereshkova had been responsible for the writing and debugging of the thousands of lines of code that were written as part of *Mir*'s shift to full automation, something Strakelov found amazing. Each new cargo ship brought along a new computerized piece of equipment that replaced old manually driven hardware. The old equipment was stowed away in the ferry and destroyed during re-entry. Tereshkova was in charge of installing the new equipment and updating the central computer program to incorporate each piece of new equipment as part of the total control system on board.

Strakelov nodded. Tereshkova was a very talented and mature young woman. After graduating first in her class at the Moscow Physical-Engineering Institute in three years instead of the usual four, she went through a two-year pilot training course at the Higher Air Force College in Chernigov. She served for three years as a MiG-29 pilot with the Frontovaya Aviatsiya, Russia's tactical air force, before she managed to get accepted at the Cosmonaut Training Center. Soyuz TM-15 was her first mission.

"Let's secure the modules, Valentina. I'll handle *Kristall*, *Kvant-1* and *Mir*. You go back to *Kvant-2* and Soyuz. We only have ten minutes."

Tereshkova headed aft as Strakelov gently pushed himself toward the multiple docking station. He reached the massive steel ball capable of docking up to five modules. Only three docking units were being used. He moved to the one on the right, *Kristall,* the state-of-the-art module containing a micro-gravity factory capable of producing a variety of semiconductor crystals. *Kristall* was also equipped with a pair of new docking units for use with the Russian space shuttle *Buran.*

He floated in the fairly spacious compartment of *Kristall* and eyed the ongoing crystal-growth experiments. He checked the timer on the equipment. The last experiment had ended an hour ago. A new experiment had automatically started. Strakelov hesitated for a moment or two before aborting the experiment and setting the machine in standby mode, to prevent the computer system from starting a new experiment. He was concerned that the sudden deceleration necessary to achieve the lower orbit might create an imperfect batch of crystals.

He eyed the rest of the compartment. Everything appeared in order. Nothing floated loose around the ship. Satisfied, he turned and headed back to the multiple docking ball. He went through it straight into the opposite side, where *Kvant-1* was docked. Unlike *Kristall, Kvant-1* had a mix of older hardware and new computer-controlled equipment. Essentially the module was also another laboratory to conduct experiments. *Kvant-2,* though, was dramatically different from its predecessor, since it was not only a workshop, but also the air lock to be used for the new *Ikar* space bicycle, similar in shape and functionality to NASA's Manned Maneuvering Unit. *Kvant-2* also had the largest of the *Mir* complex's existing hatches. At one meter in diameter, it had quickly become the permanent "front door" for all cosmonaut space walks.

Strakelov turned around, satisfied that all was secured in the module. He reached the multiple docking unit, went left, and floated back into the *Mir* module. Tereshkova was already there waiting for him, strapped into her seat. Her short black hair floated over her head, exposing her ears. Strakelov noticed she wore small diamond earrings, something that was not viewed favorably by Baikonur Control, but Strakelov did not mind. Tereshkova was one of the best flight engineers he'd seen. She should be allowed a few indulgences. A young and attractive Slavic woman having to spend months in space? No, Strakelov didn't mind at all. She deserved that and more for her many contributions to the *Rodina* in such a short period of time.

"The *Ikar* bicycles and Orlon suits are secured, Valentina?"

"Yes, Nikolai Aleksandrovich. I did a visual on the suits. They are properly strapped. The external electromagnets show nominal readings."

Strakelov nodded. The space bicycles were kept outside for storage reasons. In order to ensure they were safely strapped to *Kvant-2*'s external walls, Strakelov himself had designed an electromagnetic locking method for ease of usage and to avoid wasting precious EVA time—along with limited oxygen supply—on strapping and unstrapping the bicycles to *Kvant-2*'s exterior walls.

"Good. Time to fire?"

Tereshkova went to work on the keyboard. "Three minutes, ten seconds."

Strakelov strapped himself to his seat and reached for the radio.

"Baikonur Control, *Mir* complex."

"Go ahead, Nikolai. You are coming through clear."

"Less than three minutes to ignition. Using vernier rockets to rotate complex one hundred eighty degrees."

"Rotation confirmed, Nikolai."

Strakelov used *Mir*'s small vernier rockets to rotate the complex gently so that *Progress VII*'s engine faced forward. The original intent of *Progress VII*'s engine was to boost *Mir* into a higher, more stable orbit, but due to the change of plans, the same engine was going to be used to get the space station down to a lower orbit.

Strakelov completed the maneuver and fired the verniers in the opposite direction to stop the rotation.

"Rotation complete. One minute to ignition. Current orbit three hundred thirty kilometers. Target orbit two hundred thirty-three kilometers. One-minute burn for initial slow-down. Seven hours, twenty minutes for second ignition. Estimated five ignitions for a total of three minutes. Thirty-five seconds to ignition of *Progress VII*'s main engine."

"*Acknowledged, Nikolai.*"

Strakelov turned to Tereshkova. She kept her pressurized pen hanging off the side of her mouth as she furiously typed commands for a last-second check prior to ignition. She placed the keyboard onto the Velcro patch on the console in front of her, removed the pen from her mouth, placed it in a sidearm pocket, and then shifted her gaze toward Strakelov.

"All systems nominal."

Strakelov nodded. "Ten seconds to ignition, six . . . five . . . four . . . three . . . two . . ." He reached for the ignition button. "Ignition started!"

Progress VII's engine kicked into life, providing nearly thirty thousand pounds of reverse thrust, rapidly decelerating *Mir*. Since they faced the front of the complex, both jerked forward against their restraining harness as their bodies were exposed to a force of two Gs.

"Twenty seconds. Speed reduced to thirty-three thousand one hundred kilometers per hour. Orbital altitude three hundred eighteen kilometers," Tereshkova read from the computer display.

Strakelov kept his eyes on the digital counter in front of him while his finger lightly pressed the engine shut-off button.

"One-minute burn completed. All systems nominal. Speed thirty-one thousand. Will achieve stable orbit of two hundred eighty-nine kilometers in seven hours. Second burn in seven hours, eighteen minutes."

"*Excellent, Nikolai. The spirit of the* Rodina *lives in your flying and that of your flight engineer.*"

Strakelov smiled and looked at Tereshkova. She was smiling too. The smile quickly vanished from her face as his own face hardened at the thought of *Lightning*'s crew slowly asphyxiating in their vessel. *Up here there are no countries,* Strakelov reflected. It didn't matter whether one was called an astronaut or a cosmonaut; in Strakelov's mind they were all human beings living in outer space. They belonged to the same race, the human race. National boundaries were insignificant, or at least so it seemed while Strakelov cruised at thousands of kilometers per hour over a fragile-looking Earth. Earth was simply Earth, and not a conglomerate of countries trying to coexist. Strakelov had a new mission. A rescue mission. He was determined to succeed, but then again, he thought, he had never failed at anything he had attempted to do in his life.

NORTH OF KOUROU, FRENCH GUIANA

The paratrooper doors of the C-141 StarLifter opened and the sound that followed was intimidating. The powerful thunder of the four Pratt & Whitney turbofans, unleashing nearly twenty thousand pounds of thrust each, savagely propagated through the cargo area, deafening Ortiz and the rest of Mambo. As soon as the paratrooper door opened, the rear cargo door lowered. Each man now kept his right hand firmly gripping one of numerous handholds built in on the side walls. Ortiz was second in line right behind Zimmer.

He squinted as the setting sun made its way past the huge opening in the aft fuselage under the tail section. He could feel the vibrations induced by the increased drag from the lowered cargo door. It made the aluminum-framed floor tremble.

Ortiz felt the adrenaline kick in as he stared at the red light over the paratrooper door. Although he had over one hundred jumps to his credit, it never got any easier. The risk of a tangled parachute was always present. He placed his hand over the reserve chute strapped to his stomach, his only insurance should the main canopy fail to deploy.

As before every jump, memories from his first jump vividly flashed in front of Ortiz's eyes. That first jump had come after spending two weeks performing simulated jumps from a seventy-foot-high tower. After getting the essentials down, the real thing came. Ortiz and a group of rookies jumped from an altitude of nine hundred feet. Their parachutes were automatically opened by a static line fixed to the aircraft. That first jump had not been as terrifying as his second. After that initial jump, Ortiz knew exactly what he was going to experience, including urine-drenched fatigues by the time he reached ground. It took a lot of nerve and almost a kick in the rear for him to jump again after that terrorizing first time. *After that it got a little easier,* Ortiz thought as the light above the door turned to yellow.

"All right. It's time!" Ortiz heard Siegel scream over the noise from the wind and the engines.

With time Ortiz's confidence had slowly built up until he joined the ranks of the free-fall parachutists, a separate tribe within the Special Forces.

Zimmer turned around and smiled. "See ya down there, Tito!" Ortiz put on the goggles that hung loose from his neck. He was ready.

The light turned green.

"Go, go, go!"

Ortiz watched Zimmer rush out through the door. He inhaled, made the sign of the cross as his feet left the aluminum floor, and jumped into the abyss.

He felt the initial windblast as he extended his arms and legs in classic free-falling position. His Colt Commando submachine gun was safely strapped along the left side. Zimmer, roughly twenty feet ahead of him, moved toward The Bundle—the five-hundred-pound supply container that had slid off the rear cargo door. They would get close to The Bundle, but not too close. An aerodynamically unpredictable beast, The Bundle could easily make a U-turn and rush back at them across the sky. Ortiz moved his right arm inward while keeping his left extended. That had the effect of slowly moving him to the right. He eyed the small altimeter mounted over the reserve chute.

Thirteen thousand feet.

He checked the chronometer on his watch. Eleven seconds had elapsed since he'd jumped off the StarLifter. He had dropped two thousand feet in eleven seconds. *Right on the money,* Ortiz thought, as he plummeted at a rate of 125 miles per hour, or 183 feet per second.

Zimmer got within a hundred or so feet of The Bundle and arched his upper body to stop his momentum and maintain the safe distance. Ortiz continued his right-hand turn until he maneuvered himself thirty feet from Zimmer and also about a hundred feet from The Bundle.

Eight thousand feet. Thirty-eight seconds.

He watched the rest of the platoon assume their position around The Bundle. *Almost like clockwork,* Ortiz decided, as the altimeter scurried below six thousand feet and the chronometer showed fifty seconds had elapsed.

He waited. *Two thousand feet. Seventy seconds. Mark.* He had fallen a total of thirteen thousand feet in seventy seconds.

He pulled the ripcord handle and waited as he continued to fall. The pilot chute, or extractor, rushed clear of the fifty-pound Bergen rucksack. It had a bridle cord attached to it, which pulled the main canopy. The sudden jerk told him the main parachute had safely deployed.

A soft wind suddenly caressed his face. The sun had all but vanished below the horizon. He scanned the sky around him and spotted the parachutes in a circle around The Bundle's dual parachutes.

The dark green Earth came up to greet him. It looked majestic, serene, almost peaceful. He approached it slowly, with control. He followed Zimmer's lead toward the large clearing that Pruett had shown them on the map. It was a few miles north of Kourou. Far enough to avoid detection, yet close enough to reach their objective in two hours. Two hours, hardly enough time to hide the chutes, get the rest of their gear from The Bundle, and reach their objective. But they were Mambo. The elite fighting force. Mambo could do it.

Ortiz's thoughts quickly faded away as he landed hard on the clearing. He fell on his side and rolled twice, letting the roll absorb most of the impact. He got up and started pulling the canopy toward him.

Aboard the StarLifter, Cameron got a visual on the platoon. It had taken them exactly three minutes to reach the landing zone. He turned to Pruett.

"Looks like they know what they're doing, Tom. I couldn't have done it better even at my peak."

Pruett smiled and headed for the cabin. He opened the door and briefly examined the interior. The pilot and copilot were in their seats. To Pruett's immediate right was the navigator. To Pruett's left the flight engineer was handling most communications.

"Yes, sir?" the navigator said, turning his head toward them. He was a kid no older than twenty-five, Pruett estimated. Blond with blue eyes, medium build.

"I need you to hook the phone up back there. Got to make some hot calls."

The young navigator smiled. "No problem, sir."

The flight engineer turned around. "Sir?"

Pruett shifted his gaze to the left. "Yes?"

"Just got confirmation from Mambo. All is well."

"Good. Keep me posted if something else comes up."

"Yes, sir."

Pruett and Cameron headed back to the relatively small aft cabin, where Marie quietly stared at the clouds through a small circular window. There was a phone on the wall. Pruett picked it up and dialed a White House number he had committed to memory. He had hoped he would hear the President's calm voice answering, but instead Stice came on the line. Pruett frowned.

"Yes?" said Stice.

"The team is on the ground, sir. Two hours to target."

"Time to launch?"

Pruett checked his watch. "Just under three hours."

"Keep me posted."

"Of course."

"Good-bye, Tom."

"Good-bye, sir." He hung up the phone and stared at Cameron.

"It's gonna be real close, Tom. Real close."

Pruett massaged his chest and inhaled deeply. He reached for the pack of antacids and popped two in his mouth.

Ortiz finished stowing away the canopy under a large fallen log, one end of which dipped into the waters of a swamp. The area was filled with them.

"This is just fuckin' great, Tito," Ortiz heard Zimmer say as he approached him. "The word from Siegel's that most of th' terrain we gotta cover's swamp. We're gonna be up to our necks in shit, man."

Ortiz smiled.

"What's so funny? You enjoy havin' mud bugs crawlin' up your ass?"

Ortiz slowly shook his head. The smile on his face remained. "No, *hermano*. It's just the way you said it that's funny. Ever thought 'bout pickin' up stand-up comedy?"

"Don't fuck with me, Tito. I'm not in the—"

"All right, people! We ain't got all day! Move out!" Siegel screamed. "Tito!"

"Sir!"

"Take the lead. Stay thirty feet in front. Tommy, you cover his rear. The rest of you follow single file. Ten feet in between. Got that?"

"Yes, sir!"

Ortiz stood by the edge of the swamp. It extended ahead into the darkness. Somewhere on the other side was the target. Firmly clutching his Colt Commando, Ortiz stepped into the putrid waters. His thick camouflage fatigues were instantly drenched, but somehow it felt refreshing. The black water was cool. As long as his fatigues and sturdy boots kept leeches and other bugs away, Ortiz decided, he would be all right. Ortiz hated bugs, particularly leeches. Just the thought of them made him nauseous. *Slimy, shiny creatures!* As a kid he used to pour salt on them and watch them shrivel up. But now he didn't have to worry. The Army had provided him with protective clothing to keep the leeches off and keep his mind on the mission. After all, he was the point man for Mambo. He was its eyes and ears. His unit depended on him.

He looked at the swamp and drew his lips in a tight frown. *Fucking leeches!*

U.S.S. *BLUE RIDGE*

Lieutenant Commander Kenneth Crowe of the U.S. Navy had just fallen asleep when he felt a hand on his shoulder.

"Go away! Don't give a shit who you are!"

It didn't work. The hand remained on his shoulder. Crowe didn't move. He was just too comfortable. This was his first real rest period after a two-day rescue exercise with the Venezuelan Navy's newly acquired Sea Stallion helicopters, to provide quick evacuation support to the region's offshore oil platforms in case of emergencies.

"Sorry, Commander. The Skipper wants to talk to you."

"Ahgg, fuck him!"

"Yes, sir. Whatever you say, but the Skipper gave me strict orders to get you on the bridge in ten minutes."

Crowe turned over and sat up. "Dammit! What in the hell's goin' on? I've just busted my ass for one straight week teaching those banana pilots how to fly those damned choppers they just bought. This is my break. *My break,* and the Skipper knows that! Damn!" Hastily, Crowe got up. He wore only his underpants and white T-shirt. "Toss me that shirt, would ya?" He picked up the pants off the floor and put them on.

"Here you go, sir."

Crowe exhaled and grabbed the white shirt. It had his name tag on the right side and several ribbons over the left pocket. A pair of silver wings above them marked him as a naval aviator.

"Have any idea what's goin' on?" he asked as he buttoned up the shirt, which was a bit too tight on the arms. His bulging biceps were slightly out of proportion with the rest of his upper body.

"Ah, no, sir. Just that I had to get you to the bridge in—"

"Yes, yes, in ten minutes."

"Six."

"Whatever." He sat on the bed and put on his shoes. "I love my job, you know," he continued. "But every man's got his limitations and mine are close to the edge. I need to sleep. I'm fuckin' exhausted!"

"Sorry, Commander, but the Skipper gave me—"

"Let's go."

Followed by the mate, Crowe headed for the bridge of the nineteen-thousand-pound amphibious command ship. U.S. Navy classification LCC, the *Blue Ridge* performed a variety of surveillance jobs, including monitoring low-flying planes leaving Colombia and Venezuela in a northerly heading. The *Blue Ridge*'s primary job was that of detection only—the reason for the variety of communications aerials on the flat upper deck. The *Blue Ridge* was not supposed to try and shoot down the planes; its job was simply to detect them.

There were two helicopters on board—two Sea Stallions, among the Navy's largest and most powerful helicopters, capable of hauling fifty-five fully equipped troops for just over 250 miles.

There were three pilots on board. Two choppers and three pilots. That way there was always a rotation scheme worked out to prevent pilot fatigue, which was exactly what was occurring with Crowe at that very moment.

Still half asleep, Crowe yawned as he pushed open the metallic door to the bridge. He walked in and spotted the other two pilots standing in front of the Skipper, Captain John Davenport.

"What's going on?" he asked. "I just got off duty and—"

"I know what's on your mind, Kenny," Davenport replied, and then looked at the mate, who nodded, turned, and left the room, closing the door behind him.

"Sir," Crowe persisted. "With all due respect, I am very tired and—"

"I won't say it again, Kenny. Shut up! The *Blue Ridge* has been called in to provide support to an ongoing covert operation. We're supposed to extract a Special Forces team out of French Guiana in exactly one and a half hours. We're two hundred miles away. That means we barely have time to make it there in a chopper. I want to send both Stallions. One as backup."

Crowe could not believe it. Davenport was dead serious about sending him out without a break.

"Sir, please listen to me for the sake of the mission. I'm in no shape to—"

"No, dammit! No! *You* listen to me! See these two guys here?" He pointed to the two pilots nervously standing at attention next to Crowe. "They ain't got shit for experience! You understand that? They're good pilots but they're both rookies out of flight school. I want a veteran out there. This is the real thing, for crying out loud. I want someone out there who can make good split-second calls, and flight training doesn't teach that. Experience teaches that. Kenny, you got that experience, and I need you out there in one of the helicopters. Got that?"

Crowe gave the two young pilots a quick look and took a deep breath, trying to come to terms with the simple fact that Davenport was right on the money. This was a rescue mission. He had the experience. Real experience, that is, picking up grunts from hot landing zones all over Southeast Asia, something he'd become quite good at. He nodded and stared into Davenport's eyes. "Sir, two hundred miles each way. Our range is not—"

"We'll refuel you in midair before you get there, Kenny. A KC-97's on the way from Howard. You'll intercept fifty miles off the coast. Besides, we're steaming full speed ahead toward the Guiana coast. We should be able to cut that distance to one hundred twenty miles by the time you're ready to come back."

Crowe frowned. The Sea Stallion's range was only 257 miles. That meant that unless they got refueled before they went in, his craft would have no more than fifteen to twenty minutes of fuel after the pickup. "That tanker better show up, Skipper, otherwise we're dead meat."

Davenport smiled. "Don't worry. It will be there. Just make sure you're there to meet it."

"All right. Exactly where do we need to be . . . and by the way, where is the nearest coffeepot? Looks like I'm gonna be in for a long night."

LIGHTNING

"Lightning, Houston. Wake-up call."

Kessler rubbed his eyes as he heard Hunter's voice coming through on the intercom system.

"We're still here, Houston."

"Oxygen content?"

"Still on the nominal side, but just by a dash. Looks like our original estimates were a bit optimistic. Status on *Atlantis?*"

"We just finished rolling it up to the launchpad. Thirty hours to launch, but you'll get help before that."

Kessler pulled himself out of the horizontal sleeping station and briefly checked on Jones. He was still unconscious, peacefully snoring. "What do you mean, Houston?"

"Our Russian friends are on the way. They should be there much faster than us. You will transfer to their space station until Atlantis *gets there and we provide* Lightning *with enough juice to close the doors and patch up the tile problem. What's Jones's situation?"*

"Stable, but he's still unconscious. Any news from the spooks?"

"Ah, no. Nothing yet."

"What are we telling the public about this? How much do they know?"

"We're telling them the mission's proceeding as normal and that all systems are nominal."

"What about the fact that *Atlantis* is on the way?"

"A joint shuttle mission to practice emergency rescues."

"And they're buying that?"

"So far."

Kessler smiled at Hunter's response as he floated toward the food galley, where a variety of meals packed in different forms were carefully stored. He was starving.

"Well, Houston. Doesn't sound like there's much I can do up here but wait, so I think I'm gonna grab a bite." He opened the food galley and roamed through the selection of dehydrated, freeze-dried foods in easily identifiable plastic containers. All he had to do was add water and heat it up. He recognized scrambled eggs, and chicken and noodles.

"Go for it, Lightning. *I'll keep you posted of any new developments."*

Kessler smiled once more and closed the lid on the freeze-dried foods. Nothing looked appetizing, and since this could be one of his last meals, Kessler decided to make it count. The next container in the galley housed irradiated foods, preserved by exposure to ionizing radiation. He found bread, rolls . . . and a few rib eyes—brought on board at Jones's request. *Bingo!* He grabbed the plastic pouch that contained what looked like the largest of the four steaks, and heated it up by using the galley's food warming unit, which heated food by thermal conduction using a hot plate enclosed in an aluminum suitcase. As he heated up the steak, Kessler went through the galley's other compartments and snagged a plastic pouch of dried peaches, a plastic container with ready-to-add-water lemonade, and some chocolate chip cookies, which to Kessler's relief were sealed in a plastic pouch but had not been dehydrated or irradiated. They had been packed in their natural form and were ready to eat.

Kessler opened the cookie pouch and took a few hearty bites, careful not to let any crumbs float away. The cookies were still fresh. He added water to the pouch containing the dehydrated lemonade, shook it to mix, and put a straw through the opening on top. Because liquids in space did not slide down the edge of a glass, all beverages had to be consumed through straws. He put the straw to his lips and sucked the light-yellow liquid. It tasted relatively good and sweet.

Kessler checked his watch and frowned. Time was running out. The seriousness of the situation began to really sink in. For the first time Kessler felt the fear of dying reaching out from within him. For some reason he had been too busy before to think much about it, but now with *Lightning*'s oxygen level slowly dropping, Kessler began to wonder if they were going to make it after all . . . *Stop it, Mike!* he told himself. *You start thinking that way and you just might as well put a gun to your head and pull the trigger. You are mission commander, dammit! Act like it!*

Kessler briefly closed his eyes and inhaled. He had to fight. There was no other way. If he didn't want to do it for himself, he *had* to do it for Jones. Kessler owed him that much. He couldn't let him down again.

KOUROU, FRENCH GUIANA

Frederick Vanderhoff looked outside the window and stared at the floodlit Athena V rocket nearly a mile away on the launchpad. It was ready. All they needed was the right time to enter space at the appropriate window to intercept *Lightning*. He smiled, walked back to his desk, and grabbed a cigarette from the pack of Camels. He lighted up and took a long draw, exhaling through his nostrils. NASA was doomed. Of that he was almost certain. As long as the rocket reached its designated target. After that the American news media would handle the rest. By bombarding the American public with "investigative" reports, by giving new life to tales of NASA's failures, the American news media would drive the nails in NASA's coffin.

He shifted his gaze back toward the windows as he watched a patrol helicopter take off from the dual helipad between his building and the launchpad. He had ordered an around-the-clock surveillance of the grounds until launch time. Vanderhoff had to assume the worst, that somehow Stone had managed to reach the appropriate authorities and make known the suspicions brought to him by the former Athena scientists, before Chardon's team silenced them. Vanderhoff was not sure how the U.S. government would react to such aggression. His logical mind told him to expect the worst, whatever that might be.

SIXTEEN ★

Owners of the Night

Night, when words fade and things come alive.
                              —*Antoine de Saint-Exupery*

NORTH OF KOUROU, FRENCH GUIANA

The putrid yet cool swamp had suddenly turned into a thick, muddy mass that made every step an extreme effort. Perspiration covered most of Ortiz's face as his muscular legs burned. Rolling beads of sweat washed away the insect repellant he had rubbed on his hands, neck, and face. *But perhaps it's better to be in thick mud,* Ortiz thought, recalling a section of the intelligence report that mentioned the possibility of alligators—or rather caimans, their close cousins—in the region. He had not been very pleased in reading about that, but since the chance of finding caimans went down dramatically as the swamp thickened, Ortiz was not as concerned as he'd been at first. Thus he became more focused on the mission rather than wondering about being surprised by one of those prehistoric-looking beasts.

About two hours had passed since they had landed, yet it seemed like an eternity as Ortiz struggled to move his body forward. He kept his Colt Commando pressed against his chest, left hand under the barrel, right hand by the trigger casing. The weapon was covered with a thin plastic wrap to prevent its jamming if it accidentally fell into the swamp.

Just the sensitive sections were covered, providing Ortiz with enough control of the weapon to fire it at a moment's notice.

Long gone was the soothing feeling of satisfaction he'd felt when he'd first stepped into the swamp. He forced himself to ignore the extreme burning pain in his legs as he struggled to maintain his momentum in the waist-deep waters. The night was moonless and dark, forcing him to strain his eyes as he scanned a cluster of trees twenty-some feet ahead of him. He estimated they were less than a mile from the objective. The possibility of sentries became all too real.

Ortiz had a fairly good idea of the opposition's force from Marie's information, but he knew he shouldn't get overconfident. Given recent events, security around the complex could be much tighter than she had described. Ortiz had to assume the opposition could be everywhere, more reason to be glad that night was moonless because, unless the enemy also had access to night-vision gear, Mambo would have an edge over them. Actually, Ortiz decided, that would be the second edge Mambo would have over the enemy, the first being the element of surprise. Ortiz knew the importance of that edge. Now technically inside enemy territory, Mambo operated under an important disability—they lacked a home-court advantage. Mambo's hardware was limited to the automatic weapons each man carried plus the Javelin missiles on the two-man raft being pulled by the two trailing men. The enemy, on the other hand, could not only have hundreds of men available, but also an unlimited supply of firepower. Ortiz shook his head at the thought of their position being discovered by the enemy before the rescue helicopter arrived.

He reached the cluster of trees and twisted his body to correspond with the bends in the heavy foliage. Ortiz had never been anywhere else besides Panama, California, and the southeastern United States, but based on what he had read and what he had been told by veteran soldiers,

Guiana was definitely one of the most inhospitable places on Earth.

Damn! He reached with his right hand and scratched the back of his neck. *Fucking mosquitos!* It had not taken long for the flying invertebrates to figure out that the repellant had washed off.

Ortiz placed the Colt under his left armpit and reached with his right hand into a Velcro-secured pocket on the camouflage gear vest he wore over his fatigues. He squeezed some repellant into his hand, stowed the tube away, and gently rubbed the cool paste all around the back and front of his neck. He frowned when he felt a few lumps already growing on his skin. His annoyance with the insect bites only compounded a growing headache. Ortiz reached for another pocket and grabbed a small plastic bag. It held six extra-strength Tylenol caplets. Ortiz popped two in his mouth and replaced the bag. He took a small sip from his canteen to swallow the caplets.

Firmly clutching the Colt once more, Ortiz left the small cluster of trees behind, moving slowly forward. Every step required serious effort as he dragged his exhausted legs through the thick mud. He leaned forward to help his momentum, but still the swamp acted as a brake, pulling him back. He cleared the trees again. He felt exposed, extremely vulnerable, and doubted that he could realistically escape an attack while in the clearing.

He scanned the dark skies. They were clear, star-filled, and moonless. Ortiz reached for the battery-operated Sopelen TN2-1 night-vision goggles. Again, he tucked the Colt under his armpit, put the goggles on, and activated the thermal-imaging system. Suddenly, the dark surroundings came alive in a palette of green hues related to heat signature. The hotter the image, the lighter it showed through the goggles. He looked behind him and instantly spotted Zimmer's light-green silhouette against a dark-green background. Ortiz quickly did a three-sixty scan of the clearing. There were no anomalies in the dark green pattern.

Continuing toward the next cluster of trees, fifty feet ahead, he heard a sound he'd hoped he would not hear— the low flopping sound of a helicopter.

His mind raced through his options. There weren't that many. Actually only two. Race as fast as he could toward the tree line—something he didn't think would be successful. Or . . . Ortiz spotted the thermal image of the engine exhaust as the craft loomed above the trees.

He didn't have a choice. He was not sure what the rest of the platoon would do, but he knew what had to be done. Without a second thought, Ortiz bent his legs and lowered the upper part of his body, Colt and night goggles, down into the putrid mud.

Suddenly it all went away. The noise disappeared and a cool, soothing sensation enveloped him. Ortiz kept his eyes shut and silently cursed his bad luck. He wasn't sure how much time he needed to spend under the mud. *How long is long enough? Twenty, perhaps thirty seconds? A minute maybe?* It didn't matter. His instincts forced him down until his lungs couldn't take it any longer, and even then he squeezed out a few extra seconds. With his lungs about to burst, Ortiz pushed himself up just enough to keep his head above the surface.

"There you are, Tito. Jesus, brother! We thought you were lost or somethin'."

Ortiz was momentarily confused. Where was the chopper? Why was Zimmer next to him? Why wasn't he covered with mud like himself?

"You fucking *pendejo!*" Ortiz straightened up, nearly tore the night goggles off his head, and wiped the mud and whatever else there was off his face. "You mean to tell me that I stuck my whole body in shit to prevent the enemy from spotting us and you just stood there? I saw you, *cabron.* You were on the clearing like me. Why didn't you—"

"Tito, you overreacted, man. I saw the chopper above the trees and then I saw you goin' in. I was about to dive in also when the helicopter turned around 'n' left, man, so I kept on walkin' in your direction." He motioned for them to move toward the tree line.

Ortiz went first, reaching the safety of the trees in under a minute. He grabbed the hand-held, waterproof radio on his belt.

"All is clear to the tree line, *jefe*. Over."

"Roger, Tito. Proceeding to meet you single file. Five-minute intervals per cross, over."

"Over 'n' out." Ortiz turned to Zimmer, who stood a few feet behind him.

"*Mierda*. I can't believe I did this shit for nothin'," Ortiz whispered as he lay the Colt over a branch and grabbed a handkerchief from a pocket. He could barely stand the smell. "It's bad enough to be walking in this crap, but to have it up your nostrils . . . yech!"

"Sorry, man. I wish I could . . . oh, man," Zimmer said the moment Ortiz finished wiping off most of the mud from his face and neck. "Look at you, man."

"What about?"

"Leeches, man."

"Don't screw around. I ain't in no mood to . . ." Ortiz stopped talking the moment his fingers came in contact with a slimy-feeling object on the side of his neck. He closed his eyes and inhaled, trying to control his initial impulse to vomit. "Get the fuckers off. Get them off!"

"All right, all right, but keep it down. Don't move." Zimmer slung his Colt across his back and pulled out a double-edge, black-painted hunting knife from his belt holster.

Ortiz shut his eyes and held his breath the moment he felt the cold steel pressed flat against the skin of his neck. Slowly, the blade moved upward, almost as if he were shaving. In that short period of time the leech had already managed to attach itself strongly enough to leave behind a patch of bloody skin on Ortiz's neck.

"Got one."

Ortiz opened his eyes and stared at the disgusting-looking creature crawling on Zimmer's knife. Zimmer simply threw it back in the swamp. "Two to go. Guess you won't have to shave tomorrow, man."

"No offense, *pendejo,* but you know very well what you can do with your silly jokes. Just get these damned things off me, would you?"

"Shh . . . keep it down."

"Great. Just take all the fuckin' time in the world, *cabron.*"

Zimmer grinned and pressed the knife against Ortiz's neck, removing a second leech along with a chunk of skin. The third one had only partially attached itself to Ortiz's right ear. Zimmer removed it with his fingers.

"All right. You're back to your pretty self."

Ortiz managed a thin smile. "Thanks, *hermano.*"

Zimmer smiled back. "Anytime."

"You think this thing still works?" Ortiz pointed to the night goggles.

"They fuckin' better."

Ortiz cleaned the thermal-imaging system as best he could, put it back on, and activated it.

"Well?" Zimmer asked.

"It'll do," Ortiz responded as he scanned the area and satisfactorily noted the dark-green surroundings . . . shit!

He moved against a tree and motioned Zimmer to the same.

"What's going . . ." Zimmer stopped talking when he noticed Ortiz putting a finger to his lips. Zimmer quickly reached cover behind an adjacent tree.

Ortiz moved to the left and briefly checked the area directly ahead of them. He saw two—no—three sentries. Their light-green silhouettes shone beautifully against the stark background. He looked at Zimmer, also wearing night goggles. Zimmer nodded his head.

Ortiz reached for the radio and turned the volume down.

"Found three sentries. One hundred feet ahead. Permission for silent engagement, over?"

"Careful, Tito. Is Tommy there?"

"Yes, sir."

"All right. Permission to move out. I'll get two men in there to cover you. Hold for twenty seconds before moving."

"Roger." Ortiz holstered the radio and checked his watch. Twenty seconds. He waited.

Ortiz looked at Zimmer and pointed. Zimmer nodded and headed left. Ortiz checked his watch once more. This was it. The real thing. He warily moved to the right, always keeping an eye on the light-green figures a few feet apart from one another, his hands solidly gripping the light submachine gun. He clutched it for lack of something else. In reality he knew he could not use the Colt. That would give away his position. He wished they had had more time to prepare for the mission and maybe gotten one or two silenced machine guns, but with the two-hour notice they were lucky to have the gear they had—which was standard Special Forces.

Ortiz reached a spot over a hundred feet to the right of the sentries, and cut left to make a wide semicircle around them. He would attack from an unexpected angle, hitting the sentries from behind, from the place they would be least likely to expect any unfriendlies to come from. The sentries were near the edge of the tree line and slowly moving toward the rest of Mambo.

Suddenly a bright sparkle of green light nearly blinded him. It quickly went away and was replaced by a medium-intensity glow near the head of one of the sentries. Ortiz shook his head.

A cigarette. The idiot lit a cigarette!

That puzzled Ortiz. *Are these guys so secure in their position that they don't think anyone would dare attack from this side? Do they think that an attack most likely would come from the beach?*

Ortiz completed the semicircle and reached a spot a hundred feet directly behind the sentries, who were still moving in the same direction. He spotted Zimmer forty feet to his right. Ortiz lifted his right hand in a fist and slowly moved it toward the sentries.

Zimmer nodded and slung the Colt behind his back. Ortiz did the same, and reached for his hunting knife. He briefly stared at the swamp and exhaled. There was no other way. Ortiz immersed his body in the swamp once more, only leaving his head out. The sentries had stopped and scanned the clearing in between the cluster of trees where they were and the trees where Mambo would be by now. He blinked once more. A second sentry had lit a cigarette. *Incredible!*

Kicking his legs until they hurt, Ortiz propelled himself through the muddy hell. His neck came in contact with the swamp surface. He knew what that meant, but that didn't matter any longer. Only the sentries mattered. *If they could be called that,* he thought as he closed the gap to fifty feet. He could hear their voices. Sound traveled well over a smooth surface.

Forty feet. He looked over his right shoulder. Zimmer was there. Also up to his neck in it. Ortiz lifted one hand out of the mud and pointed to the right-most sentry. Zimmer nodded. Ortiz shifted his gaze back toward the sentries. Thirty feet. He clutched the knife's handle so hard his fingers grew numb from lack of circulation. He couldn't help it. His mind was almost on automatic as he closed the gap to less than twenty feet.

His approach was quiet, calculated. He used the noise created by the sentries to mask his own. He knew Zimmer would do the same.

Ortiz briefly gazed upward. Toward the stars. The crystalline sky looked majestic, dazzling, peaceful. He enjoyed it for another brief second before training his eyes on the left-most sentry. The one with the cigarette in his right hand. The man took another draw and turned his head to the side. Ortiz saw his profile. *A young man,* he noted.

Ten feet. Ortiz heard a few words. They were speaking in French. They were too close. Ortiz knew he had to act right away or risk detection. Would he be able to propel himself out of the mud fast enough?

He eyed Zimmer, the right-most sentry, the left-most sentry, and back to Zimmer. Their eyes locked. Ortiz held up his left hand and counted one, two, three with his fingers.

Now!

They lunged simultaneously, knives extended in front, aimed for the throat. Ortiz reached his prey in less than three seconds, catching him entirely by surprise as he was about to take another draw from the half-smoked cigarette. The sentry's hand never made it to his face. Ortiz savagely drove the ten-inch blade into the base of the sentry's neck. He heard the nauseating sound of broken bone and ripped cartilage as the stainless-steel blade went deeper and exited through the larynx. An explosion of air and foam followed as the sentry brought both hands to his neck before falling face-first into the swamp. Ortiz let go of the knife and turned to the sentry in the middle, whose face showed obvious surprise. His eyes were open wide in fear as his fumbling fingers tried to reach for the automatic weapon that hung loose from his left shoulder.

Ortiz lunged and pushed the sentry on his back and forced him into the swamp. He grabbed the sentry's lapel with one hand and pushed his head back with the palm of the other hand. The sentry let go a half scream before his head went under. Ortiz eyed Zimmer. He had disabled the right-most sentry. Ortiz shifted his gaze back toward the sentry he had pinned down in the swamp. The sentry's body was under except for his arms, which viciously flapped in a desperate attempt to free himself from Ortiz's death lock, but Ortiz kept up the pressure. He knew it was just a matter of time. The sentry had screamed before his head went under. That meant he'd exhaled instead of inhaled. The more the sentry fought the faster he would use up the little air that remained in his lungs. Ortiz was right. The arm movement slowed to a halt. Ortiz counted to thirty before letting go. When he did, he noticed the arms slowly sinking.

"Damn, Tito. You sure can be one mean bastard."

Ortiz stared at Zimmer. "Can't say I was proud of it, but we can't let their people know we're here." He reached for his handkerchief and wiped off his neck. "How many, *hermano*?"

Zimmer got close. "Just one. How about me?"

Ortiz examined Zimmer's neck. "Two."

A few minutes later he reached for the radio. "Ortiz here. Sentries compromised. Area's clear."

"All right. Let's move it, Tito. You two hide the bodies and keep moving forward. We'll catch up with you. This area is likely to be roaming with patrol choppers in a few minutes."

"Roger. Moving out." He replaced the radio. "You heard the boss, Tommy. Let's get outta here."

"You got it, brother."

Vanderhoff picked up the phone on the first ring. "Yes?"

"Sir, I think we may have a situation."

"Explain."

"A helicopter just made a patrol run a mile east of here and they can't get a response from the patrol team."

"Equipment breakdown perhaps?"

"Ah, no, sir. Each man carried a portable radio. I doubt all three are malfunctioning at the same time."

Vanderhoff inhaled deeply, trying to calm himself down. He checked his watch. Less than an hour to go before the launch. He had to keep intruders away for another hour. After that it would be over. There was nothing anyone would be able to do.

"Send all available men out!" he snapped back. "I want those two helicopters delivering security personnel out there immediately. Is that understood?"

"Yes, sir!"

Vanderhoff slammed down the phone and tightened his fists. This was the most critical phase of the operation. It was the only way to be sure *Lightning* would be destroyed. Doing it otherwise would leave too much to chance and would give NASA time to figure out a way to save the wounded orbiter.

FIFTY MILES OFF THE COAST OF FRENCH GUIANA

Wearing a set of GEC Avionics "Cat's Eyes" Night Vision Goggles, Lieutenant Crowe stared at the fuel drogue on the end of the sixty-foot-long hose hanging down and behind the tail of the KC-97 tanker. Crowe's wingman, Stallion Two, patiently took second place behind him. The advanced NVGs, secured to a bracket mounted on the front of his helmet, superimposed two smaller combiner lenses in front of Crowe's eyes. Intensified outside light, reflected onto the combiner lenses through a mirror and prism design, provided Crowe with a bright, green-tinted view of the moonless night.

Crowe lifted the collective lever and twisted the motorcycle-style throttle grip at the end, increasing main rotor RPM and also changing the rotor blade profile, creating additional lift. The maneuver empowered the 36,000-pound heavy assault transport helicopter to climb to a comfortable one thousand feet at 160 knots.

Crowe eyed the approaching drogue and then his craft's seven-foot-long refueling probe extending out from the right side of the nose. The drogue was less than ten feet away.

Crowe inched the cyclic forward. The trick was to approach the drogue fast. A slow approach would cause the drogue to be pushed down by the air from the main rotor. Crowe eyed the drogue. He aligned the refueling probe as best he could with it. Then in one move, he gently pushed the cyclic forward. It took about one second for the Sikorsky helicopter to leap forward.

Contact! The probe reached the drogue and snagged it.

"Leaded or unleaded, Stallion One?" said the voice from the tanker.

"Don't matter," he responded. "They all come from the same tank anyway. I've only got five hundred pounds of juice left. Fill it up."

"Will do, Stallion One. Are you gonna want the windows washed?"

"Ah, no thanks." Crowe smiled. Someone was in a good mood aboard that tanker.

Two minutes later he eyed the fuel gauges. "All right, guys. I think that'll just about do it. Thanks a bunch."

"Our pleasure, Stallion One. Good luck on your exercise."

Crowe raised his right eyebrow. *Exercise?* Okay, so someone had given that explanation to the tanker's crew. They—whoever "they" were—wanted to keep the number of people involved at a minimum. It made sense, he decided. That way, when things go ape-shit, "they" don't have to tell too many people to keep a lid on it. Covert operations. He'd flown them enough times in Vietnam to be able to smell them and this one stunk. The worst part of it was that he had no idea what was going on. Just that they had to pick up an Army Special Forces team. Nothing else. He had been given a rendezvous point and a time. He was to wait for no more than five minutes and would keep rotor RPM high enough to leave in seconds.

Crowe gently maneuvered his craft to the side to make way for Stallion Two. Crowe flew without a copilot. The two rookies were on board Stallion Two.

Stallion Two approached the drogue too slow. It went under.

Crowe spoke on his voice-activated headset. "Back off and go back in a bit faster."

"Roger, Stallion One."

The Stallion let the drogue move forward about twenty feet before it moved in again. This time Crowe watched approvingly as the chopper approached the drogue at a higher speed, snagging it.

"Good job."

"Thank you, sir."

Crowe checked his watch. They had forty-five minutes left.

KOUROU, FRENCH GUIANA

Vanderhoff finished dialing Chardon's private number. He heard it ring twice before the general's rough voice crackled through Vanderhoff's speaker box.

"Oui?"

"Wake up, General. We're in trouble and I need the service of a team from your elite Force d'Action Rapide. I might be getting paranoid, but we just lost contact with three of my men minutes after their deployment. There is a chance that Stone might have reached his people. We can't afford to take a chance with the launch thirty minutes away."

"You're right, *monsieur*. I'll give the order immediately under the pretext of a possible terrorist attack on the facility."

"That will be perfect."

FORTY MILES OFF THE COAST OF FRENCH GUIANA

Crowe kept his height just ten feet above the green-tinted waves at a comfortable 150 knots. He watched the KC-95 tanker disappear in the night to his north as it headed back to Howard. He eyed the fuel gauges and estimated he had roughly two hours of flying time. Just enough to go in, pick up his load, and get back to the *Blue Ridge* before all hell broke loose.

He frowned. Not only was he wired out of his mind from the several cups of coffee he'd had before leaving, but his Sea Stallion was essentially unarmed. His helicopter was strictly a rescue craft, not a light infantry division air-support craft like the Sikorsky UH-60A Black Hawk helicopter or so many other support craft. All he had to protect his chopper were two armed Marines in the back. They could use their M-60 machine guns to give the ground troops some level of cover during the extraction. Besides that his craft was vulnerable. Crowe was relying on the night and his proficient flying and combat experience to get him and the ground troops out of this one alive.

He eyed the radar altimeter and noticed it inching upward a bit. He couldn't afford to go above fifty feet for risk of being spotted. Although it was nighttime, the NVG provided Crowe with a clear image of the ocean's surface. He lowered the collective and applied forward cyclic pressure. The Stallion dropped back down to a radar-safe altitude.

Crowe looked to his starboard, to Stallion Two, also flying a few feet over the waves. *A couple of good sticks,* he reflected. Inexperienced but good.

The coastal lights became visible. He checked his watch. Fifteen minutes to rendezvous time. Right on time.

KOUROU, FRENCH GUIANA

Ortiz was the first to spot the ten-foot-tall chain-link fence surrounding the compound. He noticed that most of the compound appeared to have been created by filling in the swamp.

The edge of the swamp ended roughly fifty feet from the fence. Ortiz could not have been more relieved than he was the moment he stepped out of the muddy swamp onto solid ground. He dropped to the ground and hid behind several palm trees, obviously brought there from the coast to isolate the compound from the stark surroundings. Zimmer crawled next to him. Both removed their night goggles.

"What do you think, Tito?" he barely whispered.

Ortiz pointed to his right. Zimmer looked in that direction and slowly nodded. Ortiz then pointed to the left. Same thing.

Zimmer looked at Ortiz, who held up his hand holding out two fingers. Zimmer nodded once more and then slowly rolled to the left, Ortiz to the right. They allowed a twenty-foot gap before stopping and rising to a crouch. There were two sentries, also spaced by twenty feet. They stood guard on the outside of the fence facing Ortiz's direction. Less than thirty feet from where Ortiz was hidden in the trees, the guard was brilliantly backlit by the powerful halogens that bathed the large rocket a few hundred feet away on the other side of the fence. The lights gave Ortiz an advantage. Ortiz could see the guard but the guard couldn't see him.

Crawling on his knees and elbows over the sandy terrain, Ortiz twisted his body as he sneaked through the trees. He stopped every few feet and remained still for a minute. The guard gave no sign of alert. Fifteen feet. Ortiz removed the hunting knife from the holster and held it by the blade between his right thumb and index fingers, preparing to execute another often-practiced Special Forces technique.

Ten feet.

Ortiz slowly rose to a crouch, hiding behind the light undergrowth at the edge of the gravel road that surrounded the compound. He shifted his gaze to Zimmer, who was already waiting for him. Ortiz clicked his radio once, twice, thrice, giving the signal. He raised the knife above his head and threw it with all his might. The knife left the darkness and briefly reflected the halogen lights as it streaked across the air and savagely plunged itself into the guard's chest.

Ortiz lunged, closing the gap in a few seconds. The guard looked down in disbelief. He was about to scream for help when Ortiz jammed his left hand over the guard's mouth and fiercely drove his right knee into the guard's groin. His right-hand palm struck the knife's handle, driving it deeper into the sentry's chest. The knife stopped on something. A rib maybe. Ortiz struck it again. This time the knife went all the way in.

His gaze locked with the sentry's eyes until Ortiz saw there was no life left in them. He yanked the knife out and jumped to the side as blood jetted from the wound and the body fell to the ground face-first. Ortiz dragged the body back to the jungle and hid it in the undergrowth. Zimmer did the same with the body of the other guard.

Ortiz reached for the radio. They had achieved a "beach-head."

Vanderhoff turned his swivel chair and looked at the Athena V rocket. The restraining tower slowly moved to the side. *T minus five minutes. Just a little while longer,* he thought.

Ortiz and Zimmer helped get the raft past the palm trees and through the light undergrowth as the rest of Mambo took defensive positions near the fence. Siegel deployed his men efficiently—three teams with five men each. Siegel, Ortiz, Zimmer, and two others would remain with the Javelins. They would be Mambo One. Mambo Two would take a defensive position fifty feet up the gravel road. Mambo Three was fifty feet in the other direction. As a backup, Siegel had selected a spot near their landing zone as their emergency fallback position in case things went sour.

"All right, Tito. It's your show now," Siegel said.

Ortiz nodded and leaned over the raft. "Say, Tommy. Gimme a hand, would ya?"

Zimmer walked next to him.

"Help me take the plastic off these missiles."

The weapon of choice was the British-made Javelin instead of the commonly used Stinger for the simple reason that the Stinger was a heat-seeker, which meant there was a possibility of the missile going for the wrong target during a launch, since the hottest point of the rocket's exhaust lay several feet below the nozzle. The Javelin, on the other hand, could be manually guided to the target.

Ortiz took the shoulder-launched aiming unit and removed the protective plastic. He then grabbed the first missile-canister combination and clipped it on to the aiming unit. "There. I'm ready anytime."

Zimmer gave him a puzzled look. "What do you mean? That's it?"

"Yep. That's all there is to it."

Siegel approached them. "You guys about—"

His words were cut short by the fast rattle of several automatic weapons. Ortiz jumped back when three bullets erupted from Siegel's chest, propelling him against Zimmer. Both landed on the ground. Siegel lay convulsing.

"Jesus Christ, man! They hit Siegel. Siegel's been hit!" Zimmer screamed as he tried to drag Siegel to safety.

Ortiz grabbed Zimmer by the shoulder, pulled him away from the raft, and glanced back at Siegel, who lay still on his side, facing them. His wide-open eyes told Ortiz all he needed to know. There was nothing they could do for Siegel. As platoon sergeant, second in command, Ortiz was now in charge.

The entire world appeared to erupt around them as bullets showered the gravel road and sandy terrain. Ortiz went into a roll. He rolled as hard as he possibly could. The sky and sand changed places as he gained momentum with every roll. He had to reach the safety of the palm trees. He continued rolling. He would know when to stop. *Soon,* he thought, estimating he covered three feet with every roll. Rocks and other ground debris bruised him. He slammed hard against the wide trunk of a palm tree. It hurt but was expected. Ortiz knew what to do next.

As the ear-piercing whine of near-misses rang in his ears, he swiftly twisted his body around the palm tree and cautiously rose to a deep crouch on the other side. He rested his back against the tree and quickly shifted his gaze to the right. Zimmer was there. Ortiz looked to his left, saw no one there. Puzzled, he looked back at Zimmer, who shook his head slowly and pointed toward the light undergrowth. Ortiz understood. Three had died in their team, including Siegel. Ortiz reached for the radio.

"This is Mambo One! Situation report!" Ortiz screamed as loud as he could.

"Mambo Two. We've taken three casualties. Someone's sneaked up on us. Can't tell where the fire's coming from. Must be using flash suppressors. The bastards got us pinned down. Can't leave the cover of the trees!"

"Keep cover 'n' fire only if you got a clear target. Save your ammo. Repeat, save your ammo! Mambo Three, are you there, over? Mambo Three? Mambo Two, any word from Mambo Three?"

"Ah, negative, Mambo One."

Ortiz clenched his jaw in rage, frustration, and sheer disbelief. Mambo had lost at least six soldiers during the first twenty seconds of fighting without inflicting any damage on the enemy, not counting losses from Mambo Three. Not a very impressive record. He checked his watch. Launch was due any second now. He eyed the Javelin missile launcher assembly. It lay next to the now-deflated raft, roughly thirty feet away.

"Dammit! Tommy, can you see where's the fire comin' from?"

"Shit, no! Can't even show my nose without gettin' it blown off."

We're in the shit now, thought Ortiz.

Vanderhoff picked up the phone. "Yes? What is all the commotion about?"

"Gunfire, sir. We spotted the intruders in Sector A on the other side of the fence. We have over twenty men engaged at the moment."

"Keep it under control. The launch must go on as planned. Keep them pinned down. Is that understood?"

"Yes, sir!"

Vanderhoff hung up the phone and checked his watch. Less than a minute to go.

Ortiz couldn't wait any longer. It had to be now or never. "I'm goin' back, Tommy!"

"What? You're crazy, man!"

"That's our mission, *hermano*. That's what Siegel and the others died for! I gotta do it." Ortiz dropped to the ground and began to crawl toward the raft. Then he heard the powerful roar. The earth trembled and night became day as a huge ball of orange flames erupted from the launchpad. Ortiz didn't glance in that direction, although he did notice that the shooting had at least temporarily subsided. He kicked his legs harder and harder, gaining foot after agonizing foot of terrain, closing the gap. The raft was now a mere ten feet away. He had to reach it. He was the only one, besides Siegel, who could operate the British-made surface-to-air weapon.

Five feet. Still no fire. He dragged his body through the last few feet, and smiled when his hands came in contact with the cold aluminum canister of the Javelin system. He sat up, rested the weapon on his shoulder, and armed it. The self-contained system came to life. Ortiz quickly acquired the target in the monocular sights. The rocket was beginning to leave the ground. The cloud of smoke and debris seemed small in comparison to the space shuttle launch Ortiz had witnessed several years back, but by no means was it a minor launch.

The enemy found him. The earth exploded as rounds impacted just short. Ortiz didn't sway. His concentration focused on the departing rocket several hundred feet away, he squeezed the trigger and felt the missile come alive and exit the aiming unit. He waited. The flares fitted to the missile went off and were automatically detected by a sensor in the arming unit in order to gather the missile to the center of Ortiz's field of view.

The twenty-six-pound missile reached 1.8 Mach in a matter of seconds as it made its way toward the rocket. Ortiz kept the target centered in his sights. The semi-automatic line-of-sight guidance system generated signals that were sent to the Javelin missile's control surfaces via a radio link.

A bullet struck the side of the aiming unit. Ortiz staggered back, jerking the aiming unit toward the sky. The

Javelin responded and drifted upward.

Mierda!

He recovered quickly. He glanced toward the launchpad. The rocket was roughly ten feet in the air and quickly gaining altitude and speed. Ortiz remembered Marie telling them that the best time to destroy the rocket after lift-off was during the first fifteen seconds, before the rocket shot up at great speed.

Ortiz discarded the used canister, jumped to the raft, grabbed the second missile unit, and quickly clipped it on to the aiming unit.

Even flying at treetop level, Crowe saw the initial blast as the rocket began its launch. It was visible from miles around, creating enough light that his night goggles' automatic gain control decreased sensitivity to the point of being ineffective. He spoke into his voice-activated radio.

"Mambo, this is Stallion One, over."

No response.

"Mambo, Stallion One here. Over."

"Jesus, Stallion One, Mambo here. Hurry! The bastards found us. There's six dead. Repeat six dead. Currently tryin' to complete mission. Can you read our signal on radar, over?"

"Affirmative, Mambo. Heading your way right now."

This time it was different. Ortiz rested his head on a rock and kept the tip of the rocket lined up with his sights. The Javelin's tail of smoke went straight for the target. He saw a small explosion near the rocket's cone.

Crowe noticed something wrong. The large rocket had been slowly ascending in what appeared to be a smooth climb, but that had changed a second ago, when something had struck it. He now understood the mission of the ground team, and silently cursed his superior officers for not giving him the entire story. The Stallions were too close.

"Break left, Stallion Two! My God! Break hard left!"

Too late. The huge rocket stumbled out of control. It turned on its side and quickly accelerated toward the perimeter of the complex, straight toward them.

Crowe threw the cyclic left, forcing his craft into a wickedly tight turn. He could feel branches tearing at the Stallion's underside. He ignored it and kept the turn at the same level. The large rocket hit the ground at great speed. Tens of thousands of pounds of volatile chemicals went off at once less than five hundred feet from their position.

"We've been hit, Stallion One! Mayday. Mayday. This is Stallion Two. We're going down!"

"Keep the pressure on the cyclic, Stallion Two! Keep the pressure!" Instinctively, Crowe put both hands on the cyclic and pulled it back in anticipation of the downward shock wave. It came, forcing the heavy rescue craft down, but the back pressure kept the Stallion's nose above the horizon.

"Stallion One, we can't control it. Can't control—"

Crowe caught a bright flash to his right. It was quickly followed by a thundering roar.

"Madre de Dios, Tommy! Run for your life, *hermano!* One of the rescue choppers just blew up!"

"I'm runnin', man. I'm runnin'."

Ortiz raced back toward the swamp. The blast had ignited most of the palm trees around that section of the chain-link fence, or actually where the fence had been. The heat intensified. Ortiz himself had been lifted off the ground and thrown ten feet by the powerful explosion. He had landed a few feet from Zimmer, who had remained behind a palm tree.

Now they both ran as fast as they possibly could. The area was in flames and Ortiz was certain there would be hell to pay for this. The owners of that rocket would not be pleased to see it destroyed in front of their noses.

"What are we gonna do, man? What?"

"We move inland. Back to where we came from. Back to the—look, man, the second rescue chopper!"

"Mambo, Stallion One, here. Do you copy?"
Static.
"Mambo, this is Stallion One, over."
Nothing.
Crowe's fears were being confirmed. The explosion had occurred very close to Mambo's last tracked position. He exhaled.
"Stallion One, Blue Ridge *here. What in the hell is going on over there?"* It was Davenport's voice crackling through his headphones.
"We lost Stallion Two, sir. That's what in the *hell* is going on. It caught debris from the rocket and exploded the moment it hit the ground. Nobody could survive that. Jesus, sir! Why weren't we told about the rocket? We could have avoided the crash. Damn!"
"What about the ground team?"
"Got something on radar, but nobody answers my calls."
"Radio trouble?"
"Could be. I'll hang around for a few more minutes, sir. Maybe I can spot them."
"What's your fuel situation, Stallion One?"
"Less than a thousand pounds, sir, but there's always air-to-air refueling."
"Stand by, Stallion One."
Crowe pushed the cyclic forward and flew at less than five feet over the swamp with his landing lights on. *They have to be around here somewhere,* he thought as he constantly shifted his gaze back and forth between the radar screen and the horizon.
He hit the intercom switch. "You guys see anything back there?" he asked the two Marines.
"Ah, no, sir. Not a thing yet . . . wait . . . wait. I got something! I see a few men running away from the fence and into the swamp."

"Which way?" Crowe pulled back the cyclic and stopped in a cold hover. He added right rudder and did a three-sixty scan. There! He spotted them. About three hundred feet to the right.

"Stallion One, Blue Ridge. *Standing order is to return immediately. Repeat, return immediately!"*

"Sir, I got soldiers in plain view. They look like our men, sir."

"Have you made contact with them?"

"No, sir, but—"

"Listen up, Stallion One. This order comes straight from the top. Get your ass back here. You're low on fuel and we have no authorization to get a tanker back this way. Come home. Repeat, come home now!"

Crowe tightened his grip on the cyclic. He couldn't believe this was happening to him. Those men were so close. If only he could take a closer look, perhaps he—

"Kenny, if you ever want to fly again, get your ass back in here right now! We can't afford a second crash!"

Crowe eyed the fuel gauges. Nine hundred pounds plus a five-minute reserve. Barely enough. He hastily added power and rudder, and turned the craft around.

"Stallion One, returning to base."

"Wait! Wait! We're here! Come back!" Ortiz shouted when he watched the helicopter turn around.

"They're gone, brother. The bastards left us!"

Ortiz turned his head left. Zimmer had just come up from his right. His face was covered with mud, save for his eyes and open mouth.

"Damn! I can't believe they didn't see us, Tommy." He reached for his radio. It was gone. *"Mierda!"*

"What is it?"

"My radio. It's gone."

Zimmer looked for his. It was still strapped to his belt. He retrieved it and handed it to Ortiz.

"*Puta!* This is incredible," Ortiz said upon inspecting the hand-held unit.

"What is?"

"Your radio's busted. Look." He showed Zimmer the crack along the back.

"Try it anyway."

Ortiz exhaled and brought it to his lips. "Mambo One. This is Mambo One. Anyone out there, over?"

Not even static came through the small speaker. Ortiz shook his head.

"Well, this is just fuckin' great," Zimmer said. "Whatta hell are we suppose to do now? No wonder they left. They probably think we're dead!"

"Damn." Ortiz set the radio back to emergency-transmission mode. The unit responded with a small blip. That portion of the radio was operational. He shifted his gaze back to Zimmer. "At least they'll know where we are. It ain't much, but it's somethin'."

Zimmer shook his head. "That could help another rescue craft to pinpoint us, but what about the rest of Mambo?"

"I don't know. There were two radios per team. At our last radio check, Mambo Two had at least one working radio, but Mambo Three didn't—that's if any of 'em's still alive. So Mambo Two's our only chance. The problem's that the rocket exploded closer to them than us."

"You think they . . ."

"Don't know, *hermano*. All we can do is head for the rendezvous point 'n' hope the rest of Mambo does the same. If we can get a group of five or six, we might have a chance. Now let's go before the enemy gets here."

THE WHITE HOUSE

Stice hung up the phone. The operation had been a success but at the cost of one helicopter and a platoon of men. He would report it like that to the President.

He thought about a rescue operation, but in his mind that was too risky. Mambo was a disposable asset. They had done their job and now the U.S. government would take care of their families and at the same time issue a standard statement of denial of involvement if any part of the operation ever became public.

He closed the file and set it to the side.

LIGHTNING

"Houston? *Lightning.*"

"*Go ahead,* Lightning."

"Things are getting too critical up here. The atmosphere inside the crew module has reached a toxic level. I'm reading seventy-six-percent nitrogen, nineteen-percent oxygen, and five-percent carbon monoxide. I'm afraid our initial estimates were too optimistic. This air is already unsafe." Kessler kept his eyes on the oxygen level. A normal atmosphere was composed of seventy-nine-percent nitrogen and twenty-one-percent oxygen. Carbon monoxide was usually removed by *Lightning*'s atmosphere-revitalization subsystem, mixed with oxygen and nitrogen, and injected back into the crew module, but with *Lightning* operating only on one fuel cell and one oxygen tank, the subsystem could not maintain an adequate amount of oxygen in the air.

"*We are confirming your reading,* Lightning."

"I'm afraid we're gonna have to suit up. I'm finding it harder and harder to breathe in here."

"*We copy,* Lightning. *Don't take any chances. Carbon monoxide will make you sleepy. Get in your suits and call us back.*"

"Roger."

Kessler dove through a hatch and reached the mid-deck compartment. Jones was still unconscious. Kessler approached the large Texan on the horizontal sleeping station, removed the retaining Velcro straps, and gently pulled him toward the air-lock hatch.

He crawled inside the air lock, grabbed a folded personal rescue ball, and pushed it through the hatch into the mid-deck compartment. He unzipped it and brought it closer to Jones. The rescue ball was also made out of tough Ortho fabric over alternate layers of Mylar and Dacron.

He guided Jones into the ball, making sure that his upper body remained straight. Kessler bent Jones's legs, zipped up the ball, and activated the life-support system on its side. The ball quickly filled with oxygen.

Satisfied that his friend was safe, Kessler suited up and returned to the flight deck. In the twenty minutes that it had taken him to suit up and get Jones inside the ball, the oxygen level had dropped another two percent.

SEVENTEEN ★

Conflicting Beliefs

HOWARD AIR FORCE BASE

"So the Defense Secretary gave you the order to pull back?" snapped Pruett over the radio as the Skipper of the *Blue Ridge* gave him a status of the mission.

"Yes, sir."

"And do what? Wait?"

"Yes, sir."

"Do you know where they are?"

"Ah, no, sir. We got visual confirmation that the target was destroyed, but in the process it destroyed one of the rescue helicopters with its crew of four. Two pilots and two Marines. The second chopper hovered around the area for a few more minutes but couldn't see a thing. He reported that the entire side of the compound was ablaze, including the area where our unit was supposed to be."

"Have you tried communicating with them?"

"Repeatedly, sir, but got no response. The pilot claims to have picked up an emergency distress signal on radar. It's possible that some of the men may have made it out alive from that inferno with partially functional radio gear, but that's just a guess. It could also mean that the enemy got ahold of the radios and is trying to draw us back in. Hard to tell without proper communication with the surviving troops, again if any of them's still alive."

Pruett rubbed his eyes and massaged his burning chest. He had achieved his mission, but at what cost? Four men confirmed dead, one craft destroyed, and no confirmation on ground casualties. For all he knew, the entire team could still be intact on the ground with busted communications gear. Pruett frowned. He knew he had to proceed from that assumption. Those men, or at least some of them, could be alive and on the run, and it was his job to get them all out. *How could Stice call the chopper back? It should have remained in the area and then refueled in midair. Damn that Stice!*

"All right," Pruett responded. "Call me back immediately if you hear anything. In the meantime have the returning helicopter refueled and ready to go at a moment's notice. Got that?"

"Yes, sir!"

Pruett passed the mike to the radio operator before looking at Cameron and Marie. "Got all that?"

"Why would Stice do something like that?" asked Marie.

"I'm not sure, but I intend to find out immediately."

Cameron nodded. "You gotta get a chopper to them and get them out. Every second counts."

Pruett nodded and reached for the phone on the wall. He dialed the White House.

U.S.S. *BLUE RIDGE*

Crowe walked away from the decelerating rotor as the crew tied the Sea Stallion onto the flight deck. Although he had hardly slept at all during the past twenty-four hours, the adrenaline kept him frosty, fully awake. His thinking was clear, his determination firm. He spotted Davenport coming up to meet him.

"What in the hell happened, Kenny?"

"What do you think happened, Skipper? I was ordered to leave American soldiers behind. *That's* what happened! And that damned rocket blew up in our faces. Why didn't you tell me that a launch was in progress? Our approach would have been different! Jesus Christ, Skipper, why the secret? And why in the world did we leave them there? I had them in sight!"

"Calm down, Kenny. We all follow orders around here, and no, you *thought* you had them in sight. You didn't have any confirmation."

"Well, sir. Whoever gave you the order not to let me rescue them is a fucking moron! You tell him that. You tell him that his idiotic decision will cost the lives of American servicemen. Those men won't last—"

"Just who in the *fuck* you think you're talking to? I will tell it to you one last time, Commander. Keep your damn mouth shut and do as I tell you to! If I tell you to fucking plunge your craft into the ocean you will do it because that's an order. You got that, mister? Do you?"

Crowe didn't respond. He could see Davenport's arteries throbbing in his neck. Crowe lowered his gaze and stared at the flight deck.

Davenport exhaled. "Look, we all know that we should have stayed in the area a little longer and looked for survivors, but orders are orders. What is the matter with you anyway? Every operation has its risks, especially covert ones. You of all people should know that. You were in Vietnam, weren't you?"

Crowe inhaled deeply through his mouth, clenched his teeth, and slowly exhaled through his nostrils. Davenport was right. In covert operations, standard procedure was not to acknowledge the team until it had left enemy territory.

"Now tell me," Davenport continued, "you're sure about the blip on your screen?"

Crowe closed his eyes for a brief second and then stared into Davenport's intelligent blue eyes. "It was for real, Skipper. It lasted ten minutes and slowly disappeared as I left the Guiana coast."

Davenport didn't respond. He simply turned around and

walked back toward the bridge. Crowe followed him. "Sir, what in the hell is going on?"

"Get your craft ready to go at a moment's notice, Kenny. You're dismissed."

"With all due respect, sir. I'm ready to go right away. Those men—"

Davenport stopped walking, turned around, and got within inches from him. His voice was ice cold. "You listen to me, and listen very carefully. I just gave you a direct order and I expect you to follow it to the letter. I know about those men out there, but I also know the proper chain of command. We need authorization to go back in and get them out. Got that?" Crowe stood mute. "I said did you get that, Commander Crowe."

"Yes, sir. I got it."

"Good. That's all." Davenport turned and continued toward the bridge.

Crowe just stood there, flight helmet in his right hand. He looked over the dark sea toward the Guiana coast. Soldiers were there, American soldiers, most likely outnumbered and outarmed, and he was being asked to sit tight and wait for some Washington bureaucrat to make up his fucking mind about whether or not it was "advisable" to go back in. The old familiar pain returned. He hadn't felt it for nearly two decades, yet there it was once again. The knot in his stomach he'd always gotten when soldiers suffered the ill effects of politicians trying to make military decisions; a feeling he became all too familiar with in Vietnam. He hated it with an overwhelming passion. In a burst of rage, he threw the helmet against the flight deck with all his might, startling several mechanics. Davenport, who still was on the flight deck, also turned his way. No words were spoken.

Crowe slowly walked toward the edge of the flight deck and simply stared at the dark sea. It looked so peaceful. The stars above lazily shed their minute light on the ship's wake. He watched it in silence.

HOWARD AIR FORCE BASE

"But I need to talk to the President right away," Pruett persisted. "You know as much as I do of the urgency of the situation."

"I repeat," Carlton Stice responded. "The President is tied up with the Middle East situation at the moment and cannot be reached. He left me in charge of the operation and I'm telling you to stay put. The target has been destroyed and we're currently evaluating the situation to decide on the proper course of action."

"Who is evaluating the situation, sir? Who are the analysts? How are they evaluating the problem? How can they know more than the pilot from the rescue helicopter? How? *We* sent those men out there, sir. *We* have a moral duty to—"

"I'm telling you to stay put until a decision is made! Is that understood?"

Pruett vigorously rubbed the palm of his right hand against his burning chest. He felt like strangling the little bastard with his bare hands. He was about to say something but the professional in him slammed his jaws shut. Telling Stice what was on his mind would be the fastest way to terminate his career, and it wouldn't do those men out there any good. He breathed in and out several times, forcing his body to relax.

"Are you there, Tom?"

"Yes, sir," he managed to respond by merely moving his lips.

"Well? You with me?"

"I'm always with the President and his decisions, sir."

"Good. Keep it that way."

"Sir? If you don't mind my asking. What is your time frame to respond on this issue?"

"You'll hear from us in due time. In the meantime, stay put. Do not do anything!"

The line went dead. Pruett calmly hung up and reached into his right pocket for the antacid tablets. He popped two in his mouth, thought about it, and popped one more. He crushed them hard and fast as he walked outside the communications room, where Cameron and Marie waited.

"You okay?" asked Cameron.

"That Stice! He sure knows how to piss me off." Pruett couldn't believe the bad luck that always seemed to haunt him. No matter which Administration was in charge of the White House, he had always been able to explain his point of view to the President and most of his staff. But there always were some high-ranking persons who never saw it his way and seemed to enjoy messing up his plans. And now as too often before, it was one of those bureaucrats whom the President had left in charge. A moron who was obviously more concerned about saving face than about the lives of American soldiers in enemy territory.

"Why?" Marie asked. "What happened?"

"Stice put a hold on the operation."

"What?" snapped Cameron.

"You heard me."

"But—but there must be something you can do," Marie said. "That place's nothing but swamps. No human can survive in that place for long."

Pruett pinched his upper lip with his teeth. *There has to be a way to get them out, Tom. Think, dammit. Think!*

Marie looked at Cameron. "We can't simply turn our backs on them, can we? I mean, isn't there another way to help them?"

"You two follow me," Pruett said. "I'm gonna do this right."

"Where are we going?" Marie asked.

"To have a word with General Olson."

NORTH OF KOUROU, FRENCH GUIANA

Suffering from an overwhelming headache, Ortiz took the

lead through the swamp. He waited desperately for the two additional extra-strength Tylenol he'd taken a half hour earlier to kick in. Zimmer followed close behind, Colt Commando up and ready. Nobody was going to mess with them, and if the enemy did, Ortiz was committed to take out as many of them as he could before he went down. Yes, the enemy might have more men and arms, but they lacked the skill. And they lacked the element of surprise. The enemy would have to come looking for Mambo, and when they did, they would pay dearly.

Thick, hardened mud covered his face and neck, cooling the multiple cuts and scrapes left after the removal of the annoying leeches. They didn't hurt anymore. He had overcome that pain as he had overcome the deep burning in his legs from the non-stop retreat. Ortiz pushed on, glancing briefly back at Zimmer, also naturally camouflaged by thick, smelly mud. Neither wore night goggles any longer. Ortiz and Zimmer had opted to bury them in the swamp when their batteries died, along with all the other gear— and bodies—they could find. They'd selected specific landmarks as references, and decided that the possibility of the bodies shifting was minimal based on the thickness of the swamp. Theirs was a covert mission, and they were to leave no sign of their country of origin. No traceable evidence that the enemy could use to embarrass their nation.

Ortiz looked toward the sky and contemplated the stars. He used them to move northwest, back toward the easily defendable clearing, surrounded with thick jungle, at the edge of the swamp. The jungle would give them the mobility and protection they so desperately needed to survive what he expected would be an overpowering attack. In the jungle they would be safe, but they had to reach it before dawn. Their chances of survival during daytime in the swamp were negligible. In the large clearings between clusters of trees they would be openly exposed to the enemy.

No, Ortiz decided. They had to push themselves and reach the jungle. There was no other choice, no other way. Ortiz kicked even harder, propelled himself faster, and closed the gap between themselves and the safety of the jungle.

HOWARD AIR FORCE BASE

"You mean to tell me he called you already?" Pruett asked in sheer disbelief. Stice not only had stopped the rescue mission, but had already contacted Olson and had the entire operation canceled. *Canceled? Is Stice out of his fucking mind?* And why would Stice deliberately lie to him about "calling him back later"? Was that just a ploy to keep Pruett quiet until it was too late to do anything about it?

"He called less than twenty minutes ago, Mr. Pruett," responded a very sleepy Olson as he rubbed his eyes. "He called the operation a success and asked me to write personal letters to all the families involved. A terrible tragedy, but for a very noble cause. He said that Mambo had shown what heroes were made of."

"And you buy that crap, General?"

Olson grunted. "Not for a second. Not for a second."

"You know as well as I do that there is a good possibility that there are a few of Mambo's men out there right now, if not more than a few. Obviously without means of directly communicating with us, but they're out there. Probably waiting and wondering where in the hell we are. Are you going to tell me that you're just gonna sit there and do nothing?"

Olson's face hardened. Pruett knew of Olson's reputation as a fair officer. The rumor was that he'd single-handedly dragged two wounded soldiers out of an ambush and into a rescue helicopter during the Korean conflict, a heroic act that had made him popular among the troops and dramatically boosted his career. Pruett knew Olson had to care about his people, but he was still a soldier, and as such he was compelled to obey his superiors, even during times when he probably strongly disagreed with them. Pruett was banking on the chance that this was one such time, that Olson disagreed with the order but had no choice since it had come directly from the Defense Secretary.

"Have you any—any *fucking* idea of what it feels like to lose a soldier? Have you?"

Pruett stared him in the eye for a few moments. "I was never in the military, General, but I have lost many good field agents. I think the feeling is similar. It eats you up from inside. You feel that you have failed them. That if somehow you had planned things better, they would still be alive. Yes, General. I have been there many times, and it stinks. But in this case it doesn't have to stink all the way. There's still time to do something about it. Do something about those men stranded in Guiana . . . stranded in that hell."

Olson studied him at length. Pruett knew the old general was weighing the odds. He had obviously dedicated his entire life to the Armed Forces, and was not about to throw it all away on an impulsive move, a spur-of-the-moment decision arrived at from an emotional instead of a logical perspective.

"What's on your mind, Mr. Pruett?"

Pruett smiled inwardly. Olson was no fool. One did not get to become a two-star general in the Armed Forces by being a fool. Olson was biding his time, waiting for Pruett to make a move. If that didn't get Olson where he wanted to be, Pruett knew the general would wait for other moves. The question was, where did the general want Pruett to go? Pruett felt certain the answer to that depended on how he responded to the general's question. He leveled his gaze on Olson's.

"I want to get them out. I think I know a way to get in contact with Mambo and get them to a prearranged spot at a specific time and airlift them. *That's* what I want to do."

Olson's lips curved up a little. "Let's assume for a moment that your decision is the right thing to do in this situation.

Under that assumption answer this: How, Mr. Pruett? How do you propose doing that? Of course, without me knowing about it."

Pruett also smiled. Olson was playing ball. The general would go along by simply looking the other way. If anything went wrong with Pruett's plan and heads began to roll, Olson would be out of reach since he was not involved in it. Pruett was merely acting of his own accord. Olson couldn't lose. If Pruett succeeded, then Olson could emerge smelling like a rose. If it backfired, then only Pruett's ass would be on the line, not his. Pruett slowly nodded, accepting the unwritten terms of Olson's conditional help.

Thirty minutes later Pruett shook hands with Olson and walked outside. He checked his watch. Dawn was just over the horizon. He spotted Cameron and Marie sitting on the hood of their jeep.

"Hmm . . . that was long," Cameron said as he yawned and stretched. "What did the general say?"

Pruett smiled. "Do you still remember how to jump out of a plane?"

"What? What in the hell are you—wait a second, wait a fucking second. You're not serious about me going—"

"That's the only deal I could make with the general, Cameron. He has agreed to give us a lift to Guiana and look the other way, but he would not commit any more of his men."

"Look, Tom. I'm not the same Special Forces soldier you recruited fifteen years ago. The game has vastly improved since then and I haven't been keeping up. I know my limitations. I'm telling you, I'm not qualified. Those new Special Forces teams like Mambo can run circles around me in no time. They're much better trained than any team in 'Nam."

"Yes, but none of them has experienced battle. You have."

"What's that got to do with—"

"Everything. I think there's another reason you don't want to go. Is there something you want to tell me?"

Cameron glanced at Marie, lowered his gaze, and remained silent.

Pruett continued. "Actually, I don't want to hear your motives for going or not going. All I can tell you is that either you go and make contact with those guys, or we leave them behind. There is no time for hesitation at this point. We might already be too late."

Cameron took a few steps away from the jeep and quietly watched an F-4E Phantom taking off on full afterburners. He had dedicated his entire life to the military and the CIA at the price of writing off his personal life. *And all for what? Have I really made a difference? Do I really want to end up ill and alone like Tom?* With Marie, Cameron knew he had a chance at really living again. Why risk his life any further? He glanced back at Marie. She walked to his side and held his hand.

"You have to do what's right in your heart," he heard her say as he watched the white-hot tail of the Phantom disappear in the dark sky. Cameron closed his eyes and saw another phantom appearing in his mind. *Go, Cameron . . . I'll be all right . . . you can make it on . . .*

Cameron opened his eyes, turned around, and looked at Pruett. "All right. I'm in."

LIGHTNING

Michael Kessler stared at the stars but in his mind he saw the sea. The tranquil, blue sea. Kessler smiled when he spotted flecks of light reflecting off the swells. It was so vivid, so perfect. In his mind he was there, back on the flight deck of the U.S.S. *Constitution,* back on the number-one catapult staring at the cat officer wearing the standard yellow jersey and solemnly waving his green flashlight wand at him. The blazing sun slowly disappeared below the horizon, transforming the orange-stained sky into one with a less vivid hue. Back inside the cockpit of an F-14D Tomcat, gently applying full throttle in response to the cat officer's hand signals, Kessler felt the plane tremble as it endured the overwhelming stress just before ferocious Gs piled up on him, jamming his very soul against the flight seat . . .

Then Kessler saw Jones struggling to eject out of his wounded bomber. He heard the Air Force captain scream in agony as the F-111B's cockpit filled with flames, killing the navigator. Kessler had failed them. He had arrived too late. Jones left the blazing craft and shot upward under the power of his ejection seat's solid-propellant rocket. *I'm sorry, Tex* . . .

Kessler's mind jumped to the moment in time when he had to eject after losing his first dogfight. He involuntarily held his breath as the frightening memory overwhelmed his senses. For a second, perhaps two, he felt consumed by the terror of not being able to reach the ejection handles. Then he finally did, pulling them as hard as he had ever pulled anything in his life. Then came the savage explosion. The canopy flew up and he followed. The wind tore at him. His body was thrown up, to the side, and flipped upside down. The earth and sky changed places over and over again as the Gs pushed down on him with titanic force. Then the peace of free-falling at 130 miles per hour descended upon him. He welcomed the feeling of isolation. Kessler had never felt more alone than at that moment. Until now.

All was quiet aboard *Lightning*. Too quiet. Deathly quiet. Only the sound of his own breathing interrupted the silence. It seemed amplified in the quiet of space. Inhale. Exhale. Inhale. Exhale. Kessler's mind grasped at the edge of consciousness as he struggled to remain in control, despite the fact that his suit's oxygen supply had been nearly consumed. He thought about switching suits but decided against it. The air inside the crew module had also reached a hazardous level long ago. Besides, removing the space suit was no longer an option. Incapable of moving, he had lost physical control of most of his body, as he slowly asphyxiated in his own carbon monoxide. But his mind refused to go. It refused to take that final jump into the unknown that Kessler had always been reluctant to accept. In his opinion there were no unknowns. Everything had a simple, logical explanation. There was nothing complex in life. All was either black or white. For Kessler, the definition of life was not written in long, convoluted sentences. Life was expressed in simple terms. Simple words like freedom, loyalty, decency, friendship . . . love. That's what life was all about. Simple, logical, yet very human. Unlike most people he'd known, Kessler had always tried to remain in close touch with real feelings. With the real emotions usually found deep below self-imposed layers of pride and mistrust. He refused to take that final step, refused to leave a world he'd grown to enjoy, a world that still had so much to offer to him. There were still so many feelings he had not experienced, so many feelings he longed to make a part of his life, that the mere thought of never having the chance to savor them sent chills across his weakened, exhausted body.

He floated gently inside the flight deck, too tired to report to Houston that he was still there, still alive. Still hopeful something would happen. Something that would save him from what seemed to be his destiny. Kessler had never been very religious, but he believed enough in a Higher Authority to know that he would somehow be judged for his life on Earth. He could feel it. Perhaps it was the reason his life was quickly flashing before his eyes.

Am I already dead? Is this just an illusion? He wasn't sure any longer . . . but there was the breathing. His ears still registered his breathing. He had to be alive. He had to hang on.

He shifted his gaze toward the stars and smiled, not at the peaceful, crystalline cosmos visible through the front windowpanes, but at his own life. At the scenes that continued to flash vividly past him. They were gone as fast as they came but he remembered them all. Every single one of them contributed to the way he felt; like a small leaf on a large tree, every person, every feeling, every encounter had added something to his life.

Kessler felt a hard object against his left leg but could not see what it was. He had closed his eyes and could not open them any more. He tried once more but failed. It was hopeless. Then all began to fade away. His mind became too cloudy, too irrational. He could not control his thoughts any longer. He fought violently but it was no use. He had lost the battle and decided to surrender gracefully.

"I found the second one," reported Valentina Tereshkova as she snagged Kessler's leg and pulled him toward her.

"Is he alive?"

"Can't tell for sure. There are some readings on the front of the suit but I don't know what some of them mean. The oxygen level appears to be extremely low, though."

"Bring him in."

"Yes." Tereshkova clipped a woven line to the side of Kessler's suit and dragged him down to the mid-deck compartment where Strakelov was examining the readings on the small panel on the side of Jones's rescue ball.

"This one appears to be in good shape, at least as far as I can tell. Let's put them both inside the air lock."

Wearing their Orlon-DMA suits, Strakelov and Tereshkova placed both Kessler and Jones inside the air lock and closed the hatch. The American vessel was well built, Strakelov reflected. It had a huge air-lock section to suit up in and a large hatch for EVA activity, larger than the one on *Kvant-2*. Strakelov depressurized the air lock and then opened the exterior hatch leading to the payload bay.

He went out first and briefly glanced up toward the *Mir* complex floating a hundred feet above, between them and the Earth's surface. He shifted his gaze back toward Tereshkova and held up his right hand. "Wait, Valentina."

Strakelov gently pushed himself toward the *Ikar* bicycle and backed himself against it. After securing the suit on the backpack system with the side straps, Strakelov powered up the system. Two locator lights came on, a red one over his left shoulder and a green one over his right. The idea behind the color scheme was to be able to identify which direction a spacewalker was heading. Green on the left and red on the right meant the cosmonaut was approaching the observer. The opposite scheme meant the cosmonaut was moving away from the observer. The idea was copied from the red and green lights on the wingtips of aircraft.

He used the hand controls to thrust himself back toward the open air-lock hatch. The four primary rear thrusters of the 440-pound cosmonaut-mobility unit puffed compressed air in one direction and gently pushed him in the other. The *Ikar* backpack system had a total of thirty-two compressed-air thrusters, sixteen primary and as many backups. In the event of one thruster system failing, the cosmonaut could safely maneuver the unit back to the space station by switching to auxiliary control.

Strakelov slowly came to a halt as he got within five feet of the hatch. Tereshkova passed him a long woven line, already attached to both Kessler's suit and Jones's rescue ball. He clipped his end to a stress point on the side of the *Ikar* and turned himself around using the four thrusters on each side of the backpack system.

"Ready, Valentina?"

Tereshkova finished pushing both astronauts through the hatch and then floated toward her *Ikar*. She backed herself into her backpack system and clipped the other end of the woven line to her suit. "Ready, Nikolai Aleksandrovich."

Strakelov lightly applied thrusters to put tension on the line. He felt a small tug. Swiftly, he pointed himself up toward *Kvant-2* and fired the thrusters for three seconds. That was enough to get his caravan heading in the right direction. The short trip took less than a minute.

When Strakelov estimated they were thirty feet from

Kvant-2's opened hatch, he spoke in his voice-activated headset.

"Fire reverse thrusters."

Tereshkova, who was at the other end of the caravan, fired a two-second burst on all four primary forward-facing thrusters. Strakelov felt the rear tug as they slowed down. From there on it was a true team effort, with Strakelov firing his thrusters from one end and Tereshkova from the other to keep tension on the line as they slowly maneuvered their way to *Kvant-2*. Strakelov got within a foot of the outside wall and clipped his end of the line to a handle next to the hatch. He then piloted the *Ikar* to the external docking station, where he easily backed into the electromagnetic locking mechanism. The system engaged, securing the *Ikar* to the side wall.

Strakelov unstrapped himself and carefully crawled on the side wall back toward the hatch. Tereshkova did the same from the other end. Between the two of them they pulled both astronauts inside the air-lock/workshop module and closed the hatch. Strakelov pressurized the chamber, and quickly removed his suit and helped Tereshkova with hers.

They removed the helmet from Kessler's suit and unzipped Jones's rescue ball. They checked for vital signs. They were weak.

"Baikonur Control. *Mir* here."

"Hello, Nikolai Aleksandrovich. Status?"

"Both astronauts are alive. The mission was a success."

"Congratulations, Nikolai and Valentina! We shall relay the information to our American colleagues."

"We will take the astronauts to the medical bay. We will update you on their situation as soon as we can."

"Acknowledged, Nikolai. Good job."

Strakelov shifted his gaze toward Tereshkova, who had already unlocked the metal ring connecting the upper and lower torso section of Kessler's space suit. He smiled. Their suits were very much like the American's. He leaned over and pulled Jones out of the rescue ball.

TEN THOUSAND FEET ABOVE WESTERN FRENCH GUIANA

In full camouflage gear, Cameron quietly sat next to Marie while staring at the red light above the StarLifter's paratrooper door. Pruett had not come along this time. His stomach was in havoc. Cameron understood.

"You okay?" she asked while holding his hand.

"Well, last time I did this was over fifteen years ago in Vietnam. I hope it all comes back . . . it *better* come back, and fast. I have the feeling that things are gonna get nasty down there."

"Are you sure you want to do this?"

Cameron briefly closed his eyes. "I don't have a choice. I have to do it. It's the only way, not just for Mambo, but also for myself."

She pressed her side against his, resting her head on his left shoulder. "I know."

The door leading to the cabin swung open. A large black soldier, also dressed in camouflage fatigues, approached them.

"One minute, sir!" The soldier unlocked the paratrooper door. The light over the door turned yellow.

Cameron got up. "It's time."

"Please be careful. Please."

Cameron ran a finger over her right cheek and felt her overpowering stare reach deep inside him.

"Twenty seconds, sir!" The soldier opened the paratrooper door.

With Marie's hair swirling in the wind, Cameron put on his goggles, strapped his automatic weapon to his right leg, and silently stared at the fingers of the soldier's right hand counting from five to one.

"Go, go, go!" the soldier screamed.

Cameron took one final glance at Marie before he jumped into the abyss.

EIGHTEEN ★

Jungle Creatures

NORTH OF KOUROU, FRENCH GUIANA

Ortiz remained still at the edge of the jungle, as did Zimmer and five other members of Mambo who had made it to the rendezvous point two hours earlier. Between them they managed to piece the entire incident together, and had come to the conclusion that of the fifteen original members, six had been confirmed dead, which meant two were still missing.

Everything had been quiet until thirty minutes ago, when a plane had flown over them at what Ortiz estimated was ten thousand feet, perhaps a bit more. Now two helicopters were departing the clearing after unloading two teams of hard-faced soldiers, who definitely looked different and acted differently from the sentries Ortiz and Zimmer had taken out the night before.

Covered by a foot of wet leaves, Ortiz had scanned the group under the first rays of the morning sun. He'd counted six men in the first team and seven in the second. Thirteen well-armed men against the seven remaining members of Mambo, two of whom had lost their automatic weapons during the explosion and only had their handguns and hunting knives to defend themselves.

The soldiers had jumped off the helicopters, rolled twice, gotten to their feet, and raced for the other side of the clearing, disappearing in the thick jungle.

How did they find us? Ortiz asked himself. He felt confident no one had followed them. The Mambo team had arrived at the clearing before dawn. The chance of someone spotting and following them was small. What if someone had been captured? What if one of Mambo's missing members had fallen into enemy hands and been tortured to reveal their fallback position? He moved back into the jungle and signaled Zimmer to do the same.

"You think they know we're here?" Zimmer asked.

"Either that or they think we might be comin' this way."

"There's too many of 'em, Tito. How are we gonna get away? They don't look like amateurs to me."

"Nope, they sure don't look like rookies, but neither do we. Don't underestimate the trainin' we got under our belts. We're just as good as or better than them."

"Well, maybe *now* we still are, since we still have our ammo 'n' our individual food supplies, but after a few days we'll get tired and—"

"You listen to me. We're playin' this one smart. We'll follow 'em 'n' keep a close eye on 'em. As long as we know where they are we'll be all right. The only thing I still don't get's how in the hell they managed to get dropped so close to us. Luck? Don't know, man."

The rest of Mambo gathered around them. Ortiz scanned the group. All eyes were on him. All depended on him. He was now their leader.

"All right, listen up. We gotta assume those men know we're in the area. They probably got orders to shoot to kill. Our first priority is not to kill 'em, but to stalk 'em to make sure we know where they are at all times. I wanna follow their every move an' determine the type of gear they got." He noticed several puzzled looks, and smiled. "We only got one goal, guys, an' that's to get outta here alive. We've already accomplished our mission. Now we gotta find a way to get outta this place. Main problem is that we ain't got no means of communicatin' with our people, 'cept for this radio, which transmits an emergency distress signal. In order to get airlifted, we need a two-way communication channel, an' the only way I see of gettin' one's by stealin' the enemy's. I'm assumin', of course, that they're carryin' radios. All with me now?"

The puzzled looks disappeared and were replaced by signs of admiration. He had acted like a leader and had earned their respect. Now it was up to all of them to carry through with his plans.

Cameron had heard the helicopters only five minutes after he'd finished untangling his parachute from a nearby tree. He had managed to fold it and stow it away, along with his backpack, in record time, and was now closing in on the troops he'd seen jumping off the hovering craft.

Cameron frowned at first. He felt too old to be doing this, but the professional soldier in him resurfaced faster than he had anticipated. The jungle surrounded him once more. He inhaled deeply, filling his lungs with the smell of trees. It was a somewhat welcome feeling. Perspiration had soaked his shirt. The temperature was already way into the nineties and the sun had barely loomed over the horizon. A light fog hid the ground. It reached his knees. Cameron cruised through it as he approached the section of jungle where the group of soldiers had disappeared.

He moved in a crouch, keeping his head low and scanning the surroundings as he reached the tree line. His weapon was a silenced Heckler & Koch MP5 submachine gun, the preferred weapon of the elite British Special Air Service troopers. He kept his left hand under the sound-suppressed barrel unit and his right on the trigger. The telescopic metal butt was not extended, making it easier to handle.

Cameron remained some fifty feet behind the last soldier. *They're good,* he reflected, but it was obvious to Cameron that they had never seen actual combat before. Their moves were too "textbook," too systematic. There was no natural rhythm in their advance. Cameron decided to follow them for a few minutes to see where they were headed. He guessed they would lead him to Mambo.

Cameron checked his wrist-mounted homing unit. It automatically picked up Mambo's distress signal and indicated its closeness by the frequency with which a small red light blinked. After a few minutes the frequency decreased, which told him he was moving away from the source. Cameron smiled. The soldiers were going in the wrong direction. He stopped and turned around.

Ortiz spotted someone else entering the jungle after the soldiers, someone not dressed like the other soldiers but more like a U.S. Special Forces soldier. The camouflaged fatigues and cap were straight out of the jungle-warfare section of the training manual. The man had reached the trees, performed a brief scan of the clearing with his weapon, and then gone in among them. The weapon, though, was definitely not a Colt but something else. The thick barrel told Ortiz it was a silenced weapon of some sort, but he was too far away to make it out.

He looked back at his platoon. "Tommy, you come with me. The rest of you spread out along the edge of the clearin' an' give us cover. Don't fire unless you got a specific target, an' only if that target presents imminent danger. Even then, try to take the target out with a knife. Remember, one shot an' our concealment's gone. They'll know for sure where we are. Everybody got that?"

He saw them all nod.

"All right. Give us 'bout fifteen minutes. If we haven't come out after that, come in. If you hear shootin' also come in as soon as possible." He passed the radio strapped to his belt to another soldier. "Hang on to this till I get back. Let's go, Tommy."

Cameron smiled when the frequency of the flashing light increased. He was getting closer to the target. It was obvious to him that Mambo—or at least the generator of the distress signal—was on the other side of the clearing, which was still about a hundred feet away. He continued moving toward the edge of the clearing, carefully scanning the trees ahead for signs of sentries. Even though he felt certain that all the soldiers were moving the other way, there was always the chance of one remaining behind to provide cover for the landing zone.

The sunlight filtered through the dense trees, creating spots of light in the otherwise murky jungle. Cameron remembered to try to avoid such bright spots since they could temporarily blind him by dilating his pupils. Even with all the care he took in walking around them, a beam of sunlight reached his face. He instinctively shut his eyes but it was too late, enough light had entered his eyes to dilate his pupils. He stepped away into the shadows and rapidly blinked to readjust his vision. He scanned the jungle and frowned when he noticed several bright spots in his field of view. Cameron knew it would take about a minute before the spots faded away and he would be able to see clearly again.

He remained uncomfortably still, hiding behind a thick tree trunk, firmly clutching his MP5. Once more he scanned the terrain ahead and froze. Something didn't feel right. His ears had heard a sound that didn't belong in the jungle. Straight ahead. He struggled to see what had caused the light metallic noise. Then he saw the well-camouflaged soldier, the leaf-covered shape of a man lying on his stomach next to a tree. *Which way's he facing?* Cameron couldn't tell. His instincts told him that it was toward the clearing.

That guy's good, Cameron thought as he moved sideways. Now he had to be extremely careful to disguise his own sounds as he made a wide sweep to position himself behind and to the right of the soldier. If his experience had taught him anything it was that he definitely didn't want to approach straight from behind; the soldier had probably booby-trapped the area directly behind him to protect himself from exactly this type of attack.

As he made his approach, Cameron scrutinized the leaf-covered terrain for signs of disturbance. The only type of trap that anyone could have set up in such a short period of time was a small antipersonnel mine, easily concealable under the leaves.

He proceeded in a crouch, carefully feeling the terrain ahead with the tip of his boot. Most mines required only two to five pounds of pressure to go off. Cameron lightly brushed his foot over the terrain and moved the leaves aside to get a clean view of the hardened soil prior to setting his foot down. The procedure retarded his advance, but the alternative made it worthwhile. The soldier lay less than thirty feet away. The long barrel protruding through the leaves told Cameron the soldier was indeed facing the clearing.

A gentle breeze swayed the branches of nearby trees. Cameron took advantage of that to move a bit faster since he now had the wind to help him mask the sound he made when moving leaves to the side. Twenty feet. The sentry remained still. The wind intensified a bit. Fifteen feet. He dropped to a deep crouch and slung the MP5 across his back. He wanted to take him alive. He needed information.

Cameron curled his fingers around the plastic handle of a black-coated, serrated-edge, hunting knife. He took another step.

Snap!

Cameron froze for a brief second. The figure began to emerge from under the blanket of red and brown leaves. Cameron moved swiftly, closing the ten-foot gap in under three seconds. The soldier was about to bring his weapon around when Cameron grabbed the barrel with his left hand and pointed it to the sky, dropping the knife in the process. It was an AK-47 assault rifle. The weapon went off once, twice. Both men rolled on the ground. Cameron brought his right knee up, driving it viciously into the man's testicles. The blow had the desired effect. The soldier let go of the weapon and they both continued to roll. They crashed against a tree and separated. Cameron felt the MP5 flying to the side.

Cameron got to his feet in seconds and noticed the soldier had done the same. The man pulled out a knife from his belt. Cameron realized he had dropped his own knife to grab the AK's barrel. He saw the soldier's lips curving upward.

Cameron assumed a fighting stance—left leg forward, body sideways to the soldier—and waited. He would let the soldier make the first move. The soldier did, starting to walk in a circle. Cameron did the same. The circle got smaller and smaller, until suddenly the soldier slashed the knife out in a semicircle. Cameron stepped back. The soldier slashed it again. Cameron retreated again. This time, though, Cameron's back crashed against the trunk of a tree. He was trapped. The soldier's face hardened. Cameron knew what that meant.

The soldier lunged with the knife in front and aimed for Cameron's breastbone. Cameron reacted swiftly, pivoting on his left leg and rotating his body sideways to the attacker, missing the incoming blade by an inch. The soldier's arm went past him. The knife plunged itself into the bark. Cameron grabbed the attacking wrist with his right hand and palm-struck the elbow with his left.

"Aghh!"

The soldier stepped back and stared in disbelief at his arm, broken at a repulsive angle. Before he could react, Cameron stepped sideways, coiled his left leg, and extended it upward, heel up, toes pointing down. The powerful sidekick landed on the soldier's gear vest and pushed him down. Cameron jumped on top and sat on the soldier's chest, pressing his knees against the soldier's arms.

"Who are you? Identify yourself!"

The soldier stared back at him and in a single move, managed to lift both legs and encircle Cameron's neck, pulling him back. Cameron rolled back and easily freed himself from the lock. The soldier broke into a run. Cameron knew he could not let him go alive.

"Vite! Au secours! Au secours!" Cameron heard him scream.

Cameron jumped left, landed on his side, and grabbed the MP5. He set the side lever to single-shot, trained it on the departing French soldier, and fired once. The sound suppressor absorbed most of the noise, letting out only a barely audible spitting sound. He noticed his aim with the MP5 had not worsened through the years. The soldier was propelled forward and crashed onto the leaves headfirst. Cameron got up and quickly ran over and felt for a pulse. There was none. The bullet had entered the soldier's back and exploded as it exited through his chest, leaving a hole large enough to fit a fist in. Cameron turned him over and quickly checked for documents, but found none. He knew he didn't have much time left. The rest of the unit was probably on the way after hearing the AK-47's shots.

Cameron slung the MP5 across his back, grabbed the soldier's feet, and dragged him toward a thick cluster of trees. He turned around and froze, staring straight into the black muzzle of a Colt Commando.

"Hola, cabron. I remember you."

Cameron didn't answer. He heard a noise to his left and shifted his gaze in that direction. There stood another soldier. The first one scraped off some of the mud off his face.

Cameron raised an eyebrow. "Ortiz?"

"Yeah, *pendejo.* What took you guys so long?"

Cameron exhaled. "You shouldn't have done that, Ortiz. I could have—"

"I doubt it, man. By the way the name's Tito, not Ortiz."

Cameron smiled. "All right, Tito. You've convinced me that you're good, but if you want to remain alive, we better get the hell out of here right away. I brought some supplies with me. They're behind that tree. Where's the rest of Mambo?" Cameron headed for a rosewood tree fifty feet away. Ortiz followed him.

"On the other side of the clearin'. Where we going?"

"Home, Tito. We're going home."

U.S.S. *BLUE RIDGE*

Crowe bolted up from the bed the moment Davenport stormed in.

"Up, Kenny! We've found them."

"Found them? Where? How?"

"I'll tell you on the way. We don't have much time. From what we were told, there are seven soldiers and a civilian alive and well."

"A civilian?"

"Well, not exactly. CIA. He's the one that found them. Anyway, get dressed and see me by the Stallion in five minutes. Let's go, let's go!" Davenport left.

Crowe jumped off his bunk, pulled up his flight suit, put on his boots, and grabbed the flight helmet next to his foot locker. He headed for the deck.

KOUROU, FRENCH GUIANA

Vanderhoff stormed into the mission control room of the complex and walked past scientists and technicians working in coordination with cleanup crews by the launchpad. All of the fires had been extinguished, and workers were now shoveling the debris off the launching complex.

He reached the other side of the room, where a locked door led to another high-security room. Vanderhoff got his magnetic card out and inserted it in the slot by the door. The red light above the door turned green and he heard the locking mechanism snap. The door then automatically slid into the wall. He stepped into another room as the sliding door closed behind him. There were two technicians working there. Both looked in his direction. Vanderhoff addressed the younger of the two.

"It's time to get our backup plan into motion."

The young operator exhaled. "Sir, do you understand the implications?"

"I understand. Do it and call me when it's done."

"Yes, sir."

With that, Vanderhoff turned around and left the room.

NINETEEN ★

New Faces

MIR SPACE COMPLEX

For Michael Kessler, the world seemed out of focus. The harder he squinted and blinked to clear his sight, the blurrier things got. He gave up and exhaled as he noticed a figure looking over him. Kessler tried to move but couldn't. He was somehow immobilized.

"Astronaut Kessler? Mikhail Kessler? Can you hear me?"

Mikhail? What struck Kessler the most was not the question, but the deep female voice and the heavy Slavic accent. It almost sounded as if the woman was trying to fake it.

"Mikhail Kessler? I'm holding your hand. If you can hear me squeeze it tight."

Hear you? Of course I can hear you. Kessler squeezed her hand.

"Good, Mikhail, very good. Now listen carefully. You are aboard Space Station *Mir*. Your government asked our government for help. Do you understand what I'm saying?"

Another squeeze.

"Good. Your friend, Captain Jones, is in critical condition. It appears that he suffered internal injuries from the accident with your version of the space bicycle. We must get him to Earth as soon as possible."

265

Slowly, her face came into focus. A light olive-skinned woman with short black hair and brown eyes wearing a bright-orange jumpsuit. She smiled.

"Who . . ."

"My name is Valentina Tereshkova. I'm the flight engineer for the mission, and lucky for you I also speak English."

"How long have I—we been here?"

"We rescued you over six hours ago. You had depleted the oxygen supply of your space vehicle."

"*Lightning* . . . where is the orbiter?"

"About thirty meters below us. You know, you are lucky we found you when we did. A little longer and you and your friend would have died."

Kessler scanned the compartment. It was spacious as far as spacecraft were concerned. Definitely much larger than *Lightning*'s mid-deck compartment.

"Tex, you said he's in—"

"Tex? Are you referring to Captain Jones?"

Kessler smiled thinly. "Yes."

"Yes, we have him temporarily stabilized, but he has suffered serious internal injuries. He must undergo surgery immediately."

Kessler shifted his gaze to the Velcro straps that held him down on a horizontal sleeping station, very similar to the ones aboard *Lightning*. Tereshkova nodded and unstrapped him. He slowly moved his limbs and rolled out his neck a few times. "*Hmm* . . . much better."

Another person entered the compartment, a large-framed man with pronounced high cheekbones and square jaw. He floated next to Tereshkova and stared at Kessler.

"This is Commander Nikolai Aleksandrovich Strakelov. He speaks very little English."

Kessler extended his hand. Strakelov smiled and shook it vigorously.

"I need to get in contact with Houston Control, Valentina. There must be a way to get Tex back to Earth fast."

"We have news that the orbiter *Atlantis* will be launched in twenty-four hours."

Kessler shook his head. "Twenty-four hours? Plus another eight or so to catch up with us? In your opinion, can Tex last that long?"

Tereshkova frowned, turned to Strakelov, and spoke in Russian for a few moments. She stopped and Strakelov also frowned and slowly shook his head. Kessler understood. Jones didn't have much time to live. If he was to save his friend's life he had to act fast. There had to be a way to get him down more quickly. He looked at Tereshkova.

"I assume you came up in a Soyuz spacecraft?"

"Yes, Mikhail, but if you are thinking what I'm thinking, I suggest you think again. We had a problem during lift-off. Several of our heat shields flared open. Most fell off. The rest are still hanging onto the spacecraft. A supply ship is due here in a month with the new heat shields. Besides, Captain Jones is in a very delicate condition. He has already suffered enough inside the rescue ball. Nikolai Aleksandrovich thinks he has several broken ribs. If we move him more than necessary, he could puncture a lung. Inside the Soyuz space is very cramped and he might not endure the trip."

Kessler closed his eyes and inhaled. How? How could he get Jones back down in time to save him? He was in what appeared to be a no-win situation. *Lightning* was stranded until *Atlantis* delivered the thermal blankets he'd requested to patch up the sections of exposed aluminum. *Atlantis* would also empower *Lightning* enough to close the payload bay doors and get the oxygen to a safe level for long enough to reach Edwards Air Force Base in California safely. But with *Atlantis* over thirty hours away, Kessler decided that was not an immediate option. The Soyuz spacecraft was in no better shape, also missing heat shields . . . *heat shields? Oh, Jesus!*

He bolted up from the sleeping station. "You said there are some heat shields hanging off the Soyuz spacecraft?"

Tereshkova narrowed her eyes. "Well, yes, Mikhail. Why do you ask?"

Kessler smiled. He'd found a way. It was a long shot but he had to try. His friend's life depended on that.

KOUROU, FRENCH GUIANA

The four-thousand-kilogram Intelsat 9-F2/Athena communications satellite had maintained the same orbit since its launch five years earlier. The malfunction of the second stage of an Athena rocket booster had left the twelve-by-four-meter satellite, originally intended for a geosynchronous orbit 25,000 miles over the Earth, stranded in low Earth orbit. The original recovery plan by Athena had been to wait for the correct window in space and use the satellite's still functional third-stage boosters to reach a rendezvous with an American orbiter and haul it back to Earth. But with the *Challenger* disaster, the salvage mission had been delayed by almost ten years. In the meantime, Athena had committed to keeping the huge two-hundred-million-dollar satellite from re-entering Earth by simply firing the booster once a month to maintain a safe orbit.

Vanderhoff finished reading the report from the young technician and smiled. It was his last chance. The Intelsat 9-F2's boosters had just been fired for thirty seconds, but not to push the satellite to a higher and safer orbit as in the dozens of times before. The rockets were fired only after the young technician, via radio link, used the satellite's small vernier thrusters to turn the long satellite around. This caused the thrust to slow the satellite and force it to a lower orbit forty-five miles below.

Vanderhoff checked his watch. There was still a chance to succeed. Even with the failure to launch his Athena rocket, Vanderhoff could still pull it through. It was risky but doable.

The phone rang. He picked it up on the first ring.

"Yes?"

"Hello, Monsieur Vanderhoff."

"General Chardon, how is your team doing?"

"That's what I'm calling about. The team reported one casualty."

"Well, that's always expected."

"I agree, but a good commander is always trying to minimize casualties. I'm sending in more men to make sure everyone in the team has someone else to cover his back. The soldier that was killed was alone."

"Understood, General. Call me when your men have news."

NORTH OF KOUROU, FRENCH GUIANA

Cameron noticed the twelve soldiers standing at the other side of the large clearing. They appeared to be waiting for something or someone to come and pick them up.

He shrugged and turned back toward their landing zone four hundred feet away. He had selected the spot. Easy to defend. Two sides were muddy swamps. Mambo would be able to spot anyone coming from nearly half a mile away. The other two sides were shielded by thick jungle, making it easier for Mambo to retreat and hide if it ever came to that. The clearing itself was only about sixty feet square, just barely large enough to accommodate the Stallion rescue helicopter already on its way from the *Blue Ridge*.

Cameron reached a spot two hundred feet from the clearing, and smiled when he spotted Zimmer and another soldier setting up trip wires.

"How's it going?"

"Just a second," Zimmer responded as he tied a nylon line to a hand grenade, removed the safety pin, and carefully wedged the pear-shaped object between a low branch and the trunk of a tree. He then ran the nylon line at knee level from the tree to another tree twenty feet away. He tied the line to the tree and checked the tension. Satisfied, he shifted his gaze to Cameron. "What do you think?"

Cameron was impressed. "Not bad, Tommy. Couldn't have done it better myself."

"This is the sixth trip wire we've deployed. I think another six or seven more and there ain't nobody comin' near this place without us knowin' about it."

Cameron nodded. "It sure looks that way. Say, where's Tito?"

"He's back there, 'bout a hundred feet down."

"All right. See you later." Cameron continued walking for another minute before slowing down.

"Tito? Are you here? Tito?"

No response. He walked a little farther.

"Tito? Are you around—"

"Don't take another step or you'll be sorry, man."

"What in the hell . . ."

"We're up here."

Cameron shifted his gaze up, and was startled to see three weapons aimed in his direction. One was Ortiz's Colt Commando. The other two were the M-16s of two of Ortiz's men, both of whom had smiles on their faces. All three lay flat on their bellies over thick branches twenty feet above him.

"Stay still, Cameron. I mean it, man." Ortiz slung the Colt, crawled back toward the trunk and climbed down.

"What's going on? Why the warning?"

"See this?" Ortiz kneeled down and carefully brushed the leaves away revealing a nylon rope.

"Yeah, what about it?"

"Come, let me show you where it goes." He walked to the other side of the thick tree and pointed to a large rock suspended thirty feet in the air. "One end of the rope's connected to a net we laid out in that area over there." He pointed to the area Cameron had been about to walk through. "The other end's connected to that rock. Anyone that steps into it will wind up tangled up in the net 'n' lifted thirty feet in the air. Figure it can handle up to two soldiers at once."

"I guess they teach you guys better stuff than in my days."

"Oh, you in the military?"

"Used to be. Had four tours in 'Nam, three of them with the Special Forces. The CIA recruited me a few years after the war and sent me on a prolonged vacation to sunny Mexico."

Ortiz smiled. *"Hablas Español?"*

"Lo hablo mejor que tu, cabron."

Ortiz laughed out loud. "I doubt you can speak it better than I do, but I won't argue right now. Is there anything I can do?"

Cameron smiled. "As a matter of fact, yes. There's one thing you can do for all of us. Let's go get something out of my backpack."

Ortiz didn't like Cameron's tone of voice, but went along with it anyway. "All right. Show me."

Five minutes later, Cameron glanced at Ortiz as they walked toward one edge of the clearing carrying machetes. The young Hispanic sergeant was very talented in the art of war. At least talented enough to have survived this long.

According to Cameron's estimates, the clearing would be just barely large enough to fit the Stallion. He was simply going to buy them a few more feet of clearing by chopping down branches that extended over the edge of the jungle.

"How long before they come 'n' get us?"

"About an hour," responded Cameron as he lifted the machete above his head and landed it hard against a two-inch-thick branch. It came off clean. Cameron picked it up and threw it in the jungle. "That's assuming there's no more red tape about this rescue mission."

Ortiz busily worked on a thick branch. "Huh?"

"This rescue mission was not supposed to have happened."

Ortiz turned around and faced him. "What do you mean?"

Cameron frowned. "I don't know the entire story, but it seems as if some Washington politician didn't think it was a good idea to rescue you guys."

"That's just fuckin' great, man. I'd love to get my hands around that *hijo de puta*'s neck."

Cameron smiled.

"That wasn't a joke, *cabron*."

Cameron continued to smile. "Listen. Being part of the Special Forces in covert operations does include some risks. This kind of shit used to happen to us all the time in 'Nam. You just get used to it after a while."

Ortiz frowned. "Well, I always knew about it, man, but I guess it's different when it actually happens to you, if you know what I mean."

"I know," Cameron responded as he reached for another branch. "I know what you mean."

"Then?"

Cameron gave him a puzzled look. "Then what?"

"Then how did you get here?"

"Tito, you don't really want to know. It involves—shit, helicopters!"

The low flopping noise grew louder and louder. It came from the southeast, from the launch complex. Cameron raced into the forest. Ortiz did the same.

There were four craft in all, approaching at treetop level. One of the helicopters hovered over the clearing for several seconds before rejoining the caravan.

"*Mierda!* Looks like they're back."

"Yep."

"Think they saw us?"

"Maybe. Either that or they thought about landing on this clearing instead of the larger one on the other side of the woods. Go ahead and finish this up. I'm gonna make a call and find out how long before our chopper gets here. We're running out of time."

"What about the others?"

"They should be just about finished deploying the trip wires. I'll go get them after I make the call."

STALLION ONE

As the *Blue Ridge* disappeared below the horizon, Crowe applied forward cyclic pressure, increased throttle, and added right rudder to compensate for the additional torque induced by the main rotor. He eyed the airspeed. It was 180 knots, the maximum specified speed for the Stallion. He inched the cyclic forward and added a dash of throttle.

Up to 190 knots.

A little more cyclic.

Two hundred knots and climbing.

He felt a light vibration on the cyclic as the all-aluminum fuselage broke through the air at 205 knots. The French Guiana coast became visible under the bright sun. Crowe lowered the green visor as the cockpit flooded with light.

"Stallion One, Mambo here, over."

Crowe spoke in his voice-activated headset. "Go ahead, Mambo."

"What's your ETA, Stallion One?"

Crowe briefly checked the rectangular radar screen below and to his right. It pinpointed Mambo's position. "About a half hour, perhaps a bit less."

"Just spotted four helicopters loaded with troops. Things are gonna get pretty hot around here. Every second counts, over."

"We hear you, Mambo. Be there as fast as we can. Check back in ten minutes. Over."

"Roger, Stallion. Over an' out."

Crowe checked his airspeed one more time. He was already flying faster than he was supposed to at a mere ten feet over the waves. He inched the cyclic forward by another dash and increased power to ninety-five percent.

He briefly checked the fuel gauges and watched the digital readout, decreasing almost one and a half times faster than during normal cruising speed. He was down to 7500 pounds of fuel. Crowe did a quick calculation in his head and decided he had about a little over an hour's worth of fuel left. Barely enough to get there, pick up the troops, and head out.

He pressed the frequency-scan button on the cyclic.

"*Blue Ridge,* Stallion One, over."

"*Stallion One, go ahead,*" Davenport's rough voice crackled through his headset.

"It's gonna be close making it back. Request you guys get as close as you can to the coast, over."

"*Ah, negative, Stallion One. We're too close to Guiana territory.*"

"Christ, Skipper! You want us to fucking plunge into the ocean on our way back? We're gonna be sucking fumes in just over an hour. Over."

"*All right, Stallion One. We'll get as close as we can. You better do what you can to conserve fuel on your way out. Over.*"

"Roger, *Blue Ridge.* Over an' out."

Crowe frowned. There was a good possibility he'd run out of fuel. That in itself did not present an immediate life-threatening problem since the Stallion had the capability of landing at sea, but if the rescue area was going to be as hot as it appeared, he was concerned about being forced to hover around for some time before he could actually go in. And there were a million other things that could go wrong. If there was one thing Vietnam had taught him, it was that plenty of things were bound to go wrong during a mission that could never be anticipated. In order to maximize one's chances of success, one had to be sure there weren't any known problems or limitations going in, especially with the rescue craft.

Crowe put those thoughts aside and kept his eyes on the rapidly approaching coastline.

TWENTY ★

Returns

MIR SPACE COMPLEX

Kessler held on to the handles on the side of *Kvant-2*'s hatch, wearing Jones's space suit and backpack system, which Strakelov had retrieved from *Lightning*. At NASA's request, Kessler had opted not to use the second MMU. Although he had not seen any obvious signs of tampering, NASA didn't want to add risk to an already dangerous flight.

He now stared at *Lightning* quietly, gracefully gliding directly under the large *Mir* complex. The sight was breathtaking. A brittle-looking Earth covered most of his field of view, driving home the realization that they were indeed in an extremely low orbit. Outside temperatures were approaching 110 degrees centigrade as reported by *Mir*'s computers. At that height they were encountering a low concentration of air molecules which, when traveling at over twenty thousand miles per hour, caused enough friction to boil any exposed surface. But that was of no immediate consequence to Kessler. His Extravehicular Mobility Unit isolated him from the extreme temperatures of space while the life-support system backpack unit circulated chilled water through the plastic tubes laced throughout the nylon stretch fabric of his suit liner.

Of immediate interest to Kessler were *Lightning*'s open payload bay doors and the missing thermal tiles. He checked the display on his chest-mounted control unit and noticed he had over five hours of oxygen and suit pressurization left. He shifted his gaze to his right and saw through the gold-coated visor over his helmet that Strakelov was waving him over.

Kessler nodded and gently pushed himself toward the cosmonaut, who was backing himself into the Russian MMU look-alike system. Strakelov extended his right hand and pulled Kessler toward him, and motioned for Kessler to hold on to the right handle. Kessler complied as he got a close-up look at the midriff of Strakelov's space suit. The operating instructions and numerals applied to the suit were reversed. At first puzzled, Kessler quickly realized that unlike the easily read display on top of the chest-mounted control unit of his EMU, the Russian Orlon-DMA suit had all instructions and controls on the chest facing forward. Since Strakelov could not look straight down at them, the Russians had worked around the problem by providing cosmonauts with wrist-mounted mirrors.

Strakelov counted from five to one with his left hand. Kessler followed the fingers and firmly held on to the handle as the Russian's index finger pressed a switch on the right-hand control pod. Air puffed out the back of the *Ikar* unit, softly propelling them toward the wounded orbiter. He could see Valentina Tereshkova moving three large oxygen cylinders into *Lightning*'s air lock. They would provide enough breathable air inside the crew module to reach the Earth's atmosphere. That also meant that Kessler could now deactivate most of the environmental-control system, leaving the backup fuel cell free to power all communications and navigation equipment vital to *Lightning*'s safe return to Earth.

For a brief moment Kessler wondered if all of their efforts would be in vain. Was it all for nothing? Was he just kidding himself in thinking that he could realistically survive Earth's re-entry with tiles missing? A wave of doubt filled Kessler's mind as he continued to move toward the orbiter. Kessler eyed *Lightning*'s port wing. He stared at the American flag painted directly under the letters U.S.A. He filled his lungs with pure oxygen and his chest swelled. In spite of all the problems, *Lightning* was still there, in one piece. And so was he. He had to get Jones to safety. He owed him that. It was his responsibility to get his vessel and crew safely back down to Earth . . . just like in the Navy. Space orbiter or F-14D Tomcat, it didn't matter. A vessel was a vessel, and he was in command. A deep sense of confidence filled his whole being as he continued to stare at the gleaming, clean lines of the orbiter. The lights from *Mir* reflected against its white surfaces. He wasn't sure if it could be done, but he was willing to try. Kessler reached *Lightning* with renewed enthusiasm.

An hour later, tied to a line unreeling from an electrically powered winch under his direct control, Kessler reached the orbiter's underside, where Strakelov and Tereshkova were already hard at work stuffing sections of the Soyuz spacecraft's loose thermal insulation sheets into the six-inch-deep holes left by the missing tiles. Kessler briefly shifted his gaze up toward *Mir*. The Soyuz craft was coupled to the *Kvant-1* module. He noticed the "petal-like" protuberances of loose thermal insulation. Strakelov had merely clipped a few sheets off and hauled them over to *Lightning*.

Strakelov worked in the aft section of the underside, Tereshkova on the front. Without a reliable backpack system, Kessler felt a bit like a fifth wheel. It didn't mean that he hadn't contributed to *Lightning*'s rehabilitation. He had just spent the past thirty minutes stowing the Ku-band antenna and working inside *Lightning*'s cargo bay disengaging the actuator motors that controlled the opening and closing of the sixty-foot-long doors.

He approached Tereshkova, who had just finished stuffing several thermal insulation sheets into a six-by-six-inch hole. She had cut the thin insulation layers with a set of sheet-metal cutters in squares roughly the size of the tiles. She had then stacked the sheets four inches thick into the hole, and was now filling in the last inch with epoxy foam from *Lightning*'s tile repair kit, trimming the excess so that the epoxy did not alter *Lightning*'s aerodynamics.

"Anything I can do to help?" he asked through his voice-activated headset.

Tereshkova turned her head and slowly shook it. "*Nyet*, Mikhail. We're almost finished here. Are the actuator motors disengaged?"

"Yes."

"Good. Have you talked to your people?"

"Yes. They weren't too happy with the idea, but went along with it under the circumstances. We need to get Tex back down right away."

"There!" she said triumphantly as she squeezed the last of the epoxy foam over the last "Russian-made" tile.

"That's it?"

"There were only thirteen tiles missing. Once we figured out the best way to repair them, it didn't take long." She pointed at Strakelov, who floated in their direction. "See? Nikolai Aleksandrovich is finished too."

Strakelov approached them and pointed to his watch and then to the open payload bay doors. Kessler understood. They were running out of time. *Lightning* had less than an hour left before it would pass over the specific point in space where the primary RCS thrusters had to be used to slow the orbiter down to re-enter the atmosphere in order to reach Edwards safely.

Kessler held on to Tereshkova's *Ikar* as she propelled herself up *Lightning*'s side. Kessler floated into the payload bay, where he strapped himself to one side and grabbed the woven line that was connected to the edge of the opposite side's door. With the actuator motors disengaged, there was nothing that prevented the sixteen-hundred-pound doors from swinging freely on their shear hinges. He pulled on the woven line as hard as he could, and managed to move the large open door toward him by a few feet. He kept the tension and watched as Strakelov and Tereshkova positioned themselves over the doors, clipped lines to the edge, and slowly thrust themselves away to put tension on the lines. Kessler heard Strakelov's voice. Although Kessler's Russian was severely limited, he knew enough to realize Strakelov was counting down. He readied himself to pull even harder.

"Pyaht'. . . chetyreh . . . tree . . . dvah . . . odin . . . tepyer'!"

As Kessler pulled on the woven line, both Strakelov and Tereshkova fired their thrusters. The large door slowly pivoted on its hinges, came down toward Kessler, and stopped as it met with *Lightning*'s fuselage.

"Good job! One down, guys," he reported.

Five minutes later the second door was also closed, leaving Kessler inside the payload bay. Kessler floated toward the air lock. He reached it a minute later, closed the hatch behind him, pressurized the compartment, and quickly eased himself out of the bulky suit. He opened the crew compartment and briefly checked on Jones, who was safely strapped to the horizontal sleeping station and was breathing from a Russian portable oxygen unit. Tereshkova had brought in two oxygen cylinders in addition to the unit Jones was using. She had used the first cylinder to bring the oxygen level inside *Lightning* into the normal range. The second cylinder was a backup.

Kessler floated toward the flight deck, where he spotted Tereshkova and Strakelov through the front windowpanes. He reached for the radio. "I'm not sure how to say thanks, my friends."

"It is spasibo, Mikhail."

Kessler smiled. *"Spasibo,* Valentina and Nikolai Aleksandrovich."

"Get down safely and send us a postcard from California," Valentina responded as she waved. Nikolai waved as well. Then they turned around and jettisoned toward their own

craft. Kessler floated toward the aft crew section and stared through the upper panes at his new friends. With all his military and NASA training he'd never expected something like this to happen. It was a shame that the world might never learn of what had gone on up here. Only a handful of people would know on that day both countries had made history. They had crossed self-imposed political and cultural barriers to achieve a common goal.

Kessler verified that the payload bay doors' automatic latching mechanism had engaged and secured the doors. Talk-back lights on the control panel confirmed proper engagement. He activated the second oxygen supply cylinder and eyed the oxygen level. It was barely nominal. He thought about grabbing the small portable oxygen canister in the aft section, but decided against it. The second cylinder should keep the oxygen level out of the critical zone.

He strapped himself into the flight seat and switched frequencies.

"Houston? *Lightning*. Do you read?"

"Loud and clear, Lightning. Jesus, Michael! What took you so long? You had us worried," Hunter's voice said through the overhead speakers.

"Payload bay doors closed and secured. Missing tiles repaired as best we could. I'm coming in."

"Ah, roger, Lightning. We have worked out a new course for you. It's gonna take you a little longer to deorbit, but you'll cut down heat by about twenty percent."

"How much is a little longer, Houston? I'm not sure how long Jones is going to last."

"Just ten or fifteen minutes extra, Lightning. Besides, since you're using the RCS engines to deorbit instead of the OMS engines, your burn time just went up from two minutes to five."

"Roger. I can live with that."

"Deorbit burn in three minutes, Lightning."

"Roger. Changing profile." Kessler fired the side verniers for two seconds. The small thrusters came alive providing twenty-five pounds of thrust each. It was enough to turn *Lightning* slowly tail-first. He fired the opposite verniers the moment he'd achieved a 180-degree turn. Then he fired the nose and tail verniers and turned *Lightning* upside down.

"Two minutes to deorbit burn."

"Roger, Lightning. Looking good."

Kessler forced himself to relax. He glanced at the Mission Timer digital display on the instrument panel. One minute, thirty seconds.

"Lightning, *Houston.*"

"Go ahead, Houston."

"This is going to sound crazy but there appears to be an object moving in your direction. Same orbit, relative speed three hundred feet per second."

Kessler frowned. "What are you guys talking about?"

"Jesus. It just fired! Speed seven hundred feet per second. Thirty nautical miles south, fifteen miles downrange. Time to impact ninety seconds."

"Houston, what in the hell is going on? Are you sure that's not *Mir*?"

"Absolutely, Lightning. We're still tracking the Russians. Can't tell what it is! Good heavens! It just accelerated again. Eleven hundred feet per second. It's going to ram right into you! Time to impact forty seconds . . . thirty-five . . . thirty . . . use your thrusters, Michael! Quick!"

Kessler exhaled and reached down for the Reaction Control System primary thrusters. He knew the implications of burning early. When traveling at over twenty thousand miles per hour, a one-second mistake translated into coming out over five miles off target after re-entry. He checked the timer. He was still a minute away from the deorbit window, but only twenty seconds from becoming a permanent orbital wreck. Since *Lightning* was flying tail-first, Kessler scanned the rear. He looked in all directions. Nothing.

He waited. Ten seconds . . . nine . . . eight . . . *now!*

He threw the switches and the highly pressurized helium pushed the hydrazine from the right OMS tank through a maze of pipes down to the four primary RCS thrusters. Propellant met liquid oxygen in a hypergolic reaction, unleashing a combined thrust of 1740 pounds. Kessler sank into his seat from the mild two Gs that resulted.

"Six seconds to impact . . . five . . . four . . . Oh, my God! Look at that thing!" Kessler shouted as the tiny point in space rapidly grew. He snapped his head back as the enormous satellite zoomed past him. It was gone just as suddenly as it had appeared. "Son of a bitch! It missed. It was a damned satellite!"

"Say again, Lightning*?"*

"I said it was a satellite. It just blasted across my field of view less than a hundred feet away!"

"Looks like it's moving away, Lightning. *Continue deorbit burn."*

"Roger. One minute, thirty seconds. Helium level down to twenty percent. Hydrazine at fifteen percent."

"Helium and hydrazine levels confirmed. Two minutes to switch."

"Roger," Kessler acknowledged. The GPCs would automatically switch from the nearly exhausted OMS tanks to the smaller RCS tanks. Kessler's eyes shifted back and forth between the propellant levels and the Mission Timer. All seemed nominal, yet he could feel his heartbeat reaching a climax.

"Twenty seconds, Lightning. *Fifteen . . . ten . . . five . . . two . . . switch!"*

Kessler closed his eyes and held his breath. A malfunction now would be fatal. The GPCs completed the multi-valve operation in a millisecond, making the transition transparent to the RCS thrusters.

"Switch confirmed, Houston. RCS thrusters now operating out of their own tanks. Helium and hydrazine levels nominal. Mark four minutes."

"Roger, Lightning. *You're looking good."*

Kessler slowly exhaled. "Almost there, Houston."

"Mach thirty, Lightning."

"Speed confirmed."

"Lightning, *Houston. Warning. The . . . is slowin . . . down. Repeat, the . . . llite is . . . ing . . . hig . . . er.*"

"Houston, *Lightning.* You're breaking up. Say again. Repeat your last."

Static.

Kessler understood. With his low orbit, he had already slowed down enough that the ionized air surrounding his craft had become dense enough to prevent communications.

Hunter was warning him about something slowing down. *Could it be the satellite?* He checked the Mission Timer. Four minutes, thirty seconds. Kessler counted down the last few seconds. The GPCs turned off the RCS jets.

Kessler fired the verniers to flip the orbiter so that its underside would be exposed during re-entry. In doing so, *Lightning* faced forward in anticipation of its atmospheric glide after re-entry. Kessler saw the satellite. It had slowed down and was coming back. This time its speed was slower than before, but definitely along a collision course.

Damn! It's almost like a fucking missile!

Kessler checked his speed. Mach twenty-four and dropping. The light vibrations he felt on the control stick told him air molecules had begun to strike the underside. He pulled back the stick and kept his eyes trained on the incoming satellite. Without a copilot he had no way of knowing the exact range and time to impact.

Kessler was back piloting an F-14D Tomcat with an incoming missile. His eyes followed it as it arched toward him. He waited. With the cool professionalism he had learned in months of training and tempered in actual combat, Kessler waited for his chance. *It's only one missile,* he decided, thinking of the times he'd had two or three locked on his tail. The missile got closer and closer. There was no chaff or electronic countermeasures to help him. This was one-on-one. Man against machine.

Kessler narrowed his eyes as his fingers caressed the control stick directly connected to the RCS thrusters. For a brief second the missile appeared suspended in mid-space. No motion was apparent. Kessler saw it through the pinkish glow that slowly appeared at the bottom of the front windowpanes. Outside temperatures scurried above a thousand degrees. Just a few more seconds. The missile was close. Too close.

"All right, let's see what this bird can do," he whispered. In a swift move, he threw the control stick forward and to the side. The appropriate RCS thrusters came alive, forcing the orbiter into a steep left bank and dive. The satellite disappeared from his field of view. He waited. No impact.

Suddenly he felt the cabin temperature quickly rising. He had nearly flipped the orbiter to avoid the collision, but in the process had exposed *Lightning*'s upper fuselage tiles to a heat much greater than that for which they were designed. With both hands he centered the stick, forcing *Lightning* back into level flight, and struggled to pull the nose up. The maneuver had left him with a fifteen-degree angle of re-entry instead of the required thirty-five. Again, he was exposing the white thermal tiles of the upper forward fuselage to temperatures reaching two thousand degrees.

Perspiration rolled down his face and neck as the cabin temperature rose above one hundred degrees Fahrenheit. He pulled back hard as his eyes remained glued to the attitude indicator.

Twenty-three degrees . . . twenty-five.

The bright orange glow that had engulfed not only the front thermal glass panes but also the sides and upper panes began to fade into a light pink.

Twenty-eight . . . thirty.

Kessler eyed the interior temperature. Ninety-eight degrees. He kept up the pressure as the vibrations spiraled toward a climax. Completely focused on his task, Kessler briefly scanned the windowpanes and then turned back to the attitude indicator. Thirty-five degrees and holding. Mach eighteen. Kessler checked the timer. He had another ten minutes of this.

His mind went through the possibility of the satellite coming back again, but unless it had some level of thermal protection it wouldn't last long. On the other hand, the satellite was very large. It had a lot of mass to burn during re-entry. Kessler had two options: continue on his existing path and risk a rear collision if the satellite had not totally burned up yet, or decrease his angle of re-entry to accelerate and maybe buy himself a few extra seconds at the risk of exposing *Lightning*'s white tiles again. One exposure he felt certain the tiles could take, but two or three? He checked the timer. Nine minutes left. He decided to gamble it and kept the craft at the same re-entry angle.

Kessler glanced backward through the rearview panes, checking for any abnormalities in the payload bay. No light shone in the payload bay area. That only meant one thing. There hadn't been a burn-through yet. The Russian bandage was still holding.

Six minutes. Kessler felt he was asphyxiating. The air inside *Lightning* seemed thick, heavy. He didn't understand why. Tereshkova had provided them with enough oxygen to reach Earth safely. *Is there an oxygen leak somewhere? Maybe caused by all the explosions?*

Vibrations remained at an all-time high. Kessler kept a solid grip on the stick and his eyes on the attitude indicator. Thirty-five degrees. Speed 9.5 Mach.

Kessler checked the oxygen level. It had dropped below normal. *Why? What's happening?* It didn't matter at that point. He couldn't do anything about it anyway. He couldn't leave the control stick. Sweat ran into his eyes and he blinked rapidly, forcing them to remain focused on the attitude indicator. The angle had to be maintained at all cost. He had reached maximum re-entry temperature. Any disturbance in his flight path would most likely result in

Lightning's immediate disintegration.

Just as slowly as they had begun, the vibrations faded away, and so did the orange glow alongside the bottom of the front panes. Kessler's lips pursed suspiciously. He still had three minutes left. Why had he already broken through? It was too early. Something had gone wrong. He double-checked his angle of entry. It had been a steady thirty-five degrees for most . . . *Oh, Jesus.* For twenty or so seconds he had lowered the nose as much as fifteen degrees to avoid collision with the satellite. That was it! *Damn.*

His heartbeat increased in anticipation of what he would see. He hoped to see land, but as the noise went away and he shot below 150,000 feet at 4.5 Mach, all he could see was the ocean.

"Houston, *Lightning* here."

"Lightning, we're tracking you eleven hundred miles off course. What in the hell happened up there?"

"Had a close encounter with a suicidal satellite."

"Say again, Lightning?"

"I'll tell you guys later."

"Stand by, Lightning. We're plotting a new approach solution."

"Roger, but make it fast, Houston. Oxygen level is getting too low." Kessler eyed the altimeter. It showed 140,000 feet at 4.3 Mach. He inhaled deeply several times. The low oxygen level began to take its toll. He felt light-headed. Kessler shook his head vigorously and fought to remain in control. He now wished he had that portable oxygen unit in the aft crew station, but lacking a co-pilot, he couldn't afford to let go of the stick for even a second.

"No problem, Lightning. Avoid the S-turns. New heading zero-eight-zero. Maintain current angle of descent. At that speed you should see the coast any second now."

"Houston, oxygen level . . . in critical. Need to switch to autopilot . . . as soon as possible."

"Stand by, Lightning."

Kessler was now breathing heavily through his mouth. His limbs began to tingle. He knew he could lose consciousness in less than a minute unless he reached for that oxygen unit.

"Lightning, *there might not be enough juice left for the autopilot servo-motors.*"

Kessler didn't have a choice. It was either switching or asphyxiating. He enabled autopilot and let go of the stick. *Lightning* remained on course.

With his vision becoming more blurred by the second, Kessler unstrapped himself and bolted to the rear. Suddenly, his vision narrowed. He had gotten up too fast. He was weaker than he'd imagined, and dropped to his knees. His body had not gotten a chance to adjust to the Earth's gravity. The single G that Kessler was experiencing felt like four or five.

"Lightning, *Houston. What's your situation?*"

Kessler wasn't listening any longer. He looked up and saw the metallic door to the right of the aft crew station. He had to reach it and pull out the small emergency oxygen unit.

Kessler kicked his legs and pushed himself toward the back. His body felt very heavy. His hands trembled from the effort. An overwhelming desire to rest engulfed him, but he persisted. He had come too far to give up now. He had to fight. He was mission commander. He was in control of *Lightning*. One final push. There! He pulled open the cabinet and extracted the oxygen mask attached to a small canister through a thin plastic tube. He placed the mask over his mouth and nose and turned the knob on the canister.

Kessler took one breath of pure oxygen, exhaled, and quickly followed with three more. He coughed for a few moments and breathed deeply once more before sitting up.

"Lightning, *Houston. Come in. Come in, Michael. Michael?*"

Kessler stared at the empty flight seat, and slowly crawled on his hands and knees back to the front and strapped himself in place. He eyed the altimeter as it shot below 110,000 feet.

"I'm still here, Chief."

"Welcome home, Lightning. *We have you on TV at one hundred thousand feet, three-point-five Mach. You are positive seats. Everyone is breathing a lot easier now."* Kessler smiled. *Lightning* was safely gliding toward the dry lake beds of Edwards Air Force Base.

"Houston, you're a little garbled, say again your last."

"Positive seats."

"Roger that, Houston.

"Ninety thousand feet, range seventy-four miles, two-point-nine Mach," Kessler read out loud. "Everything looks good on board."

"Roger, we're looking at it. You can take air data now."

"Roger, Houston. Eighty-two thousand at two-point-five Mach." Kessler switched control to automatic and then back to manual, performing a series of tests before flying around the approach circle manually and then going back to automatic control for the first part of the approach-and-landing phase. The data from the tests were automatically fed back to Houston control, where powerful computers quickly analyzed them. *Lightning* was designed to use RCS thrusters in space, and elevons and rudder inside the Earth's atmosphere. As *Lightning* descended below the stratosphere, the General Purpose Computers were in the critical process of slowly transitioning from the RCS system to the elevon/rudder system for control of flight. Nearly two million operations per second computed the precise blend of RCS and aerodynamic controls to keep the orbiter on its glide path. No pilot could ever even dream of coming close to maintaining that tricky balancing act.

"Everything is looking right on the money. We have a wind update for you and a weather update. You've got a very thin cloud layer at forty thousand, the winds airborne

are as briefed, and on the ground two-one-five at eighteen knots gusting up to twenty. Altimeter setting is two-niner-point-oh-five inches. Visibility fifty miles."

"It sounds like a good ol' day at Eddie!"

"You got it, Lightning."

As the orbiter descended below 45,000 feet, Kessler noticed the computers shutting off the RCS system. The air was thick enough to rely only on the aerodynamic control surfaces.

"Hello, Lightning. Welcome to California."

Kessler looked to his right and noticed the first of the chase planes, an Air Force T-38 Talon.

"Lightning making a wide sweeping turn to get aligned with the runway. Twenty thousand feet." Runway 23 at Edwards was ready and waiting.

"Lightning, *Houston. Check body flaps to manual."*

"Roger. Body flaps on manual. Eighteen thousand feet at four-eight-zero knots."

"Lightning, *you're a little low on the altitude. Pull your nose up by a couple of degrees."*

"Roger."

"Okay, speed brake start now."

"Roger, Houston." Kessler activated the speed brake, which was integrated with the rudder and made up of two identical halves. Hinged at their forward edge, the two rudders opened and closed in response to Kessler's commands, forming a drag-producing wedge that assisted Kessler in maintaining his approach. Under a normal approach, the speed brake would have been kept one-half open, but in his current situation, Kessler kept it one-fourth open. That, in a way, acted as an engine since it allowed Kessler to shallow his approach just as he would do by increasing throttle, if he had an engine.

"Lightning, *you're still slightly low on the altitude, but looking okay. You have a 'Go' for autoland."*

Kessler switched to autoland, the microwave terminal-phase-guidance-system program that was scheduled to take over at eighteen thousand feet using information supplied by the microwave-scanning-beam landing system. Autoland would be maintained to flare at two thousand feet, when Kessler would take over.

"Roger, Houston. Brake and body flap on auto; everything on auto, thank you!"

Lightning was now entering a twenty-degree-angle glide. The air brake helped Kessler maintain a steady 265 knots.

"One minute to touchdown, Lightning."

"Roger, Houston. All systems operational."

Kessler noticed the chase planes closing in. They would call out the last tens of feet to touchdown and confirm *Lightning*'s airspeed to Hunter.

"Lightning, you're clear to land Lake Bed Twenty-three whenever you're ready."

Kessler switched off autoland and took control of the stick. As the altimeter scurried below two thousand feet, Kessler pulled the nose up and the glide angle was reduced to two degrees as they approached the sun-hardened desert floor. The landing gear dropped.

"Roger," acknowledged Kessler.

"Okay, Lightning, keep it steady."

The lake bed came up to meet him, and Kessler knew that the large elevons on the rear would make his landing difficult. He had to avoid jerking back on the stick to flare out as he would have done in a regular aircraft. A sudden jerk like that would cause the elevons to rise, resulting in a severe loss of lift, probably forcing *Lightning* to land hard.

"Two hundred feet . . . one hundred seventy-five . . ." called out the pilot from one of the chase planes.

Kessler kept the control stick steady. Autoland had planned his approach meticulously, helping him avoid corrections at the last moment.

"One hundred feet . . . fifty . . . thirty . . . ten . . . five . . . three . . . touchdown!"

Kessler felt a light vibration as *Lightning*'s rear wheels came in contact with the smooth surface of the lake bed.

"Nose gear fifteen feet . . . ten . . . five . . . three . . . touchdown! Welcome home, Lightning!*"*

The mid-morning California sun struggled to pierce through *Lightning*'s anti-reflection-coated windowpanes as both T-38 chase planes, in full afterburners, zoomed past the decelerating orbiter and rolled their wings in victory. Underneath his plastic oxygen mask Michael Kessler smiled broadly. He was home. He was safe.

TWENTY-ONE ★

Final Confrontation

In the final choice a soldier's pack is not so heavy a burden as a prisoner's chains.

—Dwight D. Eisenhower

NORTH OF KOUROU, FRENCH GUIANA

The enemy slowly approached Mambo's initial defense position—just as Cameron had anticipated—from the large clearing. Cameron and Ortiz had deployed their forces efficiently. Once more, Mambo was divided into three teams. Mambo One was composed of Ortiz, Zimmer, and Cameron. Mambo Two had three soldiers twenty feet to Mambo One's right, and Mambo Three had the last two soldiers up in the trees fifty feet from the trip wires.

Cameron checked his watch. According to his last communication with the rescue helicopter they still had another fifteen minutes. He made his decision and moved forward.

"Where you goin', *amigo*?"

"Up front. I want to get a feeling for how close those guys are. The rescue chopper will be here any minute now. If those guys are still too far away I'm pulling Mambo Three back here. No sense in exposing them unnecessarily."

Ortiz nodded.

Cameron dropped to a deep crouch and moved forward quietly, warily. Although the area was supposedly secured because of the trip wires, there was always the chance of an enemy getting by undetected. He pressed his back against a tree and looked over both shoulders. Nothing. He selected another tree a few feet away and raced for it. Again he leaned back against it and inspected the grounds. Satisfied, he moved forward once more, carefully selecting trees in advance, close enough to minimize detection between transitions, yet far away enough to maximize progress.

He scurried forward for a second, perhaps two, until he reacted to the visual image of several men moving in his direction. It all happened very fast. He dropped to the ground and rolled back to the tree. A second later he rose to a crouch, hid behind the thick trunk, and—

The loud explosion was followed by cries of pain. Someone had run into one of Zimmer's trip wires. Cameron was about to look in that direction when gunfire erupted from several places at once. Muzzle flashes were clearly visible in the murky woods. They were mixed with the horrifying screams from the wounded men and the enraged shouts from other men.

Cameron dropped to the ground again and rolled away from the tree. He shifted his gaze up toward the two Mambo soldiers, pinned down behind thick branches as a shower of bullets engulfed their entire area.

"Pull back! Pull back!" he screamed as loud as he could, but the men could not hear him. Cameron quickly moved his body from side to side, trying to bury himself in the foot-thick layer of leaves. Satisfied that he was relatively invisible, he set the MP5 to full automatic fire and aimed at the first group of muzzle flashes over a hundred feet away— the one that appeared to be firing in the direction of Mambo Three. He pressed the telescopic butt against his shoulder, left hand under the silenced barrel and right index finger on the trigger.

Another explosion. More curses and screams. More gunfire broke out from another sector to his left. *Who are they firing at?* There were only the three of them, the two Mambo soldiers and himself, in that sector. The rest of Mambo was safely positioned almost two hundred feet back.

He shrugged and shifted his gaze back toward the muzzle flashes to his left. He squeezed the trigger and made a wide sweep at waist level. The German MP5 started spitting 9-mm rounds, depleting the thirty-round magazine in under ten seconds. Some of the muzzle flashes had disappeared. Cameron quickly removed the exhausted clip and grabbed another one from a Velcro-secured pocket on his gear vest. He jammed it in place and, using his left hand, pulled back and turned upward the cocking handle located on the left forward section of the barrel. Again he unloaded the thirty rounds on the enemy. A few more muzzle flashes disappeared. He estimated only five or six attackers remained.

Another explosion. This one to the far left. The enemy was approaching from all directions. They were closing in.

"Pull back! Now! Now!"

This time one of the two soldiers snapped his head in his direction. Cameron waved them down. Both men nodded and began to crawl back. Cameron released the clip and inserted his second-to-last magazine. He set the MP5 in single-shot mode, cocked the weapon, and trained it on the remaining flashes. He briefly eyed the soldiers climbing down the tree before lining up the first flash between the rear adjustable sight and the fixed forward sight. He fired once, twice. The muzzle flashes disappeared. He moved to the next one. Same thing. Cameron glanced back at the soldiers. They were already out of sight.

He began to crawl back toward the tree when a shower of bullets nearly shaved off the bark. Cameron pressed the MP5 against his chest and set into a roll. He had gotten too close to the enemy and had attacked only one front, while the enemy had steadily approached his position from the sides. They were going to flank him. He continued to roll as the ground, the trees, and a cloud of leaves filled his field of view. Incomprehensible shouting filled the background. Cameron ignored it and kept rolling until he crashed against another tree. This time he simply looped around the trunk and rose to a crouch. He briefly inspected the area, but the murk made it difficult to see anything. He turned around and hurtled back toward Mambo's defensive position. He had to hurry. He was right in between the approaching enemy and Mambo. In just a matter of seconds he could be caught in a cross fire. He ran as fast as his legs would go. Visions of the past filled his mind. Visions of jungles, rice paddies, napalm-charred bodies. Smells too. The smell of gunpowder in the woods, of rotting foliage, of burned flesh. He was back. For a second it seemed as if he actually had never left those jungles, those hellish forests, those fields of death. *Go, Cameron. You have . . . a chance by yourself.* Skergan's voice echoed inside his mind; it reached his soul. Why did he leave him? *But it's . . . okay, Cameron. I'll just . . . hide here.* It made sense. It had seemed like the right thing to do, yet the guilt consumed him. The overpowering guilt, the pain. *Sorry, man, I'm sorry. I'm so—*

He felt something grab ahold of his entire body and propel him up with titanic force.

What the hell! Oh, Jesus!

He had run into Ortiz's trap. A sudden upward jerk and then he swung nearly thirty feet above the leaves.

Shit! What now?

He had barely finished thinking that when he saw several muzzle flashes aimed in his direction. Cameron closed his eyes and braced himself in anticipation, but the impact never came. Instead he fell. He opened his eyes and watched in utter shock as the ground grew rapidly closer.

"Aghh!"

He crashed feet-first, rolled, and landed on his back. The blanket of leaves somewhat cushioned his fall, but could not prevent him from twisting his right ankle. It didn't matter; he had to get up and continue. He grabbed the MP5, kicked with his left leg, and tried to stand up, but the moment he applied any weight to his right leg the piercing pain crippled him. He fell on his side and quickly looked down in disbelief at his tibia protruding through the camouflage fabric of his fatigues.

Suddenly he felt a hand pulling him up. Cameron looked up and watched in a blur as Ortiz dragged him toward the thick fallen log where Mambo One was stationed.

"*Madre de Dios, amigo.* You fucked up your leg big time. C'mon."

"I'm too damned old for this shit!" Cameron inhaled deeply and held it, also clenching his teeth to absorb the agonizing pain as he placed an arm over Ortiz's shoulders and began to hop back toward their defensive position.

"You're some crazy *cabron.* Tryin' to pull a stunt like that."

Cameron didn't respond, but his face showed some relief when he spotted the two members of Mambo Three to his left. They had made it back safe.

"You just lay there and let us handle this. We can take care of those *pendejos.*"

Waves of pain washed over Cameron. He spoke through clenched jaws.

"No . . . too many. They're . . . trying to . . . flank us. The clearing . . . the chopper . . . run for it . . . damn fucking leg!"

Ortiz looked at Cameron. "What are you sayin', man? There can't be any more than twenty of 'em *pendejos* out there, minus the ones that you took out!"

Suddenly all gunfire ceased. A frightening silence descended. Dead calm.

"No . . . there are . . . more, Tito. Don't know . . . where they came from . . . the chopper . . . it will be here . . . soon . . . aghh, Jesus Christ! My leg!" He bent over and continued to breathe in and out deeply, forcing his mind to ignore the pain.

Take the pain, Cameron. Take the fucking pain! he cursed at himself. *Pain doesn't hurt. Pain is good. Take it. Take it! Skergan took it, so can you!*

Focusing on the image of his friend lying bravely alone in the jungle, Cameron somehow managed to endure the pain enough to lift his head over the log. The sight was terrifying.

"Dios mio!" said Ortiz. "Where in the hell did they come from?"

"Tell your people . . . not to . . . open fire . . . yet. Wait."

Ortiz raised his right hand in a fist. "No firin' yet. Pass the word."

Cameron squinted. His vision grew blurry. He eyed the wound and noted an increase in the blood flow. The bone had definitely torn an artery. He knew there wasn't much time left. He considered a tourniquet but the enemy was too close to take the time. Every man counted. They would need all the firepower they could muster to keep the incoming mob in check until the chopper arrived. He brought his MP5 up and rested the barrel on the log. The figures were roughly a hundred feet away. His finger softly caressed the trigger.

"Wait . . . wait . . ." Cameron said. "Select your . . . targets."

Eighty feet. The figures—over forty of them as far as he could see—approached slowly. All appeared to be carrying automatic weapons.

"Just a few more seconds . . . fire!"

All seven members of Mambo and Cameron opened fire at once. Each man had a thirty-degree angle of responsibility. All enemy soldiers within that angle were his. The angles overlapped one another to cover the entire frontal perimeter.

Cameron noted that over fifteen enemy soldiers dropped in the first few seconds. The rest sought shelter in nearby trees.

"Hold your fire! Hold your fire!" Ortiz screamed. "Don't fire unless you got a specific target!"

As the fire subsided Cameron heard a low and deep rotor noise in the background. He reached for the radio. "Stallion One . . . Stallion One, Mambo . . . here, over."

"Good Lord! What in the world is going on down there, Mambo? I can hear the gunfire from up here."

"We're in a . . . shitload of trouble, Stallion One. Need you down . . . in the clearing next . . . to the swamp."

"Got it. Be there in thirty seconds."

"Roger . . . thirty seconds."

He looked at Ortiz. "Time to get . . . the hell outta . . . here, Tito."

"All right. Everyone throw me your spare clips and pull back. Pull back. All of you! Back! Back!"

Five members passed the magazine clips to Ortiz and crawled back for several feet before breaking into a run. Zimmer approached them.

"Let's go, brother!"

"All right, *hermano.* Gimme a hand with him."

Suddenly gunfire broke out again. Cameron looked back toward the forest and spotted several men moving in their direction. All three unloaded several dozen rounds until the enemy took shelter behind the trees again.

"C'mon. Let's go!"

Cameron looked at Ortiz. "You guys . . . go ahead. I can't . . . can't make it, man."

"Like fuckin' shit you can't," Ortiz snapped back. "You're comin' with us."

"And who's gonna keep . . . those bastards pinned down? Who? Now you . . . two leave me your . . . weapons and get the hell outta here . . . before we all buy it. Move it, Tito. That's . . . an order."

A few men started to move toward them. Cameron leveled the MP5 and blasted a few more rounds. As one man went down, the others jumped behind trees. They were less than forty feet away and slowly closing in.

"What are you . . . waiting for, Sergeant Ortiz? I gave a fucking direct order. Move out and take . . . Private Zimmer with you. Now, dammit. NOW!"

Ortiz was obviously stunned as he and Zimmer slowly stepped back.

For one brief moment Ortiz and Cameron stared into each other's eyes. There were tears in the young Hispanic's eyes. "God bless you, *hermano*!" They raced for the clearing almost two hundred feet away.

Cameron was alone again. The tables had suddenly been turned. *It's payback time,* Cameron reflected, knowing that destiny had finally caught up with him for what he had done in the jungles of Vietnam. A life with Marie was not meant to be. That was his penance.

He shifted his gaze toward the trees and fired several rounds at two approaching figures. He missed and fired again, missing again. His vision was going quickly.

As the helicopter's noise grew louder and louder, gunfire broke out. More figures approached. Cameron tried to fire back but nothing came out. The clip was empty. Cameron removed it and jammed the last one in while chips of wood and bark flew in all directions as the enemy's rounds pounded the fallen log. He cocked the weapon, brought it up, and fired a ten-second burst across his field of view. Five men went down. The rest disappeared behind trees less than thirty feet away.

Cameron continued to blink to readjust his vision, but it was getting to be a futile exercise. He began to feel cold. His hands trembled as he threw the MP5 to the side and grabbed Ortiz's Colt. Again he leveled it at the forest but saw or heard no one, just the helicopter noise.

He saw three, no four, men at ten o'clock. Cameron moved the weapon in that direction as muzzle flashes broke out. Wood exploded in front of his eyes, blinding him. He fell to the side, but managed to control the overwhelming desire to bring both hands to his bleeding face. Instead, he kept his hands firmly on the Colt, brought the weapon back over the log, and fired blindly. Cameron felt the powerful recoil reverberating through his whole body as he continued to unload all he had left on the invisible figures.

The Colt ran dry. He threw it over the log and wiped away the blood, regaining partial vision from his left eye. The soldiers were there, dark, impersonal figures less than twenty feet away. Weapons leveled at him for a brief moment before the entire side of the forest came alive with muzzle flashes. Cameron dropped to the ground and reached for Zimmer's Colt.

He tried to roll, but his body was overcome by shivering cold. He was losing control as blood left his body at a staggering rate. His mind began to wander. He forced himself to focus on the situation and tried to bring the Colt up, but couldn't do it.

His ears registered the roar of Stallion One's main rotor as it began to leave the ground. He had done it. He had kept the enemy back . . . a figure emerged over the log, then there were two. Cameron fired a short burst. Both figures arched back but were quickly replaced by three others, who trained their weapons on him. He was about to fire again when two loud blasts were instantly followed by a harrowing pain in his left shoulder and right forearm that nearly numbed his senses. He stared at four figures looking down at him. There was no more gunfire, just the trembling thunder from the helicopter. It seemed to get closer and closer. Cameron struggled to see the faces of the figures standing over him. He wanted to look at his executioners. Just four faceless strangers. He was temporarily confused. The rotor noise rang in his ears, in his mind. It reached his very soul as a savagely powerful windblast pinned him down on the ground.

Gunfire erupted once more. From above. The figures arched back. The noise was deafening. He tried to bring his hands to his ears but couldn't. He was too weak. Too cold. He was passing out. Then through the maddening explosions Cameron heard a voice. A familiar voice.

"Lower, lower! There! I see him! A little to the right. *Puta!* No, no! The right, the right! . . . yeah, that's it. Now a little lower. There, hold it! Hold it!"

Cameron saw another faceless figure appear in front of him. This one leaned over and pulled him up. *Why? Why bother? Can you see that I'm dying?* Cameron tried to fight him but again his muscles gave.

"Easy, *hermano*! It's me, Tito!" Ortiz screamed over the gunfire. "You didn't actually think we were gonna leave you, did you?"

Cameron tried to say something, but not even his lips would respond. He wanted to say that he didn't care anymore. That it didn't matter. That he just wanted to be left in peace, alone, to atone for past sins. It was his destiny. But instead he felt Ortiz's arms pulling him up. The young sergeant was hooking his near-limp body to the rescue cable.

"All right. Up, up! Get him up there!"

Cameron felt his feet leave the ground. He was floating. It was beyond his control. Then the pain began to subside. The throbbing from his leg faded away. The burning pain from his shoulder and left forearm slowly disappeared as a blinding light utterly smothered him. It was everywhere. He felt confused. He wasn't cold any longer. The light gave him warmth. Cameron was alone but somehow did not feel alone. There were others there. He could feel their presence. He finally began to understand what had happened to him the moment a figure emerged through the dazzling light. The figure came closer. Ortiz smiled down on him.

"You're gonna make it, *amigo*. You're gonna be all right."

Cameron smiled thinly as his vision partially returned. He stared at someone holding an IV bottle over him, and with it life slowly began to seep back into his broken body.

It was over. All seven surviving members were there. They had made it against staggering odds. A deep sense of satisfaction fell over him as he braced himself and inhaled deeply through his mouth. The old familiar guilt had been washed away by a sense of accomplishment, a sense of fulfillment. The pain of Skergan's death was still there, but he had proven to himself that he was not a coward, that he could give his own life for a fellow soldier. His eyes filled with a mix of joy and physical pain.

The skies were clear. Radiant beams flickered through the rotating blades as the bright blue sky met an equally pure blue ocean. A flock of flamingos gracefully broke into flight as the massive ship blasted over the sandy beach. Cameron watched it through tears.

EPILOGUE ★

THE WHITE HOUSE

Pruett sat quietly as the President finished reading his report on the rescue mission. This was his first time alone with the President. The President put down the stapled sheets of paper and stared him in the eye across his desk. Pruett was not sure how the President would react. After all, Pruett had disobeyed a direct order from Carlton Stice.

"Well, Tom. It seems like I may have a small problem here. On one hand, I can see why you acted the way you did. You took one hell of a chance, I tell you, because if something had gone wrong with that unauthorized rescue mission . . ."

Pruett exhaled. "I know, Mr. President. I know I was taking a chance, but there were American lives involved, sir. I couldn't just turn my head."

"Like I said, you took a chance and this time it looks like you won. You brought our boys home, and for that I salute you, but I seriously encourage you not to do it again. It could prove to be career-limiting."

"I understand, sir."

"Good. On the other hand, Tom, I have a very upset Defense Secretary. He wants me to nail you to the wall for what you did, but I can't do that."

"Sir, I didn't mean to go against the Secretary—"

"Oh, yes you did, Tom. Don't lie to me. I know you enjoyed every minute of it, and this time you lucked out. Carl is just going to have to cool off and let it go. I already talked to him earlier today about this problem, and although he didn't like my answer to his demand, he's going to go along with it."

Pruett shifted his weight on the chair. "If you don't mind my asking, sir. Exactly what is your answer to this problem?"

"Simple, Tom. We keep going in the same fashion as before. Carl stays where he is and you where you are. Both of you are doing a fine job. I understand why Carl acted the way he did. He was simply looking after the interests of this Administration. He was concerned about word getting out on the attack. But I also understand why you acted like you did. You were saving American lives, and you did an outstanding job at that. So that's it. This whole thing was kept secret from the start and it will remain secret. *Lightning* is back in one piece and NASA is on the right track once more."

"Sir, what about the other soldiers? The ones that didn't make it back?"

"I have already talked to the French President, Tom. There are going to be a few quiet changes occurring over the next few months. The Secretary of State will be meeting with the European leaders to discuss this and other issues in a closed-door session next week. Don't worry, those soldiers will be buried with honors where they belong, and the people at fault will be brought to justice."

Pruett leaned back and nodded.

"In regards to your nephew George, I'm truly sorry about what happened. I called your sister-in-law last night to give her my condolences."

"That was very thoughtful of you, sir." Pruett inhaled at the thought of his devastated sister-in-law and her two daughters. "She's trying to cope with the situation as best she can."

"A terrible thing, Tom. Such a terrible waste."

"I know, Mr. President."

The President paused for a moment. "Now, tell me. How is your operative doing?"

"Better, sir. He should be able to walk with a cane in a few weeks. According to the doctors, his leg should be almost back to normal within a year. It was a pretty bad break."

"I'm glad to hear he's going to be all right. Take good care of him."

Pruett smiled. "I already have, sir."

"Good. Men like Stone are assets to our intelligence community."

"I know, sir."

The President got up and extended his hand over the desk. Pruett also rose and shook it.

"You have done your country a great service, Tom. It's a shame that no one will ever know about it."

"Well, that's the way it is in this business, sir. Thank you, Mr. President."

"No, Tom. Thank *you*."

ARLINGTON NATIONAL CEMETERY, VIRGINIA. ONE MONTH LATER

Under an overcast afternoon sky, seemingly endless graves marked the mortal remains of the honored dead. There were rows and rows of them. Some were known, some unknown, but the men buried there had shared a common goal: All had lived and died for the preservation of democracy, of liberty, of peace. Several generations lay next to one another, from those who served in the Revolutionary War, to the Mexican War, the Civil War, both World Wars, Korea, Vietnam, Grenada, and the Middle East. All had come forth when their country had called them. All had served without complaint, without regret. All had died with honor.

Wearing a dark suit and trench coat, newly appointed Paris Station Chief Cameron Stone stood to the side with the help of a cane his doctors told him he would have to use for a long time. A cast covered his broken leg. He stared at eight coffins; at the eight members of Mambo who had perished in the service of their country. The eight bodies had been secretly returned to the United States by the French government upon completion of a joint investigation that had resulted in the removal from power of prominent figures of the French and German armed forces, and the arrest of members of the French police as well as a number of powerful European businessmen. The EEC leaders had also appointed a new Athena administration, and directed it to continue with the efforts to develop *Hermes* and *Columbus*. This time, however, under the watchful eye of government agencies. Europe would continue to grow in the field of space exploration, but it would do so along with other countries in the quest for knowledge to benefit all mankind.

Cameron frowned as the color guard folded the flags that covered each coffin and brought them to the appropriate family members. Pain drowned his soul when he spotted over a dozen kids sitting by eight women, all dressed in black. General Jack Olson was there with his wife. Cameron saw no other high-ranking officials, and he wasn't surprised. As far as the world was concerned, those eight soldiers had perished during a war exercise in Panama.

He exhaled. At least those eight broken families would never have to worry financially again. Besides the life insurance each family had collected, the EEC had secretly given each family an undisclosed, but sizable amount of money. Two words had come to Cameron's mind when Pruett told him the money was really coming from Vanderhoff's confiscated Swiss accounts: poetic justice. Cameron managed a thin smile.

He shifted his gaze to two uniformed men on the far right. Cameron didn't know them personally, but had seen their photographs in the papers. One was dressed in an all-white Navy uniform, the other wore Air Force blue. They were the astronauts who had taken *Lightning* on its historic maiden flight. Cameron smiled at the thought of no one ever actually knowing what had taken place in the streets of Paris, the jungles of Guiana, and the depths of space. As far as the world was concerned, *Lightning*'s flight had been a total success. NASA was on its feet once more. The damaged engine had been quickly hidden under the special empennage fairing NASA had put on it less than an hour after landing. The fairing was normally used to reduce drag during orbiter ferry flights. The orbiter would remain like that until it reached the Cape, where Rocketdyne workers already had another SSME ready for installation. The world would never know the difference.

Atlantis reached space a day after *Lightning* landed at Edwards Air Force Base. NASA simply stated that because of a shift in internal priorities the joint emergency drill would have to be postponed indefinitely. NASA treated the matter lightly, and amazingly enough, so did the press. After all, *Lightning*'s primary mission had been successfully completed, and as it turned out, *Atlantis* was also successful in its satellite-deployment mission.

"Are you all right?"

Cameron turned and looked into Marie's eyes as she reached for his hand and held it tight. Marie had remained by his side during his lengthy recovery. She had accepted an executive position with the new Athena in Paris. Her plane was scheduled to depart Dulles in four hours. Cameron would remain in Washington for two more weeks to complete all his medical checkups before also heading for France.

"Yes, but they're not."

"You did the best you could. At least some of the men came back . . . including you."

Cameron nodded.

"I'm going to miss you," she said.

Cameron smiled. "And I'll miss you too, but it won't be for long. I'll be in Paris in no time."

Marie also smiled.

Cameron looked up and stared at Kessler and Jones once more. He noticed Kessler turn his head toward him, and then say something to Jones, who also looked in Cameron's direction. Then the strangest thing happened. Both astronauts snapped to attention and saluted him.

Cameron smiled, also snapped to attention, and proudly saluted back.